Praise for the Khorasan Archives

The Bloodprint

"*The Bloodprint* is somewhere between N. K. Jemisin and George R. R. Martin. You're going to love it."

—Saladin Ahmed, author of *Throne of the Crescent Moon*

"*The Bloodprint* . . . is nuanced in showing the value of history and religion and the damage willful ignorance can inflict. And if it's plot twists you're after [it] has plenty of them—and an exciting cliffhanger, too."

—*Washington Post*

"Khan's latest is a tale that will grip readers from the start. With beautiful, vibrant storytelling . . . Khan's first installment in her new fantasy series is truly remarkable."

—RT Book Reviews

The Black Khan

"Khan has created a rich, well-crafted world that will appeal to readers of S. A. Chakraborty's *The City of Brass* or Erika Johansen's *The Queen of the Tearling*."

—*Booklist*

"Khan draws on her Muslim heritage and Middle Eastern history to root her dark fantasy in distressingly believable realities, and avoids the middle book slump by ramping up complex plot twists, character betrayals, and other surprises with a crime-writer's aplomb."

—B&N Sci-Fi & Fantasy Blog

"Definitely a FANGRRLS-esque read."

The Blue Eye

The Blue Eye

Book Three of the Khorasan Archives

AUSMA ZEHANAT KHAN

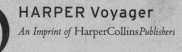

HARPER Voyager

An Imprint of HarperCollins Publishers

THE BLUE EYE. Copyright © 2019 by Ausma Zehanat Khan. All rights reserved. Printed in the United States of America. No part of this book may be used or reproduced in any manner whatsoever without written permission except in the case of brief quotations embodied in critical articles and reviews. For information, address HarperCollins Publishers, 195 Broadway, New York, NY 10007.

HarperCollins books may be purchased for educational, business, or sales promotional use. For information, please email the Special Markets Department at SPsales@harpercollins.com.

Harper Voyager and design are trademarks of HarperCollins Publishers LLC.

FIRST EDITION

Designed by Paula Russell Szafranski
Map created by Ashley P. Halsey, inspired by Ayesha Shaikh
Map background by caesart/Shutterstock, Inc.
Half title and chapter opener art by Gala Matorina/Shutterstock, Inc.
Ornament on title page and page 418 by aPerfect/Shutterstock, Inc.

Library of Congress Cataloging-in-Publication Data has been applied for.

ISBN 978-0-06-245923-7

19 20 21 22 23 LSC 10 9 8 7 6 5 4 3 2 1

For my darling Nozzie,

who would hide with me in the Cave of Thawr,
leave it all behind to follow me on hijra,
journey with me through Israa e Miraj . . .
and be waiting on the other side.

The
Blue
Eye

Prologue

THEY WOULDN'T KILL HIM AT THE COUNCIL. THE TALISMAN COMMANDers were suspicious of Daniyar, but they held fast to the rules of the loya jirga, the consultation Daniyar had asked for with the leaders of the Talisman tribes. The Shin War, in particular, held themselves to a higher standard. Their commitment to their own honor was the reason Daniyar retained any hope of returning to the Black Khan's city unharmed.

Once he returned to the safety of Ashfall, this temporary reprieve would end. Though Daniyar was one of the Shin War, as well as the Guardian of Candour—the city that was now the capital of the Talisman—he would be seen as an enemy. As such, he would be hunted with the same ferocity as the Black Khan himself, unless he could persuade the Talisman commanders that their war against the Khan was futile—that they should retreat for the sake of their own survival. For the sake of the boys who had known too much war, boys conscripted by force.

He'd passed many of those boys on his way to the Talisman's central command. Their eyes were sunken in their haggard faces, their cheeks hollow with hunger. Though they hoisted Talisman standards and readied themselves for battle, their hopelessness haunted him.

He had walked in their midst without fear, meeting each one's gaze, the Sacred Cloak flowing down his back as he passed, deliberately permitting it to brush their hands even though he knew the Talisman would consider his act a sacrilege. To take something holy that had been guarded for centuries and now allow the basest rabble to touch it was to dishonor the Cloak in their eyes. And as contemptible as that idea was to Daniyar—that some were more deserving of grace than others—he didn't think of the Talisman's legions as contemptible. As he met their eyes, eyes that were blue, green, amber-gold, or dark, midnight-flecked brown, he thought of them as his own. Shin War or not, these boys who fought the Talisman's wars, and inflicted the Talisman's cruelties, had once been his trust as Guardian of Candour.

He'd called for the loya jirga as much for them as for himself.

Somehow, they must have known it.

As he passed through their ranks unmolested, each boy bowed his head, unable to sustain the clarity of his brilliant silver gaze. Two Talisman pages leapt forward to raise the flaps of the tent as he entered. He memorized their faces and thanked them in a quiet voice.

Bewildered by this show of respect, they retreated without daring to speak. Daniyar sighed, the movement of his powerful shoulders shifting the Cloak to one side. They reminded him of Wafa, the Hazara boy under his care who distrusted any show of kindness.

Inside the tent, he was greeted by wary commanders, all of whom were armed. He searched out those who might recognize him as the defender of the First Oralist, sworn enemy to these men. The Talisman's war was as much against the women mystics known as the Companions of Hira as it was against the Black Khan. Led by the One-Eyed Preacher, the Talisman sought to bring all of Khorasan under their ruthless law. None who defied that law were spared. Women faced a darker fate, sold in slave-chains to the north. Like the Black Khan, the Companions of Hira stood in the way of the Talisman advance. Daniyar had pledged himself to their cause, and to the cause of one woman in particular: Arian, the First Oralist.

The woman he loved.

He'd fought his kin for her; he'd killed for her without a second thought.

Now, as he searched the faces of the commanders, he wondered if any might recognize him not just as her defender, but also as the rider who had killed his own cousin at the frozen city of Firuzkoh. Or if any had witnessed his killing of the Talisman leader who had roused a mob against Arian in Candour, when Arian had taken the Sacred Cloak from its shrine. Or worse yet, if any might know him from the Sorrowsong, where he'd lied to his Shin War clan mates, to further Arian's cause. The Lord of the Wandering Cloud Door had slaughtered the Shin War at the Sorrowsong, but there was always the possibility that one or more of the Shin War had escaped to sound the alarm.

But as he looked around the ring of hostile faces, no one accused him of being a traitor to the Shin War. Rather, he recognized two young men as boys he had taken into his care, now grown to manhood as soldiers capable of leadership. Though the others made no personal greeting, these two bowed their heads.

He stepped over the threshold, careful not to touch it with his boots, a sign of grave disrespect. The Talisman kept their hands on their swords. Daniyar lowered his to his sides, bowing his dark head in greeting.

The Talisman moved back, allowing him a view of the interior of the tent. Despite the exigency of the moment, the tent had been arranged for comfort, the walls lined with white felt, bright blue carpets scattered across the floor, and low cushions arranged around a steel stove for warmth, smoke from its long shaft escaping through a hole in the roof.

At the far side of the tent, a dozen women huddled together, their heads bowed, their soot-darkened faces streaked with tears. As Daniyar made his way closer to the stove, they glanced up at him quickly and just as quickly away. A closer look showed him that the women had been chained at the ankles, as were a pair of girls, although two of the women in the group had been left unrestrained to prepare food for the commanders. They performed the task ably despite their overriding fear. Rage flared behind his eyes, but Daniyar did nothing to betray it.

When tea was served in small metal cups, Daniyar was told to take a seat on the cushions. Judging from the Talisman's grim expressions, he knew none of the men would move from their positions until he did so. The sound of the Black Khan's army strengthening its defenses filled the night. Daniyar ignored it. Removing his sword and placing it away from his hand, he took his seat. The girl who served his tea glanced at him. He met her gaze frankly, not to convey disrespect, but on the chance that she might know who he was and take an instant's comfort from his presence. Her hands trembled in response, spilling hot tea on his wrist. He jerked it away without a sound to betray her, but the Talisman commanders had seen. The man closest to her, an Immolan whose beard had been dyed dark red with henna, struck a blow to the girl's back. She fell at Daniyar's feet. The other women whimpered at the promise of violence to come. Daniyar placed his hands under the girl's arms and gently raised her to her feet. This time when her eyes met his, they widened before she ducked her head. She had recognized him as the Silver Mage. The trembling of her body eased, but her dark eyes remained without hope.

"What is your name?" he asked her.

"Masoumeh," she whispered, with a frightened glance over her shoulder. A pang of sorrow seized him. The girl's name meant "innocence." And from her accent and her finely formed features, he saw that she was a girl of West Khorasan, under the Black Khan's protection, likely one of the refugees who had failed to find safe harbor at Ashfall.

The Immolan who'd struck her snarled at the girl to remove herself. Then he turned on Daniyar, the two men face-to-face, both powerful and dangerous, though Daniyar was seated with his sword set aside as an indication of his sincerity in seeking a truce. The Immolan's gaze flicked to the Shin War crest that Daniyar wore at his throat.

His face marked by a thousand cruelties, the Immolan said, "As a member of the Shin War, a woman taken as a slave should be beneath your notice." He jerked his head in the direction of Ashfall. "Or do you solicit the weak as your companions?"

The storm continued to gather in the depths of Daniyar's eyes, though his voice was even when he answered, "In violence, I seek my equals."

The insult was subtle yet unmistakable; the tension in the atmosphere deepened.

Then laughter rippled through the men.

The Immolan sliced a glare at the others, but the men fell silent only when a white-bearded elder raised his hand. He took a seat on one of the cushions. When he was settled, the other commanders copied him. The elder was in his eighth decade. He carried a staff instead of a sword, which he closed his hand around and kept near to him. His thin face was alert, eyes of charcoal gray betraying a steely intelligence as he made his assessment of Daniyar.

But it was to the Immolan he spoke.

"Have I not warned you against your misuse of the weak? The One entrusts them to our care, and this girl is nothing but a frightened child." His disapproval was plain. "You bring dishonor to your name, Baseer."

The insult was keen, Daniyar realized, for Baseer meant "one of great vision."

Baseer was undaunted. He sat across from Daniyar, close enough to convey menace.

"She is one of the enemy. I give the enemy no quarter."

To see what the Talisman elder would do, Daniyar ventured a response. "I thought you came here to test your strength against that of the Zhayedan army. Are your talents better suited to vanquishing an innocent girl?"

He laid a slight emphasis on the meaning of Masoumeh's name. And he knew that by involving the girl in his scheme, he had no choice but to ensure her escape with his own. She had shrunk down beside the other women at the back, and though the women were frightened, they had come together to shield the girl from Baseer's malevolent gaze.

Baseer spat at Daniyar's feet. Close enough to insult him, but not enough to comprise a transgression of the loya jirga.

"Baseer!" The Talisman elder issued a rebuke that Baseer met with surly disrespect, when the elder went on to add, "We have a guest in our midst."

"We have an *enemy* in our midst," Baseer rejoined. "Remember it, Spinzhiray."

The title referred to the elder's white beard, yet also encompassed more: the elder's courage, his wisdom, his skillful use of rhetoric. Though a loya jirga was a consultation of equals, the Spinzhiray held a position of seniority, one of status among the Talisman.

Daniyar observed the reaction of the men in the circle to Baseer's disrespect. The two he knew kept their eyes on him, while several of the others were openly angry at Baseer. Now and again, a few of the commanders would let their gazes drift to the cloak on Daniyar's shoulders, a touch of wonder in their eyes. Two other men shifted closer to the elder, who seemed to take Baseer's arrogance in stride. His personal guard, perhaps, but others stood at Baseer's back.

The Spinzhiray didn't respond to Baseer, his focus on Daniyar. He advanced a small clay bowl into the center of their gathering. He took a ring that featured an eagle carved from a block of blue stone threaded with streaks of white from his finger.

"A gesture of trust."

Daniyar understood. He removed the ring of the Silver Mage from his finger and placed it in the bowl. Its piercing light arrowed up through the hole in the tent's roof.

Then, obeying the rites of consultation, he waited for the Spinzhiray to speak.

The older man captured his gaze with his own, his gray eyes shrewd and deep-set in his battle-scarred face.

"I'd hoped I would not pass from this earth without meeting the Silver Mage, the Guardian of Candour. Tell me—why do you stand with the Black Khan's army?" He noted the torn crest at Daniyar's throat, the stroke of black on a field of green.

Baseer interrupted before Daniyar could answer. "How do we know he is one of our own? Or that he holds to our code?"

Again Daniyar waited for the Spinzhiray to speak. But in this case, the elder tipped his staff at Daniyar, an indication for him to answer.

Looking from the Spinzhiray to Baseer, Daniyar offered, "The Shin War I know recognize melmastia, and I am a guest in your tent." He acknowledged their hospitality by taking a sip of his tea. "Nanawatai—forgiveness. Turah—courage. Musaawat—equality. Wisa—trust. And ghayrat—self-honor." He nodded at the elder. "I place the ring of the Silver Mage in your bowl, and the sword of the Silver Mage at my side, because I have no fear in your company. I rely upon your honor."

Something in the men settled at those words. They sat back on their heels, their hands easing off their swords.

"You forgot badal. What is a member of the Shin War—of any of the Talisman tribes—without his commitment to revenge?"

Daniyar considered how best to answer Baseer. A tribal society that defended its lands from warfare found revenge necessary not only to uphold their honor, but for survival.

"What is meted out in self-defense, I see as a matter of justice, not of dishonor or revenge," he said at last.

"You think to recalibrate the foundations on which the Shin War have stood?"

Daniyar shook his head, realizing that nothing he could say would win Baseer's favor. Turning to the Spinzhiray, he said, "*Honor* is the foundation of everything we stand for." Flicking a steely glance at Baseer, he added, "You point out my omissions, but what of yours? You chose not to mention naamus."

Baseer made a show of grasping his sword.

"The honor of women?" He pretended to laugh. "Women *have* no honor."

Unexpectedly, the Spinzhiray said, *"They are garments for you, and you are garments for them."*

And having just had his involvement with the Black Khan questioned, Daniyar now wondered how a man who would recite this verse of the Claim could be in a position of leadership at this loya jirga. Encouraged, he nodded at the corner where the women in the tent had taken shelter.

"The Shin War code that I was taught defended the honor of women. Violence against those weaker than ourselves is outlawed by that code."

A murmur in the tent. He sensed the tacit agreement of the orphans he had taken in.

"Are you the champion of the weak, then?" the Spinzhiray asked, with a look Daniyar couldn't read.

His answer was straightforward. "Such was my trust as Guardian of Candour."

"Yet you are not in Candour. And I think Baseer is right to ask why the Guardian of Candour makes his stand at the Black Khan's walls."

The mood in the tent tautened once more, the canvas like the lungs of a living being, inflating and deflating with each syllable. A curl of victory shaped Baseer's lips. Yet when Daniyar made another slow sweep of the men gathered for the loya jirga, he observed a range of responses: admiration and respect from some, uncertainty and fear from others. If he was honest with them, if he spoke the truths of the Silver Mage, some might choose to ally with him. He could see from the way a few paid heed to the women at the back that the taking of slaves unsettled them. Perhaps they could still be persuaded to his point of view.

His voice rough, he said, "I am tired of war. I am tired of the desolation of our lands." He motioned with a hand, something of his grief in the gesture. "What Candour *was* compared to what it has become—you must feel it as deeply as I do." He turned his head to indicate the city of Ashfall. "It is not the way of Shin War, nor of any of our tribes, to wage war against those who do not act against us. The Black Khan seeks to hold his capital. His armies have not ventured into our lands; they haven't sought to conquer."

Baseer leaned forward so that his forearms were braced on his thighs, his face close to Daniyar's. In its harsh lines and powerful certainty, Daniyar understood that this was a man who thrived on war. And to whom the Shin War code was a tool exploited for his own purposes or discarded when it failed to serve him.

"The Black Khan's truce is a stratagem. You are a fool to believe otherwise."

Daniyar's gaze flicked to the Spinzhiray.

"Would you not hold your walls if there was an army at your gates? An army that takes your women captive?" Though it galled him to speak on the Black Khan's behalf, he added, "The Khan has his own sense of naamus."

He pointed to the young men he had tutored. They snapped to attention, their spines stiff with pride.

"Why waste their lives on this cause? Gather your men and take them home to engage in work with purpose. Allow them to build their future—restore the glory of Candour."

He made no attempt to hide the depth of his longing for this outcome.

The men began to debate among themselves, but Daniyar watched the Spinzhiray. Despite the egalitarian structure of the council, its hierarchy would prevail.

"You think our war unjust?" he asked Daniyar, under the cover of the others' voices.

Daniyar stared at the pulsing light that spiraled out from his ring. The silver light had wrapped itself around the lapis lazuli stone of the other man's ring. The carved eagle appeared ready to take flight. He took a steadying breath: an honest answer would be seen as an insult, yet the Spinzhiray would see through a lie. With great care, he posed a question instead.

"How many of the Black Khan's people have you killed or enslaved on your route to Ashfall?"

The Spinzhiray's nobbled fingers stroked the soft wool of his beard. "To spread the message of the One across these lands is an act of justice."

The Talisman commanders nodded one by one. In their renewed silence, Daniyar's sharp ears picked up a sound that filled his thoughts with urgency. The actions of the Zhayedan were intensifying: they were preparing to attack.

He'd known better than to trust the Black Khan, but what other choice had there been? Arian was behind those walls. She was determined to take on the One-Eyed Preacher, even if she did so alone.

He sought a truce with the Talisman because he'd taken on her cause as his own. He had turned from her once, then promised himself he wouldn't fail her again.

"The people of West Khorasan have long adhered to the message of the One. They named their western gate the Messenger Gate after the Messenger of the One."

The Spinzhiray's eyes sharpened . . . *hardened* . . . and Daniyar knew the battle was lost. There would be no truce with the Talisman this night. Or any of the nights that came after.

"Their court is corrupt, their practices a barbarity. The Black Khan's scriptorium houses works of the profane."

Daniyar fought not to show his outrage at this characterization of a place dedicated to the preservation of knowledge. "I have visited the scriptorium myself. Treatises on medicine and mathematics are anything but profane." He debated the wisdom of mentioning the Bloodprint, then decided to keep his knowledge to himself. "The rest is for the One to judge."

The elder's grip tightened on his staff as Baseer rose to his feet.

"The One *has* judged. We have come to carry out the judgment."

"Spinzhiray, I beg you to put the lives of your men before these notions of judgment."

The elder shook his head in disapproval. "The dunya is of no value compared to the rewards of the Akhirah."

A standard Talisman formula: the present world was only a means to gain the bounty of the afterlife. The Talisman used the formula to justify oppression. They would spend the lives of the boys in their army, boys he had once sheltered in Candour, without counting the cost.

"There will be no truce," he continued. "No retreat."

The Talisman commanders assisted the Spinzhiray to his feet. Daniyar collected his sword and sheathed it. Before he could bend to reclaim his ring, a roar shattered the night. The wind was in Daniyar's eyes as a giant boulder tore through the roof of the tent, obliterating the stove, killing the commanders closest to it.

Screams filled the air. Orders were shouted across the tent, but what Daniyar's keen hearing picked up was the cranking noise of the mechanism that raised the Zhayedan's catapults. He called out a warning to the others to flee, his eyes on the women who crouched at the back of the tent. He wasn't swift enough to act. A second boulder followed the first, its terrifying heft bringing the tent to utter silence. When the sound of the crash receded, Daniyar looked across to the back of the tent. The corner where the women had sheltered was ripped away. No one had survived, blood and bone strewn across the carpets.

He was seized from behind by two Talisman commanders who pushed him before the Spinzhiray. The elder's white robes were flecked with blood and bits of flesh. But the Spinzhiray was used to death. His hands were steady on his staff, his charcoal eyes aflame with rage.

"The Guardian of Candour engaged in rank deception—you called for the loya jirga knowing the Zhayedan would strike!"

"No!" Daniyar protested, struggling to free himself, but the two men who held him were strong. They pinned his arms behind his back. "I could not wear the Sacred Cloak and lie—you know this!"

The Spinzhiray moved close enough that Daniyar felt his breath on his face. He ripped the Shin War crest from Daniyar's throat, leaving it vulnerable and exposed.

"I know only this: you are a member of the Shin War without honor. Kill him, Baseer."

Baseer, too, was covered in the blood of others, but his eyes gleamed with unholy satisfaction. He nodded at Daniyar's captors, who forced him to his knees. He heard the sharp, metallic scrape of a well-honed sword pulled from its sheath.

He raised his head, finding the young men who had known him in Candour.

"It isn't true," he said. It mattered to him to convince them, even if he were to die here. "I came to you in good faith for the sake of our people. To barter for their lives and yours."

Baseer poised his sword at the nape of Daniyar's neck. "You have no people now. You are a traitor expelled from his clan. But that won't matter to you soon."

He raised his sword for the killing blow just as flaming arrows whistled into the tent. Fire licked up the felt walls, collapsing what remained as the Talisman tore them down. Screams scraped against the vastness of the sky. Baseer was taken by an arrow. The two men who held Daniyar released him, fleeing outside into the night.

Daniyar came to his feet in a powerful lunge.

"Run," he said to the young soldiers he knew. "Find your way to Candour."

Smoke thickened the air, slicked over his skin, and coiled up into his lungs. Flames devoured the tent, and all around him were the sounds of the Talisman regrouping for war.

One of the young soldiers looked him in the eye and spit out, "Khaeen." Daniyar flinched from the viciousness of the word. But unable to hold the gaze of the Silver Mage after naming him a traitor, the soldier turned on his heel and fled.

Daniyar knew that his own would turn against him now. They would, as the young man had, consider him khaeen; they would erase him from the history of his people. The loneliness of being severed from his clan was a wound that throbbed in his chest, achingly familiar and dull.

My course was honorable, he told himself. *No matter what they say about me, I did not betray who I am meant to be.*

He focused on the other soldier, the one he might be able to persuade.

His name was Toryal, Daniyar remembered. Toryal pulled the scarf around his neck up to his mouth, trying to lessen the impact of the smoke.

"You were the Guardian of Candour—we believed in you. We *trusted* you." He said the words in a tone so hopeless that it arrowed deep inside Daniyar. "For you to raise your hand against us—you taught us to choose the course of honor—now *your* honor lies in shreds."

Toryal pulled his scarf higher, so that his neck was exposed. A telltale map of scars spread down from his throat into his armor. He had long been a conscript of the Talisman, one of the lost boys of Candour.

While the young man deliberated, Daniyar took in the fire that blazed a trail through the encampment. The commanders who had escaped were preparing for a counterattack, while the Zhayedan's catapults continued to pound down destruction.

The devastating noise of battle was unlike anything Daniyar had ever heard. It crashed into his temples, battered his senses. Choking on the smoke, he said, "I promise you—I was not privy to this attack. But you know it for yourself, Toryal. This siege is not a course of honor. There *is* another way. Come with me instead."

The younger man blinked, reaching for his sword. Daniyar left his sheathed.

In that strange, suspended moment, both men struggled to breathe, conscious of the rush of others toward them. Whatever else he was forced to do this night, he would not harm Toryal.

"If I go with you, I'll have nothing. No clan or kin, no honor to call my own."

Daniyar held Toryal's gaze. "You'll have me. I won't leave you to stand on your own."

Toryal rubbed one hand over the marks at his throat. Awkwardly, he began to cry. Daniyar stepped closer. When the younger man didn't back away, he moved to take hold of him, wrapping the folds of the Sacred Cloak around them both. Let Toryal feel the strength that would protect him, even on a Talisman field.

As arrows burned the ground at their feet, he held Toryal until his sobs began to ease. The scent of wild honey filled the air, rising over the smoke, offering a hint of sweetness.

Toryal drew back, his blue-green eyes wet with tears.

"I would have saved the girl," he said, refusing to look over at the bodies.

Daniyar assessed him. Made a judgment. "I know you would have tried."

"How?" There was a tremor in Toryal's voice. "How can you know I speak the truth?"

Daniyar placed one hand on Toryal's shoulder, stroked the surface of the Cloak.

"You wear the Sacred Cloak. You cannot utter falsehoods under its mantle." But what he'd said wasn't enough. The boy needed more, something that didn't depend on mysteries he couldn't unravel, something beyond the sacred. "I remember you, Toryal. You wouldn't have taken this path if you'd been given a choice."

For a moment, a dazed sense of wonder appeared in Toryal's eyes. He brought his hand up to the Cloak, stroking its unfathomable texture. Silky, yet heavy as wool. Enfolding him in warmth, yet soft and cool to the touch.

Remembering himself, he dropped his hand. He stepped away from Daniyar, remorse darkening his eyes. Mourning the things he knew he would never be able to have.

"I can't follow you," he said. "There's nothing for me save this. Every man in Candour has been conscripted to the Talisman cause. There's no way out of it, though many of us have tried." His fingers ran over his scars. "Those who agree to fight are guaranteed the safety of their women. Those who refuse . . ." He dragged his tunic open, yanking at his armor.

At first Daniyar thought the pattern across his ribs were lash marks left by a whip. But the raised flesh was red and blistered, the texture of the flesh thick and waxy. Toryal's body had been burned.

A swirling torrent of rage and grief rose inside him.

"You could still come with me. You could bring those like you to the gates, and the Black Khan would give you shelter. It isn't too late for you to choose another course."

But Toryal was shaking his head, desperate and unsure.

"Don't offer me a future I know I'll never see. All I have left is my hope that my sisters will not be sold."

And, with his sword gripped in his hand, Toryal disappeared.

The strange lethargy, the almost-hope that had seized Daniyar and held the battle at bay now evaporated in a rush. He moved through the tent, stepping over bodies, searching for the bowl that held his ring. But its piercing light failed to penetrate the smoke.

Then there was no more time to search. The stench of death in his nostrils, the heat of fire at his back, he swung around to face the group of Talisman who advanced.

He drove forward into the fray, his sword flashing out into the night, the Cloak streaming from his back singed by trails of fire. The sight of the Cloak gave one of the Talisman pause; the rest rushed to meet his sword. Daniyar was heavy with muscle, but he moved with the grace of a predator, his skill in combat honed by the years he had stood against the Talisman. Bodies fell as others surged to take their place. The Talisman had no strategy beyond an inarticulate fury they intended to assuage. Daniyar took a slash to his arm, another to the opposite shoulder. It slowed him but didn't bring him down.

The fury of the Zhayedan's mangonels brought him a moment or two of rest, and then he was thrust upon his mettle again: more of the soldiers recognized him as the man who had promised a truce during the loya jirga.

Under the rage, he read their contempt for a man who could betray his own. He shrugged it aside, blocking a bold attempt at his throat, another under his armor. But in the end, he couldn't stand against them all. His arms were tiring; there was nowhere to escape to. Sweat dampened his hair, seeped under his armor. Clouds of smoke stung his eyes. There was no sign of his ring, no other powers to call upon, when he needed his every breath to fight.

But then the Talisman fell back, bodies collapsing to the ground, arrows through their necks or rising from their backs. These weren't fletched like Teerandaz arrows; they were black-tipped, lethal in their accuracy. He blinked to clear his bleary eyes. Two men were fighting at his side, raising their swords when his movements were too slow. They were sheathed in skintight leather, expressionless behind their masks.

They fought back the press of the attack, and when the Talisman's attention turned elsewhere, one of them grabbed Daniyar's arm.

"The field is lost," he warned. "The only way out is with us."

A NARROW CHAMBER LED OFF TO THE RIGHT OF THE QAYSARIEH POR-
tal. A faint scent of dampness emanated from within, overlaid
with traces of jasmine. When Arian peered inside, the sight she
encountered brought her to a halt. A moment later, her escort became aware that she'd fallen behind. Khashayar, a captain of the
Zhayedan army, signaled his men to wait. He strode back to join
Arian at the entrance to the chamber.

"Does something delay you, First Oralist?"

He spoke to her with the respect her status as First Oralist demanded. More, his manner set an example for his men, who had
balked at abandoning Ashfall while the capital was under attack.
Yet the order to accompany the First Oralist on her mission had
come directly from the Black Khan. The Zhayedan might find
little merit in chasing a holy relic while their comrades fought a
battle for survival, but they would obey their Khan, and through
him Khashayar. The city would have to hold until they returned
from their quest.

Arian raised her eyes to Khashayar's face. He was black-haired,
with dramatic dark eyes under an aristocratic brow. Though he

was no relation, in appearance he resembled Rukh, the Black Khan. He was young to be charged with escorting her to Timeback, but his youth was a matter of years, not experience. He carried his command with poise: disciplined, experienced, yet adaptable enough to recognize why Arian's mission mattered to the fate of his city.

"What is this chamber?" she asked him.

"A cistern. We use it to collect rainwater."

"There's a prayer nook in the wall."

Khashayar nodded, but his head was inclined toward the sounds of combat beyond the city walls. When she still didn't move, he said, "It was built at the request of the Begum Niyousha—the Black Khan's mother. She observed her worship here. The Princess Darya followed her example."

A shadow crossed Khashayar's face. The Princess of Ashfall had been killed during a skirmish on the walls. She should have been safe in the Al Qasr with the rest of the Khan's household, yet she'd raced to the western gate to prevent her half-brother, Darius, from striking against the Black Khan, her death as chaotic and impetuous as the way she'd lived her life.

"May I take a moment for prayer before we leave?"

Khashayar's black gaze skipped over the First Oralist's confederates—Sinnia, the Companion from the lands of the Negus, and Wafa, the blue-eyed Hazara boy under the Companions' care.

When he hesitated, Arian tried to reassure him. "The blessing is important, otherwise I wouldn't delay." A graceful hand swept out from under her cloak, the gold circlet on her upper arm agleam in the muted light. She gestured back at the square they had passed through where the impact of the battle was felt. "I will pray for the deliverance of Ashfall, as much as for our journey ahead."

Khashayar gave the order to his men to proceed. He settled himself at the entrance to the cistern, his arms crossed over his chest. "I'll stand guard."

"Don't wait," Arian said to Sinnia. "Go with the Zhayedan; I won't be far behind."

She waited until Sinnia had departed, tugging Wafa along with her. Hesitant now, she nodded at Khashayar. "I will require privacy."

She flushed a little under the keenness of his gaze.

"I won't intrude, sahabiya."

Something in his expression told her she could trust him, though all had come to chaos in both her city and his. His integrity shone from his eyes, his dedication a bond that pulsed between them in the room.

Bowing her head, she slipped past him to make her way to the prayer nook. The vaulted ceiling of the cistern sloped down to a sandstone colonnade. Lanterns in rich blue turquoise were hung between columns of gold above an elongated pool. Between two of these columns, a single pillar, almost like a plinth, had been placed in the center of the pool. The glow of torchlight shone on amber walls, whose high periphery was lined with geometries of tiny blue tiles. At the northeastern corner, a mihrab was fashioned against cold stone like the plume of a peacock's tail, feathered in emerald green, the exquisite tessellation sheened with light. Beneath it, the golden threads of a well-worn prayer rug reflected echoes of that light.

Arian knelt on the rug. She held words of prayer in her mouth until they bloomed into blessings. Benedictions sought, tumultuous griefs confided. Her fears confessed to the One.

What were they coming to?

What hope did she have of turning the tide of this war?

For years she had battled the tyranny of the Talisman and the greatest cruelty of their reign: their enslavement of the women of the east.

The Companions of Hira were all that stood between the Talisman and total devastation, fighting to preserve Khorasan's plural heritage, a battle they waged without recourse to force of arms. Instead, they relied upon the scripture of the Claim, the sacred magic passed through oral transmission; its written counterpart had vanished over time, destroyed by the Talisman's purges.

For a decade, Arian had used her gifts as First Oralist of Hira— First Oralist of the *Claim*—to disrupt the Talisman's slave-chains. Then Ilea, the High Companion of her order, had assigned her a new task: to procure the Bloodprint, the sole surviving record of the Claim. Anchored by it, the Companions would have worked to overthrow the Talisman. Months ago, Arian had set out on the trail of the sacred text, but the Black Khan's machinations had brought the Bloodprint to Ashfall instead.

Now the Talisman's war had come to the west, to the empire of the Black Khan, and battle raged at his capital. Arian could hear their cries beyond the chamber where she prayed.

Her forehead touched the carpet in prostration. Tears welled up in her eyes, drifting up into her hairline. Her questions sounded like complaints, as if she'd had a crisis of faith. She believed devoutly in the Claim, but she needed to know why she'd struggled so long to lose the Bloodprint in the end. A devastating loss, mitigated only by a new mission: to find the Sana Codex, an ancient record of the Claim hidden away in Timeback, a city of the maghreb.

As a last desperate hope, she had set out with her escort to retrieve it.

I was learning the Bloodprint, she prayed in protest. *Why let the One-Eyed Preacher take it? Though I seek the Codex as an answer to its power, is my quest likely to succeed? Do I possess the wisdom to unravel the secrets of the Claim? Will I be able to wield it against one who seems as invincible as the Preacher?*

If I fail, who will count the cost?

The prayer rug was wet with her tears now. She had already measured some part of that cost. Her family lost to her in childhood. Her sister's renunciation when they had chanced to reunite. The Black Khan's theft of the Bloodprint at the Ark. The manuscript had been in her grasp—then gone. Now two further blows had been struck: she'd been severed from the Council of Hira and divided from the man she loved.

I have Sinnia, she reassured herself. *I have Sinnia and Wafa. And this noble soldier of the Zhayedan to guide me, Khashayar, so proud and brave.*

She thought about those instances when the Claim had swept over her like a cyclone, overwhelming her conscious will. She whispered a prayer to the One.

Make me a servant of the Word. I have seen the darkness of the Claim. If I must use it to destroy, don't let it twist who I am. I seek no arcane powers; I disavow the rites of blood.

"Sahabiya." The soft reminder from Khashayar brought her to the end of her prayers.

Bless these lands, bless this city, bless the people of Khorasan. May the manifest blessings of the One descend upon those who journey at my side, those who wait for me at Hira, and those I leave behind in Ashfall.

Then she made a futile bargain, struck over the ashes of oaths she had already taken.

Keep Daniyar safe, and I'll give myself to this cause.

She kissed the spot on the carpet that she'd touched with her forehead. When she rose to her feet again, she glimpsed her reflection in the pool. The turquoise waters of the cistern seemed to collect the light—it throbbed at the base of the pool, undulating in a wave that tumbled back into itself. Arian peered into the basin. What caused the light to reflect off the bottomless depths of the pool? Was the basin tiled in silver? She couldn't tell, the sparks of light kept refracting until the mosaics split apart, an illusion that made the turquoise depths seem infinite.

A mystery she would willingly explore, but the pallor of her skin disturbed the surface of the pool, and her mind was distracted. Her face was lined with weariness, her eyes dull, her hair hanging in limp, damp trails. She'd been a queen at the Black Khan's banquet—ornamented, perfumed, beguiling, young, and alluringly feminine, a woman who belonged at a court as graceful and dignified as Ashfall's. How long ago that tranquility seemed now, how deceptive her brief transformation.

She firmed the line of her jaw to make herself appear steadfast, a trick that failed to suffice, her body and spirit bruised in too many ways to count. Now, the dullness was a thing within, the spark of her purpose extinguished. She'd exchanged one guise for another, one quest for another, her course meant to be unerring, but she couldn't deceive herself. She didn't want to leave Daniyar. She didn't trust that she would find her way to Timeback or that she would find what she was searching for in the city. The journey would take time.

What would she return to?

The green eyes that gazed back at her from the pool were bleak with worry and fear. "We must go," Khashayar said.

Must we? she asked herself.

24

"WE'VE FACED WORSE ODDS."

Sinnia's spyglass was trained on the open grasslands, a brief stretch between the hidden exit of Qaysarieh's tunnels and the rearguard of the camped-out forces of the Rising Nineteen. She grinned, a white flash against glossy dark skin. "It's usually just the two of us against our enemies, me with my whip, you with your sword and the Claim." She stretched out the muscles of her shoulders, a luxurious movement in the cramped confines of the tunnel. "This time we have a boy"—she ran an affectionate hand over Wafa's unruly curls—"and a ferocious host to accompany us." Wafa didn't smile at Sinnia, daunted by the sounds of the battle that raged behind them in the city, but he leaned into her touch.

The host consisted of ten well-armed members of the Khorasan Guard. The men looked harried by the sounds of the battle they had left, impatient to return to the defense of their city, though they knew the journey ahead was a long one. Their route would take them across the Empty Quarter to Axum, the capital of the Negus. A reasonable place to break the journey, as it would allow

Sinnia to return to the home she hadn't visited in a year. But Arian had her own reasons for stopping at Axum. If they were able to get through the Rising Nineteen and come out on the other side unharmed, Axum would be a place of refuge. Hunted by the One-Eyed Preacher, they would need that refuge.

Pausing their journey at Axum would also give her the chance to study its celebrated manuscripts. With its long history of exchange with the maghreb, there might be a clue to the whereabouts of the Sana Codex somewhere in Axum's lore, or at least some reference to the Mage of the Blue Eye, who was reputed to be its keeper. Perhaps the Negus or his queen would be able to tell her more.

Another uncertainty she faced.

If they *did* find the elusive Blue Mage, she hoped to persuade him to trust her with the Codex—to convince him that her need for it was urgent. It was the only answer to the Preacher's mastery of the Bloodprint, and she couldn't stand against him without it, no matter her proficiency with the Claim. She needed knowledge to match his knowledge, or she would have stayed in Ashfall to fight. The necessity of her return was ever-present on her mind.

Khashayar felt it too. He lowered his spyglass to speak.

"There's no cover, no means to take them by surprise. We'll have to engage them, First Oralist." His nod acknowledged Sinnia. "And despite the Companion's optimism, this is not a battle we can win. The numbers are against us."

Sinnia passed her spyglass to Arian so she could see for herself, aware that there was something different about Arian but unable to pinpoint what it was. Arian studied the open grasslands, noting the distance they'd have to clear. Passing the spyglass back to Sinnia, she turned to scan the men behind her, her gaze lighting on each for a moment, until each one lowered his gaze. All except Khashayar, who raised his chin and waited.

Arian pressed one hand against the gold circlet on her upper arm, the insignia worn by the Companions of Hira.

"They haven't moved. They're waiting for a signal from the One-Eyed Preacher."

Khashayar unscrewed a silver flask and took a sip of water. The flask was nothing like the plain leather waterskins Arian and Sinnia carried. It was engraved with ornate calligraphy in the pattern of a lush floral wreath. When he saw that the calligraphy had captured Arian's attention, he offered the flask to her. Arian read the list of blessings and offered them aloud. She returned Khashayar's flask to him without drinking from it, though his offer had been generous. She knew Khashayar would understand that as a matter of etiquette, she would not place her lips against the opening his lips had touched. He tucked away his flask without comment.

"What is your counsel, First Oralist?"

"I will provide cover." She showed him a small hillock of grass-threaded sand in the near distance. "We need to reach that hill without giving ourselves away."

Khashayar checked the spot with a frown. "Even if you *could* provide cover, it leaves us too close to their soldiers. Our circle around them should be wider." He showed her what he meant with a sweep of his hand, inadvertently brushing her arm. Her golden circlet pulsed. He was taken aback by the energy that leapt from her body to his. She shifted to allow it to pass.

"Forgive me, I meant no offense."

"You gave none." Her soft words stroked over him, and for a moment he had the sense he was being gentled as one would coax a stallion to the touch of a warrior's hand. Her answer echoed his thoughts. "We must risk it, Khashayar." She turned back to the opening again, squeezed against Sinnia and Wafa. "They have horses I intend to take."

Khashayar rubbed his jaw. He widened his stance, planting his feet.

"Horses will not survive the crossing of the Rub Al Khali. The risk is a foolish one, First Oralist."

His men murmured behind him. The noise of catapults crashing into Ashfall's courtyard sounded at their backs. The time for ambivalence was over. Either he convinced the Companions to return, or he accepted their direction.

He'd already learned that the First Oralist shared little of her thoughts or her plans. She was used to traveling without a company of soldiers at her back, unwilling to justify her actions, but something about her certainty spoke to Khashayar. Convinced him to heed her counsel.

"We must go," she said now. "The Claim will cover us all. The risk is worth it."

With no further argument, he signaled to the men behind him. They moved into position. He squeezed past Wafa, gestured at the Companions.

"I'll go first with two of my men. Follow us once we are clear."

The sound of the Claim filled the tunnel, washing the dankness from it, wrapping around their senses, its notes as close and familiar as if the men were voicing it themselves. When Khashayar and his soldiers had eased out of the tunnel, Arian and Sinnia followed with Wafa, the rest of their escort at their back. The Claim rose around them, strong and sweet, yet oddly hollow, a breeze blowing over plains of fertile scrubland. Their party moved across the grass, cocooned inside the Claim, the soft words blowing across the group of soldiers who kept watch at the rear of the Nineteen's army. Military men, professional and well-trained, alert to sounds and movement around them, their camp orderly and silent.

Khashayar tallied numbers, noted the count and caliber of weaponry, made sharp-eyed assessments of the men waiting to attack Ashfall from the west. The rearguard consisted of two hundred men. In each small group was a runner, positioned to receive messages from the soldiers yet to arrive. The entire vanguard consisted of no more than a thousand men. When spread out in a line against the plains, they had seemed ten times that number. Or perhaps the One-Eyed Preacher had used his sorcery to demoralize the defenders of Ashfall.

He counted the brushfires along their encampment. They lit the faces of small groups, though most of the men had covered the lower half of their faces with their neck scarves, in the custom of their people. He noted the looseness of their robes as a weakness—not what he would have chosen to wear as armor into battle. His own men wore leather armor that closely conformed to their bodies, their weapons at their waists, shields slung over their backs. The Nineteen may have been well-fortified, but Khashayar perceived disadvantages the Zhayedan could exploit.

As they crept ahead with utmost stealth, he considered sending a message by hawk to convey his discoveries to Arsalan, the commander of the Black Khan's army. But too many of the tribal herders who made up the Rising Nineteen had cast their glances at the sky, waiting for such a signal to give away the enemy's position. As he scanned the perimeter for a possible ambush, he noticed when two soldiers in each group raised their torches, the signal he had been waiting for.

He held up his hand to silence all movement. The Companions

came to a halt, the First Oralist at his side, the Claim a near-silent murmur from her mouth. They were no more than fifty feet from the rearguard of the Nineteen. Two of the soldiers glanced in their direction.

The breeze that brushed the grasslands whipped against their faces, forcing them to turn away.

Khashayar's smile was grim. He knew his duty was to escort the Companions to Timeback, but his mind was racing with other possibilities. With the First Oralist's use of the Claim, perhaps they could strike against the rearguard and strike hard—hard enough to gain Ashfall another night's reprieve.

Before the First Oralist could answer the question in his eyes—or before he could act on his own—a chant began in the Nineteen's camp. The soldiers beat against the ground with their torches in an accompanying rhythm. The chant was meant to terrorize the citizens of Ashfall, but Khashayar was mystified by the meaning of the words they spoke. They offered it in the High Tongue. As an elite commander, he was literate enough to understand.

"Over this are Nineteen."

Over what? What did their name signify? He lowered his arm in a signal and began to move again, letting the words sweep over the night. The First Oralist's continuous murmur of the Claim dimmed any fear he might have felt at the chant.

Over this are Nineteen.

He glanced back at his men to ensure that their course was steady. They moved with precision, a line of warriors determined to protect the Companions and the boy, weapons in hand, eyes focused on the soldiers who should have seen their movements in the open but whose heads remained turned away.

Though the temptation to strike was great, Khashayar bided

his time. He would get the Companions to safety, and then he would persuade the First Oralist of the merits of his plan.

They stole across the grass, their movements sleek and their footing sure. None looked away from the Nineteen, waiting for the silence to break, prepared at any moment for discovery.

But under the steady flow of the First Oralist's words, they made their way to the hillock and dipped down the other side. Now they were positioned on a twenty-foot dune that loomed above the Nineteen. Khashayar made a rapid calculation and was convinced: if the First Oralist used the Claim to shield them, he and his men could eliminate the rearguard.

She would caution him, he knew. Ten against two hundred. But he'd seen the power of the Claim.

Still, he had to consider the step that would come after a surprise attack. News of the First Oralist's routing of the One-Eyed Preacher at the Messenger Gate had spread rapidly through the ranks of the Zhayedan. She was a weapon they could wield. *If* she remained on their side. Angering her for a limited victory could mean losing her assistance entirely.

Too, the First Oralist had made calculations of her own. She wanted the horses the soldiers closest to them had grouped at the rear of their camp—horses whose finely shaped heads were the mark of the region's thoroughbreds. The horses could take them some distance farther west, though they lacked the stamina for the journey through the heart of the Rub Al Khali desert. At some point, the Companions would need to trade the thoroughbreds for camels.

But surely he could use that to his advantage. He would give the First Oralist her horses, if she agreed to his strike. If she helped him destroy the Nineteen's entire vanguard. He glanced over at her, expecting to find her attention focused on the horses.

Instead, her gaze had followed his, and now she watched him closely, as if she could read his thoughts. Could she? He frowned at the thought.

"First Oralist—"

She spoke to him kindly, her cloak thrown back, the breeze taking the long strands of her hair, so that it whipped at his skin, soft as Marakand silk. "I don't have the power you seek."

"You defeated the One-Eyed Preacher at the walls."

"A momentary respite."

Something in the air shifted. The chanting slowed. Deepened. Soldiers in the camp began to move. Spyglasses scanned the dunes.

Arian and Khashayar ducked down. The murmur of the Claim began again, this time augmented by Sinnia, while the boy, Wafa, crouched at their sides, his blue eyes wide with fear.

Arian shifted closer to the horses. His courtesy set aside, Khashayar's hand shot out to clamp down on her wrist.

She turned back to him, pinned him with eyes that seemed to see everything, things he didn't want her to know.

But it was the boy who wrenched Khashayar's grip from her wrist. A hard smile touched Khashayar's lips. The Hazara boy freed by the Companions had a blind devotion to them now. Nothing could rout him from their sides, or from their self-appointed Audacy.

He watched as the First Oralist took the boy's hand and pressed a kiss to his curls.

The Talisman's prejudice spilled over into his thoughts. How could the First Oralist of Hira kiss a child of the Hazara, a people too weak to defend themselves, instead of aligning herself with much worthier allies?

She answered his unspoken question. "We are all equals. We all belong to the One." Then, moving out of his reach, she skirted closer, lower down the ridge to where the horses were pastured. "If I could help you, I would, Khashayar. You'll have to learn to trust me." She nodded at the city in the distance, a glimmer of lights beyond the army's encampment. The sounds of battle were fainter far from the walls, yet still audible. The clash of steel, the destruction sowed by catapults that creaked under the weight of their projectiles, the clean whistle of arrows slicing through bursts of noise. Brilliant dots of fire flickered along the walls.

"I would understand if you and your men chose to return to make your stand at Ashfall. Just as Sinnia and I must fulfill our purpose."

She held his gaze, her own astonishingly clear.

Go with her, the Black Khan had said. *Do not leave her side. Whoever stands against you, whoever you must destroy, your foremost duty is to bring the Sana Codex to Ashfall. No matter what the First Oralist may tell you. No matter where she tries to take it. Do otherwise, and you will be party to the destruction of this empire.*

Khashayar's fingers curled into his palm. He moved to give the First Oralist cover, signaling to his men. Crawling crabwise across the hill in their descent, he felt the verses of the Claim attain an urgency. A harshness to stand against words that had no meaning for him, despite their pounding pulse.

Over this are Nineteen.

His armor was brushed by spiky tufts of grass that pricked at the skin of his throat. The breeze summoned by the Claim blew the smoke from the Nineteen's fires away from their small party back into the camp, where soldiers could be heard coughing. He gripped his sword, sliding sideways. His men remained in position at the crest. Two of his monitored their progress. The First Oralist had also motioned to the boy to wait for her return.

Now Khashayar and the Companions inched their way closer to the camp with the horses, each increment of movement scrutinized in advance.

Thirty feet. Twenty. Ten. So close now that the horses' ears pricked forward, hearing their subtle movements beneath the Claim. Sinnia's use of the Claim broke off.

"If the Silver Mage was with us, he could calm the horses for us."

She picked up her use of the Claim before Arian could answer, though Arian's shoulders tightened at the words. She changed her intonation. The Claim became more secret. When Khashayar looked up to measure their progress, his head was within kicking distance of the enemy's boots.

He rolled away. The soldier didn't stir, his gaze fixed on the stars.

Then, like a wraith trailing clouds of mist, the First Oralist flowed to her feet, her graceful movements matched by Sinnia's. She stroked the mane of one of the sequestered mares, murmuring the Claim in its ear. The horse shifted to nuzzle her shoulder, and Khashayar saw that the mares were linked together, held by a single lead. He motioned to the Companions to retreat, wrapping the lead around his wrist. His powerful body nudged the lead mare up the slope, his sharp eyes trained on the soldiers guarding the horses.

Still no movement, no awareness.

But the pace up the dune was perilously slow, the horses kicking up sand with the fussy placement of their hooves. He swore to himself, sweat breaking out on his forehead. His side was exposed to the Rising Nineteen, and he'd been forced to sheathe his sword. The horses were moving too slowly, but a signal from the First Oralist warned him against careless haste.

When the Companions reached the crest, the tension in his muscles lessened. The First Oralist took the lead rein from his hands. He fell back, counting the mares. They wouldn't need them all. A dozen would be enough; the rest could be repastured. He waited until twelve of the horses had been led down the far side of the hill before he moved to sever the lead.

But when he slid between two of the horses, he made the mistake of choosing a fierce young stallion. The freed horse reared up. When its forelegs crashed down again, they narrowly missed his head. He rolled out from under the stallion's hooves, but his unexpected movement incited panic.

The stallion wheeled, nipping the haunches of the mare he was tied to. The mares on the upslope screamed, the piercing noise cutting through the sharp-edged notes of the Claim. The mirage of emptiness faded. The soldiers closest to the hillock sprang to their feet, swords ripped from their scabbards.

Khashayar whirled to face them, even as his archers began to cut down his pursuers.

"Run!" he shouted to the Companions. "Leave the field to us!"

He made his stand at the top of the hill, sword in one hand, dagger in the other, archers at either side. Without the protection of the Claim, his men couldn't hold against so many. They were cut down on the sands where they stood. Khashayar's quick glance down at the Companions found them encircled, the horses they had stolen recaptured by the Nineteen.

"Hold!"

A powerful voice shouted the command. The Rising Nineteen went still on both sides of the hill. Taking advantage of the distraction, Khashayar plunged down the slope. When none of the soldiers attacked, he pushed the Companions behind him, his sword poised in one hand.

A member of the Nineteen stepped forward, his dark eyes gleaming under the hood of a dusty blue burnoose. He threw back his hood to show his face. An older man with rich brown skin, the hair at his temples streaked with gray that matched his beard, his posture one of a man used to having his orders obeyed. When he loosened his cloak to show them his armor, Khashayar caught his breath.

Then he counted the number of soldiers who stood behind the man.

THE ZHAYEDAN GATE STOOD FIRM THROUGH THE NIGHT. THE TEERAN-daz archers of Ashfall held it, knowing that the Cataphracts, the army's shock troops, were needed at the Emissary Gate. Cassandane, the Captain of the Teerandaz, had used her archers sparingly. She was waiting to target the sappers, who gathered at the southern wall to chip away at the foundations that fortified the Zhayedan Gate. When a line of sappers advanced, Cassandane moved archers to either side of her position.

A line to meet a line, a tactic Arsalan had taught her. She glanced down at the courtyard. The Commander of the Zhayedan was with his soldiers, cutting through the chaos with instructions to fortify defenses at all three of the city's gates. He knew his soldiers to a man. He knew the range of weapons stored in the capital's armory. Best of all, he knew when and where to disperse them. As he moved among the Cataphracts, his presence imparted calm. Without a commander like Arsalan, the city would have been lost.

A jarring noise. The gate shuddered so heavily that the ground under Cassandane's feet trembled. A Zhayedan catapult had destroyed the first battering ram; now the Talisman had brought another. The men who urged it forward were giants, heavy with muscle and just as brutally armored. The Talisman had been warned against the skill of Cassandane's archers. There were no obvious openings for her archers to target.

We will find them, she thought. *First the sappers, then the brutes behind the ram.*

She raised a hand, and the archers fired two swift strikes, their movements so rapid they blurred. The first was aimed at the soldiers who gave the sappers cover. They needed to be unseated, to open up the real targets. The second aimed at the sappers; this was the killing strike.

A return volley was aimed at the archers above the gate. But the Teerandaz were shielded by a defensive line of their own: Zhayedan soldiers whose lives were committed to them. With the first break in fire, the soldiers knelt and the Teerandaz fired again, this time with silver-tipped arrows aimed at the men who approached the gate at a run, their battering ram held aloft.

The arrows were aimed at their unprotected heads. If the soldiers survived the blows, they would try to shield their heads with their hands. The poison at the tips of the arrows would spread no matter how they tried to protect themselves, and the ram would tumble to the ground.

And so it proved.

The next rain of Teerandaz arrows carried fire. The giant wooden ram sparked and blazed to life as it burned. The assault on the gate had failed. Cassandane held up a hand. The archers waited, poised, as their captain chose another target.

Several hours later, Cassandane made a quick detour to the Black Khan's war room to meet with the army's commanders.

Arsalan gave her a welcoming nod and signaled to the others to report. When it was her turn, she was quick and concise. Her actions should have earned her praise. But the tension in the room erupted into low-voiced murmuring, even as Arsalan commended her strategy.

"Well done, Captain Cassandane. How many archers did you lose?"

"None, Commander."

The murmurs of displeasure intensified. She caught the assessing glance that Maysam, Captain of the Cataphracts, shot at her. He'd wanted her to support his maneuvers to defend the Emissary Gate. She'd refused, considering the attempt on the Zhayedan Gate the greater threat. No doubt that decision had cost her Maysam's favor.

"It won't last," she went on, ignoring the mutinous whispers. "The Talisman have numbers on their side. We'll need more than archers to hold."

Maysam shifted into her line of sight. He was six and a half feet tall, his body heavy with muscle, though for a man of such bulk, he moved with deceptive swiftness, his mind agile, his calculations complex. He was a commander of fierce ability, given to weighing the odds. Beyond these talents, he was skilled with weaponry—the sword, the axe, the fire-lance, the mace—which made him the right man to lead shock troops into battle. But more than a decade older than Cassandane, he viewed her rank as an insult to his soldiers, some nearly as skilled as her own.

Nearly. That was the critical difference.

"You have two dozen Zhayedan defending your women. No others can be spared."

Women, not archers. An unsubtle insult that elicited a soft chuckle from the Zhayedan's commanders. She ignored it, keeping her gaze fixed on Arsalan. She could handle the politics of command without his help, but she wondered at the toll the battle might be taking on him. He'd moved between the walls and the courtyard throughout the night, neither still nor rushed, his face still streaked with smoke from his encounter with the One-Eyed Preacher. In the time that she'd been at the gate, he'd overseen the evacuation of the palace and fortified the inner defenses.

And then at a critical moment, Arsalan had been absent, summoned to the Black Khan's chambers. When he'd returned, he'd been distracted. But when the One-Eyed Preacher had spread his terror at the wall, Arsalan's attention had refocused: The Black Khan's half-brother, Darius, had delivered the Bloodprint to the Preacher. And, in the struggle to reclaim it, the Princess of Ashfall had been killed.

The murder of the Princess had hardened Arsalan's determination to vanquish the enemy.

Still, Cassandane wondered now if all they were doing was holding off inevitable defeat. To the east and south, the siege had set in. And from the west, another army approached.

The Companions had given them hope against these odds, but they had since abandoned the city. Of the allies that remained, Cassandane wasn't sure she trusted them: a stranger known as the Assassin, and two of the Mages of Khorasan. But what she truly feared was the use of a power she couldn't comprehend, like the thunder that had cracked the city walls.

Were they fighting today only to die tomorrow?

Arsalan met her gaze, perhaps guessing at her thoughts. His dark hair was matted with sweat, yet his physical presence was imposing. He was not as strongly built as Maysam, but Cassandane was in no doubt of which man she wanted at her back.

Now he stood at the center of the war room, radiating a

strength of will that calmed her in a room full of men she had
learned to think of as adversaries.

"You've done well, Captain." His attention shifted to Maysam,
whose giant hands were braced on the table as he studied the
battle plan drawn up by the Black Khan's cartographer. "How
long can we hold the Emissary Gate?"

"With defensive maneuvers, at least another day. The Silver
Mage's ruse is what gave us that day. But if we don't take action,
we'll lose the eastern gate. What of your plan to ride out?"

Cassandane waited to see if Arsalan would correct Maysam
about the reason for the Silver Mage's actions. He'd called the loya
jirga in good faith—the Black Khan had betrayed him. The Khan
had ordered Cassandane to fire on the loya jirga, despite the First
Oralist's pleas to allow time to achieve a truce. But Cassandane
had known, just as Arsalan had known, that there would be no
better chance to take out the Talisman leadership. And as the
Silver Mage had made his safe return, Cassandane had nothing
to regret. She would make the same choice again, dishonorable as
it had been.

She saw the pained acknowledgment of that truth in Arsalan's velvet-black eyes. Her gaze lingered for a moment before she
forced herself to look away.

The noise of battle was heavy in the air. Boulders landing in
the inner courtyard, shouts of men under attack, masonry crum-
bling to dust. Smoke curled over the battlements. And she knew
the men were wondering at the absence of their Khan, a matter
none dared comment on to Arsalan. Not even Maysam was so
bold.

"What action would you take?" Arsalan now asked the leader
of the Cataphracts. "An offensive sortie?" It was something Arsalan had planned on himself, once he'd completed his check of

the defenses. But from the subtle shift of his stance, Cassandane thought the Commander had reconsidered.

Any such sortie would require the Zhayedan to open the Emissary Gate or to disclose the existence of the Zhayedan's secret sally ports—a series of gates they used to ambush their enemies when their numbers were evenly matched. To pursue either course now would be to yield to the Talisman the very advantage they'd been seeking. But it could be that now was the moment to expose those advantages, before time ran out to exploit them.

"Yes." Maysam pointed to a valley east of the Talisman's position. "We position archers on the high ground to either side of this valley, then draw them into an ambush."

Cassandane stepped closer to Arsalan, not stopping to weigh her words. "Such a course would be disastrous. The Talisman would overrun the gate to pick us off one by one, or they would discover the vulnerability of our inner defenses. If we were able to seal the Emissary Gate before they penetrated through, our numbers would be too small to break through to the valley. Our archers would be killed before they could gain cover. Even if we succeeded, we would only draw in the smallest portion of their army. We'd run out of ammunition before we made any gains. We *have* to hold our defenses."

"You sound frightened, Cassandane."

As he did so often to diminish her command, Maysam omitted her rank.

"Not frightened. Pragmatic." She straightened her shoulders, glanced at Arsalan again. "Without our archers at the gates, Ashfall is doomed against the Talisman."

An angry rush of protest in response to Cassandane's assertion that the city could be held only by a contingent of female archers. The Black Khan's Nizam had nurtured a quiet revolt against the presence of women in the army, though the Khan himself maintained that the Teerandaz formed a vital arm of their defense. She wondered now, in his absence, if that quiet revolt was gaining strength and would make itself known. Cassandane knew she'd been unwise to challenge these commanders, to make them seem incapable, no matter her private thoughts. But with the evidence right before them, would they risk the future of Ashfall to prove themselves superior to the women who fought at their side?

"You think well of yourself," Maysam said. "But the Zhayedan have been fighting Ashfall's wars since long before you were born. We are not in the habit of hiding behind women. Not even those who wear Teerandaz armor."

His sneering assessment of Cassandane's uniform was familiar too: the Nizam had viewed it with the same contempt.

"Enough." Arsalan moved to the windows beyond the war room, tracking the Talisman's progress. "Their army is in a state of confusion after the attack on their commanders. If there was a time to strike out, it would be now. The Black Khan—the Dark Mage—is in conference with the other Mages. If they can give us cover, we *could* send Cataphracts out into the open." He pressed Maysam's shoulder with one hand. "And *only* Cataphracts. You have your own corps of archers. You've no need of the Teerandaz."

"I still think the risk is too great," Cassandane insisted.

She was getting ready to elaborate when Arsalan offered mildly, "Do you, Captain? I was speaking to Maysam."

There was no mistaking the reproof. Cassandane flushed to the roots of her hair, her smooth dark skin aglow. This was the first time Arsalan had rebuked her in the presence of the other commanders. Maysam was quick to take advantage.

"We stand a better chance with archers from the Teerandaz," he argued.

But Arsalan overrode Maysam's objection.

"Nonnegotiable. Captain Cassandane is correct. The Teeran-daz must hold the gates. But that doesn't mean we can't do a little damage. Instead of the ambush you suggest, consider this." He pointed to a spot farther south, closer to the Zhayedan Gate. The Talisman had set up camp close to their walls for an ugly and sinister purpose. "You could achieve this, Maysam. With the Teerandaz's help."

It took Cassandane the briefest glance at the map to grasp Ar-salan's suggestion. The tightness in her chest loosened. She had deserved his rebuke. She should have known better than to think the Commander of the Zhayedan wouldn't have planned for every possible contingency *before* he summoned his council.

"You would mount a rescue of refugees? To what end?" Maysam rolled up the map and tossed it to one side, dismissing the idea. Unfazed by this show of disrespect, Arsalan smoothed it out again, pointing to the area where the Talisman had taken prisoners to use as shields.

Only then did he let his anger show, a cloud darkening his brow. He leaned forward, his face within inches of Maysam's.

"To *this* end. We do not abandon the people the Black Khan claims as his own."

When the council had disbanded in resentful silence, Arsalan called Cassandane back. She turned to face him, her hands clenched on her helmet, steeling herself for a thorough dressing-down. Her shoulders squared, she stared at the Commander's insignia: a small onyx rook mounted on silver at his neck.

"Forgive me, Commander," she said quietly. "I know I spoke out of turn."

His strong hand tilted up her chin, the hint of a smile in his eyes.

"It was a tactic, Cassandane. To pacify Maysam's pride."

He dropped his hand, giving her a moment to puzzle his actions through. Startled, she made the connection.

"You aren't certain of the extent of the Nizam's influence. But do you suspect traitors within the ranks of the Cataphracts?"

"*Especially* within the Cataphracts. If we are betrayed, it will be at their hands."

"Do you also suspect the Teerandaz?" She was an experienced soldier, but Arsalan's air of authority coupled with his physical presence made her second-guess herself. She couldn't help the note of diffidence in her voice or her desire for reassurance.

She drew a silent breath when he brushed his hand against her cheek, a gesture of comradeship, just as he had pressed Maysam's shoulder in affection.

"Of course not," he said. "I've known you far too long." His words were grimly pragmatic as he added, "The Nizam held you in disfavor."

She gave a grim smile of her own. "He thought the Teerandaz should be disbanded. Until he spoke so harshly of our competence, the Zhayedan were wont to treat us with respect." Then, not wanting to sound as if she pitied herself, when she'd been fortunate enough to have been given Arsalan's attention, she went on briskly, "Were you serious about the rescue?"

"It stands a greater chance of success than the sortie Maysam had in mind. It will also end any doubt as to where his loyalties lie."

Cassandane worked through this. "Because he'll choose his own men, and if he wishes, they'll be free to defect. We won't be able to stop him from joining forces with the Talisman."

Though his eyes were gentle on her face, Arsalan's response was pure steel.

"I have faith in your aim, Captain, so do not let me down."

4

Arian shook back her cloak to show their captors her circlets. At once, Sinnia mirrored the gesture. Both women wondered if it would matter, and if there was any hope for Khashayar, their sole remaining escort.

The man in the burnoose paused, his eyes skirting the golden bands. He called another man to stand beside him, his voice rough with command. There were eighteen others gathered on the sand, nineteen including the one who'd spoken. They were dressed in sand-colored cloaks worn over long white thobes, their heads wrapped in red-and-white headcloths. Dark-eyed to a man, their skin was a golden-brown deepened by desert sun, weathered from exposure to its relentless heat. They stood at their ease, their eyes as clear as a desert falcon's. Nothing in their appearance suggested they were men to fear . . . save for the whipcord readiness with which they had struck down Khashayar's men.

"Traders," Sinnia murmured in Arian's ear.

The man in the burnoose heard her, his eyes wandering over Sinnia's face, over the clustered curls that had begun to grow out from her head in tiny spirals. To Sinnia's surprise, his eyes warmed, as he gave her a slow nod.

"Najashi," he said with respect, to a murmur from the men behind him. "Companion from the land of the Negus. I do not know the other."

Arian gave her name. After a pause, she added, "First Oralist of Hira."

Another murmur, different in tenor than the first. It held a tinge of fear in it.

Arian observed the thick leather belts that cinched the cloaks these men wore. Each belt was inscribed with the words *Over this are Nineteen.*

She pondered the significance of the nineteen men who surrounded them; perhaps they were the commanders of the army at their back. If the man in the burnoose was the leader of the Nineteen, then the man at his side must be his lieutenant. His stance was poised, his hand holding an iron glaive, a staff with a blade that curved up at shoulder height, just above a spike that pointed outward. The lower half of the glaive was overlaid with damasquinado, a pattern of gold incised on black steel, in contrast to the naked shaft.

The man who held it glanced at Arian's circlets, then looked up to meet her eyes.

She suppressed a shiver. Though the temperature had fallen, it wasn't the night that chilled her. It was the man's gaze—amber eyes with stiletto-sharp flecks of blue and green. He held himself like a weapon, lethally honed and muscled, with an air of quiet command. His leather belt carried a complement of knives, each with a jeweled haft, as if he specialized in killing, and each of the blades he'd chosen was dedicated to a task. Beneath his cloak, he wore a fitted uniform in a color that echoed the sienna of the desert. He watched Arian with a focus that warned her he wasn't an ordinary soldier.

He was a killer who looked at her like prey.

The man in the burnoose held one hand high to dismiss the soldiers on the dune.

"Gather the horses; return to camp."

The men who remained fanned out around what was left of Arian's group to the sound of horses' hooves behind them. To distract them from her attempted theft, Arian said, "I would welcome the courtesy of your titles."

The older man spoke first. "Shaykh Al Marra." He indicated the man with the glaive. "This is Sayyid Najran, my second."

Arian considered their style of dress. Their headcloths were native to the tribes of the Empty Quarter who made their home in the boundless sands of the Rub Al Khali.

"You are far from your homes, then. What brings you here?"

"What brings *you* here, sayyidina? You have traveled far from Hira at some risk to yourself." It was a reasonable question, but it was also a dismissal of Khashayar's escort, the Shaykh's shrewd black eyes measuring the impact of his words.

Arian looked over her shoulder to the vanguard of the Nineteen. "And you have brought an army from the Rub Al Khali to the capital of the Black Khan."

The sayyid planted his glaive in the sand, startling her.

"Is the Black Khan your ally, sayyidina? A pity then, to send his men home to him without their heads."

His voice rasped like sand over stone, and she tried not to wince at the words. With the party of Zhayedan she'd had as her escort, she could hardly refute his claim. But she could try to temper it.

"The Black Khan is not my enemy, at least." She made an effort to soften her voice, using a dialect familiar to their ears, rather than the Common Tongue. "Neither are the people of the Rub Al Khali."

A nod of appreciation from the Shaykh. "Yet it is not a *friend* who comes like a thief in the night after the Marra's horses."

She understood that he referred to the people of his tribe, and not solely to himself. She was on dangerous ground: she couldn't justify the theft without giving some hint of her journey. So she used a well-known proverb to pay tribute: "The horses of Al Marra are as numerous as the sheep of Awazim."

Najran's riposte was knife-edged, a dagger shearing silk. "That doesn't give you the right to take them." He took a step forward, then in a gesture of unthinkable familiarity, he covered her circlet with his palm, his fingers tracing its script. "The First Oralist of Hira should know the penalty for theft."

Khashayar struggled against the men who held him.

"Kill him," Najran said.

"No!" Arian cried. "Wait! Tell me the penalty you speak of."

Najran's cool fingers trailed down Arian's arm to her wrist. The contact left her shaken; the Claim she harbored in her deepest self recognized that the danger he represented was something new, the aura of death around him so pervasive that she felt it sink into her bones. And yet his touch was an affront—to both the First Oralist and the woman, awakening her anger.

"Your hand, sayyidina." His hand closed over her wrist, as he fingered the emerald dagger. He moved close enough for her to count the flecks in his eyes. The green flecks had spread . . . they were glowing . . . just as his emerald dagger began to throb with light. She could feel the heat of the dagger, stark coldness from the man himself.

Wafa let out a whimper, but Arian held her ground.

"What law commands the loss of my hand, sayyid?"

His headcloth brushed her ear. "Shall I show you the verse of the Claim?"

She shifted the tiniest fraction closer to Sinnia, touching Sinnia's circlet with her own.

"*Could* you?"

She was well aware that he couldn't. No one could, save for the One-Eyed Preacher, who now possessed the Bloodprint. When the flecks of green in his eyes faded, the light from his dagger dulled, and she knew her guess had been correct.

But it likely didn't matter—she recognized the echoes of the One-Eyed Preacher's law, a code proclaimed by the Talisman. It seemed it was now the code of the Rising Nineteen as well.

She faced the Shaykh, buoyed by her bond with Sinnia.

"A boon that is granted to Hira will be remembered. My need for transport was urgent, and I feared my escort would not meet with your approval." Then, to Najran: "The law of the people of Marra does not sanction aggression. Yet here is your army, ready to begin hostilities. What should be the penalty for that, I wonder?"

The words seethed with scorn at the hypocrisy of the sayyid's application of the law. She caught sight of Wafa's frightened face. She could sense his confusion, made all the more apparent when he whispered to her in the dialect of Candour, "Make them sleep. Let's take the horses and go."

She couldn't take that risk. She knew more about the Nineteen's facility with the Claim than Wafa did. It might turn out to be disastrous to test her skills against the Nineteen's commanders at once.

The Shaykh jerked Wafa close, ignoring his panicked yelp. Holding him by the chin, he examined Wafa's face.

"Najashi I know. Talisman I know. First Oralist I know. *This* I do not know."

"Hazara," Arian answered. "A noble tribe of Candour."

The Shaykh's eyes flicked to Khashayar. His rugged features hardened.

"The Zhayedan's man stands no chance. But grant us the boy and I will gift two of my horses to the Negus. *If* that is where your journey takes you."

An unexpected opportunity presented itself, an advantage she had to seize. Arian stilled Wafa's struggles by raising her hand. "Yes. The Companion Sinnia returns to pay her respects to the Negus." She spread her hands. "But I cannot give you the boy. He is my ward. He is under Hira's protection."

She didn't mention Khashayar. She would have to try to save him by stealth.

The Shaykh held on to Wafa. "What *would* you give, then? For safe passage across the Rub Al Khali?"

Pain struck her heart at this echo of her journey through the Cloud Door. Daniyar had offered the book of the Guardian of Candour to the Lord of the Wandering Cloud Door in exchange for safe passage through the Ice Kill.

In the end, however, she had spurned Daniyar on the slightest of excuses, leaving him to the Conference of the Mages, while she charted her course on her own. She had made him believe no sacrifice he made would ever be enough, when in truth her certainties about her course seemed far less certain now.

Sinnia sensed her emotion through the bond of their circlets. She squeezed Arian's shoulder. Then she altered her voice so that she spoke in the accents of a woman from the Sea of Reeds. "We can make a suitable bargain, Shaykh. But we will need our escort's assistance to cross the Rub Al Khali."

"No." A flat denial from Najran. "There will be no bargain. Your man is an enemy combatant; he will be treated as such." He shifted the glaive so that the spike was aimed straight at Khashayar's heart. "No doubt there is much he can tell us about the Zhayedan's defenses."

Khashayar spit at Najran's feet. A single thrust drove the sharp-edged spike through the surface of his armor. A grimace that passed for a smile settled on Najran's lips.

"No one has failed to speak under the persuasion of the glaive."

And Arian knew in that moment that no matter what else happened during their confrontation, she would not permit the torture of a man who acted in her service. She marked Najran for death.

"Will you not at least hear the bargain, captains of the Nineteen? If you will permit me, Shaykh." Sinnia's voice was sunny and confident, such that the Shaykh released his hold on Wafa, who clung to Arian's side.

"What will you give me, Najashi? What might a woman, unencumbered with goods, offer in exchange for a man, a boy, and two of the finest horses bred in the Rub Al Khali?"

Sinnia's bright eyes touched each man in the circle, lingering on the belts at their waists.

"'*Over this are Nineteen,*'" she quoted. "What if I give you Nineteen?"

5

THEY WERE TAKEN TO A DESERT TENT, SIMPLE BUT EFFECTIVE IN ITS CONstruction, a guard assigned to each member of their party, only Khashayar bound. As they had been pushed forward along the sand in the shadow of the dune, Arian had brushed Khashayar's hands with hers, a message of comfort, encouraging him not to despair.

But Khashayar was a captain of the Zhayedan, brutally honed in battle. There was no fear in his eyes, nor any need for reassurance. He simply remained watchful and alert, waiting for his moment to act.

"Wait," Arian said quietly. "Wait until I give you a signal."

Whispering to Sinnia, she switched to the language of the Citadel. "What did you mean? What are you offering to trade?"

Sinnia shook her head, her smile bold and confident. Arian was taken aback. The threat was all around them, the danger to Ashfall ever-present, yet Sinnia showed no hesitation. What had persuaded her she could bargain her way out of this? Arian was still mulling over the Shaykh's decision to offer hospitality instead of death. But then such were the customs of the people of Al

Marra: honor before everything, hospitality before all, even when those who broke bread together were otherwise mortal enemies.

They were taken to a pump to wash their hands, then invited to sit in a circle in the center of the tent. Wafa and Khashayar were pushed into place on either side of Arian and Sinnia, the other men keeping some distance. In a large black cauldron, pieces of camel meat bubbled in water and salt. The pot was tended by a herder not much older than Wafa. The boy served the meat onto heavy platters, his thin arms hardly seeming capable of the task, as he stole admiring glances at the Companions of Hira.

A platter was nudged in front of Arian and Sinnia, two large pieces of meat set aside in the middle. The Shaykh pointed to the chunks of boiled meat.

"Qalb for the First Oralist. Sanam for the Najashi." An honored gesture to guests—Arian granted a piece of the heart, Sinnia a cut from the camel's hump. Arian gave a blessing that sharpened the interest of the men. She began to eat, but when she saw that Khashayar couldn't eat with his hands bound, she urged Wafa to his side with instructions to feed him. Khashayar would need his strength for the battles that lay ahead. But she'd forgotten how much hunger her Hazara companion had suffered; his blue eyes shone with distress.

She kissed Wafa's forehead. "Fine. One bite for you, one for him."

The kiss drew Najran's attention—a sudden spark in deadly amber eyes that rekindled Arian's fear. She tried to ignore him, speaking to Wafa, who tackled his assignment with gusto, careful not to reach for the piece offered to Arian. He was learning to read nuances, so he knew his greed would be an insult. She was proud of how quickly he'd adapted.

No one spoke until the meal was finished. They had eaten with their hands, and a moment at the end of the meal was taken for further ablutions. When they were ready for it, tea was proffered in little copper cups, and now camel milk was aboil in a pot covered in a layer of milky froth. The milk was poured into cups, followed by a stream of tea splashed over it like a glaze. When Khashayar refused the tea, Arian realized that even though they had shared the same food, the soldier was suspicious of poison in his drink. But she knew the Shaykh would not poison a guest he had invited to his tent. It would be an insult to his honor.

So she drank to lessen any risk of offense, then asked for another cup.

The commanders of the Nineteen watched the Companions with a fascination that spoke to legends that had been spread to their lands. With the meal concluded, Shaykh Al Marra dismissed all his men save Najran, who, though he sat poised on his heels, kept his glaive within easy reach of his hand.

Both men unwound their headcloths to reveal hair looped in braids around their skull, a custom of the people of Marra. But where the Shaykh's braids were woolly with age, Najran's were precise, evenly webbed around his skull. And Arian realized with a start that this deadly lieutenant possessed a certain attraction.

The herder cleared the platters away, leaving the tent in silence.

The Shaykh nodded to Sinnia. "Tell me of your Nineteen."

Arian intervened, pressing Sinnia's hand. "A question, if you will permit me."

He fingered the rough growth of beard at his jaw. "As you wish, sayyidina."

"Why has your army come to Ashfall? Are you governed by the One-Eyed Preacher?"

The questions were meant to remind the Shaykh of the fierce independence of the tribes of the Rub Al Khali.

He sat back on his heels, his legs folded beneath him. "The people of Marra govern themselves. The First Oralist should know this."

She made her tone conciliatory. "I did not think the Marra would serve a foreign master. But I cannot account for the presence of your army outside the gates of Ashfall."

"The Shaykh owes you no explanation."

The Shaykh waved Najran's warning aside. "We come to honor our own convictions. It may be that these are convictions the One-Eyed Preacher shares, so for the moment, our purposes align."

The herder who'd cleared the tent now brought the Shaykh the apparatus of a shisha. The Shaykh leaned back on his elbows to inhale from the pipe. He passed it to Najran, who refused it with a word of thanks. No offer was made to Arian or Sinnia, and none expected.

"The Nineteen assert they are guided by the Claim. How do they reconcile their beliefs with the Preacher's commands?" A careful question from Arian.

Najran leaned forward, resting his elbows on his thighs. "The *Preacher* is guided by the Claim."

Arian let her power echo in her voice. "Yet none know the Claim as well as the Companions of Hira. None know it as *I* do. And my knowledge of it does not sanction your war upon these lands."

Najran made a dismissive gesture. "A woman has no authority over the Claim."

Wafa spat out his tea. Arian patted his back.

"Do you deny the authority of the Council? Do you refute the Companions of Hira?"

Najran fought back. "Do *you* refute the supremacy of the Rising Nineteen?"

A dialogue of opposites. A contest of conviction played out for the benefit of an audience of one: the Shaykh, who smoked his shisha, quietly biding his time.

"Can you recite the Claim?" Arian asked Najran with genuine curiosity.

"No."

"Then how can you assert the supremacy of the Nineteen?"

Najran's hand slipped to one of his daggers, this one adorned with sapphires. He glanced at her throat; Arian recognized the threat. Horror struck deep and hard, reminding her of the collar that had stolen her voice in Black Aura.

"You speak in riddles." A growl from Khashayar deflected Najran's attention. "What supremacy can any man claim compared to the First Oralist of Hira?"

The look in Najran's eyes promised Khashayar death. "The Nineteen comprehend the perfection of the Claim. Its verses, the mysteries of its arrangement—they give us the miracle of Nineteen."

"What miracle?" A contemptuous dig from Khashayar. "The First Oralist is the only miracle in these lands."

Najran barked at the herder. "Tell the guard to chain him outside."

Khashayar scrambled to his feet. Najran did the same, removing the opal-edged dagger from his belt. A white line bisected his pupils. The little herder shrank back, hurrying to carry out his orders.

Rising, Arian looked to the Shaykh. "Enemy or not, you received my escort as a guest."

Two men entered the tent and grabbed hold of Khashayar. The Shaykh waved his pipe. "Hold him. Do not harm him." Then, to Najran: "Sit. I would hear the end of this debate."

As Khashayar was led outside, Najran sheathed his dagger, the white line fading from his eyes. He had shed his robe. Under his uniform, his lean frame was honed to an edge.

"Your soft heart will not save him," he said to Arian.

"Your dark arts do not matter. You have no power against me."

He smiled suddenly, a stern slash across his face. "Shall we see, sayyidina?"

He waited for her to sit before taking his seat again, wearing his menace like a shroud.

Speaking to the Shaykh, Sinnia echoed Khashayar's words. "I do not understand either. We know of no miracle of Nineteen in the lands of the Negus."

The Shaykh set down his pipe. He pointed at Sinnia's arms.

"The inscription on your circlets are the opening words of the Claim."

Sinnia nodded, still puzzled.

"Nineteen letters. The opening verse occurs nineteen times throughout the Claim, the opening *word*—one hundred and fourteen times, a factor of nineteen. The opening word is absent in only a single chapter of the Claim. Nineteen chapters occur between the place where it is missing, and the place where it re-appears *twice*. The number of the Claim's verses are a factor of nineteen. The number of the Claim's chapters, a factor of nineteen. The first revelation . . . nineteen words. The last revelation . . . nineteen words. Should I go on?"

The Shaykh's fervor was that of a true believer, of a man who, though illiterate in the Claim, could inspire others with his passion.

Arian responded with a scrupulous observation.

"The *total* number of verses are only a factor of nineteen if you choose to disregard two verses of the Claim."

"Irrelevant," he snapped, no longer lounging on his cushions. "The verses you speak of are heretical. They stand apart from the Claim."

"Do they?" Arian asked, certain in her knowledge as First Oralist. "Or have you declared them heretical in order to preserve your miracle? There is no metaphysical truth to 'nineteen,' aside from the meaning you assign it."

"Sacrilege," he whispered through dry lips. But even though the Shaykh wanted to deny her—to dismiss her without measuring her erudition—he couldn't denounce the First Oralist's claim to knowledge. He looked to his sayyid for confirmation of his beliefs, receiving a nod of reassurance in return. A sly smile curved Najran's lips, as he took heed of Sinnia.

A prickle of awareness crept along Arian's spine. Najran wasn't an ideologue or an impassioned believer. He was a paid assassin. With all an assassin's tricks.

Speaking to Sinnia, he said, "You claimed to have proof of Nineteen."

Sinnia didn't hesitate. Linking her hand with Arian's, she began to recite, her low, throaty voice rich in its offering of beauty.

"Mention in the Book, the story of the Adhraa when she withdrew in seclusion from her family to a place in the east. She placed a screen to screen herself, then We sent her Our Ruh, and he appeared before her in the form of a man."

The Shaykh paused, letting the words sink in. Then he motioned for Sinnia to continue.

"She said: 'I seek refuge with the One from you, if you fear the One.'"

She looked to Arian, who added, "The spirit of the Ruh announced to the Adhraa the gift of a righteous son."

Though her eyes were bright with tears, Sinnia finished the

verse: *"She said, 'How can I have a son, when no man has touched me, nor am I unchaste?'"*

Najran cut across the spell woven by Sinnia's words, speaking solely to the Shaykh. "She comes from the land of the Negus. Small wonder she spins these fables that honor the Esayin. The Najashi are Esayin—they learn fables from birth that hold no meaning for us."

Arian rose to her feet, bringing Sinnia and Wafa up with her.

"The Najashi may have their own scriptures, but they are also people of the Claim. Sinnia gave you the *nineteenth* chapter of the Claim, which is the story of the Adhraa."

Now the Al Marra had proof of their knowledge of the Claim. And in all his veneration of the miracle of Nineteen, the Shaykh could not discount the honor bestowed upon a woman by the nineteenth chapter of the Claim. It stood not only for the Adhraa herself, but as a lesson as to how women were meant to be treated by the people of the Claim.

Her hand was bound to Sinnia's, memory flaring of their journey to the Golden Finger, the minaret where two rivers met. The minaret had been inscribed with turquoise bands of calligraphy, and circling the tower, Arian and Sinnia had found verses that told the story of the Adhraa's utmost esteem in the Claim.

Najran helped his Shaykh to his feet.

"As I said, the mother of the *Esayin*." Those strange eyes flicked over her face. "The Claim grants women no such honor."

Her time was running out. Najran's influence over his shaykh was too powerful, his menace all-consuming. She would have to call upon the Claim as something other than recitation.

"Then why is it women who were chosen as its guardians?"

Najran's fingers moved over the daggers at his waist. "Because we took the Council of Hira at its word." He gripped one of his daggers and drew it from his belt, the hilt concealed in his hand. "But now *our* truths are ascendant: '*Over this are Nineteen.*'"

Arian had no answer. The verse was an obscure one. She had puzzled over it for months; she was still no closer to deciphering it.

The one thing she knew with certainty was that it could not have reduced the grandeur of the Claim to a numerological miracle. Not if it had to deny other verses of the Claim to do so.

If she could show them the Bloodprint, she could shred the Nineteen's heresies with irrefutable proof. The fact that she couldn't was a weakness Najran was prepared to exploit.

"The Bloodprint confirms it. *Over this are Nineteen.* What does the Council of Hira have to offer in response?"

His arrogance assailed her, confirming her suspicions. The Nineteen and the Preacher were inseparably linked if the Preacher had given them word of his theft of the Bloodprint. She shuddered at the thought of the manuscript left to the Preacher's care. Of the use he would make of it in his overarching design. *Was it possible Najran had seen it?*

"The *One-Eyed Preacher* confirms it, you mean. Because if you had read the Bloodprint, you would know it says no such thing," she told Najran.

"Do you offer a *written* proof?" An insult. A subtle repudiation of her word.

She turned it back on him. "Is the sayyid able to read?"

A rough laugh, the scrape of silk and sand. The hilt of his dagger flashed blue. He'd chosen the blade for her throat, which meant she had run out of time.

Releasing Sinnia's hand, she called down the Verse of the Throne. This time she shaped it differently, spacing the words to give each one the power of a hammer pounding at quartz. But she did it almost soundlessly. A violation of their hospitality served in

Ausma Zehanat Khan

response to the murder they had been invited to, which was cause enough.

The words drove both men to their knees and held them there, frozen. Sinnia searched the tent, returning with a length of the rope they used for tethering their livestock. She bound their feet, and then she tied their arms to their torsos while Wafa kept an eye out for intruders.

The little herder who had served them stumbled into the tent, his eyes wide at the scene before him. He had an instant to decide—to sound the alarm, to slip past Wafa. Or to allow the Companions to pass from the tent in peace. Even as Najran's daggered gaze threatened him, the boy sank to his knees before Arian. One small hand reached out to seize the hem of her cloak. He buried his face in its cloth. "Sayyidina. Please say a blessing for my soul."

Najran would kill him, she thought. But she could save the boy from that fate by killing Najran herself.

She knelt and kissed his cheeks. "May the One keep you and all of your people safe." She nudged him from the tent. "Disappear inside the encampment. Look for a place to hide."

He didn't listen, darting around her to stand before Najran, whose face was mottled with rage, his lips sealed shut by the Claim. The boy's hands unlatched the belt with the daggers. With the same dexterity he'd shown serving up their meal, he wound the belt around his waist.

A word broke free of Najran's throat.

"Traitor."

Traces of blood leaked from the corners of his mouth. The colored flecks in his eyes mutated to crimson. She thought of the Authoritan. She thought of the Claim in his mouth, darkened and degraded.

62

Arian shivered. They had to move quickly to free Khashayar without alerting the soldiers gathered outside.

The little herder rolled up a flap of the tent at the rear. He cast a glance at the iron glaive, then wisely decided against it.

The sound of gravel in his throat, Najran forced out a threat. "When I find you, boy, I will take my daggers back, flay your skin from your bones, then cut out your heart with my glaive."

Losing the little of his color that remained, the boy ducked out of the tent.

"Kill him," Sinnia said to Arian. "He'll hunt us to the ends of the earth."

Arian had reached the same conclusion. "Take Wafa. Assess our chances of escape."

When they slipped out of the tent, she turned to the men on their knees.

She couldn't murder the leader of the tribes of the Rub Al Khali—he may have been misguided in his aims, but he wasn't an evil man. So, without occulting it, she used a word she had learned from Lania to stun the Shaykh into unconsciousness. He slumped to his side, his body held by the ropes.

Najran struggled against the ropes that bound him, an unforgiving predator, his eyes crimson and amber, the color of dancing flames with a white-hot tinge of blue at the center. She could have used her knives against him, but she kept up the thrum of the Claim.

He faced her with savage defiance, gritting out a response. *"Over this are Nineteen."*

Taken by surprise, she stumbled back a step.

He shouldn't have been able to speak.

She used the verse she had used against the High Companion, giving it a sharper edge.

He answered her again, his voice a thing of blood and ice.

"Over this are Nineteen."

Stunned by the power that flared from his words, the crimson thrust bold and bright against her face, she fell to her knees before him. She tried to grasp one of her weapons, but her hands were frozen at her sides.

His answering smile was lethal; he knew that she feared him now.

She couldn't risk a merciful response. She slashed at him with the Claim, cold, clean fire, spun from an inner conviction; his eyes rolled back in his head. Just as his breath escaped from his body in a long, stuttering exhale that signified his death, Khashayar threw back a flap of the tent. He made a soldier's instant assessment.

"You killed them? Good."

She didn't correct his mistake about the Shaykh for fear that he might finish him off.

"Come, sahabiya, we have to move quickly now."

She gestured at the glaive, a question in her eyes.

"Leave it." The firm line of his lips pursed in distaste. "I have no use for the enemy's dishonorable weapon."

He reached for Arian's hand and pulled her from the tent.

6

DANIYAR ENTERED THE ANTECHAMBER THROUGH A PAIR OF DOORS carved with maghrebi stars, the Black Khan leading the way down a short flight of marble stairs. The room was twice the size of the war room, one wall lined with wooden shutters that opened to the eastern plains. These were carved with star-centered lattices in patterns that throbbed with distant light.

The room itself was thick with the musk of scattered petals. Candelabra gleamed on the floor, their light picked up by the crystal loops of a glittering chandelier. But with the doors and windows closed, the chamber was dim—preserving an aura of mystery. Pages hurried to do the Black Khan's bidding: arranging small tables at intervals, setting a tall mirror edged in gold against one wall. A towering torchiere, dripping with crystal loops, was placed beside it, throwing light upon an alcove in the room, screened by panels of amethyst silk. Several more mirrors and candles were placed around the room to foster an aura of intimacy.

In the center of the room, a space enclosed by four towering columns, two of the stronger pages set a heavy copper pan upon a black-lacquered table. The curled lip of the pan was engraved with Khorasani script, crimson petals strewn across the water in its depths, the fragrance subtle and rose-edged.

Watching these preparations, Daniyar said, "The Conference of the Mages requires nothing other than our presence."

The Black Khan ignored him, motioning to his pages. They placed four stools cushioned in silk around the table.

When their preparations were complete, he answered, "Perhaps you are used to simplicity, but grandeur is Ashfall's great art." A subtle glance at the Silver Mage's tattered uniform, at the absence of a crest at his throat, turned his claim into an insult.

Daniyar examined Rukh in turn. He was dressed in Zhayedan armor, embellished with silver epaulettes that stretched over broad shoulders, still perfectly groomed, his hair pomaded and sleek. At his neck was his imperial symbol, though its jeweled ropes had been replaced by brooches that betokened martial honors. On his right hand he wore his onyx ring. On his left, an assortment of sapphires and pearls. The attention he paid to his appearance should have made him seem as much a pleasure-seeking dilettante as any of his lesser courtiers. Instead, furious, concentrated power burned in his midnight eyes.

Easy enough for the Khan to dismiss Daniyar's appearance when he hadn't been trapped in the midst of Talisman fighters with boulders crashing from the sky.

Charismatic and clever, he could enjoy his presumed superiority for the moment. This did not move Daniyar to trust him, nor would he underestimate the Black Khan's duplicity again. It was time the Khan learned as much.

"What I am used to is integrity. When I give my word, I keep it."

"You would have done the same in my shoes."

"Violate a promised truce by disrupting the loya jirga? Would I have?" He glanced at the pages scurrying to set the stage for what the Black Khan imagined a Conference of the Mages entailed. The pages were young and inexperienced, their fear of battle evident. They reminded Daniyar strongly of the boys in the Talisman camp at the moment when the truce had been broken. Their blood may not have been on his own hands, but the stain on his honor was unlikely to wash away. "I agreed to act as your emissary because of those on *both* sides of your walls."

A page knocked over a brass lamp on the floor. Rukh banished him with a scowl, then said to Daniyar, "There are only enemies on the other side of the wall."

Daniyar moved closer to Rukh, a swirling storm in his eyes, his pain transformed into anger at what the Black Khan had cost him. "They are not *my* enemies. I took you at your word. You repaid me by calling my honor into question."

Rukh snorted. "Your claim to honor was forfeit the day you made your stand with Arian."

The use of Arian's name was a provocation too far. Daniyar's hand shot out, gripped the Black Khan's throat, and pressed the weight of the onyx rook back into it. Rage flared along his nerve endings, the furious temptation of violence, the satisfaction of finally having the means to avenge Arian's suffering at the Ark. And his own deep sense of loss, dishonored in the eyes of his tribe. The Black Khan may have been a Mage of Khorasan, but he wasn't an ally or friend. Daniyar squeezed harder, feeling the rook cut deep into his palm.

The pages leapt back in alarm. Two of the Khorasan Guard raced from their post at the door. The sibilant slash of steel brought their swords to Daniyar's throat.

Rukh watched Daniyar, saw the brutal warning in his face. He waved his guards aside, making no defensive moves.

"She renounced you." Though Rukh's breath was faint, satisfaction glistened in his eyes. "Do you still claim her as your own? When you returned from the battle, you were holding the High Companion's hand." A hint of curiosity, a soft insinuation of disloyalty.

Daniyar's grip tightened. Hard enough to bruise. Not hard enough to crush, as he wanted. For the injuries Rukh had inflicted, a price would have to be paid.

"When this is over, you and I will have things to settle."

He released his grip on Rukh's throat. The Black Khan sank down on a stool unperturbed, a small smile playing on his lips.

"The badal of your forebears? Your primitive instincts amuse me."

The Black Khan considered the graces of his court and the richness of its traditions superior to those of the rest of the lands of Khorasan. His scriptorium surpassed the Library of Candour, even at the pinnacle of its accomplishments. But one thing Daniyar knew with certainty: the tribes that answered the Talisman call held fast to their code of honor. When their word was given, they kept it.

"What you call revenge, they see as a matter of justice." He moved away from the table to lean against a column. He flexed the hand he had used to grip Rukh's throat, the gesture a promise to himself. "As do I."

Cold rage echoed off the walls in the Black Khan's response. "Where is the justice in their war against my capital or in their murder of my sister?"

Daniyar straightened. Concern sharpened his voice. "Has something happened to Darya?"

"The *Princess* of Ashfall is dead. She was murdered by the One-Eyed Preacher, whose teachings inform your kin."

Daniyar murmured a prayer, his anger swiftly curbed.

"This city needs more than your prayers." A contemptuous dismissal from Rukh.

"Then let's begin. Where is the Golden Mage?"

"I do not know."

Daniyar shifted out of the path of a page who set a candelabra at his feet. In the spaces between gold ornaments, pages scattered armfuls of petals across the floor.

"This is theater," Daniyar warned Rukh. "It serves no purpose in the Conference."

The Black Khan slammed his hand down on the table. Water spilled from the copper bowl, from the table onto the floor.

"Go!" he said, dismissing the pages who were listening to every word. Then, to Daniyar: "It serves *this* purpose: those who prepared it, those who observed it, will spread the word to others. Whispers will soon become fact. Magic will be unleashed by this Conference. Because of it, Ashfall will survive. You and I may know otherwise"—a savage smile—"but my people need to believe that their city will not fall. Theater merely entertains. This is politics, so do not presume to instruct me in what would serve my people best."

Daniyar snorted, his eyes narrowing, but said nothing.

The maghrebi doors pushed open. The Golden Mage had arrived.

She had changed from her battle armor into a gown that echoed the colors of the room: an outer robe of amethyst studded with dozens of tiny crystals, an inner gown in crimson that clung to her delicate frame. The outer robe was layered in tiers that ended in an amethyst train, its high neck embroidered, its sleeves flaring out at the wrists. Her thick gold hair was bound in a series of intricate coils, on which rested the diadem with the single sapphire at its center.

Another role enacted in the Black Khan's theater, Daniyar thought, beginning to understand the nature of it. She looked imposing, her spine a steel-forged line. Rukh rose from the table to guide her to her seat. She flicked a glance at Daniyar, one golden brow aloft.

He came to the table and took his seat. He had things to say to the Golden Mage when time and circumstance permitted. He could no more count her as an ally than he could trust to the word of the Khan. Yet he would not turn away from the Conference.

When they were seated around the table, the three Mages linked hands. Rukh's sleek palm against Daniyar's much rougher one, both men gripping hard in a show of strength until Ilea said, "This posturing is tiresome. Need you bolster your egos at the expense of this war?"

Rukh gave her a lazy smile. "Perhaps we do it in your honor."

"Spare me your tribute then. Call the Conference to order."

The Black Khan hesitated. When he didn't speak, it became clear that he didn't know how to proceed. Daniyar stepped in, raising their linked hands.

"*In the name of the One, the Beneficent, the Merciful*, guide us in our efforts. Infuse the spirit of the One in the risen Mage . . ." He nodded at Rukh to fulfill his portion of the rite.

"Rukh, the Dark Mage and the Black Khan, Prince of West Khorasan."

Daniyar looked next at Ilea.

"Ilea, the Golden Mage and High Companion of Hira." The honeyed voice of the Golden Mage wound around the senses of both men.

"Daniyar, the Silver Mage and Guardian of Candour."

With the ritual complete, Daniyar closed his eyes. The others followed his lead. There was an interval of silence. Then he began to feel the flicker of his power. A line of silver fire arrowed up his spine. It spiraled down his arms, a tingling in his fingers that made the hands of the others jerk, although they didn't let go. Then the ring of the Silver Mage—recovered by the Assassin from the ruins of the loya jirga—became a band of white fire around his finger. Lightning flooded his veins, an incendiary flare that pulsed in an echo of the light from his ring. It spread outward from his jugular vein, thrusting up through his skull, sparking a web inside his mind. His power raged incandescent, until he forced it under control.

His thoughts shone with new clarity. The warmth that pulsed from his hands to the hands of the other Mages was answered by the Golden Mage. He knew her signature, recognized the golden surge underlined with steely power. It twined with the tendrils of light from his ring, reflecting his power twofold, as lethally honed as a blade, as boundless as the warmth of the sun. But from the Black Khan there was no pulse of energy beyond the strength of his grip. The magic that leapt from Daniyar's hand to Ilea's couldn't complete its circuit. Their power was mutually reinforced, but there was nothing else beyond it.

He opened his eyes to study the Black Khan, to find Ilea frowning at Rukh.

The Black Khan's eyes were fixed on the petals floating in the copper bowl. His hands were tightly clenched on theirs, his jaw a harsh line, his brows lowered in furious concentration, as if by simply willing it, the power of the Dark Mage would rise.

A litany fell from his lips.

"*In the name of the One, the Beneficent, the Merciful.*"

His gaze moved from the copper bowl to the light that pulsed from Daniyar's ring. Then to Ilea's diadem now ablaze in sheets of gold. He pulled his hand from Daniyar's, studying the ring on his own finger—an onyx-carved rook on silver to mirror the emblem at his throat.

"Perhaps this is the wrong token. There *is* no such thing as dark light."

The others dropped their hands. A hush fell over the room painted in flickers of candlelight.

Ilea's response was unsparing. "Those who attempt the dark rites should expect their powers to be tainted."

A black scowl from Rukh in response. "How did you hear of the attempt? Neither Arsalan nor Arian would have told you."

"Do you still not understand how the power works?" A haughty tilt of her head. "I felt the ripples of it through the continuity of our magic. Just as the Silver Mage would have."

Daniyar shook his head, dark hair brushing his nape. "I was fighting for my life. When I was brought back to the walls by the Assassin's men, the One-Eyed Preacher's thunder served to uproot my magic."

Something moved behind Rukh's eyes. Not uncertainty. Perhaps the regret that his attempt to use Arian's blood in the bloodrites had stripped him of his abilities.

"You *reclaimed* your power," he said to Daniyar. "I felt its pulse in my veins. Why can I not feel my own?"

Daniyar edged back from the table. "This is your first attempt. Give yourself more time."

Rukh swore to himself. "What time do you think I have? They're battering the Zhayedan Gate. Soon the Talisman will move east. If we lose the gates, we lose the city." He made a swift calculation. "How far does your power extend—the Golden Mage and Silver Mage in concert?"

But Daniyar was shaking his head. "Not far enough to hold the city."

Rukh turned to Ilea. "What of the Bloodprint, then? You read from it. You copied a verse you said would serve to defend the Citadel. Use it here, first."

There was no softness in the golden eyes that dwelt upon Rukh's face, nor any of the indulgence of a former lover. Her gaze was mesmerizing . . . predatory. The skin over Rukh's cheekbones tightened in response. But she ignored his request, speaking to the Silver Mage.

"The only thing that will aid you is the dawn rite. You know it as well as I do. Arian taught you the verse." It was a signal to Rukh, as well.

Rukh threw back his chair, striding across the room to throw open a pair of windows. A thousand watchfires rose against the darkness, showing them the depth of the Talisman's forces.

"You think a single verse will hold the Emissary Gate."

Daniyar came to stand beside him, his gaze picking out the bloodstained flags dotted about the camp.

"*Five* verses. Each backed by the power of this Conference."

Rukh's hands balled into fists. "I cannot *summon* it."

And he wondered then if the Conference of the Mages had failed because each of the Mages was an enemy to the others.

"You have yet to try." Daniyar motioned to Ilea. "High Companion."

She moved to join them, her eyes on the Talisman advance. "They will devour everything in their path, if you do not stop them here. You should have forced the First Oralist to stay. The Codex—if it exists—will not deliver you in time."

Rukh left aside the fact that the only person in the room with the power to command the First Oralist had chosen to disavow her, expelling her from the sisterhood of the Council of Hira.

"*What. Of. The Bloodprint.*" He ground out the words through his teeth. "You studied it. Your knowledge could deliver us!"

Ilea held up both hands, the ends of her sleeves belling out. With a cutting smile at Rukh, she said, "Your search for easy answers will not avail you, but I will give you what you seek. If only to show you a truth the Council of Hira has long known."

Eagerly, the Black Khan stepped forward.

"Tell me your truths *after* you have offered your benediction to my city."

"Very well." She turned away from him, calling out an incantation.

"*When the sky is shrouded in darkness . . . when the stars lose their light . . . when the mountains are made to vanish . . . when the seas boil over, and when all beings are linked to their deeds . . .*"

Hot white light inside the chamber, the coils of Ilea's hair catching fire.

"*. . . And when the girl-child that was buried alive is able to ask for what crime she was slain . . . when the scrolls of your deeds are unfolded . . . when heaven is laid bare . . . when the blazing fire is kindled bright, and when paradise is brought into view; on that Day, every human being will come to know what they have prepared for themselves.*"

Though chilling in their meaning, the words were curiously devoid of impact.

Then Ilea's arms jerked forward, forming a V. Her trailing sleeves caught fire, and the fire lanced straight from her arms to cut through Talisman lines. A pale gold tinged with crimson, the fire burned two lines through the camp, searing all in its path. It blazed brightly for an instant—a gilt-edged sword shearing through the final hours of the night. When it vanished, it left two blackened tracks on the ground. She had killed perhaps twenty men all told, but the Talisman rapidly regrouped.

Rukh glared at her. "Is that all?"

Sly acceptance. "That is all."

He grabbed her shoulders, shaking her.

"Then do it again. Again and again, unto a world without end."

Daniyar wrested Ilea free of Rukh's bruising grip. "Even if she did, you would still be facing an army of thousands at your gates." Rukh paused. Deliberated. Turned his back to them both, a gesture considered offensive at his court. But it *was* still his court. He may have failed as Dark Mage, but he was still the Prince of Khorasan.

He looked out over the path of Ilea's deliberate destruction. She had recited verses of the Claim—more in number than Arian and Sinnia combined. Deadly and more threatening than anything he had heard fall from the First Oralist's lips. Because the Verse of the Throne was an assertion, not a source of annihilation.

Why, then, had Ilea's recitation had so little impact on his enemy? If Arsalan had been with him in this room, he might have known the answer. Arsalan's calling to the Claim was sincere, richer and deeper than Rukh's.

At that, a door opened in Rukh's mind. He entered a room filled with light. He raised his face into the light—it pushed at him, moved through him, penetrated through to his cells, blinding and calming in the same calamitous instant. Throbbing like the answer to a question he'd forgotten to ask. The light expanded outward into his mind, pricked at his fears, made nonsense of his certainties, mocked him for his stubborn refusal to see it for what it was. Part of him. All of him. That was when he understood.

Ilea's warning . . . the taste of Daniyar's fear . . . the significance of Arian's absence. All trace of pretense fell away.

He turned back to Ilea, ignoring the Silver Mage. He raised a hand to untangle the golden coils of her hair, a gesture she allowed. When they'd fallen free of their intricate arrangement, he brushed back a lock from her forehead. Then he pressed his lips to her diadem and whispered, "It isn't just the words, is it? It's the qari who recites them—the gift given to the First Oralist."

She blinked, and he finished softly, "A gift you do not share."

Bitter acknowledgment in her golden eyes.

"Tell me your truth now, Ilea."

He had already guessed at the answer. The High Companion could recite verses from the Bloodprint, but without the depths of Arian's conviction, without the gift for language that had seen Arian rise to the rank of First Oralist, she would never be able to harness the power of the Claim as Arian had done. She couldn't bend it to her will.

She wound her hands around his wrists, removing them from her hair.

"My gifts are aligned to Hira. Ashfall must rely on the strength of the Dark Mage."

She told these half-truths to the Black Khan without compunction. *Why?* Daniyar's thoughts moved swiftly. *Because of Hira.* The Black Khan had delayed her return to the Citadel. And with Arian and the High Companion both absent, Hira *was* at risk. Ilea would know as well as he did that the Black Khan would not relinquish any advantage to his city. Whatever the extent of the Golden Mage's powers, Rukh would try to keep her at his side.

What Ilea had shown him—what she had done with the Claim—was designed to prove to Rukh that her talents would serve him no further. She couldn't do what Arian had done.

A misdirection the Black Khan would accept, knowing that of all the Companions of Hira, only Arian's gifts existed to serve more than her allegiance to the Council. Arian had shown him as much with her defense of the people of Ashfall. Though her Audacy was directed by the High Companion, she had chosen her own means of fulfilling it. And even after Ilea had stripped her of rank, she hadn't given up the fight. Daniyar felt a fierce throb of pride at Arian's defiance of Ilea. Her service on behalf of the Council wasn't that of blind adherence. Her calling was to the Claim—and the ethics that underlined it.

No *ritual without purpose,* she had whispered to him in another life, the whisper tinged with love.

And he had understood. Without a commitment to the values they espoused, rituals meant little to Arian, a position that often placed her at odds with the Council. Even the story of the Night Journey, a sacred visitation to the heavens, Arian viewed as an allegory, and not as a physical voyage, as so many of her sisters did.

No *form without substance.* No *sacred duty more hallowed than the worth of a single life.*

The words had meant more to him after the fall of Candour. They defined them both in opposition to the Talisman.

In whose name was our heritage set to the fire? Daniyar had demanded.

And the Talisman's acolytes had answered, *In the name of the One.*

He pushed down the familiar ache caused by Arian's absence. It was a weakness Ilea would exploit, at the moment he needed to turn her to his purpose. Which was to keep her in Ashfall, until Rukh could learn to harness his abilities as the Dark Mage.

He'd felt something stir at the way Rukh watched him, a prickling of his nerves along the tendrils of his magic. An awakening that the Conference of the Mages would fulfill. He recalled the Conference he'd been summoned to in Timeback, where he'd visited the scriptorium and sifted through its manuscripts, including one where the arguments of theologians had gone around in circles, perhaps like this Conference now. The memory passed from his thoughts as suddenly as it had come.

"Let us return," he said, holding out Ilea's chair. She pressed her lips together in refusal.

"Why try again?" Rukh asked. "The High Companion's powers—"

Daniyar cut him off. "The High Companion lacks the First Oralist's ability with the Claim, but she is still the Golden Mage. She *can* awaken your gifts. As she said, Ashfall must rely on itself. It needs the power of its Mage." And now he made use of the Black Khan's persistence to further his own resolve. "Your power is merely dormant. I felt it stir, as you must have felt mine." They could and *would* hold the Emissary Gate. "The Golden Mage can help to bring your powers to life. As can I."

A narrowing of Rukh's eyes. A hand at Ilea's elbow, as he urged her back to the table.

"You used the Claim to open the Conference," he pointed out.

Daniyar nodded. "A ritual." *No ritual without purpose.* "Just as the dawn rite is a ritual."

"Wherein lies its power?"

A question that cut to the heart of things. One for which he had the answer.

"In the strength you have to wield it. In the use you would make of it." His silver eyes shone, his words deadly as a blade. "Can you think of a suitable use?"

Eyes of midnight glittered in response.

A KNOCK ON THE DOOR TO THE CHAMBER. THIS TIME ONE OF THE Zhayedan's runners came to bring news of the Talisman's maneuvers and of Arsalan's response.

The Black Khan excused himself—no closer to retrieving his power—leaving Daniyar and Ilea alone in the room. The closing of the maghrebi doors cut off the cries of battle as suddenly as a blade thrown at an unprotected throat.

The High Companion reached for Daniyar's hands. Silent and watchful, he let her hold them. The act reinforced their mutual power; otherwise he wouldn't have permitted her touch.

"You still don't trust me." His hands clenched on hers, a betraying gesture. He eased the pressure of his grip, but not before they both felt the rise of their magic. In a few more hours, it would be dawn, and the dawn rite would be possible. That was all that was holding him in Ashfall. Were it not for his commitment to the Conference, he would have been on Arian's trail.

That didn't mean he needed to respond to the High Companion with anything other than the truth. "Why would I trust you, Ilea? You've stood between me and Arian from the first."

She looked into eyes like frozen silver lakes, eyes that had gazed into the void. But what *was* the void to Daniyar? The Talisman's desolation of his city? Or the loss of the woman he wanted for his own? Her fingers stroked his callused palms, the touch deliberately careful to contrast with pitiless words.

"One man's desires cannot undo centuries of tradition. There is no place for a man at the side of a Companion of Hira."

"Liar." Her hands jerked at the accusation. "How long after you arrived at the Citadel did you take the Black Khan as your lover?"

"He is a tool I use to further the Citadel's aims; he means nothing to me beyond that. What you seek from Arian is something else entirely."

She studied the flawless arrangement of his bones, wondering how to unsettle a man as dangerous as he was beautiful. One who had every reason to oppose her.

He proved that with his response. "You seem to have forgotten my gift."

Ilea *had* forgotten. For the Silver Mage possessed the ability to discern the lies she told from the truth, a gift given to those who held the title of Authenticate.

"You tore her from me," he said now. "With no thought to her needs when she'd already suffered such loss. Your duty as High Companion is to serve the Companions of Hira."

"You need not teach me a duty I have never failed to honor."

"How can you claim to honor it, when your actions serve only yourself?"

"Oh? And what of you, Daniyar? When I sent Arian to Candour more than a decade ago, *your* duty was to teach her of the manuscripts of Candour. Not to train her in war. Nor to take her as your own. It was you who betrayed *my* trust, before I raised a hand against you."

A contemptuous glance from eyes silvered over with frost. "My commitment to Arian was never a threat to Hira."

"Your *seduction* of Arian was meant to sever her from the Council—you knew our traditions; you swore to defend her honor. Instead, you took her, claimed her, *kept* her."

"No man keeps the First Oralist. She followed your dictates to the end. She gave me up to do so."

There was a primal beauty to his rage, to the dark brows that slashed down over eyes of arctic fire. And Ilea was not insensible to it. So she marshaled her words against him.

"You only *think* you know her." Her head tilted toward the sound of the Black Khan's voice beyond the door. She was gathering information, another tool to exploit. Despite the warmth that pulsed through their linked hands, she felt the chill of his response in her bones. "You think you know a history even Arian doesn't know. But as I warned you when you asked for dispensation, Arian is First Oralist. I will not cede her powers to your base desires."

She made sure he heard the truth in her words. A rawer form of her magic raced along her arms, rippling through her veins to flare around the center of her power, vibrating with fire. But she knew he was too arrogant, too certain of his claim to be deflected.

"Your insults cannot diminish the loyalty that binds Arian to me." His shrug was careless. "Besides which, you no longer have the power to command her. You dismissed her from the Council."

She gave a crystal-edged laugh.

"What future are you imagining, Daniyar? That the two of you will leave this war and flee to a place of safety, so you might finally have the chance to prove to her your devotion?" A mocking reproof. "Are you no longer Guardian of Candour? Have you no other obligations beyond your undisciplined desires?"

His thoughts flashed to the Damson Vale.

When it was done . . . when he had passed on the trust of the Guardian of Candour, he would take Arian to his secret valley in the mountains.

She caught the thought from his mind with a hissed incantation of the Claim.

"So the limit of your ambition is the vale you deem an earthly paradise?" She laced the words with contempt, her nails digging into his palms. "What a parochial fate you would choose."

"Only for someone who doesn't know how to love."

He felt her stillness in his own bones, knew the words had found their mark. The doors to the chamber opened, the Black Khan stepping inside. He perceived the tension between them without a word being said.

Ilea released one of Daniyar's hands to raise a palm in invitation. Rukh moved to take it.

"Did I miss something?" he asked.

She made her voice low and inviting as Rukh pulled his stool to the table, leaning over the fragrant copper bowl. "How fortunate that you differ so greatly from the Silver Mage."

"Oh?"

A sensual smile on her lips as she scored her nails against his palm.

"His pledge keeps him here at your side, when in truth he is longing to chase through the night after his beloved." Her gaze moved between the two men, measuring one against the other, confident that in her ambition, she was greater than both. "But there is no place for honor in war, a truth you illustrate so well."

Rukh dropped her hand. There was no merit to him in such a comparison, but angry at himself for allowing Ilea to provoke him, he picked up her hand again and kissed it.

"No doubt, I am to the Silver Mage what you are to the First Oralist."

An unexpected glance of appreciation from Daniyar, even as Ilea turned her fury at the comparison on the Silver Mage.

"She's not coming back to you." The hit cold and precise.

Daniyar reached for Rukh's other hand, completing the necessary circle. But it was also a gesture of fellowship.

"She doesn't need to."

"Oh?" The disdainful arch of a fine gold brow. "And why is that?"

"Because nothing that happens in Ashfall could keep me from her side."

So confident, Ilea thought. *So certain of his powers of attraction. So certain of the bond between Arian and himself.* When she returned to Hira, her actions would sever that bond with the cold finality of truth.

She felt her power rise, augmented by his.

And savored the strike to come.

8

KHASHAYAR HAD WASTED NO TIME. HE'D FREED HIMSELF AND SLIT THE
throats of the two men left to guard him. Quiet prevailed over
the Shaykh's tent as they stole out into the night to cross a wide
ridge of sand, disturbing only the rest of cape hares burrowed
deep in the grass, under a night of no moon, with stars flung up
against the stony darkness.

"Horses?" Arian whispered to Khashayar.

He forged the path ahead, his footsteps sinking into sand, setting a harsh pace.

"It's too risky to head back. We could be intercepted." Arian
kept pace beside him, though Sinnia was the more sure-footed
over sand. Her steady hand propelled Wafa along, the boy stumbling more than once, as he kept glancing back to the camp.

"We'll be discovered," Sinnia warned. "We can't outrun
them."

Khashayar herded them over another rib of sand, moving them
farther west.

"I did some scouting earlier. They've set up a supply depot just
south of us. There are camel herders there. If we can reach it in

time . . ." He shot a grim glance at Arian and Sinnia. "Let me carry the boy."

Without waiting for permission, he scooped up Wafa and settled him on his back.

"Hold on." Then, to the Companions: "Now run."

Wafa's arms fastened around Khashayar's neck in a death grip that he adjusted with a grimace. He set the grueling pace of a soldier trained from birth to overcome physical discomfort. His strength was enormous, his pace unflagging as he found a depression between two ridges of grass-feathered sand, its surface nearly flat.

Arian stumbled on the downslope of the ridge, falling to her hands and knees. Khashayar grabbed her under the arm and set her on her feet without breaking his rhythm. Sinnia flew beside him. When Arian brushed off her knees, she found herself staring at a startled caracal, whose tawny coat had camouflaged its hiding place in the sand.

She kept moving, hearing sounds of discovery break out in the camp behind them.

Not enough moon to trace their footprints in the sand, but all it would require to track them was a torch. The army of the Nineteen had men enough to spare to follow several different trails at once. Or they could save themselves the bother and ride the Companions to ground. A simpler method still: they could loose their hunting falcons on the night. It was what she would have done in their place.

All these thoughts raced through her mind as the wind whipped her hair against her face. She was the slowest of their party, Khashayar moving with deadly grace and Sinnia as though born to these sands.

Arian made her way across the depression, picking her steps

with care over the swaying grass. She couldn't see the depot ahead and was trusting to Khashayar's instincts. She'd had a moment when she wanted to tell him to cut his losses and run—to return to Ashfall, to lend his strength to his Khan. But she needed him. She wouldn't be able to cross the desert without him.

He cut south across the sand, Wafa clinging to his back. As the ridge dipped southward, the roof of stars cast a sharp orange flare against the sand. Her heart in her mouth, Arian feared they had fallen on a desert-dweller's campfire. But the light dimmed with the curve of sand, and she realized what she'd seen was a field of orange poppies.

Her relief was short-lived. Angry voices carried across the sand, followed by the thunder of hooves. Desert horses trained for speed and agility. And guided, as Arian had feared, by the telltale cry of a hawk.

The Nineteen had found their trail.

His voice gravel-edged and deep, Khashayar urged them to hurry. "We have to reach the supply depot before the guards hear the alarm."

They sank into another valley, but Arian knew it for a losing battle. They couldn't outrun the Nineteen's horses. And the pursuit was too close to give her time to conjure a mirage. Wind snapped her hair against her face again, and she caught the glimmer of an answer.

"Go," she said to the others. "I'll meet you at the depot."

"No, sahabiya. My orders are to stay at your side." Khashayar grabbed hold of her arm.

Arian shook herself free. "I'm not helpless, Khashayar. Trust to my use of the Claim."

He didn't argue further, her self-assurance persuasive.

When Sinnia hesitated, Arian urged her on. "Khashayar will

need your help. If I need you, I'll call you back." She pressed her circlets; Sinnia did the same.

They split up without further discussion, though Arian heard Wafa's broken cry of protest.

She moved through a maze of gullies, seeking the valley of sand's center. A band of caracals followed her high along one ridge, their golden eyes aglow in the dark. She used them to pinpoint her progress, the sound of hooves at her back. A red fox froze as she crossed his path, its black eyes sharp and curious. It darted away again at the earsplitting cry of a hawk.

She was almost at the center of the valley, bringing the riders with her, leaving Khashayar's way clear ahead.

She moved along curled eddies of grass deep into the valley of sand. The riders approached, a party of six astride the mares that were bred in the heart of the desert, their arrow-straight manes tossing in the wind, their heads thrown up high and proud.

Five commanders of the Nineteen hooted at her in triumph. One man remained silent, dried blood at the edges of his lips, the glaive in his hand starkly poised. Their eyes met, and she knew his strike would be fatal. But the thrill of fear she felt wasn't because of the glaive. It was at the realization that she'd failed to kill him with the Claim, as she'd thought she'd done in the tent of the Al Marra. She must have faltered in her resolution or in the way she'd shaped the verse—*but how could that be when she had seen the breath whisper from his body?*

Or had she?

How had Najran been able to resist the verse she had used to strike at him? What powers did he possess?

Then she noticed something else. His hips were girded with his belt of jeweled daggers, the tip of his glaive spiked with blood.

"You killed the child?" she cried in protest.

His eyes hooded, he answered her, "I put a traitor to death."

His voice was the scrape of a blade, metal crunched against bone.

The group of riders circled her, drawing closer, the hooves of their horses stirring up clouds of sand. The caracals crept closer on the ridge, predators who now assumed a hunting crouch. She met the eyes of one and motioned it away with a wave. The black tufts of hair at the tips of its ears quivered before it bounded down the far side of the ridge, its packmates following behind.

Arian kept moving, one slow step at a time, her eyes on the man with the glaive. His eyes struck sapphire sparks as the riders tightened their circle.

"Fall back," she warned them, the promise of the Claim beneath her words.

Najran raised his glaive, his head cocked to one side, listening.

Her tone gentle, Arian called up the Claim. *"Would any of you wish to have a garden with date palms and vines, rivers flowing underneath, and all kinds of fruits?"*

A soothing whisper chased at the edges of the dunes. The riders nodded to one another in answer, loosening the reins of their mares.

Arian motioned at them, just as she had motioned at the caracal. The horses drew away, giving her space to maneuver.

And still Najran watched her with those sapphire-studded eyes, his fingers loose and relaxed around the glaive.

The whisper in the valley rose into the air, gathering traces of sand, the silver pathways of the stars dimming above their heads.

"But you would be stricken with age, your children too weak to tend it, your garden struck by a whirlwind, lashed with fire until burnt."

Najran raised the glaive high above his head.

But it was too late now for him to undo the power of Arian's spell. The crests of the dunes that surrounded them exploded in a tornado. The distance between Arian and the riders increased as the vortex rose around them, pierced by ribbons of flame. Hot winds from the north mixed with cold winds from the south: the aesar of the desert put to the test of the Claim.

They were smothered by sand, while fire roared in their ears until it had swallowed their cries, burning the riders to ash, their horses scattered to the winds.

In the eye of the storm, Arian waited until the whirling sand subsided, a shimmering waterfall of fire that circled her until it ebbed into a single line—a wall between the encampment she had escaped from and the uncharted distance ahead.

Flames spun orange-gold patterns on the sand—it was over; it was done.

But when she looked up, one man remained on his horse, his weapon poised in his hand as he watched her across the veil of fire. He lowered the glaive, his gleaming eyes fixed on hers.

She finished what she'd come to say.

"So does the One offer clear signs so that you may reflect."

The sapphire glint in his eyes dimmed to amber, as he acknowledged the words. He wheeled his horse around, searching for a way through the whirlwind her voice had summoned from the sands. When he realized there was no path that would allow him to cross, he spit out a lengthy curse. Then he bowed at her in respect.

"Until we meet again, First Oralist."

She nodded and left him on the sands.

ARIAN FOUND THE OTHERS ON A RIDGE ABOVE THE SUPPLY DEPOT, where most of the camp was asleep. A handful of guards were near a small armory, another one asleep at the foot of a trio of camels. The Nineteen had grown confident to leave so few here, but it was more likely that they had dozens of similar depots dotted about the desert.

"Wait here," Khashayar told them. He disappeared down the ridge.

"How did you know to call the aesar?" Sinnia asked.

She hugged Sinnia close to her, the warmth of the contact easing the chill of her encounter with Najran. "From those stories you told me of your childhood. Those tales of warriors who crossed the Sea of Reeds to summon up the firewinds."

"Those were fables," Sinnia muttered, aghast. "That was quite a risk."

"Surprising, I know," Arian teased. "Given our adherence to only proofs we can see."

A pause. Then Sinnia's bold grin. She squeezed Arian harder.

"Wretch."

Arian smiled too. "I'm sorry, I couldn't resist."

She noticed Wafa staring at the pair of them, mildly indignant that the Companions had found anything to laugh at in their near escape.

She stroked a hand through his curls, kissing the top of his head.

"Don't be frightened," she reassured him. "Have faith in Khashayar."

Wafa snorted in disgust, which she apprehended as his general disgust at men of every stripe, save for the Silver Mage. At the thought of Daniyar, her spark of amusement subsided. The depth of her longing for him remained acutely painful.

She took a sip of water from her waterskin, then offered it to Wafa, meeting Sinnia's eyes. Using the language of the Citadel, she told Sinnia what had happened in the valley.

"Twice now, I've been unable to kill Najran."

Sinnia's eyes swept the supply camp for signs of renewed activity. There was no sign of Khashayar, a black blade against the night.

"Najran is the Shaykh's sayyid. He wouldn't have risen as high as he has if he wasn't uniquely gifted."

Arian's exhalation was a sigh. "Perhaps. But I failed to kill him with the *Claim*. I split the Registan with my voice and killed dozens of Ahdath at the Clay Minar. And together, we held off the One-Eyed Preacher. How could *Najran* have resisted the compulsion of the Claim?"

"There *is* no compulsion in faith," Sinnia reminded her.

Sinnia was right, but it was beside the point. The real question was whether Arian had now encountered someone more powerful than the One-Eyed Preacher. Like the Nizam of Ashfall, Najran was a whisperer who had the ear of power. How far did that power extend? Could there be something to the Nineteen's numerology—a hidden message contained within the arithmetic of the Claim? If there was, why had Najran then denied the power of the Nineteenth revelation? Why had he dismissed the story of the Adhraa as a story of the Esayin?

She had a more practical concern, as well. How long would the veil of fire hold before Najran tracked them again?

"Let's go." Khashayar's gravel-edged voice. He'd crept up to them without a trace of noise.

Sinnia hissed in surprise. "You'll be the death of me, Khorasan. Next time give us a warning."

A corner of his mouth jerked up. "That warning would come with blood that I'd prefer not to spill."

The words might have softened his image as a member of the Zhayedan, but when Sinnia scanned the supply camp again, she saw that the guards lay dead upon the ground.

"What of the others in the tent?"

"Don't ask." He pulled both of the Companions to their feet, easier now with physical contact. A camaraderie was building between them; neither woman rebuked him. Keeping his voice low, he added, "I've damaged their armory and spoiled their food supplies, though I set some aside for our journey. The camels are ready. I can add your packs to their load."

Arian and Sinnia helped him load their supplies, careful to divide their waterskins evenly between their three mounts. Unlike Sinnia, Arian hadn't ridden a camel before. Their strong smell and snorting breath came as a surprise, as did their long, thick lashes. Camel spiders scurried around their hooves. Arian suppressed a shudder. Wafa shrank back from their dun-colored mounts, his expression frightened and forlorn.

"Do you want to ride with me, boy?" Khashayar offered. Wafa

shook his head with a scowl that bordered on rudeness. He clung to Sinnia's hand, making his preference clear.

"So this is your thanks for the way I carried you across the desert. Ruffian."

Khashayar's grin flashed against the darkness. He boosted Arian up onto her camel, swinging into his seat with easy masculine strength. Arian kept pace with him, Sinnia and Wafa at his other side. It took them some time to adjust to the swinging gait of their mounts, but Khashayar rode without difficulty.

"You've done this before," Arian observed.

"Training," he answered briefly. He wouldn't tell her more. The Zhayedan protected the secrets of their army.

"We should make for the Gulf of Khorasan. If we cut through the gulf, we'll be at the court of the Negus much sooner than we planned."

A sharp shake of his head. "I overheard the guards." Faint contempt in the words. The Zhayedan wouldn't be so careless discussing their plan of battle. "The Nineteen hold the Gulf. They've set the ports ablaze, which means there's no safe place for us to cross. We'll cut southeast, travel overland, skirt the far edge of the Rub Al Khali. Then we can cross the Sea of Reeds. If we journey south on the water, we'll be able to make up some time."

Arian considered his plan, conscious of what he'd chosen not to say.

"If we take the longer road, by the time we reach Timeback, Ashfall may have fallen."

A grim twist of Khashayar's lips. "Not as long as there are Zhayedan left to fight. I have my orders from the Khan. I won't allow myself to fail them."

Too tired to argue with his Zhayedan stubbornness, Arian subsided in her seat.

He glanced over at her, his gaze skirting the shadows under her eyes, dropping lower to the pale curves of her mouth.

"You should rest, First Oralist. I can lead the camels while you sleep. We'll be easier to spot come daylight." He reached for Sinnia's lead too. "You as well, Companion. Neither of you have rested since your arrival at Ashfall. Nor long before, I suspect."

Sinnia snatched back her lead with a sinuous twist of her shoulders. "I can manage."

But he knew how to persuade her. "The First Oralist will not sleep if you remain on guard. Will you permit your contrariness to add to her fatigue?"

Glaring at him, Sinnia passed him the lead.

Khashayar swallowed a smile. "I've anchored your carrier. If the boy doesn't jostle you, you should be able to sleep."

Sinnia settled back with thanks, Wafa fitted against the sleek curves of her body.

A quiet question from the First Oralist disturbed the silence, as Khashayar linked their reins together. "Does it ever rain in the desert, Khashayar?"

"This isn't true desert," he answered. "These are small dunes over scrublands—they collect their share of rain. When we cross the Rub Al Khali, you'll be able to tell the difference."

She'd eased back in her saddle, still alert, the rich color of her eyes silvered at the edges by starlight. A soldier to his bones, Khashayar's senses tingled at this touch of the supernatural.

"Will you offer a prayer for Ashfall?" A storm of emotion in his eyes as he thought of his burning city.

She leaned over to take his hand, her palm soft under his. "May the unrighteous fail to prosper, may no harm come to the believers. May Ashfall stay safe for all the nights to come, may the One protect the Guardian of Candour." Her voice went quiet. When she let go of his hand, his retained the warmth of her touch. Another sign of who she was.

Her eyelids were heavy now; he urged her to rest again.

She settled back in her seat.

Then he had the night to himself.

10

THERE WAS TOTAL DARKNESS IN THE COLD ROOM BENEATH THE Qaysarieh Portal. Its walls were lined with nooks that ran from the ground to the vaulted ceiling above. Each nook could be piled with the bodies that fell in war, until a moment of respite allowed for burial rites. In the center of the room was a giant table whose surface was formed of a marble slab, cool and dark and at least three feet thick. Along one wall of the room was a heavy set of double doors that led to a similar chamber on the other side, this one staffed by healers, busy with care of the wounded. Thus far, the doors had remained closed. There was only one body in the cold room.

The delicate form of the Princess of Ashfall was laid upon the marble slab atop a silk divan with silver handles decorated with obsidian rooks. Her thick dark hair fell in spiraling curls from the slab to the floor, a lock at her temple as white and jagged as lightning.

The Assassin lit a torch and placed it in a brace by the door, so that soft gold light danced over the Princess's face. Her body had been washed and dressed in a burial robe, which fit too loosely on her slight frame.

The same insult in death that had been offered her in life.

"No more," he whispered, bending to her ear. He brushed aside the curls clustered around her forehead, slipping off his gloves to wind the single white lock around his finger. The lock singed by the One-Eyed Preacher's fire felt brittle to the touch, not silky like the riotous curls that spilled in abundance to the floor.

The Assassin let his gaze caress Darya from her forehead to the soles of her feet. Releasing the lock twined about his finger, he raised his sensitive fingertips to open Darya's eyes. They stared straight up at the ceiling, black as onyx, the pupils striated in shock. A faint odor of death emanated from her body, proof of the onset of decay.

But she was not yet lost to the Assassin.

He unsheathed a blade made of bone from a strap at his waist, running the tips of his fingers along its edge. The knife would do.

There were three sources of power in the chamber: The chill of the cold room. The flickering light of the torch. And the Assassin himself. He sheared off part of the white curl of hair with his blade, setting it on the table not far from Darya's head. Then, running the edge of the blade over her robe, he slit the flesh over Darya's heart. He pressed the blade into her flesh until a single pearl of blood welled up over its tip. An act of preservation he had thought of from the moment he had spied the Princess on her bier. A careful exhalation and the blood drop on the tip of his blade settled on the shorn white lock.

Next he took Darya's wrist in his hand, pushing up the sleeve of her robe. He studied the delicate carpus, the two rows of bones that knotted her wrist together. Angling his blade with care, he made an incision through flesh. On the proximal side, he sliced swiftly until a shaving of bone curled up on the tip of the blade. Placing her wrist gently back on the table, he nicked the shaving with two of his fingers so that it landed on top of the drop of blood.

Then he took his blade and used it to etch a six-point star into the marble. His preparations were complete.

He bent over Darya again, pressing his thumb to her lips. Its curves were still resilient. Nodding in satisfaction, he angled Darya's jaw to leave her mouth wide open.

The sound of raised voices came to him from the chamber across from the cold room. Their efforts with the wounded were failing. Soon the healers would require this room.

He moved quickly, calling up the verse of the Bloodprint he had taken the time to memorize in the hour the Black Khan had spared him at his fortress.

The Assassin was not a traitor to the Khan. He had studied verses from the Bloodprint as promised, to aid in the Black Khan's defense. But he had also done more. He had sought the answer to a riddle that had long defied his understanding.

The living cannot be called forth from the dead, except on the Day of Resurrection.

If they could, the powers of his tribe of Assassins could grow to unparalleled dimensions. The question was not whether the Assassin *could* raise the dead. The question was whether he ought to: whether having raised the Princess from her bier, he would then be able to command her. To restore the Princess to the role she should have occupied as the right hand of her brother.

He'd sensed the power of the Claim inside the Princess, just as the First Oralist had, when Arian had thought herself unobserved with Darya in the Black Khan's scriptorium.

He'd witnessed Darya's vision as it appeared in Arian's mind. He permitted himself the familiarity of her name because he was gifted in the Claim himself. His gift bound him to any who were similarly bound or inspired, and with Arian—

He'd caught her words, perhaps because he was uniquely disposed to hear them.

You are a child of Hira.

You belong *to us.*

A regretful smile at the limits of Arian's vision. Arian thought she'd found another disciple of Hira who might be made literate, when Darya's power was at her fingertips. Where it could and *would* serve Ashfall.

Then there was the question of the Assassin. The Black Khan owed him a debt, one the Assassin hadn't claimed. Until this moment with the Princess.

He hadn't sought the Khan's permission because he knew the Khan would not refuse him. Not after everything the Assassin had offered in the Khan's service.

And he hadn't yet begun.

He would give the Black Khan more, offer him *true* fealty, if he could have the Princess.

To an end he would share with no one. Not even the Khan he admired.

He had enemies in common with the Khan. And for the moment that was reason enough.

He murmured the verse he'd selected from the Bloodprint. He whispered it three times over his small pile of relics, and then he waited. Fire struck the lock of hair, sparked crimson with the drop of blood, acquired the blade-sharp edge of bone before dissolving into dust. He gathered the odorless dust onto the tip of his finger. Then he dropped it into Darya's mouth.

He leaned close and pressed his lips to hers, breathing into her mouth.

Once, twice, a third time . . . until the wooden legs of the table rocked against the floor and the slab of marble cracked in two.

Movement. The soldiers in the other room were shifting the metal bar that locked the door between the chambers.

There was little time to act.

He whispered the final words.

"Breathe, Princess, and rise."

11

Cold sleet against her skin in the dark of unsettled night. Bones that felt fragile, breakable with a breath. Skin stretched across sinew. And unfamiliar movement, fingers curling into soft, wet palms, untouched by the hardship of labor.

Who am I? she asked from the quarry of nightmare.

Princess of Ashfall, came the answer.

Then where is my brother?

Fighting a war that only you can end.

Memory returned in broken pieces. A princess at the edge of the court, who found herself in disfavor. The eager desire that clamored in her blood to win her brother's approval. A handsome man in uniform who sat at the right hand of the prince. His name came to her mind.

Arsalan.

He is not for you, Princess.

Cold rejection in her soul. Arsalan was hers, and she would claim him.

Where am I?

Open your eyes, Princess. Discover the truth for yourself.

Her eyelids drifted apart. She was sitting on a stone bench under a night sky streaked with shining sleet, the stars above her polished to silver blades. Petals of snow bloomed against her skin. Her head was . . . free . . . light, her neck open to the cool kiss of the wind. Her hair was undressed, flowing over her shoulders like a cape. When she pressed her hands to the bench to raise herself to her feet, the sound of bells didn't follow. She was unencumbered.

On the stone bench across from her, a figure watched her from the shadows. Waited for her to take in her surroundings. A park inside the palace, a green garden lush with groves of almond blossoms and plane trees. A place for lovers to meet to give in to clandestine desires.

A sudden throb of emotion.

Was the man who watched her from the shadows her lover?

They were enclosed in a secret copse among a dozen others in the garden, this one perfumed with jasmine. Utterly peaceful in the haze of midnight, the scent of jasmine rose around her body and calmed her.

The man who watched came to his feet in a sleek and silent motion.

Was it Arsalan, the general of her brother's army? Would he touch her, kiss her, take her for his own?

Arsalan—

What do you remember, Princess?

He stayed in the shadows so she couldn't see his face. But Arsalan's voice called to her, sang to her across the wall of sound that crashed down over her memories.

What was the sound? Was it the sound of battle?

Weaponry loaded and fired. The urgent voices of men calling across the courtyard. Stone against stone . . . a battering rush of noise.

Her name. Her name called by a man who loved her.

And a blue-eyed boy chasing at her heels, his small hands reaching out to catch her.

Why was she at the walls? Why did she race to the Messenger Gate, her bells chiming a frantic alarm?

Why was there so much smoke . . . where had the thunder come from . . . a roar of fury and terror . . . ?

She covered her ears with her hands, sinking onto the bench, the quick collapse jarring bones that moved without coordination. Unbalanced, she slumped to one side.

And still the man in the shadows watched her, utterly without pity.

But why would she need pity? She was the Princess of Ashfall, sister to the Black Khan.

Strong male hands that gathered her close to a body honed for battle. A cry of loss, as he pressed her face to his own—touching her freely, giving her what she'd longed for when she was no longer able to ask for it.

And a roar that silenced the night—proof of her brother's grief.

She wanted to go to him, to reassure him, to offer her help in any way she could, but how could she? He wouldn't want her. He was angry at her; he had banished her to Qaysarieh. But she had redeemed herself, hadn't she? She had obeyed the Nizam's order to free her half-brother from the dungeons. She had brought him to the Emissary Gate to use his gifts as Dark Mage to fight in Ashfall's defense.

Your brother Darius is dead.

The man from the shadows was speaking in her mind, his voice cool and precise, a blade slicing through snow, a cadence to cauterize wounds.

But how could Darius be dead?

An image in her mind, brutal in its clarity. The Nizam . . . Darius . . . herself . . . racing to the Messenger Gate. Something wrapped in Darius's hands, something of vital importance . . . something she should have protected.

The Bloodprint.

The One-Eyed Preacher has it now.

The memory came as a blow.

She tumbled from the bench to the ground, sensing the disarticulation of her spine, as her limbs jerked out of sequence. Her breath touched her lips, faint and icy. She forced the paralysis from her right hand and pressed it hard against her heart, searching for a rhythm.

Nothing.

Just a cold, empty space at her core.

Finally, the man in the shadows was moved to offer his assistance. He raised her to her feet and held her against the armor that fit his body like a skin. Magnetic eyes gleamed at her through the openings of a mask engraved with a script that was foreign to her.

Yet Darya could read the script. She knew who the man was.

Assassin, she whispered in his mind. *Why have you called me to life?*

Are you alive, Princess?

A touch of mockery in the question. But nothing there of pity.

He was holding her weight between his hands, as she couldn't support herself.

She had breath but no heartbeat. Thought without the gift of speech.

You are able to speak, Princess. You merely have to decide.

"Do I?"

It didn't sound like her voice, which was sweet and girlish. The pitch of her voice had changed. It was . . . riper. Smoothly inviting. Nothing like Darya at all.

You see? You've begun your transformation.

Terror opened up. Of the lightning that had stolen her life, of the One-Eyed Preacher's infinite power, throbbing like a drumbeat in her skull, draining her of that which made her Darya, snuffing out her soul like a spark.

Stop. Those firm hands continued to hold her. *You have nothing to fear from him now.*

What have you done to me?

What needed doing.

"No!" She struggled against his unyielding grip. "You shouldn't have done this! You should have let me go. You've turned me into something I shouldn't be."

She felt . . . wrong. Her bones, her flesh, her manner of movement, it was all wrong. She was overtaken by panic, but the tears she wanted to shed wouldn't come. Despite her fear and confusion, her face was as smooth and cold as a sculpture carved from ice.

"They'll laugh at me!" It wasn't her voice. *This* voice didn't seem to mind. "They'll call what you've done to me an outrage. You've made me an object to be pitied—a monstrosity!"

Are you a monstrosity, Darya? Did Arsalan think of you so?

He placed another image in her mind—this one accompanied by sensation. Darya shivered in his hold, as the touch of a man's hands imprinted itself on her skin.

Those same hands slipped to her feet, removing the anklets she wore, stowing them beneath the breastplate of his armor. She glanced up to see who it was. Arsalan's face wore a mask of sorrow, graven lines beside his mouth, heaviness on his brow.

For you, Darya. All for you.

"What do you want from me? What use do you think you can make of me?"

The icy touch of the Assassin's mind against hers.

You will stand beside your brother at the gates. You will oversee his council of war. You will awaken his powers as Dark Mage. You will become who you were always meant to be.

It took every ounce of strength she had to wrest herself from his hold. Her footsteps lurched out of rhythm, one forward, one back, the spacing unequal. She pressed both hands to her diaphragm and drew a shuddering breath.

Traces of snow trailed down her face, mimicking tears she couldn't cry.

"You won't do this to me. You *won't* command me."

The Assassin curved a hand around her neck, pressing down on a pulse that didn't throb.

You have nothing to fear from coming into your power. I will be there to guide you—nothing more.

She didn't believe him. And then she was distracted, as an image of Arsalan flashed into her mind, one she had conjured for herself, shielded from the Assassin. She was wrapped in his strong embrace outside the door to her chamber, and Arsalan was kissing her as if she held the key to his salvation.

Something hot and dark unfurled inside her thoughts. Warmth ignited at her fingertips. She ducked under the Assassin's arm, her sinews finding their rhythm, her footsteps slipping into place. She caught the glint of surprise in his eyes.

I do not require your guidance. I have already chosen the man I wish to have at my side.

Princess, you move too swiftly. Arsalan will not come to you like this.

The sensual curve of a smile on her lips. A shimmy of seduction in her shrug, as she turned to leave the garden, gliding lightly down the path.

He has no say in it, Assassin.

Come to it, neither do you.

12

It took Arian's party almost a week to cross the Rub Al Khali, and the geography of their travel was not as Arian had learned it from the histories of Hira. Distances were shorter and steeper, crushed together by plates that had realigned, with gaping holes cut from the map of the world that had existed before the wars. As they edged closer to the ruins of the holy city, the metallic scent of the wars of the Far Range lingered in the air.

Yet not in the air, precisely. As Arian tipped up her head to taste the wind, she was conscious of that lingering scent as if it were a memory reawakened, something conveyed to her during her long years of study. She set the thought aside; she could also smell the thousand scents of the sea—salt crystals, iodine, the rich ochre of the seabed tangled with so many others—and it wouldn't be long before they reached it. Just as well. They were perilously low on supplies, the land too dry and damaged to yield much in the way of the hunt, though Khashayar had proven adept at digging up scorpions.

Their last taste of fresh water had been six days ago; their stores were nearly finished. Wafa was weak with thirst, so she and

Sinnia had alternated in giving him their portion, keeping it secret from Khashayar, who would have done so in their stead. She and Sinnia were used to privation, and they needed Khashayar at full strength. Arian hadn't told the others, but just as she was conscious of the pull of the holy city, she sensed the danger at her back.

Najran would find them again, unless they reached the shores of the Sea of Reeds first.

The blazing sun that beat down on them hadn't made matters easier. They moved at night and rested in the shadows of hillocks or under the shade of palm trees in daylight, but these shelters had been few along the journey. And Khashayar was looking back—counting the days, the hours, the minutes until his duty was discharged, so he could fly to Ashfall's defense.

Despite his impatience to return to his city, he'd been good company on the journey, spinning tales of the court of Ashfall in its days of glory, though careful not to touch on any subject that could occasion a betrayal of the Black Khan's secrets. He spoke of the Princess Darya's fondness for tragic tales of romance found in the Book of Kings. He told them of the Zhayedan's prowess but not of their method of training. He spoke of beautiful white horses captured from the lands of the Russe. Of himself, he said little, but when he spoke of Arsalan, the Commander of the Zhayedan, it was with great respect.

"He taught us the meaning of loyalty; it is loyalty that binds the empire."

When Arian pressed him on the subject of Darius, Khashayar fell silent after saying, "Ashfall has only one Khan."

He frowned as Wafa's head drooped to his chest. He gestured at the boy. "We should stop at the holy city. We are bound to find hospitality somewhere in its environs."

"Does anyone live there still?"

"I'm not certain," he admitted. "I haven't been this far west. But it's unlikely that an area with access to water and shelter would be entirely abandoned."

Arian was about to respond when she felt the tremor beneath the sands. The ground shifted; the camel she was riding faltered. Sinnia and Wafa fared worse. Their mount stumbled to its knees, sending them tumbling from its back.

The wind began to stir across the dunes, flinging sand into their eyes. Sinnia led the animal by hand.

"Hurry," she urged the others. "Something unnatural is coming."

The sands continued to shift, giant dunes collapsing in their path.

"Make your way to lower ground!" Khashayar shouted the words into the wind that had whipped up with sudden fury. "And ride hard; use your crops. Companion!" he called to Sinnia. "Get back on your mount at once."

They began their descent, struggling to drive their mounts as they wrapped their cloaks around their heads. Sand rose up before them in waves, whipping hard at the camels, who crashed to their knees and refused to move another step.

Arian heard Wafa's quickly stifled wail. She understood his pain when particles of sand slipped into her lungs. Within moments, they were all coughing, sheltered behind the camels, trying to summon the Claim as they choked on bits of grit and dust.

A new sound echoed in their ears—an eerie whistle, as if the winds had been called into song, before a harsh, thunderous roar pounded against their skulls.

How could it have struck so swiftly? Why had there been no warning?

She clutched Sinnia's hands, trying to see. She could make out Wafa's body huddled under Sinnia's arm. But Khashayar she couldn't see at all. He'd driven his camel to its knees at a spot where it served to shield Arian and the others from the wind, but of his own strong form there was no sign.

The wind raged and raged until Arian thought it would flay her flesh from her bones, leaving her raw and exposed. Her breath was choked by blowing sand, her lungs pushed to their limit. She buried her head in her knees.

She was helpless, unable to search for Khashayar, unable to do anything to protect the camels that served them. And still the wind raged on, until—with a stinging breath—it died as suddenly as it had sprung up, leaving silence in its wake.

Arian coughed up a mouthful of sand. She tried to wet her lips, but her tongue was as dry as bone, her lips blistered and cracked. She struggled to her mount, who had tucked its head into its chest. She found her waterskin and squeezed water onto her tongue.

She shook out her cloak before she stumbled back to Sinnia and Wafa. Sinnia was on her feet, her dark curls gilded by sand. She shook her head and sent sand flying in all directions. Arian ducked her head.

"Look!" A hoarse shout from Sinnia. Arian followed her pointing finger.

They had made it halfway down the dune, but high on the crest she caught sight of Khashayar. She opened her mouth to call him, but all that came out was a croak.

Khashayar wasn't alone.

His sword raised in his hand, he was facing another man who stood some distance apart, his feet firmly planted in the sands at the crest of the dune.

The man's head turned toward Arian, and she caught the

amber glint of his eyes. When he shrugged his shoulders, sand fell from his cloak to expose the belt of daggers at his waist. In his right hand, he held the iron glaive.

Najran!

Khashayar was at his mercy.

"Sinnia!"

Arian grabbed Sinnia's hand, and the two of them began to scramble up the dune to Khashayar's rescue.

"Stay back!" Khashayar shouted.

The Companions didn't listen.

Najran tipped his head to one side, watching their climb, his lips curved in a smile of utter malice. He looked from Khashayar to the Companions and measured the distance between them.

Then he did something unexpected.

He raised the iron glaive and plunged it down the side of the dune.

He'd aimed it at a spot behind Khashayar, but at a distance where it struck neither the Zhayedan soldier nor the Companions of Hira.

Arian paused for a moment as the glaive trembled in the sand, and then she and Sinnia continued to climb. There was too much grit in her throat for her to summon the Claim, but perhaps by the time she reached the crest, she and Sinnia could stand against Najran together.

He must have read the thought in her eyes, yet he still didn't reach for his daggers, that peculiar smile playing on his lips. Instead, he opened his mouth to issue a series of sounds, followed by words in a language that verged on the familiar.

The words spun out like a poisonous web that shrouded the distance between them. Dark words, black words . . . yet words that contained within them the seeds of something pure.

For a moment, Arian thought her heart was thundering in her chest, before she realized it was the sands of the dune that had shifted beneath her feet in an amber, oceanic wave. She lost her footing beneath it, sliding all the way back to slam into Khashayar's camel. Sinnia slid past her down the dune. Waves of sand collapsed around them.

The shuddering, sliding sound went on and on until Najran's voice fell silent.

When the ringing had subsided in Arian's ears, she staggered to her feet.

Khashayar and Najran loomed up on the crest far above her head once more.

From the point where the iron glaive had landed in the sand, a canyon had opened up, a crevasse that stretched for miles, separating the men from the Companions. Sand poured into the canyon, skittering down over iron red walls. The fissure was twenty feet across, and there was no means of bridging the gap. Najran couldn't reach them, but neither could Khashayar. Najran had achieved his purpose: he'd stolen their escort from them. Now he would strike at Khashayar, who, despite his fierce ability as a warrior, was no match for a foe like Najran.

"Get the camels," she muttered to Sinnia. "Get Wafa and go. I'll be right behind you."

When she heard the sounds of Sinnia's movement, she shouted up the dune to Khashayar. "You can't help us now—go home to Ashfall! Leave the sayyid to us."

"No! My sworn duty is to protect you!"

Najran flung a blade at his head. Khashayar barely ducked it in time.

"He'll have to find a way across. Go, Khashayar! Your commander needs you!"

But Khashayar wasn't easily governed, and Arian watched in despair as he raised his sword. Then he seemed to change his mind, feinting to a spot behind him. Arian watched him move with quicksilver cunning as he reached for the glaive in the sand.

A clever move, but Najran was too canny to be outmaneuvered. Two daggers flew straight at Khashayar's heart; there was nothing Arian could do to shield him. But hearing her low cry, Khashayar twisted aside in time, grasping the glaive under its spike. A mercurial movement, the swift bend of his arm, and the glaive was flung into the crevasse. He brought up his shield to guard his chest before Najran could strike at him again.

A grating cry emanated from Najran, who now rolled down the dune to the gap. Arian braced herself against any other secret powers Najran might command, but to her shock, he lowered himself into the crevasse, following the arc of Khashayar's thrust. In a moment, he had disappeared. Arian knew better than to climb closer to the edge to see where Najran had gone.

Khashayar had no such reservation. He clambered down the dune, as close to the edge as he dared, his shield held high before him. His search yielded no answers. The canyon's depths were impenetrable; no movement betrayed Najran's whereabouts.

Khashayar looked across the canyon at Arian. Sinnia had gathered the camels; now she placed a lead in Arian's hand. She gave Khashayar a sad salute.

"I will miss your stories, Captain. You were starting to grow on me."

"Like fungus?" Khashayar said drily, but there was self-reproach in his eyes. He stared across the gap at the Companions.

"Go home before he finds you." Arian's voice was still rough with sand. "Don't linger at the gap. There's no way across for miles. By the time you find a place to cross, we'll be at the sea." A gentle look in her eyes, she added, "You brought us this far, Captain; your duty has been fulfilled. But you know as well as I that your heart is calling you to Ashfall."

Khashayar made up his mind. "Go. Get to the sea before Najran resurfaces." He looked ruefully at his mount on the other side of the gap. "I'll make my own way home."

His eyes blazed with sudden, fierce emotion. He went down on one knee.

"It was my honor to serve the Companions of Hira. May your journey be fruitful; may your return to Ashfall be victorious and proud."

Tears lit Arian's eyes. "May the One bless your return. May your journey home be safe."

Khashayar rose to his feet and moved away, as Arian climbed onto her mount. He waited until she was settled before he said, "There are rumors of a fresh-water source at the center of the holy city." His gaze touched Wafa. "The boy will need it soon."

As would they all—including the Zhayedan captain. Khashayar's supplies were on Arian's side of the gap. She couldn't imagine how he would survive the journey across the desert without them, but his resilience had surprised her. Once she regained her voice, she would send him the blessings of the Claim.

He raised his hand in farewell.

She hoped their paths would cross again.

13

"ARSALAN."

His name was a husky caress on a woman's lips.

On the walls above the Emissary Gate, Arsalan turned to look. The light above his head was breaking, the sky a misty pearl tinted with shades of rose. Dawn had come, but the Mages of Khorasan had yet to stir from their Conference. The dawn rite would not be wielded to hold the gate this day—a bleak realization. A flutter of crimson chats arrowed across the sky like a harbinger of blood, underlining that thought.

But Arsalan believed only in the fate he fashioned with his own hands.

They were holding the gates against the Talisman assault, desperately tired from the past days' efforts. Every few hours he rotated out a division of the Zhayedan and called up another in its place. He could afford no such grace to the Teerandaz, though matters of rota were left to Cassandane. Ashfall needed its elite corps of archers, and now as he watched a changeover of the corps, he was fiercely grateful he had doubled their numbers at Cassandanc's request. She forecast like a general. Were Ashfall to survive, she might rise to that rank one day. But with blood and flame and noise all around him, he fenced in the hope in his thoughts. This night, the next day, he would look no further until he had word from his Khan.

"Arsalan!" The voice sounded again, this time more imperative, as soldiers shifted out of the way along the wall, giving him a line of sight.

He didn't recognize the voice, but he was stunned to recognize the face.

He staggered back a step, tearing off his helmet to wipe a hand over his eyes.

"Darya?"

A woman stood at the edge of the flight of steps that led up the Maiden Tower, her black hair a mass of curls with a long white lock falling over her breast. She wore a dress of deepest crimson, its fine silk molded to her curves. She pushed the hair from her shoulders to reveal a neckline that plunged almost to her navel. The pearl she had worn on her forehead now hung between her half-naked breasts from a shimmering rope of sapphires.

"I borrowed the necklace from Rukh. I didn't think he'd mind."

Soldiers turned to look as she passed; then, recognizing the Princess of Ashfall, they turned their eyes away.

Her gait was smooth and sinuous as she walked to Arsalan to brace her hands on his forearms. Her mouth was richly painted in the same shade of crimson as her dress, her eyes outlined with layers of kohl. But there was a film over the clarity of her eyes, and even her touch—firm and possessive—didn't feel like Darya at all.

"Who *are* you?" The words gruff, uncertain.

"Don't you recognize your betrothed?"

Her throaty voice curled around his senses, fastening onto his fear.

"The Princess of Ashfall is dead. I laid her on her bier myself."

"Poor Arsalan." She cooed the words at him, her hands shifting from his forearms to run freely over his chest. When he would have shaken her off, he found he couldn't move his hands. "I heard you took my anklets for yourself. Was the gesture meant to honor that foolish girl who loved you? Did you *want* to remember the child who threw herself at your feet?"

He felt the coolness of her breath waft against his throat. He tasted blood-tipped frost. He tasted the resonance of *death*.

"*What* are you?" A note of fear from a man who rarely gave in to it.

A wave of darkness swamped his senses—a thickening, as if she spoke to him at some deeply buried level, and in that communication something gravely unpleasant unfurled. A tremor of wicked joy. He was trapped. He thought of the First Oralist. He needed the Claim in his ear.

The woman's scarlet-tipped nails slashed swiftly at his jaw.

"Don't think of another woman, my warrior. My fragile heart cannot bear it."

But when the woman who could have been Darya pressed his hand over the curve of her breast to her heart, Arsalan felt nothing at all. Not the warmth of living flesh, nor the faintest throb of a pulse. Her skin was icy to the touch, just as it had been on the bier.

"You *will* call me Darya," she said.

Arsalan shuddered. "Who did this to you, Princess? Who sought to unmake you?"

Whoever had raised this corpse-like specter would find himself without a head.

"That isn't nice." Her crimson lips pouted at him. "The Assassin gave you a gift."

"Whatever you are—"

Her voice became a shaft of steel. "You know my name. Say it."

Arsalan found his lips moving, heard a sound forced out from his throat. *"Darya."*

"Better." She reached up and kissed his mouth, nipping at his lips. "Touch me."

Stiff and unbending, his arms came up to embrace her. He jerked her close to his armor before he knew what he was doing. Part of his mind witnessed the astonishment of the soldiers on the wall beside him.

"Turn away," the strange voice whispered. The soldiers turned their backs.

"Kiss me," she said, and Arsalan did, but the taste of her lips wasn't sweet—it wasn't soft and enticing. She tasted of decay. His mind shouted in protest, but he couldn't make his body obey. She took and took from him, and as she did, cold shivers broke out along his flesh, stirring the hairs at the back of his neck.

Through it all he could hear the noise of battle, the calls of his men asking for instruction. Cassandane interrupted them, astonishment in her eyes as Darya broke away to face her, displeasure plain on her face.

"Princess?" But despite her amazement, Cassandane was a warrior of the Zhayedan, and she turned her attention to Arsalan. "Commander, we need you at the Tower of the Mirage."

Movement from Darya. Unusual and not quite coordinated, to place herself between Arsalan and Cassandane, her back to Arsalan's chest.

"You can't have him," she said with mock sweetness. "My need is greater than yours."

Shock widened Cassandane's eyes, but she kept her focus on Arsalan.

Freed from the constraint of Darya's embrace, Arsalan prodded Cassandane. "What's wrong? What's happened?"

"Another contingent of Talisman have arrived. Their army has cleared the salt plain. We need to rethink our strategy. You'll be able to judge better from the tower."

Darya lunged forward, drilling a finger into Cassandane's chest. The ice-cold stroke burned a hole through Cassandane's armor, leaving a scorch mark so that Cassandane gasped.

"Darya, no!" Arsalan caught Darya's hands and held her to his side. His eyes flashed to Cassandane as her fingers pressed to the burn. "Are you hurt?"

"It's nothing. Princess, why—"

Arsalan shook his head. "I'll deal with it." Then, to Darya: "Ashfall is at war. You must let me attend to my duties."

Darya pouted up at him.

"You speak of your duty to this city. What of your duty to me? Your duty to satisfy my needs? I won't allow you to choose"—a contemptuous wave of her hand at Cassandane—"whatever *she* represents over me." A narrowing of those hollow eyes. "Your archer seems to be more man than woman; perhaps it is that which pleases you."

A flush rose up under Arsalan's skin, mirrored by Cassandane's discomfort.

"You forget yourself, Princess. And you insult my captain."

Darya closed her fist, and just like that, his entire body was immobilized, his lips frozen around anything else he might have chosen to utter.

"She's not just another of your soldiers," Darya hissed. "She's your prize pupil, your steadfast devotee. She's in love with you,

Arsalan. She thinks she has a chance at your heart, something I won't allow."

He wanted to warn Cassandane, protect her from Darya's strike, but he stood by with his arms anchored at his sides, his strength of no use in a battle of the arcane arts.

Cassandane swallowed and said, "That's not true, Commander. I'm no different in my respect for you than any of the men under your command."

Trying to alert Cassandane with his eyes, it took every bit of strength that Arsalan could summon to nod his understanding. Darya had taken one of his hands in her own, and he felt the coldness of her touch spread from his fingers to his arm, then sideways across his chest, splintering up to his throat. But deep in the wariness that froze him, he understood that Darya meant her actions not as a sign of possession but as a means of assuring him of her love. A winter-edged darkness glowing with ruby streaks flashed up against his mind.

Her head raised proudly, Cassandane addressed Darya. "I meant no trespass, Princess, but the risk to Ashfall is severe. I need to confer with the Commander."

"Oh, very pretty," Darya drawled. "Very pretty words, indeed. But I've seen the way you look at him. Don't think I don't know what you want."

She raised her hands above her head. Confused but alert, Cassandane stepped back as soldiers crossed around them, their attention fixed on Arsalan, who stood powerless and silent, a captive of Darya's sorcery.

Before Darya could strike, a man's voice barked out a harsh command.

"Your breath is mine, made of blood and bone and hair."

Darya froze in place, her hands arched above her head in a

pose that resembled a palace dance, except that Darya had proven unable to master any of Ashfall's arts. Clumsy to a fault, she had never learned how to dance.

The Assassin strode along the wall. When he reached the Princess, he eased her arms down and stared into her olive-tinted face. A shadow moved in her eyes; otherwise her body was still. A crash beneath them in the courtyard shattered the quiet on the wall.

Arsalan shouted orders to the Cataphracts to strengthen their positions. His cloak whirling about his shoulders, he grabbed the Assassin's arm. "What have you done to her?"

Smoothly, the Assassin answered, "Nothing that can't be undone. But first she has a part to play. I'm taking her to the Khan." He shook off Arsalan's grip, removing the strange silk lace from one of his elbow-length gloves. He used it to bind his wrist to Darya's. "Come, Princess. Your brother is waiting for you."

Arsalan blocked his path. "No! Whatever alchemy this is, you will not allow it loose in the presence of the Khan. I don't know what you've done to her, but Darya poses a danger."

Amusement sounded in the Assassin's voice. "Because she kissed you? She *is* your betrothed, after all. Perhaps she sought a little comfort from a man unsuited to give it."

Fury placed a blade in Arsalan's hand before he jerked back his arm. He couldn't allow the Assassin to provoke him. Before the Nizam had usurped him, Rukh had turned to Arsalan for his counsel. He wouldn't permit the Assassin to maneuver himself into the Nizam's seat.

Cassandane cleared her throat. "The tower, Commander."

His head swiveled back to her. "For now, target the soldiers operating the Talisman's catapults. They're striking too hard and too often." He surveyed the damage in the courtyard, a giant boulder having fallen close to the Illustrious Portal, the entrance of the royal palace. He found it difficult to focus and shook his head to clear it of sorcery. "By the Last Day, I thought the attack on the loya jirga would have gained us more of an advantage."

Cassandane had been assessing the field since the attack began. "No matter that they accuse the Silver Mage of treachery, I think the Talisman had a plan of their own. There was a second rank of commanders ready to step in, if anything happened to the first." A sound strategy, and one she approved of as a soldier. "Meet me at the tower when you can."

A curt nod of dismissal. Her eyes drifting back to the Princess, Cassandane hesitated.

"Commander—"

"What is it, Captain?" Impatience in every word.

Her cheeks hot, Cassandane forced herself to meet that adamantine gaze. "I truly meant no trespass against you or the Princess. I am well aware of my place."

She was stunned when Arsalan's hand shot out to yank her close. His forehead braced against hers, he breathed his fiery response almost into her mouth.

"Your *place* is Captain of the Teerandaz. Your *place* is at my side in the Zhayedan. Your *place* is to die defending the honor and glory of Ashfall. I've never had any doubt of it."

Aflame with joy at his pride in her, she fought back childish tears.

"I will not fail you, Commander."

She strode back along the wall to the tower, raising her bow as she walked.

"The Princess was right." The Assassin's observation wasn't meant to goad him. "There's strong feeling there."

Arsalan's eyes snapped to his. "It's called loyalty." He took in the Assassin's possessive hold, Darya acquiescent in his grip.

"What necromancy did you cast to achieve this? The Black Khan will not thank you for bringing the Princess to ruin."

Arrows of flame fell along the wall. Arsalan's shield flashed up to shelter Darya from harm. She didn't move, didn't register the wind that carried the arrows, the scent of smoke that burned at points along the wall, or the cries of soldiers who had suffered the rain of fire.

A thrill of premonition chased up Arsalan's spine. "What have you done to her?" he asked again.

Inching closer to the edge of the wall, the Assassin considered the strength of the Talisman army. "Whatever I had to." His voice held a quiet intensity. "The Conference of the Mages failed. There will be no relief this night, nor the nights to come. But the Princess—the Black Khan's sister—*can* awaken his powers. The Dark Mage must rise, or Ashfall's glory will fade and come to an end. That is why I raised Darya, but you have no need to worry. I used a particular verse of the Claim." A private smile behind the mask that Arsalan couldn't witness. But he wasn't a fool.

"You raised the Princess so you could test the extent of your abilities. Dark arts have dark ends." Bitterness in Arsalan's voice. "I know this better than most. Your efforts will end in grief."

The Assassin tugged at Darya's wrist, pushing her along the wall to the steps of the Maiden Tower.

"Strange that a man of war should also be a believer," he said over his shoulder.

Arsalan wiped his hands over his face. Then he unsheathed his sword.

"I cannot let you take her."

The Assassin paused and looked back, measuring the threat.

"If you harm me, her power will rise unchecked. You've had the merest taste of it. Would you leave her untrammeled when you're fighting a battle at the gates?" The Assassin glanced past Arsalan. His grip on Darya eased. He shook his head at Arsalan with pity. "Soldiers know nothing of such matters, and now your objection comes too late."

A figure moved from the Maiden Tower to the wall with a grand sweep of his cloak, silver epaulettes glinting in the torchlight that glimmered from the wall.

"What have you done, Hasbah?"

To Arsalan's dismay, the Black Khan's voice resounded with *joy* as he glimpsed his sister.

14

Rukh's arms closed around Darya as he rained kisses on her head, oblivious to the icy touch of her flesh. His fingers caught at the trails of her hair. He buried his face in her neck in a gesture of profound gratitude.

He was woken from his joy not by the counsel of the Assassin, nor by Arsalan's grave caution. Instead, he became aware of how his sister was dressed. He gave in to a familiar impulse, removing his cloak to drape it over her gown.

"Darya, why are you dressed like this?" he asked, a frown on his aristocratic features as he studied her face. "Why is your face made up as if you belong in a pleasure-house? You are the Princess of Ashfall—clean off your face at once."

The light of battle sparked in Darya's eyes. But she didn't move, didn't speak. Didn't acknowledge either her brother's affection or his admonition, made no gesture of obeisance.

His eyes snapped to Arsalan, who managed to say, "Rukh, you must beware—" before the Assassin cut him off.

"I give your sister back to you, my lord."

Rukh glared at the Assassin, his earlier joy forgotten. "Did I ask this of you? Did I grant you my permission to practice your arts on my sister? Did I say I wanted Darya's purity darkened by your sorcery?"

A sidelong glance at Arsalan showed him Arsalan's approval of this castigation. But then Rukh and Arsalan had fought a similar battle in the private chambers of the Khan.

The Assassin bowed before Rukh. "You promised me payment of my choosing. You said that I might ask for anything I desired."

Rukh's sharp eyes dropped to the silken thread that bound the Assassin to Darya. His voice became low and dangerous.

"And do you desire my sister when she is Arsalan's betrothed?"

The Assassin's breath sighed out through an opening in his mask. "No, my lord. I would not presume myself worthy of the sister of the Black Khan." He weighed whether he should say more in the presence of the Zhayedan's commander. But the Black Khan changed his stance so that Arsalan was at his back, a gesture of total trust, so he continued.

"Your sister is a child of Hira—perhaps you did not know this. Neither did the One-Eyed Preacher. When he used the Claim to strike against her, he wasn't able to kill her."

"She was dead," Arsalan barked at him, anxious now that the Assassin's words might have some power over Rukh. "I held her in my arms. Her spirit was stolen from her body."

The Assassin's hand came up to separate out the white lock of Darya's hair.

"How remiss of me to forget that you profess yourself a scholar of the Claim, Commander." Arsalan made to respond to his mockery, but Rukh held up his hand, indicating the Assassin should continue. Smiling beneath his mask, Hasbah said, "A true child of Hira cannot be harmed by the Claim. Her spirit was in abeyance. There was time to call her back."

"You knew this?" Rukh demanded. "You knew this and didn't tell me?"

"I . . . suspected, my lord. I could not give you false hope when my theory remained unproven. Even as a scholar"—he looked at Arsalan—"I cannot claim to have mastered it. Testing it for myself was the only payment I sought."

Rukh's eyes warmed. The Assassin's actions were reckless, but he'd undertaken them on Rukh's behalf. And in doing so, Hasbah had brought his sister back to him.

"Do not heed him," Arsalan insisted. "Believe me when I tell you that this *isn't* Darya."

The chill of Darya's flesh now penetrated Rukh's awareness.

"*Is* this my sister?" Cold censure in his tone, a warning to both the Assassin and Arsalan. He raised Darya's chin with the long fingers of one hand. "Darya? Answer me."

The Assassin whispered a word, and Darya spoke.

"Brother. Have you found a use for me at last?"

Rukh hesitated. Looked to the Assassin for an explanation, but once more Arsalan stepped in.

"She was dead, Rukh. We saw it, felt it. This is a facsimile—a macabre trick of sorcery. She may walk with Darya's bones, clothed in Darya's skin, but this isn't the Princess."

Darya's eyes shifted to Arsalan's, a promise in them that she wasn't done with him. The Assassin touched her throat, and sullenly, Darya looked down.

Something stirred at the back of Rukh's mind like a panther raising its head to test the wind for scent of prey. His body shifted under his armor; his head turned to Arsalan.

"The Conference of the Mages continues to fail." He kept his voice low, nodding at the soldiers who responded to the crisis around them, the moving parts of the machinery of war, rigorously trained and battle-hardened.

Arsalan drew Rukh away from the Assassin and his creation, not wanting either to hear.

"Did you give it enough time?" He knew Rukh's impatience too well, just as he recognized his jealousy of the talents of the Silver Mage.

Rukh's jaw tightened. Arsalan took that for an answer.

"Your Assassin is about to promise you the answer to your prayers. He thinks this shadow of Darya will awaken your latent abilities."

He watched Rukh glance over his shoulder at Darya with renewed interest.

"Don't take it. Don't trust it. She will overthrow your mind . . . just as she did mine."

Two soldiers of the Zhayedan hurried past them, carrying munitions from the armory.

"What's happened?" Rukh's black eyes swept the wall. "Why do the Zhayedan panic?"

Arsalan considered the wisdom of keeping his mouth shut. But when the black gaze of the Khan pierced his, he realized the point was moot. "The Talisman's reinforcements have arrived." He shifted responsibility back to Rukh. "What of the dawn rite? The Silver Mage suggested that it would gain us an advantage. We could certainly use it now."

"Not unless I come into my powers as Dark Mage." Rukh shoved at Arsalan's shoulder for a better view of his sister. "Hasbah doesn't act without purpose, and I do not believe he wishes me—or Ashfall—harm. If he raised Darya from her rest, there must be some profit in it."

Angrily, Arsalan responded, "Listen to me, Rukh! Darya is *dangerous*. And if the Assassin is the power behind her, she is more dangerous still."

The Black Khan laughed. "Darya is no more dangerous than a child."

Arsalan struck one fist against the other. "Darya held the commander of your army helpless before her with a word."

Now Rukh paid attention. "What do you mean?"

"The dark rites empowered her with an echo of the Claim. Her voice holds a powerful magic." He squeezed Rukh's shoulder, a gesture of commiseration. "I know it is painful to lose her again, but you *must* send her to her rest."

He was expecting the insult Rukh flung at him. "Do you wish to be free of her so badly that you would deny me my sister?"

Cassandane signaled him from the far end of the wall. Impatience warred with his sense of impending danger. "I'm trying to protect you from your own worst instincts." He searched for the appropriate example. "What the Assassin has raised is a ghul from our legends, and the ghul are notorious for gluttony. This ghul that possesses Darya will seize everything you hold dear."

"Children's tales," Rukh said. "Hasbah commands her, even if she *is* as you fear."

Arsalan saw that this battle was lost. He called for a runner, focusing on the things he could control. His love for Rukh—his fear for him—made him utter a final warning. "Before you proceed with your shortsighted plan, perhaps you will ask the other Mages for the wisdom of their counsel." He gave Rukh a cursory nod, headed to the tower.

He'd warned his prince about Darya. Now he prayed for the Zhayedan to hold.

15

RUKH'S ATTEMPTS TO RAISE THE DARK MAGE HAD RESULTED IN FAIL-ure. This was his chance at something greater than glory, a chance for Ashfall to survive. If he had to use a ghul to do it, he wouldn't hesitate, even if it sullied the memory of his sister.

In life, he had spurned her desire to be of value to his reign. In death, she would earn her glory and her rightful place at his side.

"Come." He took Darya to the scriptorium, clearing the hall of scribes but keeping the Khorasan Guard in place. They passed by the pedestal that had so briefly held the Bloodprint, coming to a nook in a small alcove, lit by brass lamps in the section where manuscripts on alchemy were stored. The vast pink halls of the scriptorium that was the pride of Ashfall were reduced to light flickering on shadows around a table where the Warraqeen practiced the strokes of their calligraphy. Here he told the Assassin to wait within earshot.

Alone with his sister at last, he said, "It pleases my heart to see you, Darya."

He was rewarded with a look of such impertinence that he knew he was looking at the ghul.

"Does it, brother?" A broken laugh, its notes discordant. "Then this would be the first time."

"You used to call me Rukh." Another attempt to charm away her bitterness.

That jarring strain of laughter sounded again in response. "*Did I? Are you a phoenix then, brother, rising from Ashfall's ashes? Or merely a pawn in that game that you and Arsalan excelled at?*"

Her cunning riposte played on both meanings of his name.

Phoenix: the first meaning. The knight's castle: the second.

"Whatever pleases you most, Darya."

"What would please me most is having Arsalan in my bed. But your general continues to elude me."

The bold-faced insolence of Darya's response silenced Rukh. His sister had been known as much for her modesty as for her timid enthrallment with her betrothed. He peered at her, discerning the movement of shadows behind the film that glazed her eyes.

"Darya?" Her name was a forlorn sound.

"Rukh?" Ridicule in her reply.

Fighting down his anger, he forged ahead, remembering what he stood to gain.

"Our enemies are moving against us. Ashfall would welcome your aid."

She sighed. A languorous stretch threw his cloak from her shoulders. The rope of sapphires that he'd worn to ornament the onyx rook at his throat caught his attention. She fingered the stones with a laugh.

"You don't approve? You'd rather I wore the headdress that nearly snapped my neck in two?" She leaned forward slightly, the huge white pearl that descended from the necklace swaying between her breasts. "This is more compelling. Your soldiers couldn't look away."

"Behave yourself, Darya! You know the scriptorium is hallowed!"

She glanced about the nook with a dismissive sniff. "The alchemy alcove, I see. Hardly a sacred place. Besides, dear brother, what do you find unholy about a woman's body? You've known more than your share."

Rukh's hands clenched into his fists, a rare rage rising in his eyes. Seeing it, Darya smiled. But with the thick paint that covered her lips, it was more like a crimson snarl.

Bitter in turn, he said, "You always were incapable of the arts of beauty. I see that nothing has changed."

Now the snarl came from her throat. "What do you want, brother? You keep me here against my will."

"The Assassin claims you are ensorcelled. I want you to stand with me against the Talisman. I need you to summon my abilities as Dark Mage."

"Your twisted ambition *murdered* the Dark Mage. Do you not recall that you left him to die on the wall? Shall I summon another ghul to aid you in your efforts?"

Unable to bear this description of their half-brother, Darius, he lunged across the table and ripped the sapphires from her neck.

"How dare you insult me, ghul? How dare you take what is mine?"

The strand of sapphires snapped, gems spilling over the table and onto the floor, the heavy pearl rolling to a stop near his boot. He crushed it without a thought.

"My lord—"

The Assassin's warning came too late. Darya flew at him in a fury of teeth and nails, her hands at the vulnerable skin of his throat, teeth as sharp as a wolf's sinking into his neck. He shoved her back, but she held on with demon intensity and strength, nails clawing at his chest. She was brought to bay by a blade at her throat, held by one of the Khorasan Guard.

She tilted her head, smiled her painted smile at him . . . then slashed his throat with nails grown into claws. When a second guard approached, she bit clear through his wrist.

She raised her head to glare at Rukh, blood dripping from the corners of her mouth, nothing of Darya in her eyes.

The Assassin lunged at her, placing himself between Darya and Rukh, the strange silver thread wound tightly around one hand. He spoke the verse he had used to control her, to rein in her demon instinct.

She laughed in her brother's face.

Faster than Rukh's eye could follow, the Assassin spun out the thread so that it wound around Darya's neck. She screamed in fury as the thread dissolved into flame. When she clawed at the rope of flame, all she served to do was to scratch deep grooves into her skin.

The Assassin spun a verse, then another, then a third, backing Darya into a corner. Her bones finding that odd coherence, she crouched low, then leapt over his head, racing to the door. The greater the distance between them, the more his recitation failed.

The rope of flame faded to ash at her neck. She tipped her head to one side, flicking away the ash. For a moment, her eyes held Rukh's.

"I wanted to help you, Rukh." Her voice was that of an abandoned child. She tugged at an invisible binding, her eyes swirling with flame. "But it won't let me. The ghul won't let me, Rukh." Then speaking to herself, "I shouldn't be here. It isn't safe. *I'm* not safe."

Her spine snapped back then forward, her arms stretched out

to the vaulted ceiling. Fire roared to life in her eyes, spread out from her fingertips to lash out at both men, pinning them in place, unable to move to defy her. Unable to *stop* her.

The ghul mocked him in his sister's voice.

"Ashfall is lost without Arsalan. And Arsalan belongs to *me*."

16

I⊤ TOOK ARIAN, SINNIA, AND WAFA ANOTHER DAY TO REACH THE HOLY
city, with no sign of Najran in pursuit. They left their camels at
the city gates, telling Wafa to stay alert. His sunburned skin and
cracked lips spoke of his need for refreshment. If they didn't find
water somewhere in the ruins, Wafa would not last another day.
Nor would Arian and Sinnia fare much better.

Arian searched for water amid the ruins of a place she hadn't
thought to see. The air they breathed may have been poisoned,
but in her bones she felt the grace of the One. She offered a prayer
for Khashayar's safe return, just as she bound Wafa in the protections of the Claim.

She proceeded with care. Ten centuries later and still nothing
had grown, not even the patches of grass that scrubbed the dunes.
An eerie quiet over the flattened hills, the low valley between them
formed a bowl pushed into the earth. Mortar and steel had been
carried away by sweeps of raiding tribes searching for anything of
value. All that remained of a once-grand complex was the green
eye of a clock tower, broken and tumbled to its side.

Skirting the edges of the bowl, Sinnia said, "This entire area has been decimated. What weapon was powerful enough to wreak this kind of destruction?"

"A weapon of the Far Range." Arian swept her spyglass over the rim. "This is where the Claim was rent from us. Where its history was savaged." Yet she knew there was more to the loss of the Claim than the actions of the Far Range. Yes, the armies of the Far Range had made the air unbreathable and the ground uninhabitable, much as they had done to the Plague Lands. But the seeds of the destruction of the holiest of holies had been sown by its own guardians. With their corruption of the Claim, with actions that refused to recognize the oneness of the Claim's adherents. They had been guilty of exploitation, with an ordering of the world that demanded the oppression of women. The kings who ruled the city had stripped all others of freedom, practitioners of a creed that would inspire the cruelties of the Talisman: a creed of form without substance, of ritual without equity or justice.

Long before the weapons of the Far Range had crushed the city into dust, its keepers . . . its *guardians* . . . had erased from its environs those symbols that generations of believers had clung to as their own. The guardians had delivered their history to the fires of a raging pietism, while those who sacrificed all they had to reach the holy city were received by its keepers with contempt.

The eye of the fallen clock tower was the blind eye of commerce and greed. The losses of the people of the Claim had begun long before the cataclysm caused by the Far Range. In the aftermath of their apocalypse, they had even lost their language, the words of their ancient tongue melding not only with the dialects of Khorasan, but also with that of their conquerors. As Hira's only linguist, Arian held to herself the secrets of the High Tongue and its new iterations.

Though she doubted she'd hear it uttered in the deathly silence of this place.

But though sorrow subdued her thoughts, Arian felt the echoes of the Claim on the wind that swept over the rim. It awakened the inner promise that bound the Companions to the Claim, reminding her that those who sought the guidance of the One were never entirely lost: if she sought, she would find.

She gathered her courage, and gingerly, she and Sinnia picked their way over broken stones gathered in towering piles. It took them some time to make their way down to the center, Wafa's desperate need weighing on their minds. Breaking off in different directions, they began to search. But what they were hoping to come across in their search for water, Arian couldn't have said. The cube-shaped house of the Claim? Fragments of the shroud that concealed it? Vertical loops of verses of the Claim stitched in gold upon black? Or the arcade of arches where worshippers had taken refuge from the heat of an unforgiving sun?

Or would they find nothing, as she feared?

Because nothing remained of the ancient past—nothing that would nurture the agony of Arian's nostalgia. Here in this holiest of cities, a slate had been wiped clean, just as the written word and the equity it promised, had been stolen by deliberate design.

And what the One-Eyed Preacher hoped to revive in its place was a darkness that would snuff out any remaining hope.

"Look, Arian." Sinnia pointed south of her position. "There's an alley of stones here. Am I imagining it, or is that raised ground on either side? Do you think it holds some significance?"

Arian mapped the distance between the elevations. Something painful shifted in her mind, waking a dormant memory . . .

She was staring through the fountains of the All Ways. Making her way out of the Council Chamber to a passageway along the walls, deep into the heart of the Citadel, until she reached the antechamber of the scriptorium at Hira.

Under her hands, ancient scrolls unfurled, kept at a distance from the light. The Companion Ash stroked a hand over Arian's hair and read the history out loud. She showed Arian a drawing of the House of the One and the glories that sprang up around it. Then, with a teasing smile, she said, "Should you ever find yourself in this valley, running between two hills, look for a small spring."

"Is it a miracle?" the child Arian had asked.

And Ash had nodded wisely, pressing a kiss to her cheek. "The lord of the angels struck the ground with his wing; a blessing rose from the earth."

"What was the blessing?"

Ash smiled down at her, not minding the persistence of her questions. This was Arian, the precious child of Hira. Her questions were guided by the Claim. The knowledge she sought from Ash would serve all of Khorasan one day.

"Water in the midst of the desert, the blessing of the women of our history, though the histories speak only of men. Find it once, my child, and you will not thirst again . . ."

"Look for a spring nearby."

Sinnia shifted her weight on the balls of her feet. "Any source of water we find here might carry the poison of the Far Range."

Arian smiled at this caution. Though she'd had a similar thought, she knew something about this source of water.

"Sinnia." Her wondering tone snapped Sinnia's attention to her face. "You've found the path of the Saee."

Sinnia's head swiveled around, measuring the distance between what could have been two hills. She considered the alley of stones. Bending down to peer at the stones, she caught glimpses of crushed white powder . . . pulverized marble, perhaps.

Sinnia's graceful body went still, angles tucked in, head tipped to one side.

"Go." She motioned to Arian. "Let me search for the source of the spring."

Sinnia squared her shoulders, touched her circlets, kissed her fingertips. Her face was unusually solemn as she walked the path between the hills. As Arian descended into the bowl, her last sight of Sinnia was of a woman with ebony curls and sable skin beginning a sacred pilgrimage. An echo of a history too beautiful to be borne.

Sinnia would cross between the hills seven times, whispering to the One of the need of the boy in her care. Then she would find the place marked by the angel's wing. Perhaps in their extremity of need, their prayers would be answered, and Sinnia would find the Well of Zamzam.

"The One is sufficient for you in all things," Arian promised herself, refusing to reflect on her weakness against Najran. Or on her fear of his malice.

She wouldn't allow doubt to creep into her heart, no matter that the legacy of her people lay in ruins at her feet. She climbed down the rim of the bowl with care, edging closer to the fallen clock tower, pausing beside its eye, giving her body a chance to rest.

She swept her spyglass across the ruins . . . once, twice, a third time. In the distance opposite the tower, she caught a flash of light. The gleam of the sun's rays bounced hard off metal. Straightening at once, she crossed ground that burned beneath her boots. Ten minutes passed before she reached the place where she had seen the flash, but as she moved closer, it disappeared.

She tucked the spyglass away, searching the piles of rock with care.

Still nothing. Then her hand brushed something hot enough to burn. She flinched, jerking her hand away. She'd found it. The jagged edge of metal—silver glinting through centuries of tarnish. She kicked at it with her boot, and it rolled away.

Her pulse beating in her ears, she dropped to her knees and began to dig within the rubble. But what she sought was firmly welded to the stones that covered it. She used the knife at her waist, stabbing away at the crust that had formed around the unfamiliar object. When she'd finished, she blew away a layer of dust from the stone she held in her hand. Large, smooth, and round, its midnight surface glittered with silver streaks, a reddish corona at its edges. It filled her hands, and though it should have weighed them down, the stone weighed nothing at all.

Tears left dusty tracks on her face. She knew what she had found.

She was holding the Paradise Stone.

Some said it was the remnant of a meteor striking the earth. Others thought it was formed of basalt or agate, others still a kind of liquid glass frozen in its current form. It did not float in water, and it would not burn in fire. The guardians of the city had warned against the veneration of the stone, calling it a form of idolatry.

But as its cool exterior pressed against Arian's fingertips, she knew the caresses of thousands of believers had made its surface smooth and even. Her palms tingled at the touch; her breath, when it came, was a sob.

She raised the stone to her lips and kissed it. Then she pressed it to her heart.

"If the power of the One resides in you at all, help me find the Sana Codex."

She considered what to do with the stone. She could return it to its hiding place and trust that it would not be desecrated by raiders. Or she could take it with her and gift it to the Citadel, where it would be treated as a holy relic. But she could be ambushed on her journey, and just as the One-Eyed Preacher had taken the Bloodprint, she had to consider what would happen if he captured the Paradise Stone.

It belonged in the holy city, guarded by an archangel's wing.

As soon as the thought formed in her mind, she knew what she had to do.

She scrambled to her feet, settling the stone inside her pack. Now it pressed against her back. Her journey to the top of the rim was easier, her footsteps flying over rocky ground.

As soon as she cleared the rim, Sinnia's voice called out to her. She followed it until she found Sinnia crouched over a spot where the earth was dark and healthy, in the lee of the southern hill. She knelt beside Sinnia, peering down into the murky depths of a deceptive opening—as small as a copper pan, as rich and deep as the center of the earth itself. Sinnia's hand touched hers. Her fingertips were wet.

Side by side, they dug at the earth, until their nails were torn and their fingers were bruised. After some time, their efforts were rewarded. From the opening's mysterious depths, a jet of the clearest water shot up and arced over their heads.

They turned their faces up to its rain, uncaring that rivulets of water worked their way beneath their armor. They hugged each other in speechless delight, pulling out their waterskins.

"Arian!" Sinnia's golden laughter warmed the air. "I completed the Saee; I found the Well of Zamzam! I followed the path of the Mother of Believers!"

Arian laughed with her, her face alive with joy, echoing Sinnia's wonder. They kissed each other's cheeks, wiping water from their faces. Then Sinnia remembered Wafa.

"Wait a moment, Sinnia." Arian emptied her pack to show Sinnia the black stone. Quickly, she explained her discovery. Then she raised the stone to Sinnia's lips so she could kiss it, unbearably moved when Sinnia began to cry.

"The Well of Zamzam *and* the Paradise Stone . . . Did the Negus foresee this for me when he chose me as his emissary to Hira?"

"Did we imagine we would see *any* of the wonders of the Audacies we set out on?"

They both thought of the Bloodprint, and in that moment, they resolved anew that they would not fail against the Preacher.

The same thought occurred to Sinnia that had troubled Arian. "We cannot take the stone from here—it's the cornerstone of the House of the One. But if raiders find it—"

Arian nodded, a tearful smile on her lips.

"You've thought of something." Sinnia followed Arian's gaze down to the fountain that had sprung up from the Well of Zamzam.

"Will you help me?" Arian asked her.

Sinnia moved her hands under Arian's to help her cup the stone. They lifted it above the opening of the well, then let it fall to its depths to be reclaimed by the earth.

"It will still be a touchstone of this city."

"Do you believe in angels?" Sinnia asked.

Arian wasn't certain how to answer. She paused for a moment, allowing the water to sink through her hair, so that long black tails fanned around her throat, cooling her heated skin.

"I believe we were tested as those who came before us were tested." She licked a drop of water from her lips. "In the ruins of the holy city, we found a moment of grace."

They hurried back to Wafa. After they'd made him drink water at a moderate pace, they pulled him to his feet to guide him to the well. His blue eyes cleared of the bleariness that had clouded them for days. He ducked his head under the spring, but Sinnia's hands were at his clothes. Abashed, he pushed her hands away.

"Fine," she said. "We'll turn our backs to give you privacy. But, boy, you're going to bathe every inch of dust from your body until you're soaked to the skin. Then you're going to drink some more, and when you're feeling better, you'll load water for us to carry."

While Wafa hurried to obey her, she and Arian conferred. They fed and watered their animals, took some nourishment themselves, stocked up their supplies, and when all else was done and their bodies were covered in sweat again, they rinsed out their clothing and bathed in the water from the spring.

It was more than a momentary respite, more than an offering of grace.

It was a miracle of peace given to them by the One.

17

THEY FOUND THEIR EXIT FROM THE CITY BLOCKED BY A GROUP OF BARE-
foot children dressed in colorful caftans with patches of embroidery that denoted the range of tribes that surrounded the Rub Al
Khali.

The children were loud and boisterous. They scrambled to
surround the Companions and Wafa, who tried to beat them back
with a stick. The children weren't threatening; most hadn't lived
to see their first decade, though they cheerfully hollered at Wafa.

"Where are your families?" Arian asked in the Common
Tongue. A girl of perhaps thirteen years shouted at the others to
hush. Her hair was a mass of wild dark curls, her skin the polished bronze of the sands, her eyes as tawny as a caracal's. She put
her hands on her hips.

"*This* is our family." She growled low in her throat at Wafa,
aiming at his stick with a well-placed kick of her own. Arian held
him back with one hand.

"You're on your own?" Arian's smile had no effect on the girl's
antagonism.

"Who are *you*?" she demanded rudely. She deigned to acknowledge Sinnia with a nod. "Najashi, I know, we trade with you. But you—*what* are you?"

Arian shifted back her cloak. Sinnia copied the gesture. As the sun struck glints of gold off their circlets, the children shrieked with joy.

For all the world like a tiny soldier, the curly-headed girl bent her knee.

"Sahabiya." A nod at Arian. "Sahabiya." Another at Sinnia. "Did you come here to bring blessings?"

Arian considered the children's attire. They looked as dusty and thirsty as she and her companions had been.

"Go to the other side of the hill you see there."

When the group would have tumbled over the hill, the girl who was their leader shouted them into silence. "Wait!" She moved cautiously around the hill herself, and Arian's heart turned over. This girl truly was the leader of her small contingent, allowing them to venture no risk that she didn't bear herself.

From the corner of her eye she saw Wafa glaring at the girl as if she were a devil of the sands.

"All of you, come!" The children tumbled away, and the girl ran back to Arian. Arian noticed that the girl hadn't stopped to drink the water from the spring.

"What's your name, child?" Sinnia asked.

The girl's scowl became ferocious. "Not child. *Sayyid*. You can call me Rim-Sarah."

Arian hid a smile. The girl had taken a man's title to herself. But if she commanded this pack of ten or twelve children, perhaps she had that right.

"Rim-Sarah, you said you trade with the Najashi."

The girl nodded, her tawny eyes bright.

"We're headed to the lands of the Negus. Can you tell us a safe route to the sea?"

"What will you give me if I do?"

"What do you want?" Arian asked, enjoying the girl's unashamed willingness to bargain . . . and to ignore the fact that Arian had just directed her to a source of water. However the girl had been raised, her spirit hadn't been harmed.

Sinnia grinned at the girl. "I know you too." She rubbed her chest, indicating the pattern of embroidery on the girl's scarlet robe. "You're Bani Shira'a."

Rim-Sarah affected a sigh. "Our camp is at the oasis."

Arian and Sinnia exchanged a glance. "Is the oasis close?"

"North," the girl said. "You're going south." She jabbed a finger at Sinnia. "To Axum?"

Sinnia nodded, alert. "You know it?"

"I told you. We trade with Najashi." She frowned at Arian, tracing a pattern on the sand with her toes. "Stay away from the Rub Al Khali. The spiderlings are there."

"Spiderlings?" Arian echoed.

The girl shivered with dramatic flair. Then she raised her arms up high and shifted so that her legs were spread wide, trying to imitate the grasp of a spider. She shuddered copiously again.

"You should take the sea." A sly smile crept into her eyes. "Traveling by camel, it will take too long for you to get to Axum. The sea will take you there by tomorrow's moonrise."

"How far is it to the sea?"

"If you want a faster way, a safe way, what will you trade for it?"

The happy cries of children frolicking in water drifted over the hill.

No longer setting aside the miracle of the wellspring, Arian said, "Wasn't giving you water a worthy trade? You're in my debt, Rim-Sarah."

The girl grimaced, her small hands curling into fists. "If it was for *me* to decide, I would honor the trade. I would take you to the sea and bring you back if you asked."

"So who *does* have the power to decide?"

The girl shrugged. She let out a piercing whistle. Two boys raced back to join them. Their robes were soaked with water, their faces shiny and wet.

"Bring the sandsail," she told them.

Neither questioned her order. The girl's feet danced in a semi-circle. Crooking her fingers at Arian and Sinnia, she urged them to follow her out of the city back to the sea of sand. Hopping back and forth, she pointed at a dune to the south.

A pair of dark heads appeared above the ridge.

The girl grinned, waiting for Arian's reaction.

As Arian watched, a huge white sail rose above the crest. Sinnia clapped her hands.

"You're not just Bani Shira'a—you're a *Sandrider*!"

The girl's smile widened to show them a chipped front tooth.

"Yes," she said modestly. "The best one on these sands."

Sinnia turned to Arian. "She can take us, if she agrees, and in a fraction of the time. The sandsail will fly across the dunes. We'll reach Axum as quickly as she says."

The boys pushed the sandsail over the ridge, and now Arian saw that its billowing white sail was attached to a shallow sand skiff with a curved outer hull.

"Will it carry us all?"

Rim-Sarah counted on her fingers. "Four. I can take four."

The cunning smile returned, a glint of mischief in her eyes. "But no camels."

Now Arian understood what they would have to trade. Sinnia leaned over to whisper in her ear. "They drive a hard bargain, but Sandriders are as good as their word."

Arian nodded. "We keep our packs," she cautioned the girl.

Rim-Sarah gave an elaborate shrug, pretending not to notice Wafa. "And that strange thing, too, if you want."

Arian choked back a laugh. "You surely don't mean my friend Wafa."

"Straa-aange," the girl repeated, drawing out the word. She planted herself in front of Wafa, puffing out her breath. "Did you steal *fayruz*?" she asked him.

He scowled back at her, indignant. "I didn't steal anything! Wafa is not a thief."

Arian tried not to laugh and failed. Looking into Wafa's eyes, she explained, "She means your eyes. She thinks they're blue like turquoise."

The girl skipped over to the sandsail. "Blue," she said easily. "We don't have blue in Bani Shira'a."

She spoke her own language to the two boys, who stripped the camels of the Companions' gear with practiced ease and stowed it inside the skiff. One of the boys whistled, and the rest of the children rejoined them, jostling for a seat on the camels.

"Are you sure about this?" Arian asked, not at all reassured by Sinnia's reckless grin.

"How many times can we die?"

"Let's not put that to the test."

Rim-Sarah crooked her finger, and they followed her onto the skiff, Arian and Sinnia side by side, Wafa seated behind them.

The girl laughed at his crouched-over posture.

"No one sits," she told them. "All of you must stand."

She wrapped her hands around a sturdy mast that was used to rig the sail.

"How does it move?" The wind that blew over the sands scarcely stirred the rigging of the sail, which was made of some kind of canvas.

Sinnia shook her head. "Do you remember the firewind?"

Arian shifted her position, gripping a wooden pole. "This girl can summon a vortex like the one I conjured with the Claim?"

"Not quite." Sinnia adjusted her weight so the skiff was balanced. "The Sandriders sail the sands like waves—almost as if they magnetize them. Like the parting of the Sea of Reeds, in the ancient myths. It's a gift they developed in the wake of the wars of the Far Range."

The thought of such a gift was mystifying to Arian. But perhaps it was no different than any gift rooted in the earth over which the Claim governed. In the environs of the holy city, how much stronger might that power be?

"Are all the Bani Shira'a so gifted?" she asked.

"No." Rim-Sarah jumped up onto a small runner that extended from the hull. With a cheery chipped-tooth smile, she waved at the gang of children who were leading the camels away. "Just me and a few other girls. Those whose mothers gave birth close to the eye of the clock tower."

"Wait." Arian pointed to the other children. "Won't any of them come with you?" She didn't want to frighten the girl, but Najran was on their trail, and he'd already shown her the limits of his mercy when it came to his treatment of children. "Someone should come with you to make sure you are safe. You shouldn't journey home on your own."

"I have someone." Rim-Sarah looked confused. She pointed to the Companions. "I have you and you." A mischievous nod at Wafa, who ignored her. "And *fayruz* too."

Arian explained about the sayyid of the Marra. She described Najran's daggers, the thrust of his spike-tipped glaive.

The girl nodded solemnly. "We know of the Najran." She made his name a title. "But the Marra and the Bani Shira'a are allies."

When Arian still wasn't convinced, Rim-Sarah said, "The sands will keep me safe." Stamping one foot, she demanded, "Do we go to the sea or not?"

Arian nodded. But silently she covered the girl in the protections of the Claim.

18

Two Teerandaz archers stood at attention beside Cassandane, paying careful attention to the plan that she and Arsalan were working out between them.

Even if the Cataphracts were successful in their sortie, the Zhayedan had few options but to wait for the Talisman to breach their walls. But from the Tower of the Mirage, Cassandane had spotted a weakness in the Talisman's approach.

And Arsalan remembered what the First Oralist had told him.

"They have nothing except numbers on their side. It is the Zhayedan who will conquer with their mastery of tactics."

He raised his spyglass and gave Cassandane coordinates for what he wanted her to see.

"Too far." Her answer was firm. "We can't reach it in the numbers we'd need to strike a true blow."

"The Cataphracts could do it."

"Impossible. And I thought the refugees were your immediate priority."

Only Cassandane spoke to him so frankly. Neither her tone nor her words were disrespectful, but she had the rare gift of treating him as an equal. He was glad that the Nizam's open dis-respect had not diminished her confidence.

He put his spyglass away, nodding to runners who came and went between the gates. In the courtyard below, he saw that May-sam's Cataphracts were ready to implement his plan.

Could Maysam be trusted? He needed another commander like Cassandane at his side, but his senior captains had assignments of their own, and Khashayar had been sent to escort the First Oralist to Timeback. He knew well enough that the idea of an escort as protection was illusion. He'd witnessed the First Oralist's mastery of the Claim; her skills would suffice to protect her. But perhaps his men would be able to get her closer to her goals.

Cassandane's impatience called his attention to the matter at hand.

"There might be another way," he said. She waited for him to continue, her bow resting at her feet. "Do you recall the armillary sphere in the war room? It might serve us in this instance."

"How? Doesn't it chart the movement of the stars?"

Arsalan grunted in satisfaction as he watched one of the Zhayedan's mangonels strike at the Talisman's defense. A Zhayedan soldier approached with a request to take action against the sappers at the eastern gate. Arsalan took a moment to orga-nize that response. Cassandane didn't rush him, using the time to issue her own instructions to the Teerandaz's secondary corps.

"Will you burn the sappers with oil?" she asked when Arsalan had finished.

He shook his proud dark head. "They're too close to the walls, and the fire might affect the gate. Water will muddy the ground, mire them in their tracks."

"Others will climb over them. They'll use their bodies for trac-tion."

"Then those are the ones we'll burn before they get too close."

He took no pleasure in it. He'd seen the faces of his enemies, most of them young men, inspired to fanatical devotion by the One-Eyed Preacher's edicts. They would kill, they would die, and to the Talisman and Preacher alike, their lives would have no merit. They were simply servants to a cause.

But while a better part of his conscience would mourn them, he couldn't afford mercy. He had people of his own to protect from the Talisman's unholy fury. And they had brought the fight to Ashfall.

He told Cassandane of his plan.

"When Darius usurped the throne of the Black Khan, he did so with his talents as Dark Mage. He took his studies more seriously than the Khan, he spent time in the scriptorium—he was more thoroughly literate."

It was an explanation of how Darius had been able to claim his birthright as Dark Mage, while Rukh still struggled to accept who he was destined to become. A warrior, a strategist, a prince who wove a thousand cunning schemes while giving himself over to pleasure, devious in matters of faith despite his partiality for tokens. If Rukh's powers as Dark Mage were locked inside himself, those machinations would be the cause of it. A better man would have served the empire more nobly, but a better man wouldn't have been able to wrest back his throne from the half-brother who had usurped it.

"Darius was obsessed with one of the legends of the Claim: the Night Journey and the Ascension. Do you know it?"

Cassandane nodded. "The Messenger of the One ascended to the heavens on the back of a winged creature, where he was gifted with knowledge. Why did that interest Darius?"

Arsalan thought of Darius, driven to dark sorcery, overthrown by it in the end.

"Darius experimented with his gifts as Dark Mage. He sought a means to ascend to the heavens, just as the legend described. He thought he could make this journey by opening up a portal, but during the course of his experiments, he made a discovery he didn't anticipate. He harnessed the power of the stars—he created a weapon that could be used in battle. And I've thought of a target— one that could be significant." Almost to himself, he added, "But timing will be everything. We'll have to hold the walls until the Black Khan comes into his own." Because once Rukh did, he would be able to use the sphere to mark out Arsalan's target.

"Darius trusted you?"

The question reflected Cassandane's recognition of his bone-deep loyalty to Rukh.

"He shouldn't have, but he did."

"I won't make the same mistake."

The cutting remark didn't come from Cassandane. It was the ghul who spoke. Arsalan watched the ghul approach from the Tower of the Mirage, ranks of Tecrandaz archers parting to let her pass. Bloodstains encrusted her mouth, her eyes bright with a feverish glint, her hands clenched into fists. When she reached him, she didn't touch him, didn't seek to compromise his authority before the Zhayedan. Yet she held him with her voice, her finger crooked in his face.

A merciless glance at Cassandane warned him of her intentions before she voiced her threat aloud. "Come with me or I'll strike her dead before your eyes."

"We're fighting a war, Darya." He knew better than to look at Cassandane.

"I don't care." Each word separate and precise.

A black darkness moved behind his eyes. It plunged inside his armor, burrowing into his chest to grip his heart with its fists. Swallowing his anger, he forced himself to remember that he was dealing with Darya, the girl whose love he had spurned. It was Darya he needed to reach.

"What would you have of me, Darya?"

The grip on his heart eased at his tone, the ghul's voice becoming playful. Her fingers patted the corners of her lips, picking the blood from her face.

"Come with me to my chambers. I would have you to myself."

Flickering tendrils of darkness danced before his eyes, as she waited for his response. He knew what she was asking for, felt a heaviness settle in his bones. He didn't want this. He didn't want *her*. It wasn't that he hadn't taken women as his lovers in the past. He was grateful for the warmth they'd shared when he had been in need, but there had been no tenderness in it, no true intimacy, no moment when Arsalan had been taken as himself until the First Oralist had gazed into his eyes and pressed her hand to his heart.

There are many paths to the One, and the One speaks only of love.

"Give me a moment, then." He made the request of the girl he had known. "I must assign command to one of my soldiers."

"Not Cassandane." The ghul pouted.

"Not Captain Cassandane," he said firmly. "Be about your duties, Captain."

As Cassandane returned to her archers, Arsalan shouted to a Zhayedan soldier who wore two silver rooks on his shoulder. The soldier hastened to obey, his curious eyes on Darya.

"Captain Esfandyar. You have command of the walls until my return."

Esfandyar had proved his skill in battle with knowledge of tactics to spare. Like Cassandane, he was a keen and independent thinker, though young for the rank he held. He was also a bashful admirer of the princess. Now his fascinated eyes dwelt on her.

"Maysam is more senior than I am, Commander."

He didn't say what both men knew. Esfandyar's command would be open to Maysam's challenge if his tactics failed.

"I won't be away long."

He shouldn't be going at all; he shouldn't leave the walls until the fate of the city was decided. His mind was filled with turmoil at the thought that it might be his absence that decided it. But he wasn't certain that he had any choice—the ghul gazed at him with an unchecked hunger that demanded a sacrifice. He needed to remove her from the walls. In the urgency of these circumstances, he hadn't had time to determine which of his commanders had sworn loyalty to the Nizam and might be working against him. Esfandyar was junior in rank, but Arsalan had trained him himself. He had the benefit of Arsalan's trust.

Which gave Arsalan a window of time to deal with the Darya-ghul—a battle that needed to be fought privately if he stood any chance of winning it. He was thinking also of Rukh and the care Rukh would want him to take with his only sister. Later, when he counted the cost of what he was being coerced into giving the ghul, he would deal with the Assassin, who had raised her from the dead, as he hadn't dealt with the Nizam.

Darya's arms wound about his waist, her voice husky in his ear. "I wouldn't make promises you won't be able to keep."

Her darkness pushed at his mind, showing him if he hadn't

already guessed, how fragile a construction it was. The ghul could override him at will, and it would, feasting on Darya's innocent yearning for him. So instead of reproving her, Arsalan swept out his arm to show her the army at their gates.

"I would hold this city for *you*, Princess. I would give it to you as a gift."

Joy sparkled in the ghul's hollow eyes—Darya's joy tainted at the edges.

"A wedding gift!" She clapped her hands. "Come, then. We will speak of the rest later."

Dismayed at his going, Esfandyar looked to his Commander. Arsalan shook his head, appalled by the choice the ghul had forced him into but too proud to explain.

"Deal with the sappers, Esfandyar. I must attend to the Princess."

19

DARYA TOOK ARSALAN THROUGH THE AL QASR, THOUGH HE KNEW SHE hadn't intended to humiliate him, not when she claimed him as her own. She wanted to show him off, wanted to show the women who had made her life at court a torment that she had developed the sensual attraction to bring her lover to his knees.

He nodded at the women of the Black Khan's family sequestered in the Al Qasr, under the protection of a contingent of the Khorasan Guard, who waited outside the door.

The Begum stepped forward to block his path, imperious and disdainful, as was her right as matriarch of the court, the eldest aunt of the Khan.

"Why is the Commander of the Zhayedan lurking in the women's quarters when the city is under siege? Don't tell me this wayward child presumes upon your attention?"

He had no answer for her. But he needed to distract the ghul from the Begum's flagrant scorn. He clasped Darya's hand in his and drew it to his lips.

"A momentary respite, Begum. There are others at the gates."

The Begum didn't budge from her path, frowning as she took in Darya's dress.

"What kind of *respite* do you seek, Commander? You are not yet wed to the Princess."

Before he could prevent it, Darya raised her finger to the center of the Begum's forehead. The Begum sputtered in response.

The ghul spoke. "This is the last time you censure me, old crone."

Fire pierced bone, arrowed to the back of the Begum's skull. She collapsed in a heap on the floor, the Al Qasr filling with screams.

Darya touched Arsalan's chest, freezing him in place. Then her eyes searched through the ranks of the courtiers, of the cousins who had taken pleasure in humiliating Darya at court. Her right hand became a claw, fire arcing from its tips.

"Darya, no," he managed, horror gnawing at his mind. What was the ghul doing to the girl he had loved as the sister of his prince?

The ghul stopped. She searched for women she knew Arsalan had taken to his bed. The fire arced up above their heads and then drove down straight through their hearts. Bodies fell amid shrieks of fear, while the Khorasan Guard pounded at the doors that the ghul had sealed.

"No more, Darya." Arsalan forced up a hand to cover hers. "Don't taint the time we have together with this fury of blood and death."

She studied him with suspicion. "You'd shield those you have lain with from my wrath? Do these other women mean that much to you?"

"I'm thinking of *you*, Darya. Of the time I would spend with you. Take me to your chambers."

His heart pounded as she raised her arm to strike, a cold sweat on his skin. But then her expression softened. "You won't refuse me again?"

"I swear it. Let me show you what it could be like."

He wanted his actions to be guided by his compassion for her, but all he could taste was the bitterness of defeat. This wasn't who he was. It wasn't what he deserved.

"I don't trust you." Her voice changed, becoming soft and girlish—Darya's voice. "You said I couldn't attract you—you said you didn't want me."

He hadn't lied but also hadn't wanted to hurt the princess. But she could not be his confidante—she was too young, too unsure of herself, too untested to survive the intrigues of the court, where his true desires would be utilized as a weapon against him. And now he had to anticipate what the ghul might be driven to do if she learned who it was that he loved.

The ties of loyalty that bound him had never cut so deep.

He tried to calm her.

"Remember when I kissed you at the door to your chambers? If Rukh hadn't summoned me, I would have proved my faithfulness that night."

The ardent declaration made her let him go, and freed from Darya's power, he bent his head to kiss her. This time he tasted Darya in the sweetness of her lips, a taste tinged with sadness and regret. Her body became pliant, her breath coming faster, a flush of color settling over the unnatural paleness of her cheeks.

She took his hand again, leading him through the Al Qasr to the palace beyond. The chorus of mournful cries that followed echoed Arsalan's thoughts.

"Shall I wear these for you?"

Darya snatched the gold anklets he had laid on the table beside the bed hung with oyster-colored silks. The silks shimmered with iridescent tones, enclosing Darya's bed in an aura of intimacy that was sweetly feminine and should have been alluring.

Darya had lit candles on the surfaces in the room, small jeweled tables, her intricately carved little desk, the lacquered chest that Arsalan had brought back for her from his travels in the east. She also lit the maghrebi lanterns that swayed above his head, mirrored bits of glass casting colored patterns on a floor of smooth white marble.

The princess undressed without shame and watched as Arsalan did the same.

He answered her question with a nod, touching the fine filament of bells, a gift of gold from Rukh. She had strung them along her delicate ankles, then bent her legs to display them.

"There should be music when you take me."

He nodded again, his movements mechanical, aware of the sounds of war that boomed beyond the doors of her chambers. His thoughts were scattered, distracted . . . taking him out of a moment he wished he could delay . . . prevent . . . upend somehow . . . without causing harm to the Princess. Without destroying himself. Harsh lines of worry marked his brow. Would Esfandyar hold the Emissary Gate? Would Maysam follow through on his instructions to the Cataphracts? Had the Teerandaz won back the respect of the soldiers along the walls? Would Cassandane be able to command them, if not?

And where was Rukh? Had the ghul that had overtaken Darya managed to beat the Assassin? Had Darya harmed the Khan? There had been so much blood . . .

He would have felt it, he thought. If something had happened to Rukh, something irreversible, it would have pierced straight through his heart.

Determined fingers closed on his jaw, angling his proud head down. Darya was watching him, a glint of suspicion in her eyes that belonged to the ghul. But when he looked at her more closely, when he searched her gaze with the unaffected love he had always felt for the Princess, he could see the awakening of her remorse. Her lashes fell to her cheeks, a reflection of her uncertainty.

Did *Darya* want this at all?

In submitting to the ghul, would his actions be harming the Princess?

A bitter twist to lips that should have ripened with sensual awareness.

Because he knew the answer to his question, too painful in this moment to face—the greater harm was to himself.

Later, when it was done, he held Darya close, feeling the tremors that rocked her. He had tried to be gentle with the Princess, but his urgent need to return to the walls had not allowed for finesse.

"You shouldn't have touched me." A plaintive cry in the aftermath of their encounter, her knuckles pressed to her lips. He wondered what had come to Darya's mind and whether the ghul would let him leave now that its desire had been sated.

"How will they accept me at Hira after my transgression? A betrothal is no grounds for dispensation—a ceremony is required."

"I'll marry you, Darya, you needn't fear." Though he didn't know what the rites of Hira demanded in this respect.

"Here and now?" She looked up at him wide-eyed.

"Whenever you choose." What choice had the ghul left him, after all?

A long pause as her hands smoothed down over the strength of his arms.

"Why do you sound so sad, if our marriage is something you want?"

He wondered if he could tell Darya the truth without arousing the ire of the ghul. But even as he considered it, he dismissed it. There was no compulsion of the ghul's that would make him risk his place at Rukh's side.

"I was wondering if Ashfall will see another dawn, a dawn where I might marry you."

He eased from the bed to dress. Darya let him go. Suddenly self-conscious, she pulled the sheet up over her body. She faced him as he fastened his boots.

"Why didn't you choose me when you had the chance, Arsalan? Were the women you courted more appealing? Should I have studied the arts they used to seduce your attention?"

Leaning over her, he brushed back tendrils of her hair from her face, noticing how she held on to the sheet. It was too late to regret giving in to her, but he knew she was still Darya. Nothing he'd done when he'd taken her had tipped the balance to the ghul.

"You are perfect as you are. I've just had . . . other . . . considerations on my mind." He kissed her on both cheeks, then straightened from the bed to tell her, "I've loved you as Rukh loves you."

"More kindly," she said with a frown.

"More kindly." His harsh expression softened. "I would have sent you to Hira."

"To keep me at a distance? To win your freedom from me?" She snapped the words at him, the sheet falling to her waist. He nudged it up to anchor it behind her shoulder, feeling her blush heat the skin of his cheek.

He was overcome by the knowledge of how constrained his choices had been. If he *could* have loved her, everything would have been different. They would have found their place. They would have had a home in each other.

"No, Darya. Because it would have given you joy. And that, more than anything, is what I wish for you." This at least was the truth. And more, perhaps, than he owed her for what her unchecked longing had wrought.

A crash from the grounds beyond the palace; he could spare her feelings no more time. Careful with the innocence he had taken, but even more careful with the ghul, he asked, "May I have your leave to resume my duties?"

The sharp eyes of the ghul looked back at him without blinking, but it was Darya's hand that rested on his and Darya's soft voice that said, "Please come back to me when you can."

20

THE CATAPHRACTS USED THEIR SECRET SYSTEM OF SALLY PORTS TO break out of Ashfall at dawn.

With Maysam at their head, they arranged themselves in a wedge, the wide edge at the forefront, sharpshooters tapering to the back. Protected by black and silver shields, they rammed through a section of the Talisman army southwest of the Emissary Gate.

A separate contingent of Cataphract archers occupied slits beneath the parapets. They mirrored the movement of the wedge, their concentrated fire throwing the Talisman's lead troops into stunned disarray. The Talisman parted around the Cataphracts, their panic such that they didn't at first grasp that they could close their forces around the advance to lock down their enemies' progress—a reminder that for all their numbers, the Talisman were not soldiers trained in battle but men caught up in the One-Eyed Preacher's net, on a course they couldn't control.

The Cataphracts took advantage of the confusion as the Silver Mage and the Golden Mage gave what assistance they could from high above the Emissary Gate—fires broke out and were swiftly doused with wet furze, as the Talisman adapted their tactics in response. But the efforts of the Mages were enough to distract, aided by the fact that the company that had broken out from Ashfall was too small to attract the attention of the bulk of the Talisman army, whose front ranks were occupied with giving cover to their sappers.

The Cataphracts used all of this to their advantage, turning the wedge so that it punched through the group of soldiers that guarded the villagers the Talisman had taken prisoner. The Golden Mage burned an arrow of fire through their camp, cutting the guards off from their prisoners. The wedge began to separate at the head, allowing a space for the Cataphracts to pull the prisoners between the safety of its two flanks.

The maneuver was succeeding when a shout went up in the camp. A Talisman commander had caught sight of them. His horn sounded before an arrow caught him in the throat. The horn was echoed by others up and down the Talisman formation.

It was enough.

Before the Cataphracts could re-form their wedge, soldiers who had been sheltering the Talisman's sappers turned back to form a wall, cutting off the Cataphracts' retreat. Further progress was hampered by the panic of the villagers trapped between their flanks.

But it did create an opportunity.

"Fire!" a Cataphract archer shouted from the wall, seeing the unexpected opening.

A line of sappers fell dead, but others rose in their place, their shields sheltering their heads. A second volley failed against their shields, the sappers settling into place.

The Golden Mage attempted another strike of fire to open up the Cataphracts' retreat, to little effect. The wedge was surrounded in minutes, as more and more Talisman soldiers raced to aid their comrades. Considering the Cataphracts' options, Daniyar came to the same conclusion that Maysam must have considered: settle in for battle until not a single Cataphract remained alive on the field or turn the wedge on its axis to invert it—allowing the Cataphracts to batter their way back to the gate. Either option would defeat the purpose of their dangerous sortie, though the second would have some chance of success, if the Dark Mage bolstered the Mages' efforts from the wall.

All they needed was time.

Maysam chose the second option, calling out a series of commands. The wall of Cataphracts broke apart, Maysam leading the charge. Soldiers flowed down both flanks, re-forming the wall at their rear, while the sharpshooters now had point. But Maysam's decision left the villagers exposed, causing confusion in his ranks. Within minutes the Talisman had slaughtered them, leaving a handful of soldiers to batter their way to the gate. A spear raised high in the air aimed at Maysam's back. The Silver Mage cast the light of his ring deep into Talisman ground. The spear-carrier was momentarily blinded, the Cataphracts stumbled through the sally port, the Zhayedan sealing it behind them.

One hundred men had set out. Fewer than a dozen returned.

Not a single refugee had been delivered to safety, a total failure of their plan.

Beyond their walls, the Talisman shouted in victory.

Ashfall's dead were collected, their severed heads pitched over the wall, their bodies doused in flames. The disposal of the dead was merciless, as the Zhayedan roared from the walls.

Maysam charged through the courtyard, ripping his helmet from his head. He made for the steps to the Tower of the Mirage, a litany of curses on his lips.

Daniyar looked over at Ilea, noticing for the first time that neither Rukh nor Arsalan had taken command of the wall. His glance fell on a soldier with an insignia of rank on his shoulder. He was shouting orders at the Zhayedan who surrounded him, but they were slow to obey.

Daniyar strode over to stand with the soldier, first demanding his name.

Esfandyar made short work of his explanation. "The Princess of Ashfall has been reclaimed. She has some . . . power . . . over Commander Arsalan. He didn't have much time, so he asked me to take command." He glanced over at the opposite tower, where Cassandane was at work with her archers. "None of the Zhayedan will take orders from a woman, though the captain knows what she's doing."

Daniyar sorted through this as best as he could, asking, "Where is Arsalan now?"

"The Princess took him to her chambers."

"What of the Assassin and the Black Khan?"

Esfandyar shook his head, falling back to his men. "I haven't seen them, I don't know." He didn't panic, but his voice was grim. "How will we hold without them?"

Daniyar's reply was adamant. "Your general will return. And your Khan must be found. Send someone to look for him."

Maysam's rage was such that he tore Cassandane's helmet from her head. He cast a quick look around, searching for Arsalan. When he didn't see him, he roared an accusation at Cassandane.

"*You* did this! First you influenced Arsalan to your wishes, and then you refused to support us with your archers. Most of my men are dead—sacrificed for those who stood no chance." He grabbed Cassandane by both shoulders and shook her. "Where is Arsalan?"

Behind him, chaos reigned. The Teerandaz waited for orders, and down the other wall, the Silver Mage and Esfandyar raced to Cassandane's aid.

"Get your hands off me!" Cassandane struggled in Maysam's grip. She might have been able to disarm him with a thrust of her sword, but to do so would be treasonous: it would set off a reaction she wouldn't be able to control. Instead, she kicked out at his knee, but he was too strongly built to feel the blow. He raised her off the ground so that she dangled in his grip like a doll.

"Where is Arsalan?"

"Captain!" A shout from Esfandyar, Daniyar just behind him. But before Daniyar could caution Esfandyar not to speak, the young soldier called out, "Commander Arsalan attends to personal matters at Princess Darya's request."

"Darya?" Maysam's head swiveled. His grip on Cassandane's shoulders loosened, and she tore herself free. Backing up, she nodded to her second-in-command to follow through on her strategy for the defense of the Zhayedan Gate.

Maysam's rage cooled. Now he took in the chaos along the walls, the hapless movement of the Zhayedan, both on the parapets and down in the massive square. Only the Teerandaz acted with purpose, their aim and attention unflagging. A small contingent of the army commanded by a woman—and as for the rest? Did a pup like Esfandyar believe himself in charge?

When the Silver Mage approached at Esfandyar's heels, Maysam waved him off. "This is an internal matter. Your presence isn't required."

"Your Khan asked for my assistance; I promised him my aid."

Maysam's eyes flicked to where Ilea still wielded her magic above the Emissary Gate.

"I fail to see how your gifts have served us. The Zhayedan prefer their swords to your arcane rites." He unsheathed his sword. "How can the Princess be alive?"

Daniyar hesitated; it was enough to make up Maysam's mind.

"More of your demon magic. I suggest you return to the Khan. And as for you—" Here he gripped Esfandyar by the throat. "Did Arsalan assign command of these walls to a novice?"

Esfandyar choked in his grip. "The Princess didn't give him a choice."

Maysam let him go in disgust. "I'm assuming command. The defense of Ashfall will proceed as it should have from the first." An angry nod at Cassandane. "Move your archers to the Emissary Gate."

Cassandane froze, not daring to glance over at the Silver Mage.

"Captain." Her tone was conciliatory. "We can't leave the Zhayedan Gate exposed." She gestured down at the ground. "The Talisman have raised another contingent of sappers."

Maysam struck her hard enough on the shoulder to drive her to her knees.

"Not a single Zhayedan would dare to question my orders. You are relieved of duty." He pushed Esfandyar forward. "Take her to Qaysarieh. Find Commander Arsalan, and then report to me. Is that understood?"

Esfandyar gave him a quick salute, prodding Cassandane with the tip of his sword.

Maysam focused on Daniyar. "Interfere and you'll be joining her."

He didn't wait for an answer, his eyes searching out Cassandane's second-in-command.

"You. Woman." He pointed to one of the archers, whose face was dark with anger at his treatment of her captain. "Move your archers east; be ready to strike on my command."

Despite Maysam's threat, Daniyar attempted to intervene. "You need to listen to Captain Cassandane. The threat to the Zhayedan Gate is imminent; you must not weaken its defense."

But Esfandyar was already leading Cassandane down the steps of the Tower of the Mirage. Neither he nor Cassandane resisted Maysam's orders, obedient to the chain of command. The Teerandaz began to position themselves above the Emissary Gate as directed by Maysam.

"I have tolerated you," Maysam said to Daniyar, "because my Khan had need of you. But I know where your true allegiance lies. If you persist in interfering, my men will not hesitate to send you to your Talisman brothers."

Daniyar's thoughts raced. Maysam's overturning of Arsalan's careful plans didn't necessarily signify betrayal. Maysam commanded the Cataphracts; at the present moment, he was the senior-most captain at the walls. He had the right to give orders and perhaps even to determine strategy in Arsalan's absence. Which made Arsalan's return all the more urgent.

Could it be true that Darya had bewitched him? If the Princess had been reanimated, there could be only one explanation. The Mages had been in one another's presence; it was the Assassin who was nowhere to be seen.

He gave Maysam a sharp nod, indicating his acceptance of Maysam's right to command.

Then he had another thought. He raised his right arm to the sky. His silver ring flared to life, its light glancing over Ilea. She looked back at him, bringing her power to bay.

He pointed to the Zhayedan Gate, stripped of its protection.

When she moved to take up its defense, he made for the square below.

21

THUNDER BOOMED IN THE SKIES ABOVE ASHFALL, A RAVISHED, UNSPEAK-able moment as heavy clusters of clouds descended over the capital, shielding the army's view of the Talisman advance. In the courtyard, uncertainty prevailed. The Zhayedan's defenses fell quiet. They couldn't read signals from the parapets. They were remembering when the thunder had struck before, cracking the city walls. They had just repaired those defenses.

Lightning streaked through the clouds, ribbons of flame that struck through the square without warning. Wooden catapults burned, then a storehouse at the rear. Commanders shouted orders into the chaos, but what response could be made when they couldn't penetrate the mist?

Cracks of gold then appeared, arrow-sharp and swift. A break in the cloud cover revealed the Golden Mage, rapid strokes of her hands piercing through white drifts of fog. It wasn't as much as they needed, but in this moment, it was enough. The noise of battle resumed, Cataphracts assembled for a strike, the Teerandaz poised to give them cover.

Just outside the royal chambers, Arsalan's path crossed Rukh's.

The Khan was dressed in full armor, the Shahi scepter in his hand. For once, the Assassin wasn't skulking at his side.

"Where have you been?" A rough demand from Rukh, his eyes ablaze with anger.

Arsalan glanced back at the route to the royal chambers. His voice gruff, he said, "I'm surprised you don't know."

Rukh's black eyes turned sharp as he followed Arsalan's gaze. When he looked back at Arsalan, his face was dangerously neutral. He considered his next words with care. "This passage leads to my sister's chambers."

"Yes." Refusing to explain himself, Arsalan asked, "Did Darya awaken your gifts?"

Rukh's response was rash. "Did she awaken *yours*?"

"How dare you ask me that, Rukh?" Fury coated each word. Rukh knew Arsalan's desire—had forcefully made it clear that desire would never be fulfilled.

"We are speaking of my *sister*. I have a right to know."

They paused as another crack of thunder shook the palace.

His handsome face bleak, Arsalan said, "She didn't give me much choice." His shoulders straightened with purpose, as if he sensed a rebuke. "But you needn't worry; I have pledged myself to Darya, as you wished."

Something shifted behind Rukh's eyes. His fingers clenched the Shahi scepter.

"I hadn't planned to tie you to a ghul."

"Perhaps you had as little choice as I did. Though I thought you believed the ghul *was* Darya. What happened to change your mind?"

Rukh hesitated. But he had never lied to Arsalan, never hidden anything from him—nor allowed another to come between them, despite his dependence on the Nizam or, latterly, the Assassin. Arsalan had Rukh's trust. He had his deepest loyalty. So he described what had happened in the scriptorium, conscious of Arsalan's unwavering attention, his dark eyes fixed on Rukh's face.

When he'd finished, he added, "If the ghul forced you into something you didn't want, I am sorry for it."

The words couldn't begin to convey Rukh's anger or remorse at his refusal to accept what his sister had become, so desperate had he been to believe. Or at the choice his actions had forced Arsalan to make—scarcely a choice, at all.

Another crack of thunder. Arsalan wiped a hand over his face.

"Didn't *want*? The city is under attack—do you think I would willingly abandon it? Don't you know me at all?"

Rukh let the Shahi scepter fall. It struck hard against the floor and rolled away. With its crown of gold and its diamond-encrusted staff, the scepter was priceless beyond what it signified in terms of his right to rule. But he didn't consider it now.

He moved to embrace Arsalan, while his eyes stared blankly down the hall. He sensed Arsalan's shock at the intimacy of the embrace. Time spiraled out, the moment enduring, separate from the battle that raged beyond their gates. Then Arsalan gripped him back, his face turned into Rukh's neck.

"Forgive me," Rukh said.

For insisting on Arsalan's marriage to Darya. For leaving him to the ghul's mercies. For accepting Arsalan's fidelity without being willing to requite it. For a long list of sins that would only grow, if Arsalan stayed at his side.

"You could leave," he told his friend. "I don't have the right to hold you. I can't give you what you want."

Arsalan drew back to look at him, his dark hair brushing Rukh's jaw. "Would you grant me my own fiefdom?"

A lazy spark lit Rukh's eyes. "Assuming we make it to dawn, I'll grant you anything you ask."

A smile tugged at Arsalan's lips before a darker expression replaced it. "I won't be forced from your side. If you want me gone from Ashfall, you'll have to banish me yourself."

Rukh scowled. "Do you take me for a fool?"

"Not a fool, Rukh. Perhaps just not willing to accept where your choices might lead."

The teasing note in Rukh's voice vanished. Soberly, he said, "There was no choice for me in this. Ashfall must have a queen, and I will not dishonor her with my open disloyalty."

"No?" They were standing face-to-face, still bound in the embrace of brothers. Then it altered, as Arsalan edged closer to brush Rukh's mouth with his own. He outlined the firm edge of Rukh's lips with a slow sweep of his tongue. Rukh's lips parted. For long moments, he allowed the kiss, giving Arsalan the taste he wanted. Testing it for himself. Until Arsalan raised his head to ask, "Does this feel like disloyalty?"

A scream of fury rent the air.

The two men broke apart to find Darya rushing at them, tears streaking her face with inky trails of kohl. Her lips parted in a snarl as she rounded on her brother, her hands raised high, her fingers twisted into claws. She snatched up the Shahi scepter and brandished it like a mace.

"Arsalan is *mine*!" She shrieked the words in his face, aiming the staff at Rukh's head. He evaded her strike by a breath, and then Arsalan was there, pushing Rukh behind him, wrenching the Shahi scepter from her hands.

"Stop this at once, Darya! It is treasonous to lay your hands upon the Prince!"

Darya's sudden movement was oddly fluid, sinews twisting in

a manner that offended the eye, her thin white robe falling from her body. Arsalan shivered. She caught his gesture of abhorrence. This time when she raised her hands, the strike was aimed at him. She spat out words that slashed his face, scratching out trails of blood.

He grabbed her hands and twisted them, tugging her robe back up. She hissed at him like a feral cat, rage pouring from her lips.

The more he fought to restrain her, the more she struck at him with words. He tried to knock her unconscious; she froze his hands at his side. Her claws slashed down, tearing at his chest, one bloodthirsty strike after another, until she'd brought him to his knees, armor riven, chest painted in blood.

Rukh sprang at her from behind, his hand covering her mouth.

The ghul bit through his hand, white foam edging her lips. Arsalan forgotten, she whirled around to Rukh. This time as her rage roared to life, Rukh bore the brunt of her attack. Whips of flame stung his face and then arrowed down his body, plunging into his chest. With the clawing motions of her hands, something tore behind his ribs.

It should have hurt him; it should have broken him in two. But the sight of Arsalan bloodied on his knees turned his bones into steel. Ashfall could burn to the ground, as long as Arsalan survived. Scorching fire sprang to life inside his chest. It seared his heart and then ignited his body with lightning-quick streamers of flame.

Raising his own hands high, he lashed out with verses of the Claim—verses he had uttered at the Conference of the Mages. The verses pushed the ghul away from Arsalan, one jagged step at a time. The flames that issued from Rukh's fingertips singed the ghul's long hair.

Power swamped him in a wave, but it wasn't as before, when

he'd been darkened by Arian's blood. Then, the power had controlled him, swallowing his will. This was something *he* controlled, something cold and precise that seethed with righteous fury. The robe of the ghul began to burn. She withdrew from him inch by inch, her cries wild and inhuman.

Rukh pressed forward just as Arsalan staggered to his feet.

"Rukh, no!" He flung an arm out at Darya. The ghul was sliding up one wall, tearing her robe from her limbs. Rukh raised his hand to strike again, when Arsalan tugged down his arm. Arsalan yanked him around as the ghul retreated. "Rukh, it's still *Darya*!"

The Black Khan's hesitation was all the ghul needed. Her lips twisted in furious pain, she disappeared down the corridor. But not before Arsalan had seen traces of the Darya he knew, the agony in her eyes undercut by her sense of shock. She knew at last why Arsalan did not love her—why he would never love her. And she recognized now how deeply their encounter had damaged the man she loved. Repentance . . . grief . . . untenable shame . . . covered her face before the sight of her was lost.

A shadow appeared in her place—the Assassin, masked and cloaked in black, the laces on his gloves striking sparks of antique fire. He took two steps after Darya, then turned back to the Black Khan and waited.

Rukh brought both arms down and crossed them over his chest, murmuring an incantation known solely to the Dark Mage.

"You were right," he said to the Assassin. "I know who I am now; she was able to awaken the gift. Go after her and bind her, but do not do her any harm."

The Assassin nodded once. Smokelike movement and he was gone.

Before Arsalan and Rukh could confer, the Silver Mage hailed them from the entrance to the palace. His appearance was accompanied by the earsplitting groan of iron chains—the only sound ominous enough to drown out the thunder outside.

His silver eyes blinding them, he warned, "Maysam gave the order to open the Emissary Gate. There was nothing I could do to stop him." His eyes met Rukh's and held. "But there may be something *you* can do."

Rukh closed his hands into fists, fulfillment a riot in his blood.

The ghul's vicious attack on Arsalan had served to set Rukh free.

Or perhaps it was Arsalan's kiss that had finally unchained him.

No matter the reason behind it—the Dark Mage had risen again.

22

Three gates, three Mages, the sky an ecstatic color that heralded a riotous dawn. Livid clouds climbed to a perilous height, a miracle of atmosphere that cloaked the entire city.

Rukh looked over at Ilea. The Golden Mage waited for his signal above the Messenger Gate. The Silver Mage held the Zhayedan Gate to the south, but Rukh had claimed the Emissary Gate for himself. It was time for him to face the Talisman, time to show them who he was. His father hadn't been chosen as Dark Mage, but his belief in Rukh had been steadfast. He'd favored Rukh over his half-brother, Darius.

One day you will rule all of Khorasan. I have prepared the way.

Courtiers had been purchased, and soldiers trained from youth to protect Rukh at all cost. His loyal cadre of followers had ensured his ascension to the throne. But perhaps his father's greatest gift to him had been the sheer scale of resources he'd devoted to the scriptorium. The gifted tutors whose only charge was to educate the future Khan. There, too, his father's wisdom had prevailed. Knowing that Rukh would grow restless at prolonged and solitary schooling, Arsalan had been assigned to study with him, sowing the seeds of lifelong friendship. The difference was that the schooling had taken with Arsalan, aided by the fact that Arsalan's mother was a Companion of Hira. Rukh had studied the forms; Arsalan had learned the substance.

But now Rukh had mastered both, as the Talisman would soon discover. He waited for the first tinge of dawn to pierce through the heavy cloud cover. Arsalan was in the square, where the first ranks of Talisman fighters began to push through the gate. They were met by a Cataphract brigade, and amid the clash of swords and the raging fury of resistance, brutishly strong Zhayedan soldiers struggled to wind the gears of the mechanism that would close the gate.

Power pulsed along the link that bound Rukh to the other Mages. Impatient, urgent, *glorious*. Threads of silver and gold twining along ribbons of black that lashed out like fire from his fingers. He nodded first at Ilea. Then over at Daniyar.

The Mages raised their arms, their fingertips aimed at the sky.

Rukh looked down at the Talisman army. Reinforcements were banked along the salt plains. And in that quick survey of the sheer scale of the assault, he apprehended the weakness first spied by Cassandane. There was something he could do—a strike that would even the odds.

But first he had to hold the gate that Maysam had opened to the enemy, certain of the success of the strategy he'd outlined to Rukh privately. Free to give it rein with Arsalan's unexpected absence. A ruinous mistake. But one they might recover from.

If this newfound power could be brought to bear.

Rukh let out a bloodcurdling cry. The Talisman at the forefront of the attack halted. Streaks of flame pierced the clouds, burning the sky with depths of light.

The black-gold-silver thread wound around the three Mages, a glorious ribbon of fire.

The dawn rite had begun.

His voice amplified by his recitation, the Dark Mage intoned, *"Say I seek refuge in the Lord of Daybreak, from the evil of that which the One created, from the evil of the black darkness when it descends, from the evil of those bent on occult endeavors, and from the evil of the envier who envies."*

His voice trembled as he spoke of sorcery—the verse of the dawn rite condemned his earlier actions, his attempt to use the First Oralist's blood to awaken and augment his powers. But then Daniyar and Ilea joined in, echoing his recitation, underlining his strength by purifying his intent. He felt their power wrap around him, accelerating and amplifying his, an unparalleled source of the deepest communion: the Conference of the Mages as it was meant to be.

The fiery thread that linked them now erupted into flame. Into volcanic fury that painted the sky a molten red. The Mages lowered their arms in concert.

A conflagration blazed through the armies gathered at Ashfall's gates.

The vanguard of the Nineteen burned. At the southern and eastern gates, Talisman soldiers threw down their weapons and fled. Those who weren't swift enough to evade the annihilating fire disintegrated into dust.

But others pressed forward, pushing hard at the Emissary Gate, and Cataphracts and Talisman clashed in the square below. The heavy chains dragged forward. The gate began to close, even as a small company of Talisman were driving a catapult forward to jam the gears of the gate. If they succeeded, the gate would freeze and Ashfall would lie open to the east.

Rukh called up the dawn rite again, this time arrowing his hands straight down.

The golden thread was still twined with his, but the silver thread had faded. He glanced over at the Silver Mage, whose concentration was broken. Daniyar was following a line of Talisman who approached under a separate flag. Chaos reigned around this line, the Talisman uncertain where to strike. Daniyar's voice fell silent. He'd left his post at the Zhayedan Gate—he was headed straight to Rukh.

The dawn rite faltered. The Talisman catapult advanced, as the Emissary Gate juddered slowly to a close. Deprived of Daniyar's steadying assistance, the black thread began to suffocate the gold. Bolts of lightning streaked through Rukh's veins. His chest began to heave under the weight of his armor, soldiers to either side crying out at his appearance. By the time the Silver Mage reached him, blood had darkened his face.

But still the fury of the fire raged, burning wherever it struck, though twice now he had failed to target the catapult on its wheels.

"Wait!" Daniyar's shout cut across the dawn rite.

Rukh turned crimson-streaked eyes on him, his voice a double-edged blade. "No! We're losing the gate!"

Another strike at the ground, another narrow miss. The catapult rumbled on, and cutting across its path was a small contingent of the enemy under an unfamiliar flag. White lines of script traveled across a field of green, in a language Rukh couldn't read.

Then Daniyar's hand gripped his and wrested him around.

"Let them pass!"

"*What?*" Rukh's awakening stilled, the fire in his veins contained. "Why?" He was stunned by what he read in the Silver Mage's face. Neither fury nor demand. Instead, there was desperation in those eyes like diamond rain.

The Silver Mage had acceded to Rukh's authority, and now he was seeking a dispensation.

Underneath it all, the Golden Mage's power thrummed like a dual heartbeat in his chest.

Daniyar swept his hair from his eyes. He pointed to the flag below.

"The standard they bear is mine. They come to you not as enemies; they seek refuge. The man who leads them, Toryal, was once a boy in my care. I swear it on my honor and my life."

He unsheathed his sword and showed its script to Rukh, reciting his motto aloud.

"Defend the truth in the face of all dishonor."

The battle continued to rage. Daniyar's plea was succinct. "I promised Toryal sanctuary during the loya jirga. I ask this of you, Mage to Mage, Guardian to Guardian."

The power that surged through Rukh's body now took another form, the crimson receding from his eyes, to leave them sharp-edged and clear.

"What if they strike us from within?"

Epochs of ice in blinding silver eyes. Nothing but the clarity of truth.

"Look within yourself as Dark Mage."

The catapult breached the Emissary Gate. Soldiers poured through the opening headed for the mechanism that operated the gate.

The hypnotic power of the truth burned through Rukh's indecision. He was left with a choice to make, a moment where he had the upper hand. Where he could bargain with the Silver Mage for whatever he needed most.

But a fourth thread wound around the edges of his power. Gold for Ilea. Silver for Daniyar. This newest link was like the gentle fall of rain. Jade rain with a strident edge of steel. A woman's determined voice spoke to him from memory.

"Why do you never allow me to trust you?"

His power surged to life. He nodded at Daniyar.

"Deal with the catapult; leave the rest to me."

He sorted through the different groups who pressed forward. Raising his arms in slashing gestures, he burned a path clear behind the catapult. Then he set up a line of fire between the Cataphracts and the breakaway Talisman soldiers, allowing them to pass through the gate.

The Silver Mage turned to face the interior courtyard. The verses of the dawn rite fell continuously from his lips, shaped by years of hardship, hardened by unshaken faith. Instead of targeting the Talisman, his strike set their catapult aflame. The gate shuddered to a close, and trapped inside with the Cataphracts were two separate groups of Talisman, Maysam's attack against them indiscriminate.

The Dark Mage stood with the Silver Mage. He drew an incantation on the wind.

The black ribbon expanded and rocketed through the square. It moved from body to body until its fire was extinguished. Dizzied by the surge of energy, Rukh stumbled at Daniyar's side. Daniyar caught him, staring down at the courtyard where Talisman fighters lay dead.

Save for those who carried his standard, a black rook etched upon their foreheads.

A smile of immense satisfaction shaped the Black Khan's lips. "They bear *my* mark now. And I will use them as I choose."

The power drained from his body as the blue of the sky broke through.

23

WHEN RUKH WOKE, ILEA WAS AT HIS SIDE, HER HANDS CARESSING HIS face.

A quick glance showed him he'd been taken to his chambers, the sounds of battle dull at the periphery of his hearing.

"The dawn rite?" he asked her.

"Ended with the dawn. It happened as you'd hoped. You won Ashfall a reprieve, despite the foolish tactics of your captain and the ill-timed absence of your general."

The Golden Mage was dressed in her battered armor. She'd taken the time to bathe before she changed back into it, and her sultry scent teased his senses. He grasped her arm, tried to pull her down to the bed; she was quick to ease out of his reach.

"You cannot leave for the Citadel," he said, before she could speak. "I need your assistance with the dawn rite."

She bent down and kissed him, her lips lingering on his. He responded at once, possessively holding her nape. She let him kiss her at his leisure before she drew away.

"There is more to your abilities than the dawn rite. You must learn to harness your gift."

Rukh swung his legs over the side of the bed. "How will you get to Hira undetected? The Talisman have us surrounded."

Ilea's smile was sleek with self-assurance. "I've had use of my abilities since childhood. I am also the High Companion—you need not fear for me."

He caught her hand, gripped it. "My fear is for Ashfall."

To his surprise, Ilea raised their hands to her lips. She pressed a kiss to his knuckles. "I've done what I can for Ashfall. You cannot expect me to allow the Citadel to burn."

Silence fell between them. The weight of fatigue upon him, he felt the truth of her words. His power *would* rise again . . . His gifts would expand. He needed nothing and no one else.

Except Arsalan. One corner of his mouth quirked up. He'd yet to fight a battle without Arsalan at his back. Though the ghul had overtaken Arsalan, Arsalan was still the one he trusted. The one he wanted at his side.

"I'll send word once I reach the Citadel." Ilea helped him to his feet. He was surprised to find himself steady enough to return to the walls.

"The Silver Mage?" he asked her.

"You won't hold him here long." Bitterness tinged her smile. "His love for the First Oralist is his true allegiance." Her expression became thoughtful, as she guided Rukh to the door. "But as you aided him with the lost boys of Candour, he considers himself in your debt. Don't hesitate to use that."

She parted from him at the Illustrious Portal, where she turned to look back. "Will you truly grant these Talisman sanctuary?"

Rukh's smile was sharp and guileful.

"Come back to Ashfall and see."

24

Rukh was accompanied by two of the Khorasan Guard. They waited outside the war room, where Arsalan, Maysam, and a handful of Zhayedan commanders rose from their seats when he appeared.

He glanced around the table with a frown. "Where is Cassandane?"

"Later." The warning from Arsalan was clear, but something else sparked in his eyes. Pride. Pride at Rukh's success in winning them another day. Another glance around the table showed the same pride reflected in the faces of the Zhayedan commanders. Their posture was straight, their heads held high, their faces firm with belief. His actions had given them hope.

He listened to casualty reports, but his focus was elsewhere. How much of a reprieve had they had gained? What use could he make of the defectors? And there was a third matter that he would discuss with Arsalan and Maysam—after he issued the reprimand that Maysam's tactics had earned.

Arsalan summarized the Zhayedan's activities, then offered a final conclusion. "The Talisman disarray is temporary. We've gained a few more days, at most another week. Unless you plan to enact the dawn rite up until their army is defeated."

"Tactics must be our strength, but I will lend my aid where I can."

A rumble of approval around the table, which he silenced when he asked, "Where are the men the Silver Mage placed under his protection?"

"Under guard in our barracks." Maysam's voice was stiff with knowledge of his failure.

Rukh tapped the table. "Not a long-term solution. We can't spare the men to keep them under guard. Nor can we afford to allow them to wander unchecked."

A murmur of agreement that fell quiet when the Silver Mage stepped into the room. He'd dressed in fresh clothing, his pack strapped to his back. Just as Ilea had predicted, though she'd forgotten one thing. The Silver Mage carried the Sacred Cloak in his arms.

"I've spoken to Toryal. He's pledged his allegiance to you." A hard look came into Daniyar's eyes. "I am in your debt, Prince of Khorasan. The debt will be greater still if you care for the lives of these boys. They were conscripted by the Talisman; they didn't come here by choice."

"Will they help us against their masters? Will they divulge the Talisman's strategy?" A hard demand in return.

The two Mages locked eyes. "They will do whatever is needed to bring the Talisman down." Daniyar paused, weighing his words. "They've given me warning of the One-Eyed Preacher's expected return."

Rukh rose to his feet, Arsalan beside him. "How can I stand against the Preacher on my own?" He touched Daniyar's pack. "How will you repay the debt you owe me, if you leave?"

Fear pulsed along the bond that linked the Mages. But Daniyar's grim expression eased.

"I know what Ashfall needs. The same thing Hira and Candour need. The return of the First Oralist. Can the Zhayedan hold Ashfall until we're able to return?"

A chorus of confident replies. For Rukh's ears alone, Daniyar murmured, "The gift needs tending. Do not nurture it with darkness. The Sacred Cloak will aid you."

Another pulse along the bond of the Mages. A promise of loyalty for loyalty given. And then Daniyar placed the Sacred Cloak on the table in front of Rukh, covering up the map.

A hot pricking behind Rukh's eyes at this unexpected sign of trust. A trust he'd yet to earn, when no man present would dispute Daniyar's right to take the Sacred Cloak as his own.

Rukh followed Daniyar to the door, where he made a difficult confession. An admission of wrongdoing—a grudging acknowledgment of guilt. The words didn't come easily, but he knew he had to speak them—it was what Arsalan demanded of him. Integrity before all.

"I regret my deception about the loya jirga, when you took me at my word. I will allow no one to harm these Talisman under your protection. I will take them as my own."

The two men didn't embrace, but the silver-black threads that bound them were reinforced a thousandfold by the pledges they'd made.

DANIYAR WAS STOPPED TWICE ON HIS ROUTE TO THE QAYSARIEH POR-
tal. The first time was by the poet Alisher, just outside the scriptorium.

"You're going after the First Oralist," Alisher guessed.

"Stay safe in the scriptorium; there are others who can fight."
Daniyar gripped the poet's hand and said a prayer. *The ink of a
scholar is more precious than the blood of a martyr.*

Alisher bowed his head, humbled by Daniyar's gift of grace.
"I'll do my best, my lord. I have something for you, as your journey is bound to be treacherous." He held up a leather satchel that
fit across his chest.

"I appreciate the gesture, Alisher, but I need to travel light."

Alisher unfastened the lower part of the satchel and pressed
it into Daniyar's hands. "Its contents are essential . . . It's a me-
dicinal salve I devised from the Marakand loess. Its properties
are invaluable in wound-healing. And I've included other healing
aids I've derived."

He explained their uses, and Daniyar listened, knowing that
Alisher had prepared the supplies for Arian, having missed the

chance to give them to her before her departure from Ashfall. He took the pack with thanks, bidding the poet farewell.

He was interrupted again at the entrance to Qaysarieh, this time by a man who moved like a sleek black shadow, an apparition who could disappear as soundlessly as he appeared. He saw that the Assassin was dressed for travel, a pack slung across his back.

He began to move through the tunnels of Qaysarieh, the Assassin a whisper of darkness at his side.

"The Black Khan needs you more than I do."

"You've needed me at every step along your journey."

Daniyar stopped cold. The Assassin echoed his movement, and in that fluid gesture, there was something that stirred Daniyar's memory. He tipped his head back, and the memory vanished. He tried to read something behind the Assassin's mask or in his voice but couldn't.

"Show yourself," he demanded.

"It wouldn't do you any good . . . yet."

The Assassin began to walk again, directing Daniyar down through the maze of murky tunnels that had been Arian's escape route out of Ashfall.

"Then explain. How did I need you? Where have I encountered you before?"

The stench of decay filled his nostrils as the Assassin led him deeper. There was rot and putrefaction in these tunnels, yet the Assassin was unfazed. Perhaps his mask protected him. Daniyar drew up his cloak over his nose and mouth.

"I sold you a manuscript in Maze Aura. The one that described for you the graces of the Verse of the Throne."

A chill settled in Daniyar's bones. That manuscript had been sold to him by a native of the city, a young man in a bookseller's traditional garb, more than a decade ago.

"Then the mask you wear is a disguise. I would know your face if I saw it."

The Assassin ignored this. "When you went to plead for dispensation for Arian at Hira, I was there in the shadows."

Daniyar halted again. "You show your disrespect when you take the First Oralist's name." But it wasn't the Assassin's familiarity that was his chief source of anger.

The Assassin kept walking. "I have a right to her name. More so than the Guardian of Candour." He waited for Daniyar to catch up, and when he did, he added, "I stalked the Bloodless in Marakand, until I learned the whereabouts of the clues to the safehold of the Bloodprint. I told the High Companion where those clues could be found. I arranged for Captain Turan to be sent to the Sorrowsong to wait for Arian there."

Turan had rescued Arian from her house on the night of her parents' murder and delivered her safely to the Citadel of Hira. He'd been sworn in Arian's service from that night and had fulfilled that pledge by giving his life for her in Marakand.

His voice grim with fury at this emotionless reference to a friend, Daniyar grabbed the Assassin's arm. "How could you have arranged that? Turan was Shin War. He owed no allegiance to you."

The Assassin twisted free of Daniyar's grip. Tonelessly, he said, "Let us say that I removed anyone who would have been appointed in his stead."

"Why?" A rare torch lit their path ahead, the ground muddy and damp beneath their feet. The Assassin's mask was burnished bronze. His eyes gleamed through its slits.

"Why?" Daniyar insisted. "Your loyalty is to the Black Khan. Why pretend otherwise?"

"Is it?" The Assassin navigated a turn in the tunnel smoothly, cautioning Daniyar. "Then why did I bring you your tokens?" He nodded at Daniyar's sword. "Why did I have my Assassins rescue you from the Talisman camp?"

"Those are my questions to *you*. Why do you seek to accompany me, when the Black Khan needs you here? I have no reason to believe that your loyalties are torn."

Daniyar locked his hand around the Assassin's arm, using his full strength. But an instant later, the Assassin was behind him, his breath cold in Daniyar's ear.

"Don't turn this into a battle. Don't try to look behind my mask."

Daniyar shifted to face him. The man moved like smoke; he didn't try to touch him again.

"Then answer my question. Answer *all* my questions."

Light illuminated the lines of script on the Assassin's mask. The unreadable letters seemed to dance in Daniyar's vision. He blinked the vision away.

The Assassin cleared his throat. When he spoke, his voice was lethally soft. "I rescued you because she loves you. I walk this path beside you because I owe a debt to Hira. This is how I choose to repay it."

Daniyar pressed him further, but when the Assassin would tell him nothing else, he made up his mind to turn his companion back.

"You'll hinder my ability to slip past the Rising Nineteen."

The Assassin's shoulders shook. In anyone else, Daniyar would have thought he was suppressing amusement.

But there was only arrogance in the Assassin's reply. "Without my assistance, you'll be captured and killed at once."

Daniyar read the other man. The Assassin was telling the truth. Daniyar chose to accept it, and he was about to agree when a shadow stepped into their path. The Assassin's knife was at the newcomer's throat before Daniyar could blink.

"Who trespasses?" The Assassin pushed the intruder into the path of the torch. Its amber light burnished a soldier's injured face. But even disfigured by blood and dirt, Daniyar recognized Khashayar. He gripped him by the shoulders, pushing the Assassin aside.

"Where is the First Oralist? You were meant to defend her with your life!"

Khashayar's words tumbled out.

He told them about Najran.

26

RIM-SARAH PILOTED THE SANDSAIL WITH APLOMB, HER SMALL HANDS using the tribal gestures of her people to summon and skirt the winds, her head thrown back, her face alight with joy as her long curls danced in the breeze.

Wafa didn't share her joy, his hands locked onto the forward mast, his features tight with discomfort and more than a trace of fear. Sinnia was steadier on her feet than Arian, who kept glancing behind her for signs of Najran's pursuit, even as she recited prayers for Khashayar's safe return. With every dip and curve of the sandsail, they skimmed the dunes with terrifying speed, edging closer to a range of rocky cliffs that circled the holy city. But Rim-Sarah's confidence did not falter.

Arian had wondered at the freedom granted to daughters of the Bani Shira'a—the freedom to ride the dunes at will, venturing deep into the heart of the desert. But Sinnia had told her that just as with the Shin War, the codes of the tribes of the desert were set in stone, their laws of honor upheld: no one would touch a Sandrider, no matter how tempting it may have been to try to suborn their gifts.

It was near dark, and Arian could almost taste the sea when

she felt it. The thunderous sound of sand rising and falling in waves, ground lost beneath the sandsail, swallowed by a yawning nothingness.

Najran.

He'd found a way to cross the canyon. And from the shuddering tumult of the sands they skimmed over, he'd also recovered the glaive.

The sturdy sandsail skidded to a stop, Rim-Sarah caught off balance, her curls falling into her eyes. Wafa yelped with fright as the sandsail plunged down the slope of the dune. It faltered to a stop at the base of a stone-studded hill. Rim-Sarah tried to right the sandsail, but the wind had risen in a curtain behind them, trapping it against the hill.

Arian wheeled around on the deck. Najran was just below them, the glaive raised in one hand, as he waited to see what she would do.

Arian banked the Claim in her throat, cursing herself now for failing to deal with Najran in the tent of the Shaykh Al Marra. The curtain of sand parted: she looked straight into Najran's eyes. He glanced past her, first to Wafa, then to Rim-Sarah, the girl who commanded the sands. The roar of sand abated, and he said, "Interesting. The girl might be of use."

He rolled the glaive between his fingers. Arian leapt from the deck, a plan formed in her mind. She would meet the others at the shore of the Sea of Reeds. But she would end Najran's pursuit, here and now, at the foot of these rocky cliffs. She eased back toward the hills, drawing Najran with her, when Rim-Sarah shouted out a warning.

"*No*, sahabiya, no! Jabal Thawr is forbidden!"

Arian caught the shift of Najran's eyes to the mountain behind her. She'd already spied several openings that led to caves inside.

Rim-Sarah begged Arian to stop, Sinnia echoing her calls.

"I can deal with him," she told Sinnia. "I've done it before. Go on ahead; I'll find you." She outlined her plan in the Companions' language. Hearing Arian's certainty, Sinnia didn't hesitate. One of them had to reach the Sana Codex.

She braced her hands on Rim-Sarah's shoulders and told the girl to set sail.

Arian hummed the Claim, luring Najran to the caves.

The sandsail rose from the ground to a wail of protest from Wafa. It lurched over the dunes through the whirling curtain of sand. Najran let it go, his eyes tracking Arian, a secret smile on his lips, as she retreated into the caves of Jabal Thawr.

He raised the glaive, and she flung an incantation at him, her low voice edged with gravel.

A thin seam of blood split the skin between his neck and shoulder.

To her horror, he smiled again, as his eyes moved beyond her to the entrance of the cave.

She backed away into the mountain, fazed by sudden cold as icy darkness enclosed her. The Claim was constant in her throat, but the attack came from a place she didn't expect. Najran's strange murmuring crumbled the rocks above her head. She was forcefully struck on the shoulder. As she stumbled to one knee, Najran moved with lightning speed, the glaive coming down hard.

A sharp rasp of the Claim deflected the glaive from her heart. It struck her shoulder instead, the same shoulder that had taken the brunt of the rockfall. He ripped the glaive free to strike again, and a cry of pain escaped her lips. She threw up one hand, letting the Claim fly free, her voice turning hard and dark. Najran circled behind her. The arm that raised the glaive was frozen. Arian turned and fled deeper into the heart of the mountain, as a giant cavern opened up, frigidly cold and dark. From the corner of her eye, she caught sight of something strange—a silver-thin thread of color. The minute she stopped reciting, Najran's footsteps followed her, gaining with every step.

Her eyes adjusted to the dark. Tunnels spiraled off to the left and right, but ahead were a dozen narrow paths that led upward through the cavern, draped in the same silken threads. They brushed her face as she raced forward, Najran in close pursuit.

Her voice rasped low in her throat, but it wasn't enough to slow him. She felt the tip of the glaive prod her back through her cloak. Najran could have struck, but he was playing with her. Waiting for an opening to engage her.

Her shoulder throbbing with pain, Arian climbed as high as she could, until the ledge evened off. It wound around a sheer face of rock, dark, solid and cold, with the faintest twist of silver dangling from a rugged roof.

What was it? What had Rim-Sarah tried to warn her against?

There was no time to ponder it. She could sidle around the cliff face where the ledge was perilously narrow, but she'd be making herself a target. The glaive could strike her down; the ground was so far below now that she'd break apart on the rocks. Unless there was a way to leap to another ledge. Her eyes blurred slightly—the ledges were so similar that she didn't recognize the one she had climbed to the top. Just as she couldn't tell which of the handful of openings below had led her into this cavern.

She turned to make her stand, chanting the Claim without reprieve.

Najran shrugged off his cloak, dropping his belt of daggers. Leanly muscled and deadly, he balanced the glaive in one hand. Arian gripped her sword, her body moving with the fluid ease of her training. She used both weapons in tandem: the Claim, harsh on her tongue, and the sword in her hand, raising it to block the glaive.

The glaive locked by the Claim, she was able to strike at Najran, a slash across his ribs, that didn't penetrate through because he twisted away to one side.

She raised her voice, the Claim surging hard and bright, giving her another chance to strike. But somehow he overcame the power of her gift and used the glaive to block her sword, using the spiked edge to trap it and wrest it free of her hand.

It didn't matter. She had a dagger at her hip.

But now it was Najran who spoke—that unfamiliar language, though she thought . . . was it *possible* . . . that it was threaded with bits of the Claim? With stories and verses she knew?

Najran's voice was as sleek and pointed as Arian's was rough, her larynx ravaged by sand. She tried a short, sharp strike of her voice. He answered with a sinuous chant, his voice falling into a rhythm.

She aimed the Verse of the Throne at his throat.

He raised his own voice in answer.

Her vocal cords seized up, the verse strangled in her throat.

She couldn't recite. *This* was the power he wielded, an arcane yet strangely familiar magic that the Claim was insufficient to withstand. A gap in her years of study, a weakness she hadn't known she possessed.

He recognized her weakness at once. His amber eyes glinted, the pupils tinged with blood. When she reached up to ease the grip on her throat, he lunged, pushing her back against the cliff. He feinted low, the glaive striking her thigh, tearing into her flesh. When his chanting stopped, giving Arian a reprieve, her knife slashed his wrist.

He jerked his hand back, dropping the glaive, and then he was on her, locked in a physical struggle, rolling back and forth at the very tip of the ledge. She punched the wound in his ribs. He retaliated with a knee to her thigh. She sliced at his neck with her knife; he ripped it from her hand to throw it over the ledge. Both their bodies were slippery with blood; otherwise his hands would have locked around her throat. His irises shattered into myriad colors, as he tried to land a killing blow. His fists hammered swift and fast at her arms, her ribs, her unprotected back, battering her without mercy.

But she twisted in his grip until she had thrown him off her body.

Before she could stagger to her feet, he pivoted on one heel and stepped onto her injured thigh. Her scream shattered the silence. His taunting composure gone, he moved around her body, kicking viciously with his boots until every part of her felt broken. He gathered the glaive, striking her head with its solid base. Blood dripped into her eyes. He jerked her body up with his free hand, wrenched at her battered shoulder, then let her drop to the ledge again, limp and unprotected.

He raised the glaive for the final blow, staring down into her face.

She wanted to stare back at him, proud and undiminished, but the pain that seared every corner of her mind left her fractured and begged her to surrender. She dragged in a shallow breath, feeling it rasp through her lungs.

He aimed the glaive at her heart, and Arian knew she'd failed.

And in this final moment, all she wanted was Daniyar. Daniyar's touch, his warmth, his promise of devotion. Her stubbornness and pride were poor consolation now.

"Wait." She croaked out the single word, pushing aside strands of hair that were sticky with her blood.

To her surprise, he listened. Leaning the glaive against the cliff face, he refastened his daggers at his waist. Then he took up the glaive again.

"Strange," he said. "I thought if anyone could stand against me, if anyone could give me a fight worthy of the name, surely it would be you. But here you lie broken at my feet."

A painful truth to accept, with answers she wouldn't find now. No time left to ruminate on failure, the glaive bearing down to her breast.

From the One I came, to the One I return.

A thought for Daniyar and the Damson Vale, another for the Citadel at Hira.

And then she caught a movement at the edge of her vision: a stirring of silver-thin threads, the agile grace of a shadow.

A choked cry from Najran.

Arian kicked out with her foot, heard the clanging fall of the glaive to the cavern below, followed by a heavier thud.

Silver thread, silver light. A memory of a story from the Claim.

And then her vision went dark.

ARIAN STOOD BEFORE THE WATERS OF THE ALL WAYS. Its waters were purest turquoise, its ever-unfolding patterns drawing her in. She reached out a hand and heard its voice.

Come to me, child of Hira.

Hira was her home. She longed to return with all her heart . . . but a slight shift of her body made her conscious of pain, most pressingly in the arm that hung limp and broken at her side.

A quick look down showed her that her armor had been damaged in the battle with Najran. Her clothes were rent, her body throbbing with bruises, her shoulder and leg sticky with blood that had dried. At some point she must have wrapped the wound at her thigh with a bandage she'd fashioned from her clothing.

She eased herself into a sitting position. She'd lost her cloak in her battle with Najran, but his was near to hand, though the man himself was nowhere to be seen. Wincing at the pain the movement caused her, she wrapped herself in it, drawing his hood over her face. The cloak dwarfed her, but it was warm. Her head fell back against the cliff face as her eyelids fluttered closed.

She wouldn't give up—Sinnia and Wafa waited for her at the

sea. She would rest and recover, using the Claim to aid her. She hadn't survived the tortures of the Authoritan to be defeated by the Nineteen. Najran may have beaten her bloody, but she was the one who'd triumphed. Her thoughts were hazed and foggy, her perceptions distorted: she couldn't remember *how* she had killed Najran. Or if she had defeated him at all. She remembered the movement of silver threads across her vision. She had a moment's confused recollection of a story her mother had told her of a cave hidden within Jabal Thawr . . . the Cave of Thawr. And she knew that nothing of this world could have saved her from Najran, unless it was shepherded by the spirit of the Claim.

Her head lolled on her shoulder. Her thoughts drifted to Daniyar.

He was watching her, a question in his eyes, his black hair worn like a shroud.

"Are you ready now? I've been waiting for you for so long."

She reached out her hand, his image faded from sight. Darkness crept over her brow, the taste of it dull in her mouth. What she'd seen was an illusion—*he* was an illusion—so she closed her eyes and slept.

The next time she woke it was to the sound of voices below— she could hear movement, as if the cave was being searched. She couldn't gauge how much time had passed, but she came awake, alert to danger, a crust of grime around her mouth that told her she needed water.

She peered at the wound in her thigh. The gash had stopped bleeding, but any movement would reopen it. Her arm throbbed at her side. Its ache had been persistent in her dreams, and when she tried to lift it, a gasp escaped her lips.

The sun was rising, light piercing its way through tiny cracks in the mountain. Splinters illuminated the far end of the ledge.

Her position would soon be visible to those who were moving through the cave. The sound of their voices grew louder. At least two men were searching the cave; perhaps others waited outside at the entrance to the mountain.

Sweat broke out on her brow. In the dark, she'd been able to see little of the cave's interior. Now as the sun rose, she had to consider whether those who searched below would be able to track her to the top. Had she left a trail? Would they follow it to her? If she rolled to the edge of the ledge to look below, she might give herself away. If she didn't move, their search would bring them to her.

If she sought out a different place to hide, assuming she could move her body at all, the intruders would hear her. Her thoughts harrowed by pain, she considered her options. If she *hadn't* killed Najran . . . if he'd found reinforcements . . . her fear of him surged up in her throat.

Her palms damp, she waited. She heard a note of urgency in the voices that spoke to each other, as the footsteps below picked up speed.

Please, she prayed.

There was no answer from the One.

Her eyes snapped open again. She wouldn't give in like this. She wouldn't let Najran torture her before he killed her and tossed her away.

With movements that were agonizingly slow, she reached for the knife that was strapped to her back. When she managed to pull it loose, she stabbed it into the ground, using it as leverage to stand. Slowly, she climbed to her feet. She tested her weight on her injured leg and let out a breath when it held.

The knife gripped in her hand, she took a careful step.

Pain seared through her consciousness. She pressed a fist into her mouth. She fell back against the wall, making her first mistake. The hilt of the blade struck stone. The sound rang out through the cavern. Her breath puffed out in harsh gasps, the strength draining from her body.

Silence below, before a voice called out. The sound of running footsteps. And then the intruders were climbing. But there were many paths to choose from—had they found the one that led to her hiding place?

Sheathing the knife at her waist, she wiped the sweat from her face. She had to round the cliff face using the narrow ledge. A maneuver that was bound to fail, but what other choice did she have? Her body was drenched in sweat, in contrast to the dryness of her mouth, aching from Najran's assault. Each turn of her head brought a fresh wave of nausea, her vision blurred at the edges. She forced her leg to take the weight, dragging it with her as she inched across the ledge.

Ahead on the left, the cliff curved around. If she made it across, she would find a way to summon the Claim, though the muscles of her throat had seized up.

Too far, she thought with despair. *They're gaining on me too fast*.

Her sole hope was to find an alcove where she could take at least one of the men by surprise. Her aim would have to be true; she had only enough strength for a single pass with her knife.

Memory flared through her mind, brilliant and beautiful. Daniyar had taught her how to use a knife. He'd bent one arm behind her back, his free hand holding his blade to her throat. She'd looked up into eyes like two endless wells of light and wondered how to respond. His strong hand had shifted to clasp her own, showing her how to turn his blade. He'd made her practice until she'd learned to force him to yield.

"Stay with me," she whispered to the memory, edging around the cliff face to find the shelter of an overhang. Past the overhang, the ledge jutted away. If one man went ahead to search the rest of the passage and the other remained behind, she would do her best to overthrow him.

She unsheathed her knife again.

If she couldn't kill the intruder as Daniyar had taught her, she might be able to trip him into a fall, just as Najran must have fallen. Unless the silver threads had caught at him and made him fall. She shut down the thought, waiting for the intruders to approach.

They were working methodically, scouting the path as they climbed.

Then one of them called out to the other.

The intruders had found her trail.

She shut her eyes in a moment of stark, unreasoning terror. Her palm was perspiring so heavily that her knife slipped. She adjusted her grip, her heart pounding in her ears, over the sound of footsteps moving closer.

The waiting was agony. She had to remember to keep her weight on her uninjured leg, had to remember to pivot with a single, sharp thrust to the neck.

The knife felt leaden in her hand.

Rays of sunlight splashed the cave, and now she could see the shadows of her pursuers. They loomed, large and ominous, over the ground below. A sob caught in her throat.

She couldn't see a way out of this. She couldn't think through it at all.

A murmur passed between the men. One stopped inches from her hiding place. The other followed the sharp turn of the ledge to disappear into the shadows.

A faint spark of hope worked its way into her heart. She couldn't have fought them both, but this way she stood a chance.

The man who had inched closer dropped into a crouch. His palm was spread upon the ledge. He was studying her tracks. In a moment, he would know where she was.

He moved toward her, his stride wary, checked. He didn't call the other man back.

She understood. He thought he could avoid warning her of his approach. He knew she was trapped beneath the overhang, so Arian brought up her blade.

The man edged forward with care, until he was right in front of her.

She stepped out to meet him, her knife slashing at his throat.

He met it with the ring of steel.

She was face-to-face with her pursuer, though both of them were heavily cloaked. He blocked the sweep of her blade with a thrust so powerful that it jarred her entire body, throwing her off balance. She managed to stay on her feet, swinging around and raising her blade again. The intruder met it with his sword, the strength of his lunge shattering her desperate defense.

Her leg was bleeding freely now, a stump she carried into battle as she tried to force him to give ground.

She could see nothing inside his cowl, just the gleam of his eyes. If she'd had a moment to think, she would have seen he wasn't pursuing the offensive. Each time he brought up his sword, it was to block her blow. He was patient, waiting—circling her. He had spotted her weakness; he was waiting for her to yield.

The other man sprinted back; she wanted to fall to her knees. Anything to get past the physical agony of struggling to stay on her feet. She forced herself to a last assessment of her options, the Claim locked tight in her throat, her thoughts hazing over . . .

Then everything was shifting, sweat dripping into her eyes. An unexpected advance; she struck the intruder's leg. He let out a cry, and she threw her weight forward onto her uninjured leg, her momentum toppling them both.

She fell on top of his body, pinning him beneath, while his sword lay trapped under her injured leg. She raised her blade; his hand came up to block her. Locked in a furious struggle, they rolled to the edge of the drop-off.

A grunt of pain escaped her lips as she felt her leg fold beneath her. The sound disarmed the intruder. He hesitated, and quicker than the eye could follow, she had the knife at his throat; a second more and she would have speared him.

But that second was lost to her.

Her arms were yanked behind her, her knife dropped over the ledge. The wrenching of her arm completed the break; her body seized with pain. She was lifted like a doll off the man beneath her and shoved against the cliff face, her head crashing back to the wall.

Her period of grace was over.

28

"Tell us where the First Oralist is. Tell us what harm you did her." The man Arian had pinned to the ground snarled the words in her ear. The curse was accompanied by a rough jerk on her arms, and this time she screamed in response. She was glad her hood masked her face, or they would have seen she was crying.

Then she heard a name she knew—one that should have been impossible for her to hear—as the man who had come running to the first man's rescue shouted out, "Daniyar, don't!"

Her head snapped up in shock. Time fell away, or maybe she was the one falling through a long, dark tunnel.

Other words followed, but she couldn't make sense of their meaning. The arms holding her released her, and unable to stand on her own, she faltered to her knees. As she did, her hood fell back, revealing a face wet with tears. Her hair was matted with blood. One arm hung at her side, useless, while the cloth binding her leg was soaked through with crimson, just as useless in her moment of need. Her hand wiped dust from her eyes as the stranger threw back his hood. She met agonized silver eyes in a longed-for, familiar face. Daniyar was with her again, the Black Khan's Assassin at his side.

Her perceptions shifted, her mind taken by phantoms. Why would the Assassin be in Daniyar's company? This was an illusion that had twisted in on itself, borne from the sense that she had known the Assassin, the premonitory warning that somehow he was linked to Daniyar. She wanted it to be real, but the part of her mind that was lucid knew that it couldn't be. Her anguished cry filled the silence in her mind and echoed through the cave.

Both men flinched at the sound, but how could a phantom of her mind respond to her involuntary cry? No, the men *were* real, one might even be the Assassin—but the other was a stranger who had taken Daniyar's form.

If the Assassin was real, and if his companion had assumed a guise that was beloved to her, they had come on the Black Khan's behalf. They thought her in possession of the Codex; they had followed her into the mountain to try to steal it from her. They saw her as an enemy, someone who stood in their way. But perhaps she could persuade them out of further cruelty, out of battering her to death.

"Use the sword," she said harshly.

The two men stared as if her words made little sense. She'd spoken in the language of Hira, and once she realized that, she tried the words again.

"Use the sword," she said, this time in the Common Tongue, in a voice broken by Najran's cruel magic. "Just—finish it."

The two men exchanged a glance, but her eyes were fixed on the silver sword, its gleaming edge lit by the sun. Tears slid down her face. She retreated into silence.

The Assassin knelt before her, his hand moving over the wound on her leg, but she looked away from his actions, her eyes fixed on the sword.

The sword. Daniyar's *sword. Why hadn't Daniyar come?*

"Arian."

Instead of drawing her eyes to the stranger, this tender use of her name made her cram her fist into her mouth.

The Assassin tried to touch her, to help her in some way, but her entire body shrank back, sobs escaping around her fist.

Her body began to shake.

"Move aside." Cold command in the voice of the man who was not Daniyar. Meeting her eyes while he did it, he eased her hand from her mouth.

She was shaking too much to resist him.

For a long moment, he did nothing but hold her hand, surrounding her with his warmth. His fingers stroked over the back of her hand, establishing a rhythm. After a time, her breathing quieted.

When that happened, he eased closer, and her heartbeat sped up again.

He began to speak in the dialect of Candour, a clever move that made his subterfuge complete. But who he was no longer mattered. Her eyes clung to him as if he were the north star in a world spiraling into chaos. There was no struggle for her to respond. She let his words wash over her ears, until he slid his arm behind her shoulders, preparing to take her weight.

A signal to the other man. The Assassin moved away to spread his cloak on the ground. He had found a wider space just beyond the overhang.

In a movement that sent the world spinning, the man who was not Daniyar lifted Arian with care. The hand he held tightened in his own, as she tried to break away. Daniyar was the only man she would permit to embrace her.

But he repeated his healing incantations, using her name to focus her attention. Then he set her down on the outspread cloak, careful not to jar her leg.

She wanted to react—something in his voice stayed her panic. The Assassin was on the periphery of her thoughts, but if her mind strayed to the reasons for his presence, fear would consume her entirely. Her blind terror subsided, replaced by a dull fatigue.

The pain flooded back in full force.

How fragile bone and sinew were, how capable of dishonoring the spirit that breathed them to life.

She didn't know that the man who was not Daniyar was looking over her battered frame with despair, struggling to decide which injury to attend to first.

He laid a gentle hand on her cheek, bringing her attention back to him. With utmost care, he turned her head from side to side. He frowned as a gasp of pain escaped her. His fingers probed the area around the bruise on her temple: she lost the little color she had.

He turned to look at the Assassin. "Tell me what to do."

"The wound on the leg," the Assassin answered. "You need to stop the bleeding."

The Assassin's metallic voice gave Arian the impetus to try to move away. The hand on her arm did not stop her, and intuiting the reason for her panic, Daniyar sent the Assassin to search for a source of water.

When he was gone, Daniyar used the light pressure of his hand to halt her incipient flight.

"You will injure yourself, jaan." She froze at the term of affection, at the sound of the voice that uttered it. Questions filled her mind, but pain gave her no room to pursue them. She lay back on the cloak, conscious of the breadth of the shoulders looming above her, the strength in the arms that could break her if they chose, the eyes that gleamed brighter than the stars that shimmered over the dunes.

"I failed," she whispered, though she didn't know why she spoke the language of the Damson Vale. "I failed at everything I tried."

"No." A soft rebuttal underscored by faith. This man, whoever he was, believed in her. She felt his hands move over her body and shuddered at his touch. Had she killed Najran in the cavern below? Or had he crawled back to life and used his sorcery to weaken her mind? As her teeth began to chatter, the man who was not Daniyar drew away from her, concerned.

"I seek to check you for damage, Arian."

She didn't answer, squeezing her eyes closed as she felt his hands resume their exploration. They stilled on the arm that hung limp at her side, moved over the bruises on her torso, then turned to unwrap the bandage on her thigh.

He exhaled sharply at the sight of the wound.

"Arian," he called. Her eyes remained closed. His grip on her face tightened, and her eyes flew open. Shadows within shadows, but no answers.

"I need to cut your clothing away. The wound must be cleaned before it can be bound."

"No!" she cried, and it sounded so loudly in the emptiness of the cavern that the Assassin came running.

"What's wrong?"

The two men spoke in a rapid undertone. Arian was holding on, but just barely, trying to protect herself from the threat she sensed was coming. She was powerless to stop the stranger from taking her in his arms, this time following the Assassin across the ledge to the far side of the cavern.

"Here." The Assassin's voice was disembodied. It floated to Arian from a hollow behind the wall. The cracked stone of the cavern split apart. Water slipped over the fissure, glittering in the light.

The man who was not Daniyar set her down on her feet. The Assassin moved to stand behind her; she would have fled if she could have overcome the pain that gripped her body, but she was trapped between the two men.

"What are you doing?" she asked, a thin whisper of sound.

If they heard her, no one replied. Again the two men spoke, their voices too low for her to catch. And then the stranger's hands were on her shoulders.

"Look at me." The compulsion in his tone made it impossible to disobey. But even as her eyes met his, she was conscious of the threat behind her.

"Don't touch me—" she began, then there was blinding pain. The Assassin wrenched her arm. He shoved her forward with such force that her head collided with the stranger's shoulder.

The pain was so sudden, so unexpected, that she didn't cry out. She fell limply into the stranger's arms, and when the mist over her thoughts cleared, she understood that he was bearing her weight in his arms.

She tried to look up at him. Unable to raise her head, her forehead pressed to his breastbone. The scent of him was Daniyar's.

"Why?" she wept, her tears sliding down his skin.

"Forgive me, jaan." He cradled her head against his shoulder, letting her see his eyes. "Your shoulder was out of joint. That's why you couldn't feel your arm."

"You hurt me," she whispered. "Daniyar wouldn't hurt me."

She closed her eyes again, telling herself she didn't see the sheen of moisture in his eyes.

"Hasbah."

The Assassin laid out his cloak, this time near the waterfall. A series of images passed through Arian's mind, of the time she had spent with Daniyar at the Library of Candour. The memories hurt, so she pushed them from her mind, trying to soothe herself with a murmur of the Claim, a murmur that punished her throat. Her shoulder pulsed with pain, but true to the stranger's word, sensation was returning to her arm.

She was laid down on the cloak again, but she tangled her fingers in the opening of his armor to prevent him from leaving her with the Assassin. Her torn nails scraped his chest, and he winced. His hand came up to cover hers.

"Don't—don't—" She couldn't find the words for what she wanted to say, but he seemed to know. He nodded at the Assassin. "Leave us."

He brought his face close to hers and kissed her brow. His lips were soft against her bruised skin, but all she could see was the determination in his eyes. Then he pulled away the remnants of her shirt.

"Forgive me, love, but I must."

She shoved at his hands with her own.

"Don't fight me, Arian. I'm trying not to hurt you."

"Who *are* you?" He smelled of pomegranate and wild mint. His hair was dark as nightfall and his eyes—his eyes were a shimmering silver-blue that could have been the waterfall's reflection. She'd seen that color before, only once. What if it *was* Daniyar? Daniyar, who touched her so gently, who tended her with such care. Who bathed the grime from her skin before he dressed her.

Moments passed, the silence broken by the rustle of the stranger's clothing as he moved over her, his hair sliding like the muted rush of silk on her skin. She let him tend her, thinking of Daniyar.

"I would have given him what he wanted," she said at last.

The silver eyes pierced her. "Who?"

"My lord Daniyar. I swore that if we found each other again, I would give him anything he asked for. I would hold no loyalty higher than my loyalty to him."

The hands that were tending her stilled, a frown marring the pristine beauty of his face. His head lowered until his lips brushed her ear. She shivered at the touch.

"Don't you know me, jaan? I'm here with you, Arian."

The tension drained from her limbs. So many words struggled for expression on her tongue that she could utter none of them. She knew that the stranger had wrapped her in a cloak, but the pain in her shoulder meant she couldn't draw it up.

"I'm cold," she said. And then after a moment's consideration, when the stranger had wrapped the cloak around her and pulled her into his embrace, she added, "I need water."

He reached for a flask in his pack. He brought it to her lips.

Her thoughts drifted. Two warm hands slid firmly to her back. She stiffened at once, but when the hands didn't move, the tension eased from her spine.

The stranger was speaking, telling her something. His deep voice was pleasing, so she closed her eyes to listen. He'd called her jaan, she remembered. And as her thoughts continued to drift, she realized that once he had called her the heart of his heart.

Her misgivings began to fade under the warmth of his hands, the deep voice speaking healing words. Or was he reciting the Claim? No, these were words of praise, of encouragement. She let the words wash over her, let herself believe it was Daniyar who wrapped her in the shelter of his voice.

He was looking at her again, and now he ventured more, a careful hand smoothing the hair back from her forehead in a gesture that promised absolution if she could just hold on to it.

His eyes met hers, a shimmer of silver fire, and she let him take her in his arms, let him cradle her, while her hand reached up to touch his beard.

He didn't stop her, just leaned closer to reassure her. She stroked him, telling him of her love. A teardrop seared her skin; her fingers traced the moisture on his cheek.

"Why?" she asked simply.

A low growl from his throat. "Because I let this happen. My pride mattered more than your welfare. I let you go and now—"

Because he sounded so wounded, she turned her cheek into his chest, pressing her face against his heart. "And now?"

Hard hands caressed her hair, tilted her face up, looked deep into eyes whose thoughtful clarity had dimmed.

"And now you don't know me, do you, Arian? You don't trust that it's me."

The strength of his pain hurt her—she felt its echo in her bones—but she was half-asleep, her thoughts confused and mercurial.

"Kiss me and I'll know."

Her words were light, teasing.

"Arian—"

She chided him with a soft look. "Daniyar would kiss me." She looked down at herself covered in the stranger's cloak, her body sprawled in his lap, her hands trespassing into intimacy, as she petted his beard. She nuzzled his chest with her face.

"You feel like Daniyar, smell like him—do you taste like him, I wonder?"

Another growl in response. But he didn't give her what she wanted, not even when her fingers played lightly over his lips.

"What's taking so long?" The arms holding her had tightened to bands of steel.

The stranger muttered to himself. "I can't take advantage of you when you don't know who I am."

Rueful laughter as her body stirred in his arms. "You *must* be Daniyar. Only he would scruple so with a willing woman in his arms." She turned her face into the hand stroking her hair and kissed his palm. When she looked up at him, her eyes were clear.

"I knew you would come, Daniyar."

And then shadows claimed her as her voice trailed off at last.

The Assassin returned to find her curled up in Daniyar's embrace, her limbs heavy with sleep. Daniyar shook his head at the other man, a dark resolve in his eyes.

"Keep this to yourself. Don't ever divulge that you saw her in this state."

The Assassin fingered the lace of his gloves, winding its loose ends in a pattern.

"What makes you think I could harm her?" Before Daniyar could stop him, the Assassin bent down to kiss Arian's forehead. "I would be harming my own."

29

ARIAN WOKE TO FIND HERSELF HELD IN THE STRANGER'S ARMS, HIS chest a hard wall behind her, his hair brushing her neck. Though her arm still throbbed and a hot band of pain was wrapped around her thigh, her thoughts were lucid and focused, conscious of where she was.

When the Assassin ventured into view, bearing a bowl of food he must have prepared, her memory of his dark presence was clear. Not so the stranger. She struggled out of the stranger's hold so she could turn to see his face. Sleepy silver eyes stared back at her, his hold tightened, and she was tugged without ceremony back into his lap.

"Who am I?" he asked softly.

She blinked. "My lord, the Silver Mage, the Guardian of Candour."

His eyes narrowed in warning so she added with an uncertain smile, "Daniyar, whose love for me defies all explanation."

Shifting her in his arms, he tilted up her chin. "*Now* I'm going to kiss you as you asked."

He seized her mouth with a raw male hunger that stole the

breath from her lungs. She kissed him back with wrenching need, sinking into the hard lines of his body, her hands sweeping over the muscled arch of his back.

The Assassin cleared his throat.

His eyes met Daniyar's over Arian's head. Daniyar grimaced.

"Not that I'm not happy"—a protest from Daniyar and she changed it to—"*overjoyed* to see you, but the pair of you make for an unlikely source of rescue." And then finding her rhythm as First Oralist, she remembered where they must have come from and demanded of Daniyar, "Ashfall—what's happened to Ashfall? Has the city fallen?"

"The siege was ongoing when we left."

"Then how were you able to leave?" Another thought struck her, and she added, "How did you find my trail?"

Daniyar kissed her temple. "Questions for another time. First you will tell me what happened to you in this cavern. Who dared attack the First Oralist?"

Arian shivered under the impact of those eyes. "You didn't find him in the tunnels or in the cavern below?"

Both men frowned at her now. "Who?"

"His name is Najran." A lick of fear as she thought of how he'd locked her voice in her throat, of how, even now, she felt the residual pain. "He's a commander of the Nineteen."

At her tremor of fear, Daniyar coaxed her back against his chest, his other hand raising a flask to her lips. She recognized the engraving on its surface. Her wide eyes flew to his.

"Khashayar?"

"Safe at his Khan's side. We passed him in the tunnels beneath Qaysarieh. He gave us word on the road you had taken; Hasbah did the rest. Now drink."

He made her drink until the flask was empty, his eyes on her face, his hand rough yet indescribably gentle as he angled her jaw to make drinking from the flask easier. Only when she finished did he ask her to tell him more.

Gathering herself, she described the time that had passed and the events that had led her to the Jabal Thawr. As she spoke, she became aware that despite his close attention, Daniyar was pressing kisses to her hair, possessiveness in every breath. She pushed at his chest to gain some distance, aware of the Assassin watching them.

"Daniyar."

He raised her hand and brushed a kiss over her palm, defeating her efforts at propriety.

"You swore an oath to me," he reminded her. "You hold no loyalty higher than your loyalty to me."

The words broke something open in her mind. She caught his hand in her own, staying him. It was like holding back the leap of a leopard with the gentle breath of a sigh.

"I didn't imagine it? You were here?"

The throbbing ache in her shoulder renewed; pain grayed the color of her irises. His strong hand massaged the ache.

"I didn't mean to hurt you, my love."

The Assassin placed the bowl at her elbow. "There's medicine in it. It will ease her discomfort and hasten the healing of her wounds."

Though her position in Daniyar's lap was hardly befitting her dignity as a Companion of Hira, Arian straightened her shoulders. "Don't speak of me as if I'm not here. I can hear you perfectly well."

There was no change in the Assassin's expression, but how could there be? He was wearing the steel mask, horizontal lines of script moving from right to left across his face. It bothered her, so she said, "Why don't you take off the mask?"

"Why don't you speak of Najran?" he said in return. "How did he rob you of the Claim?"

Hasbah knelt in front of Arian, the aura of menace about him not dimmed by Daniyar's sanction of his escort. A frisson of Arian's fear transmitted itself to Daniyar. He shifted her body farther over his lap, angling his own so that he was positioned between Arian and the Assassin.

"Careful," he warned the other man.

"What must I do to prove to you that I would never harm her?" A sigh escaped from behind the mask. The Assassin moved back a little. "We'll need to know the answer if he's still on Arian's trail."

Arian paled, surprised that Daniyar chose not to rebuke the Assassin's familiarity. "You didn't find his body below? I thought— I thought I killed him."

The Assassin jumped to his feet, the movement so fluid it frightened her. He moved like mist . . . like smoke . . . like danger she couldn't see until the knife was at the wound.

"Shhh." Daniyar dropped his voice, gentling her. It only served to make her angry.

"I'm far from helpless," she informed him.

She felt his smile against her cheek. "Then for my sake, indulge me. I spent the night cleaning the blood from your skin." She had wanted intimacy with Daniyar—craved it—but not this kind, not with him seeing her maddened or helpless. When she would have raised a protest, he silenced it with his kiss. She touched the lines of strain beside his mouth and thought of his suffering at the Ark.

"You have bound yourself to someone who brings you nothing but torment."

Another kiss, this one hard with demand. Then he offered her a verse of poetry: "*'She is a refuge and a haunt for beauty.'* She could ask everything I have, I would find more to give."

The Assassin paced the length of the ledge, his eyes searching the area below.

"How will we recognize this Najran?"

She tried to struggle to her feet to show him, but Daniyar held her fast.

"Describe him for us, instead." His snarl was for the Assassin, and Arian was hard-pressed not to laugh. So much for her illusion of endless suffering—she was safe, she was loved, and soon she would be whole. She relaxed into Daniyar's embrace, savoring the warmth of his body. His tension eased, he cushioned her against his chest.

Quashing her traitorous desires, Arian described Najran. When she came to the jeweled daggers and the spike-tipped glaive, the Assassin's head whipped around.

"I found no trace of those weapons below."

Daniyar rose to his feet, cradling Arian in his arms, refusing to allow her to test her weight on her injured leg.

"You know him by another name," he said to Hasbah, guessing at the truth from the Assassin's voice.

The Assassin nodded, unsheathing the dagger at his waist, his eyes making a sweep of the secret corners of the cavern. "You may know him as well. They call him the Iron Glaive. In the Rub Al Khali, he is known as the Angel of Blood, in the Aryaward as the Bone Shadow. His particular gift is death."

Arian slipped free of Daniyar's hold to lean back against his chest and brace her leg against his. "Some might say the same of you."

A flicker of something behind the Assassin's mask.

"I do not kill without purpose." A subtle shift of his shoulders to indicate Daniyar. "And I know the meaning of loyalty."

"Tell her who you are." Daniyar's hands were firm on Arian's shoulders. "I won't keep secrets for you."

The Assassin's eyes continued to search the shadows. He

shook his head in warning. "It would weaken her further—the Iron Glaive isn't dead. We would have found his weapons or his body if he were."

"I may have pushed him from the ledge," Arian said. "Something distracted his attention, something that gave me an opening."

They heard the sound at the same time, a scurrying of small creatures across the ground. Arian rubbed at her shoulder.

"They won't harm you," she said, letting Daniyar take more of her weight. "The silver threads that float through the Jabal Thawr—they're cobwebs. This cave is full of spiders."

She said it absently, not taking in the import of her words.

"We know."

She caught the edge of wonder in Daniyar's voice. She turned fully into his arms.

"*How* did you know where to find me? Why the entrance to this cavern instead of any of the others? The Jabal Thawr is riddled with openings."

The Assassin unwound the laces from his gloves. In the sunlight striking off the waterfall, the laces glimmered like netting. Akin to the silver threads she had found drifting through the cavern. She stared at them, perplexed. Thinking that it *couldn't* be.

Daniyar's voice was gentle in her ear. "This was the only cavern whose entrance was wholly sealed."

"Then how did you know to search it?"

The Assassin completed a complex gesture with the silver laces from his gloves. "A spiderweb covered the entrance to this cave, as well as the path that led to you, the pattern so complex, it would have taken weeks to weave. It's clear now that the web was woven as a protection for you, should the Iron Glaive return. If he lost track of these tunnels, he wouldn't have searched a place where a web was undisturbed."

A note of wonder in her voice, Arian said, "But *you* thought to search here."

"Because I read it as a sign," Daniyar said. "From a creature of the Claim."

As was Daniyar's gift.

And now the spinning of the web sharpened the recollection of the story Arian's mother had told her as a child: the story of the web spun to protect the Messenger of the Claim, who—accompanied by a trusted companion—had fled the pursuit of enemies to the safety of Jabal Thawr. A place their enemies had left undisturbed because of a flawless web, finely and intricately wrought.

"Is this a hallowed place?"

"Did you recite the Claim in your battle against Najran?"

He must have known that she'd done so, but Arian nodded to confirm it.

"For as long as I was able to." Her fingers briefly traced the bruising at her throat. "Najran found a way to silence me. That's how he was able to defeat me."

"*Defeat* you?" The Assassin wound the silver thread of his laces around one of Arian's wrists. "But *you* are here and the Iron Glaive is nowhere to be seen."

Arian tested the strength of the laces with her unadorned hand. She couldn't explain Najran's disappearance; all she could offer the Assassin was the truth.

"I don't know how I survived."

His ornate mask dipped toward her.

"Don't you? *You* are a child of Hira . . . a cherished child of the Claim. Like the one who came before you, *you* invoked the protection of the creature who wove this web."

30

As if the Assassin's illumination of Arian's connection to the Messenger of the Claim had unlocked the power within her, it surged up in Arian's veins to wrap fierce hands around her heart. It spilled from her lips without effort, the obstruction that had silenced her against Najran gone as if it hadn't existed. A verse came to her thoughts, then to her lips, memory beating like a gong. She was in her parents' scriptorium, her mother reciting the verse, her family helping her practice until her recitation was perfect.

"The likeness of those who take to themselves protectors other than the One is that of the spider who builds a house."

The aura that surrounded the Assassin lightened. His voice as calm as hers was rich with emotion, he offered, *"But the most fragile of houses is the spider's house, if they only knew."*

Through the shining mask, the Assassin's eyes held hers. Her heart pounded in her ears.

"But not in your case, First Oralist . . . as your protector is the One."

Through stiff lips she asked him, "How could you know that verse? How could you know it as the answer to the other?"

Her memories unraveling, she gave him no chance to reply. "My mother taught me those verses. I was a child in my parents' scriptorium when . . ."

Her voice faltered. Daniyar slipped one arm around her waist. His free hand closed over hers, their fingers threaded together.

The Assassin tipped his head forward; the act gave nothing away. The mask he wore shifted, its script flaring to life in the shimmering reflection of the waterfall. The script she hadn't been able to read transformed into words that were secret and familiar.

"Do not grieve, for surely the One is with us."

She whispered the words in the High Tongue, the language of the Claim. But pronounced in the accents of her family's scriptorium, a singular beauty in the words.

The Assassin answered her again. She could hear the note of learning in his voice. The note of *teaching,* infused with soft reassurance.

"What could happen to two when the One is with them as a third?"

Arian gasped in recognition. The Assassin had quoted the epilogue of the legend of the Cave of Thawr—the story her mother had told her. A story she'd never heard elsewhere.

Arian pushed away from Daniyar, settling her weight on the leg that could bear it. She lurched forward a single step. The Assassin held his ground. Her hands uncertain, she reached for his mask and tilted it down so she could read the letter on his forehead. The open bowl with the diacritical mark pinned above it like a dot.

ن

Nun.
Inkwell.

The name of her parents' scriptorium.

She staggered back and Daniyar caught her, her shock a painful echo of his discoveries the night before.

"Tell her," he said grimly.

The Assassin pulled off his mask. He stepped from his place of hiding. Fingers of rich gold light stroked his face, throwing into relief a network of raised scars that burned in shades of amber, a map of fire made flesh. A mask of incessant agony that should have disfigured him beyond recognition, but what she beheld was the echo of a man she'd once known, his scars gentled by the curve of his mouth, by the soft green sea of his eyes.

Her nails marked Daniyar's palms. She let him take her weight, unable to pretend a moment longer that she was the unconquerable First Oralist.

"I watched them kill you." Words torn from her heart. "I saw you cleaved by the blade."

For answer, the Assassin ripped off his breastplate and dropped it beside his laces. He pulled open the shirt he wore beneath it, showing Arian the scar.

It ran down the center of his torso, raised and raw, an angry arrow that pointed to his navel. On either side of it was a tracery of scars as brutal as those that marred his face.

"I swear by the galaxies revolving their courses. By the night as it recedes, and by the morning as it breathes."

The Assassin's words were an oath, a promise that he spoke the truth.

Daniyar confirmed it with his gifts as Authenticate. *"The speech of a noble messenger."*

Arian stared at him blankly, then she began to cry, shuddering sobs that tore through her frame with the force of a desert storm.

"Arian . . ." With Daniyar unable to console her, the Assassin tried again. "First Oralist . . ."

She launched herself at him, flinging her arms around his neck. "If you are truly my brother, call me by my name!"

Puzzled . . . reluctant . . . bewildered, Hasbah's arms came up to bear her weight.

"Why couldn't I read your mask before this?" A broken murmur sobbed into his neck.

"You didn't want to, little sister. You were protecting yourself at Ashfall—a natural instinct, perhaps."

"Where *were* you, Hudayfah? Where have you been all these years?"

He didn't answer. He'd warned the Silver Mage there were secrets he wouldn't share, secrets that spoke to the fate of his house, to the years he'd spent seeking to learn why Inkwell had been designated for destruction. He'd found his answer by stealing into the Citadel to gain access to the Khorasan Archives, Hira's treasury of manuscripts. The archives spoke of the schooling he and his sisters had received from their parents, scholars of the Claim who were once renowned throughout their lands for their learning.

And therefore, a threat to the One-Eyed Preacher, who'd struck first and struck hard, not knowing that Hasbah had survived or that Arian had been delivered to the Council. Until Arian had taken his war back to him, fighting the Preacher on his own ground with the Claim spilling forth from her lips.

Then the Preacher had learned of his mistake: the daughter of the scholars of Inkwell had survived to become the First Oralist, more gifted in the Claim than any who had come before her, more dangerous to the Preacher than any other enemy he faced.

The secret of Arian's survival, and of her growing power, had been kept for that very reason, a reason Hasbah accepted as the price of his sister's security. He'd learned of it himself only by chance, the first time he'd stolen into the Citadel to visit his family's graves. For within the cool stone walls of the mausoleum erected to honor his family, the graves of his parents were as closely entwined as his parents had been in life, but of his sisters' passing there was no sign, nor any marker to honor their names.

He'd stumbled from the darkness of stone to the warmth of Hira's gardens. How long he'd stood under the shelter of the trees, his head bowed in thought, his mind preoccupied with questions, he couldn't say. Long enough to hear the Companions recite their morning prayers. And from their recitation, one voice had soared above the rest, pure, distinctive, clear.

Hearing it, his head had jerked up.

He'd slipped deeper into the shadows of the surrounding arcades.

And then he'd seen the novice and recognized her face at once.

A young Companion of Hira whose voice resounded with the Claim, stronger now, but just as rich as when Arian had spoken as a child.

A thousand thoughts rushed to the surface of his mind, but he brought himself to order with the discipline of an Assassin.

His sister was hidden at Hira.

And at the Citadel of Hira, she was safe.

That was his only thought then. To leave her to her peace. To keep all knowledge of her from the One-Eyed Preacher by directing the Preacher's attention to the threat posed by Ashfall or to the subtle maneuvers of the fortress of the Assassins.

When Arian's decision to confront the Talisman's slave-chains had made her abilities known, and her identity had come to light, that choice was taken from him. Even then, Hasbah had remained in the shadows, where his concerns were best served. The strike *he* made in response to the Talisman's war against his family would be made from the Black Khan's side, with the Zhayedan at his back. A strike he was poised to make because of the secrets he'd kept.

Raised in a court of intrigue, the Black Khan would not have tolerated a hint of his divided loyalty. He would have suspected Hasbah of conspiring with Hira through his connection to Arian. And as for Arian herself—her calling to Hira was such that she may have betrayed Hasbah's identity if she deemed that doing so would serve the Council's aims. He'd chosen not to take that risk. To lose the place at the Black Khan's side that he'd worked for or to be used as a pawn in the game between Hira and Ashfall—that would not be his fate. He had kept his counsel and his silence, paying the price of his loss.

He said nothing of this to Arian now, who pulled back to look at him, as if with the depths of her gaze, she could penetrate his secrets.

"You won't tell me why you waited so long to come to me?"

"It wouldn't serve you now."

He tried to set Arian away from him, but she grasped the edges of his linen, her nails curled into her palms.

Her voice was flat with the sum of her losses when she looked at him again. "Will you renounce me like Lania did? Is that why you hid the truth? Perhaps you didn't *want* to claim me because you blamed me for all you had suffered."

It wasn't true. So he gave Arian what he could.

"I would never hurt you." The soft words echoed the promise he'd made to the Silver Mage the night before. He picked up his mask. "I sent you a gift, little sister. Before you embarked on your Audacy, I sent you a gift as proof that you have never left my thoughts."

"I received no such gift."

His fingers played with his mask, his eyes gentle on her face.

"I sent it to Hira with the Black Khan. He called it *his* gift, perhaps, but I was the one who sent you a manuscript that recorded the history of our family."

Hasbah had searched for the manuscript for years, following rumors that it had survived the burning of his family's scriptorium. He'd hunted many Talisman on its trail, but when he'd found the manuscript displayed as a desecrated trophy in the home of a Talisman commander, he hadn't traded for it: he'd killed for it.

Then he'd taken the time and care necessary to restore it before sending it to Arian. Perhaps even then, some part of him had wanted her to know he'd survived.

Arian looked to Daniyar. He read the subtle signs that she sought Daniyar's confirmation that he was still speaking the truth. When he nodded, she took hold of Hasbah's hand.

"You sent the manuscript with the Black Khan—does *he* know who you are?"

He shook his head. "Consider, Arian. Your allegiance is to Hira, mine to the Black Khan. They may be allies of a kind, but they are also rivals."

She drew a shaky breath that it pained him to hear. But she gathered her composure, considering what he'd revealed with the discernment of the First Oralist.

"Then why choose to tell me now?"

His hand reached out with unaccustomed tenderness to stroke a tendril of her hair. "You had need of me, I came. You were losing hope, I gave you something to believe in. You had no reason to trust me . . . I offered one." He hesitated, knowing he'd placed his fate in her hands. "Assassins work best from the shadows. May I ask that you leave me there?"

He'd been right to be wary of her perception—she was shaking her head, still scrutinizing his motives.

"What you have with Rukh isn't feigned. You *are* loyal to him. It would aid me to know why."

He couldn't tell her . . . He *wouldn't*. That was his to keep, the memory of a man who'd stayed by his side during his recovery from the Talisman assault, when all he'd been able to measure was the depth of his unending loss.

His rescue from the ruins of Inkwell had been effected by the Shah, who had taken Hasbah under his wing and treated him to the care of his physicians. The Shah had overseen his progress, indulging him with a benevolence that Hasbah couldn't comprehend. Hasbah had trained with his soldiers, and then he'd been sent to the Eagle's Nest, to study with the Assassins.

"If you desire to strike against those who brought about the downfall of your house, learn the secrets of this sect," the Shah had urged him.

Hasbah had mastered those secrets, rising to the rank of Assassin, transforming the sect into something deadlier, until he was both leader and founder. He'd tried to repay the Shah by putting his new skills at his guardian's disposal. Instead, he'd been asked to pledge his loyalty to the Shah's son who was still in his minority. Hasbah had given his word . . . swearing to serve a boy named Rukh.

When Hasbah had asked Rukh's father—for the Shah was the Khan of Khorasan—why he'd chosen to rescue him, he'd finally learned the reasons behind the Shah's indulgence.

"When I began to collect manuscripts, I asked for your father's assistance. Ashfall's scriptorium owes its foundation to him. Your father refused to accept payment for his work; he considered the sharing of knowledge his duty. To thank him, I assigned soldiers to guard his house—an action I undertook too late. My soldiers found you in the ruins of your home. By rescu-

ing you, I repaid the debt I owed your father, but if your wish is still to serve me, pledge yourself to my son. If Rukh should come to have need of you—"

"I will serve as his strong right arm."

On his deathbed, the Shah of Khorasan had smiled. "My son already has the loyalty of one who stands in that position. You will be his Assassin, assisting him from the shadows."

"I swear it to you, Great Khan."

The oath Hasbah had sworn honored the link between his father and the Shah. A link given life by Ashfall's scriptorium, the beating heart of the city, where his presence was still urgently required.

But for the moment, he focused on Arian, who was saying, "I should have read the manuscript you sent—I should have made sense of your gift, I should have *known*."

But how could she have? When he'd kept his secret for her sake and his own?

The scar tissue around his lips distorted his grimace as he counted that cost now. Arian's pain at witnessing it made him slip the mask back on.

"There's no blame in this, little sister. We met when the time was right for us to know each other again."

And when she still looked unconvinced, he murmured a verse of the Claim. *"Nothing can ever befall us except what the One has ordained."*

He forced himself to accept her touch when she raised a hand to his mask, her voice weighted with her unanswered questions. "Whatever your reasons for keeping your secrets, I'm glad you came to me now."

His face frozen behind the mask at her unexpected generosity; he prayed no action of his would cause her to change her mind.

31

SINNIA WASN'T EXPECTING TO FIND SHIPS AMASSED ON THE NORTHERN shore, their vast sails still and silent in the utter absence of wind. She counted a dozen vessels, each with a complement of more than a hundred men. Some of those men were drawn from the tribes of the Rub Al Khali, others from the fishermen who made their livelihood at the Sea of Reeds. Black men, brown men, men from cultures and tribes whose ancestors had intermarried. Some held their traditions separate; others had merged together as evidenced by their dress or by their tribal markings.

This was something common to Sinnia's lands, particularly in the aftermath of the Great Forgetting, when the north and south had given up their rivalry for the sake of a common peace. A hundred different traditions were represented in the lands of the Negus; all were welcome at his court. But the presence of the men at the Sea of Reeds didn't bode well for their crossing, especially since the ships were warships commanded by the Nineteen.

Rim-Sarah led them to a Bani Shira'a oasis, thickly sheltered by palms. The Sandrider had been greeted with cries of delight by children who crowded around the sandsail, before offering their hospitality, which proved generous in the extreme. Their party was plied with food and drink, Wafa indulged as a child of the tribe. Sinnia left him in the care of the Bani Shira'a, while she and Rim-Sarah found a secluded spot on higher ground to spy on the Nineteen's flotilla. Her teeth sank into her lower lip. Her people were a seafaring people—did they know about the ships? Were they ready to defend their port? She didn't think the Nineteen planned to cross into the open waters of the Aryaward. They were headed to the southern shore, and what they wanted there, it wasn't difficult to guess.

Two days and a night had passed. She'd had no news of Arian, though she'd felt a kind of rupture when she tried to use the Claim. It made her worry for Arian's safety, but she knew without the sandsail to transport her, it would take Arian at least an extra day to reach the Sea of Reeds. In the meantime, Sinnia had found a boat to take them across to Axum, though its departure point was worryingly close to the ships of the Rising Nineteen.

One problem at a time.

A commotion from the oasis drew her attention to the grove. The children had gathered around two riders. Sinnia's heart began to race. She tugged at Rim-Sarah's elbow, and the two of them climbed down from their hiding place to run back to the grove.

She came to a sudden stop as she found herself staring at a black-cloaked man whose face was covered by a mask—the *steel* mask of the Assassin.

Sinnia's hand moved to the whip at her waist. He jerked his head in response. Following the movement, she found Arian in the center of a group of children, Wafa's arms around her waist. And standing beside Arian, the sun casting shadows on the sculpted lines of his face, none other than the Silver Mage.

Her bones settled, satisfaction easing out in a sigh. But when she took a closer look at Arian, her sense of relief disappeared. There was a bruise on Arian's temple, her right leg was heavily bandaged, and she carried her body stiffly, easing from the children's grasp.

Quick courtesies observed, Sinnia led them to a private tent with flaps that were open to the breeze. Terse explanations were offered while the Assassin stood guard. When Sinnia had heard what was necessary of the battle at Ashfall, and of Najran's attack, she told them of the Nineteen's flotilla. "We should slip away in the dark, if you are well enough to travel."

Her glance at Arian was doubtful, though Arian had ridden to the oasis with horses the Assassin had procured.

"Daniyar tended me with Marakand loess. The rest will heal in time." With slow, precise sentences, she explained about the Assassin and finished by telling Sinnia, "He stitched up my wounds with the netting from his gloves." Wonder in her voice, she stared at her brother's back, Sinnia silent at the import of revelation. For here was another child of the Nun scriptorium. What use might he make of the Claim?

But no. The thought secretly defiant. *Only women serve as Companions.*

Rim-Sarah hesitated at the entrance to their tent, carrying a wooden tray filled with tiny cups of coffee.

"Let her pass." Sinnia gave the order, but the Assassin waited for Arian to confirm it. He watched while the others took their cups with thanks, declining a cup for himself. His steel mask dipped at Daniyar. "I should take a look at those ships."

Daniyar swallowed his coffee. Rim-Sarah passed him another tiny cup, her eyes entranced on his face. He drank the second cup as well, nodding to the Assassin. "I'll stand guard. Watch for the Iron Glaive."

By the time a meal was served to them and consumed, the Assassin had returned.

"What's the matter?" Some undiscerned ability must have linked Arian to her brother, because his cold steel mask gave nothing away of his thoughts.

"A night crossing won't guarantee your safety. The Nineteen have set up minzars on their decks. They'll sweep the sea, inspect every boat. There's also a moon tonight."

Sinnia set down her cup. "The Nineteen don't own these shores. They don't own the Sea of Reeds."

The Assassin's response was blunt. "You've been away too long." His head swiveled to face Daniyar.

Daniyar rose to his feet. "You have a plan."

"We burn their ships. We offer a distraction that allows the Companions to cross."

"No!" Arian struggled to her feet. Daniyar eased her back down with a frown.

"Rest, Arian. There's nothing to worry about." He turned to Sinnia. "Is your boat ready?"

"Yes, but how can two men disable a dozen ships? They'll capture you, my lord. Capture you and kill you."

Sinnia saw Arian's lips tremble in protest, and she reached down to help her up. Whatever decisions they made, Arian's voice would be heard. She looped Arian's arm around her shoulders, taking half her weight.

The Assassin interjected. "I have two men at the shore."

A hard look from Daniyar. "Assassins?"

The steel mask dipped in acknowledgment.

"Your men are everywhere, it seems."

"It's a foolish man who waits for the hammer of oblivion to fall."

Daniyar didn't argue.

"We can manage a strike at a handful of ships—that should be enough to distract them. Hasbah and I will follow you, once the strike is complete."

"My men will burn them all." It wasn't a boast. It was a reflection of Hasbah's certainty of his skill and his confidence in his Assassins. "But I won't be crossing the sea." An impatient gesture of his shoulders, a rare giveaway from a man who made no unnecessary movements. "The Black Khan awaits me in Ashfall; I've left matters there unattended."

Sinnia gasped at this. The Assassin intended to circumvent the Nineteen's army *again*.

"Will you stay and assist me?" The Assassin put the question to Daniyar, who nodded at once, though at Arian's murmur of protest, he leaned over to murmur in her ear.

"The Sana Codex is paramount; our time is running out. I won't be far behind you, but the decision is yours. If you want me with you, Hasbah must manage on his own."

But the Assassin wouldn't have asked for Daniyar's aid unless he needed it, so Arian made the only choice she could.

"It won't be dark for another hour. Make your preparations, then come and say good-bye. I'll take the time to rest." She let Sinnia help her back down onto the cushions, closing her eyes against her need. The Sana Codex *was* paramount. What she wanted would have to wait.

She was alone and asleep on the cushions when Daniyar returned to wake her, while Hasbah waited outside. She looked into Daniyar's eyes, at the haunting precision of his beauty, and couldn't find it within her to offer him words of farewell. He was honoring her choices, taking to heart the words she had flung at him in Ashfall's throne room.

Love me for who I am, or your love means nothing at all.

He had found her at her lowest point in the cave of Jabal Thawr. Yet he still believed she possessed the resolve to see her Audacy through. He'd accepted her duty as First Oralist, just as she had demanded.

He trusted her. Now she would have to trust herself.

He enfolded her in his cloak as he kissed her cheeks, her temples, her lips.

"Try not to stop my heart again."

"I could say the same to you."

He cupped her head in one hand, caressing the black silk of her hair.

"I'll find you in Axum. And if not in Axum, then on the road to Timeback."

She nodded. "I'll be waiting."

She meant it as a vow, and she saw from the sudden joy in his eyes that he'd understood.

She glanced over his shoulder to make a request of her brother. "You'll take care that he comes to no harm?"

The Assassin bowed in what was becoming a familiar gesture. "Utmost care." An odd hesitation. "I know what he is to you."

"The gift you gave me was priceless." A glance at Daniyar, who refused to relax his hold. Another thought occurred to her, and she voiced it. "Why does the Black Khan call you Hasbah? Do you not trust him with your name?"

Hudayfah's eyes gleamed through the slits in the mask.

"The Khan has a sense of history. He means it as an homage

to Hassan Sabah, the founder of the Assassins. I didn't give him my name because our names—yours, mine, Lania's—are too dangerous for others to know. Our family was targeted for a reason—the One-Eyed Preacher conjectured that our power would rise."

Confused, Arian said, "That power is not through blood. There is no hereditary gift."

Her brother nodded. Arian sensed he was pleased. "The gift was in our training, in the years we spent at Nun, in the teachers we learned from. You are correct, Arian. Our aptitude with the Claim does not depend on blood."

"Because it comes from love." At this reminder of their parents, Hudayfah clasped her hand again. He might have said more, but Arian was distracted by Sinnia's reappearance.

Sinnia gave them a jaunty grin, excitement coloring her voice at the thought of almost being home. "The boat is ready. We can be on our way when you choose."

The Assassin gestured at Wafa, wedged at Sinnia's side. "Keep the boy safe."

Arian followed his gaze. She knew the Assassin terrified him; he was counting the minutes until Hudayfah was on his way.

But she caught some other meaning beneath her brother's words.

"Why?" she asked again.

He glanced at Daniyar, then shrugged.

"I sense something in the boy that transcends his attachment to you." He paused, thinking. "Or perhaps it is because of his attachment to *both* Companions of Hira." Another cryptic glance at Daniyar. "You took him as your ward. Now his destiny is bound to yours."

He nodded at her, collecting Wafa and Sinnia to give her privacy with Daniyar. The tension in Daniyar's body tightened at the impending separation.

It was her turn to calm him. She placed her hands on his heart, looking up into the solemn beauty of his face. She was wrung by the wrenching need that had overwhelmed her in the cave, the same need reflected in his eyes.

"For you," he said. "Everything I do is for you."

She attempted no caution, no reminder of who he was as Silver Mage, his destiny and duty separate from hers. He didn't deserve that from her. They had moved beyond it.

She pressed her lips to his, breathing the Claim into his mouth.

He watched her with a warrior's patience, waiting for her to finish.

"What does it mean?" He spoke against her lips, claiming her with each word, wrapping her in his warmth, as if he already knew. A new thought tumbled to the forefront of her mind. What if this was how it was meant to be? Not a woman alone as a Companion of Hira, nor a man alone as a Guardian, but a man and woman side by side, held by a sacred bond, creating a perfect whole. Because how could a Companion be alone? How could a Guardian have no one to protect? It would give new meaning to the edicts of the Claim—setting forth an example that would heal the Talisman's prejudice. Or perhaps this was where the Claim had always been guiding her.

A future she and Daniyar could build.

Another kiss to remind her that he was waiting for an answer.

I am your garment, just as you are mine.

Heat blazed from his eyes, as color rose under his skin. His voice rough, he told her, "You make it impossible to leave you."

She moved her hands from his heart to link them around his neck.

"I wanted you to know. I wanted to give you something that was a blessing of the One's, something that was *ours*."

"Your gifts, Arian." He watched her with such sensual intent that she buried her face in his neck. "Say it to me again, one day in the Damson Vale."

A kiss as soft as a breath, and he was gone.

32

ARIAN, SINNIA, AND WAFA REACHED AXUM BY EARLY EVENING, WHILE sunset blazed through the sky in a radiant arc of gold. They had crossed the sea without incident during the night, waves lapping against the hull to the timeless symphonies of turacos. Sinnia had piloted their watercraft with such speed that they were halfway across the Sea of Reeds before the ships of the Nineteen were set alight, burning like the secret glow of braziers against the black waters of the sea.

The panic and noise of the crossing left behind once they reached the southern shore, they trekked over plains that were richly green with rivulets of blue streaking through irrigated fields. Everywhere there was evidence of well-tended agriculture, stone wells popping up against the horizon where families tended their crops.

Children called out greetings as they passed, kissing Sinnia with great affection. As they moved into the heart of the city, they acquired a train of followers. Children with warm brown skin and densely clustered braids tied with colorful fabric chased after them, clapping their hands. They glanced shyly at Arian and

Wafa, but when they noticed Sinnia, their faces broke open with delight.

Sinnia recognized many of the children, picking them up one at a time, kissing their earth-soft cheeks, teasing them in their own dialect, as they pressed their hands to her circlets, then ran them over their heads.

"They're anointing themselves with the blessings of Hira." She tossed a smile over her shoulder at Arian, who followed her lead. "They can't wait for a proper reception, the scamps."

A long line of women fell in behind the informal procession. Arian took note of their regal eyes and hands, the elegant arch of their necks, and the vibrant colors of their dress: splashes of fuchsia and peacock blue, greens to rival the plumage of parrots, and reds that burned like the halo around the sun. Some gathered their children and hugged them, while others moved up to fall into place beside Sinnia, welcome in their smiles. And something more as they took in Arian's presence—a deep sense of pride in the woman the Negus had chosen to send to Hira, the woman who bore the status of Companion of Hira.

Look at her, their dark eyes seemed to say. *How worthy is the one we sent.*

Arian bowed her head to show them both her gratitude and her appreciation of Sinnia's importance. The women's smiles warmed. They nodded in return, their attention all for Sinnia—a clamor of questions and gentle chiding for sending no word of her return, interspersed with bits of news about happenings in Sinnia's absence.

As Arian absorbed the atmosphere of joy, she smiled down at Wafa, who was staring in fascination at the children who stared back at him, making up games universally known to children. She was surprised but utterly pleased when he fell in with a group who had teased him into a game. It allowed her to slow her pace to accommodate the bruising of her body, the ache of her wounded leg still a dull, dark throb—the ache in her heart deeper.

They passed from the aromatic grasses of the countryside into the well-organized plan of the city, a pair of stone gates standing alone in the earth without the benefit of a wall to defend the city from an onslaught. Just as the countryside seemed at peace, the gates led to a city about its business, unaware of the wars that ravaged other lands. Arian took a moment to absorb the unfamiliar feeling—to bask in the utter peacefulness of it, as Sinnia halted at the gates. Their collection of companions waited for Sinnia to speak.

Painted over the gates was a beautifully rendered mural in the same vibrant shades as the women's clothing. It depicted the assassination of the king of Axum by a giant serpent who demanded a diet of maidens. A warrior crossed the Sea of Reeds to challenge the snake in battle, but instead of battle, the warrior fed the snake a poisoned goat. His reward for slaying the serpent was the throne of Axum. He ruled over the people wisely, married into the populace, then raised a daughter whose portrait was at the mural's center.

The portrait was of a queen with skin that glowed bronze under a crown of curls that reached her waist. Her white dress was embroidered with bands of gold at the arms, neck, and waist, down the center of her body, to end in a pattern of crosses.

"Queen Makeda," Sinnia recited in her own language. "May your blessings continue to rain upon the people of the Negus."

The procession that followed them to the gates responded with a chant. "Blessings from Queen Makeda on the people of the Negus."

Arian was fascinated by the mural. A memory stirred of a

manuscript in her parents' scriptorium, taken to Hira for safe-keeping. It contained a portrait of the Axumite queen, similar to the one on the gates. But now Arian noticed that high up in the left-hand corner of the mural, a giant wooden ark was etched on top of tumbling waves tipped with curls of white. At the bottom of the mural was another unusual addition: four strongly built men carried a large golden chest upon two rods, the chest itself surmounted by a fanfare of crosses.

As their escort halted at the gates, two striking black women pushed the gates outward to plant their spears in the ground. Wafa ran up, wedging his wiry body between Arian and Sinnia, as if he recognized a threat.

The soldiers knelt at Sinnia's feet.

Embarrassed, Sinnia looked over at Arian and said, "Kneel only before the One as I do."

She urged the soldiers up. They stared at her with solemn faces, the golden chains that followed their hairlines strung with tiny medallions. Sinnia kissed them on both cheeks. The soldiers clasped Sinnia's hands, and knocked their shoulders together. The three women stood together in a huddle, hugging one another close.

"Who are you showing off for?" Sinnia teased.

"You've been gone so long, we thought we'd greet you as if you were a visitor of repute," the taller of the two women said.

"If I recall correctly, *you* convinced the Negus to send me across the sea." She grinned at them, then introduced them to Arian and Wafa. "Nuru, Kamali, this is Arian, the First Oralist, and Wafa, her ward."

The two soldiers bowed their heads as Arian greeted them. The awe that characterized the response of most strangers to meeting the First Oralist was absent, though Nuru said with obvious sincerity, "The First Oralist is welcome in these lands."

Kamali barked an order at the procession: the women and children dispersed. Then one at a time, Nuru and Kamali clasped Arian's right arm near her elbow in a custom of deference.

"Come," Kamali said in the Common Tongue. "We will take you through the city to the Negus." Her tone diffident, Kamali asked, "Do you mind if we steal Sinnia? It's been too long since we've seen our cousin."

Seeing Arian's surprise, Sinnia grinned at her. "I told you about them, but it must be different seeing it in reality. I have seventeen cousins. We come from the Tigra and Amhar clans—all our women are warriors."

"And one Companion of Hira," Nuru said proudly. Arian studied Sinnia's cousins. Nuru's face was narrower, her huge brown eyes shimmering with flecks of gold. Kamali was the younger of the two, her face still holding the roundness of youth, her eyes a gleaming anthracite, her skin a burnished bronze. But young as they were, the two women moved with the discipline of warriors. They wore long cotton tunics over narrow trousers, too light a costume for battle. Embroidered bands at their necks may have signified rank.

"Ceremonial attire," Sinnia explained. "The last war these lands have known are spoken of in our oral histories. We haven't faced the struggles that have come to other peoples."

Arian nodded to herself, content to store up her observations as Sinnia chatted with her cousins, catching up on news of home. They passed through streets that radiated out from a central house of worship, adorned with murals similar to the one painted on the city gates. In the outer ring were homes separated into spaces for family and livestock, their conical roofs thatched. Moving inward, homes and small shops were built of fieldstone, with cornerstones of some distinction set in mortar, each with a different design.

Bustling markets showcased the trades from which Axum had drawn its renown: a tapestry of stalls selling grain, skins, animal horns, rock crystal, cowry shells, pottery, frankincense, and coins. One lane was dedicated to chalcedony and carnelian, with elaborate stone-studded strings hanging from sturdy wooden frames. The lane opposite specialized in goods that had been traded to Axum from other lands, mainly clothing, glassware, and iron, but also bottles of olive oil and wine. Though she looked for them, there were no manuscript stalls and no signs of skins being scraped to dry as parchment.

As far as Arian could tell, the residents of these lands were divided among three occupations: the tending of livestock and agricultural land, a vigorous trade in the city's markets, and participation in sacred rites centered on a house of worship called the maqdas. Many of the people she passed wore a shalmas, a gauzy length of fabric draped over their heads and torsos, while around their necks were talismans that carried special charms. In Candour, these charms consisted of holy words wrapped into armbands. They were colloquially known as tahweez, after the circlets of the Companions of Hira. In Axum, the charms were held in lockets that bore the secret names of the One, described as the Asmat. In both cases, the talismans were meant to call upon the power of the One to protect against illness or misfortune.

When the plague had come to the lands north of the Wall, the dead had been wrapped in shrouds covered in holy incantations. Having failed the people of the north, the tahweez charms were given up. But here in Axum, they seemed to be a commonplace, part of general attire. Nuru and Kamali wore similar lockets, and as they conferred with Sinnia, their fingers touched the lockets often.

Seeing the absence of materials for calligraphy, Arian wondered if the lockets contained anything more than scraps of cloth or bits of dried hide without the promised protection of written benedictions.

As she walked, she took hold of Wafa's hand, glad to see his curiosity as his head turned from side to side in answer of friendly greetings.

"What do you think of Axum?" she asked.

He shook his head, uncertain. "It's hot here. And there are lots of birds and so many children, too many to count. With their . . . guardians."

He tried out the word, having heard her use it to describe her care of him, and also in the context of Daniyar's governance of Candour.

"Their mothers," she said with a smile. "Their fathers, also. Those whose joy it was to bring them into this world."

Wafa stared at her, all eyes.

"You don't remember your mother? The woman who held you, nursed you, raised you?"

He answered as she expected, and her heart ached for him again. "I remember Talisman. I don't remember seeing . . ." He searched for a word, and when he couldn't find it, his face became tight with frustration. Arian stroked his cheek.

"Families. We haven't had much experience of family life in our travels, have we?"

Wafa considered the word. Compared himself to the Axumites, whose bonds were on view everywhere he turned. He seemed to think for a while as they moved deeper into the city, until finally he nudged Arian's shoulder and pointed to Sinnia, a few steps ahead of them. "Are we a family?"

Arian hugged him again. "Yes. And the Silver Mage, as well."

He accepted that without protest, his small body slackening in her hold. But with typical possessiveness, he tacked on, "Not those two."

He scowled at the backs of Kamali and Nuru.

Arian swallowed a smile. "Sinnia has family in Axum. *Lots* of family. That doesn't mean she can't be our family too."

Wafa skipped ahead a pace, scowling at a little girl who toddled across their path. When Arian blew a kiss at the girl, he asked, "Can families be big? As big as tribes?"

She knew what he was trying to ask and sought a way to answer. "Yes, I suppose that's true. Families can be those who share your blood—that's what they usually are." His face fell so she hurried on. "But they can also be those you *choose* to love, those you trust. Families are loyal to you but do not fear to tell you the truth when you do something wrong. As with Sinnia and me."

"And me," he said at once, cheered by this description. A boy his own age skipped up beside him and offered Wafa a spinning toy wrapped in a length of blue cotton. He pointed to Wafa's eyes with a grin.

"Thank you," Arian said on Wafa's behalf when all he did was scowl. "That's very kind of you." And to Wafa, "He likes your eyes. He thinks the color is pretty."

Puzzled, Wafa looked up at her. "His eyes are black and shiny. More beautiful than me."

Touched by this description, Arian translated the words for the boy's benefit. His face broke into a grin as dazzling as Sinnia's, though he was missing two of his front teeth.

"Ajani," he said, offering his hand to Wafa. Wafa brushed his own hand on his shirt to clean it, then reached forward to take the other boy's hand. When he gave his name to the boy, Ajani leaned forward to knock Wafa's shoulders in an easy gesture of friendship.

The boy waved and ran off as Wafa watched him go.

"Maybe later you can find Ajani and play. After we are taken to the Negus."

"We're almost there." Sinnia fell back into step with Arian and Wafa, guiding them to the left, where a long avenue climbed a modest rise. Perched at the top of the rise was a building that was more courtyard than standing stone, framed with palm trees and vines in a garden of designs that were beautifully complex, with soft blue channels of water weaving through their path.

"A palace of water and sky," Arian said, as Sinnia linked arms with her.

"And sun, wind, and trees. Not so monumental as Ashfall, but suited to our climate and our needs."

Sinnia's voice reflected pride. She wouldn't have changed the capital of the Negus for the illimitable glories of Ashfall, nor for the quiet beauty of the Citadel. This was home, with its glorious warmth and color, steeped in eons of tranquility. Though Sinnia returned to Axum with the weight of war on her shoulders, she felt engulfed by its peace. Here at last was a place where no one would utter epithets that condemned the color of her skin. She'd heard the words *"Kill the black"* too often in Talisman lands, a loathsome phrase uttered by those whose prejudice had passed into law. She'd made light of it in Arian's company, but the words had not only hurt, they had *damaged* her. No son or daughter of the Negus would choose to set down roots in a land that cultivated hate—small wonder she hadn't encountered any of her own during her time in the south. She had a deep sense of solidarity with Wafa; the Hazara people had suffered the brunt of the Talisman's intolerance.

Sinnia knew her duty as the emissary of the Negus. But there was no dereliction of that duty in taking time to rejoice at returning to her people and her home.

"We're in the midst of a festival," Kamali warned.

Feeling young and free, Sinnia clapped her hands. "The Festival of Manuscripts?" She squeezed Arian's hand. "This is something you have to see. There's a procession that will take us right into the heart of the maqdas, where the treasures of the Negus are stored."

Sinnia waved to Nuru and Kamali to cross through the screen of palm trees to the second layer of the gardens. Soft, warm air caressed their arms and faces, their circlets glinting gold, as they made their way past green pools luxuriant with river reeds. Their swaying lines were broken by colonies of orange lilies with dew-cups that glittered in the grass. The feathery strands of trees Arian couldn't name formed a canopy over their heads, as they climbed an inlaid path that shimmered in gold and bronze. For the dozens of species of trees in the gardens, there were groves of ravishing wild flowers, and above all these the persistent cries of birds whose plumage flashed amid the green.

Twilight deepened the velvety shadow of the gardens. Arian caught sight of women who wore white dresses embellished with tribal embroidery at the throat and the wrists, with gold pieces fastened at their hips. The women were tending the gardens, cutting back wayward growth, but they paused to call out greetings to Sinnia, their voices warm with respect.

Arian took hold of Sinnia's hand. "You've been too modest, Sinnia. Why didn't you tell me of the place you hold among your people?"

Sinnia shrugged. "It would be unseemly to boast in the presence of the Companions of Hira, let alone in *your* presence. Especially as I am hardly literate."

"That's not true at all." Arian smiled as one of the women in white nodded at her. "Several of the Companions are novices in the early stages of their training. Not only do your skills in most areas supersede mine, I have witnessed your mastery of the Claim."

"Salikh," Sinnia said at once. "It was his doing, not mine."

"You were the one who wielded it, so do not attribute your abilities to him."

Instead of the smile she expected, Sinnia looked troubled.

"What is it?"

Birds streaked from tree to tree, as they climbed through a maze of silver waterways. For the briefest instant, Arian had the impression the birds were tracking their course.

"Things are different in Axum than under the Talisman. Our society is modeled on partnership—we are not at war with each other." A glance to see how Arian received this. "In every aspect of our society, men and women work side by side."

Arian's steps slowed, the Companions falling behind as Wafa scampered ahead.

"Does it seem to you that I think of men as my enemy? Or as enemies of Hira?"

Sinnia's teeth sank into her lower lip. She brushed away filaments of goldenrod that caught at the hem of her cloak. "Things were brutal in the south, so I'd understand if you did. That isn't why I raise it."

Their eyes met, and Arian had a hollow sense of what Sinnia would say.

"The terms you set with the Silver Mage allow little room for his feelings or his needs. You seem . . . lacking . . . in empathy for one who proves his devotion with every action he takes."

Arian's indrawn breath was audible in the silence of the gardens. She was shocked when Sinnia finished by saying, "Were he mine, I would not treat him so."

Hurt and anger vied for expression on Arian's tongue. This was the first time Sinnia had spoken to her like this; she hadn't presumed the standing that would permit her to do so.

What had Salikh *done* to Sinnia?

But even as Arian asked herself the question, she was overcome by shame. Was she arrogant enough to think her behavior beyond correction? Did she resent the evolution of Sinnia's power, or was she jealous of Sinnia's stature among the people of the Negus? Did her proclamations of sisterhood ring false when it came to her practice?

She calmed herself with the Claim, made herself think through Sinnia's words—to think through why she'd found it necessary to say them. An undercurrent of longing had shimmered through Sinnia's words. Hira's traditions were austere, demanding a great deal from the Companions. Perhaps Arian's closeness with Daniyar had awoken Sinnia's yearning for another kind of life, a consort of her own at her side. But she could also be misinterpreting Sinnia's motives. Perhaps Sinnia simply feared that Arian's aloofness would alienate the Negus.

Nuru and Kamali waited at the top of the tiered gardens for the Companions, so Arian spoke quickly, tamping down the hurt she felt at having her behavior questioned.

"You must have heard me reproach Daniyar in the Black Khan's throne room."

Warily, Sinnia nodded. "You said if he didn't accept your

choices, he couldn't love you at all. That seemed . . . narrow . . . to me, when he's bled for you more than once."

Her head raised and her spine held straight, Arian moved ahead on the path. Sinnia matched her pace.

"Perhaps you are right, but you were not present in the throne room. You didn't see what the Mages of Khorasan wanted. I couldn't think, I didn't have time to reflect on all that had befallen us since we left the Ark. Truthfully, I haven't had time to accept what happened to us *at* the Ark." She sounded like she was making excuses. "I was angry that Daniyar allowed the High Companion to influence his thoughts of me. I didn't think he would doubt me."

"Yet *you* doubt him all the time."

Sinnia's observation was a trespass too far. Her voice now edged with anger, Arian said flatly, "You weren't there to hear the promises I made him." She drew a little away. "What Daniyar and I feel for each other is a matter for us to resolve; it doesn't require your scrutiny. Trust I will treat the Negus with the respect that he is due."

During this exchange, Wafa's head jerked back and forth between the Companions, his blue eyes shadowed with concern. Their sudden discord worried him, revealing as it did the fractures in his newfound family.

He couldn't know that, for most families, conflict was as natural as love.

33

A BUILDING OF CONSIDERABLE BEAUTY STOOD FRAMED BY AN ARCADE OF palms. With a climate as warm and tropical as Axum's, the main business of state was conducted in the open courtyard before it, where fountains played in maghrebi-influenced patterns, and low divans cushioned in the region's rich textiles rested on rods of pure gold.

The Negus held court in the center, a man of great age whose face was shielded by a turban, dressed in a linen robe embroidered with the emblems of each of Axum's tribes, who despite their frequent intermarriage, remembered their individual heritage—their colors were displayed proudly, yet not in competition. Somehow, the people of the Negus had achieved interdependence, a more amicable version of the tribes gathered under the Talisman's bloodstained flag.

As Sinnia had described, the courtiers and advisers of the Negus included a mixed company of men and women, each with equal access to their king.

Sinnia reached for the hands of the Negus. She kissed them and pressed them to her eyes. "Your child of Axum returns, bearing the trust you honored her with, in company of great distinction."

A tender smile softened the austerity of the Negus's expression, his eyes jewel-bright in a face lined with hard-won experience.

Arian brought her hand to her heart. She spread out one arm in the greeting of the Companions.

"Your Eminence. The Council of Hira thanks you for your gracious reception."

She felt a flicker of worry as he answered without more than a nod, without any of the courtesy the First Oralist of Hira would normally have been due. "We shall see." Ignoring Arian, he said to Sinnia, "Come sit by me and tell me of your adventures at the Council."

Then, with a careless gesture, he indicated the seating area to his right, where a woman of the same great age sat on a divan covered with cushions, surrounded by attendants in elaborate robes.

"Queen Zoya of the Negus receives you, First Oralist."

"Your Eminence," Arian murmured, as gentle hands led her to her place. She hesitated, wondering if it was appropriate to sit on the same divan as the queen, but the woman's eyes twinkled at her with a welcome warmer than the Negus's. The queen wore a necklace of layers of weighty gold coins. A headpiece at her hairline covered most of her forehead and made a mystery of her fine dark eyes. Her hair was woven in a crown of braids that was topped with a white veil. When Arian looked closer, she saw that the coins around the queen's neck bore effigies of Axumite royalty, depicted wearing their crowns. But the coins on the queen's forehead showed royalty veiled in headcloths.

The queen patted the spot beside her, and gratefully, Arian sank onto the divan, relieved to see that Sinnia had scooped up

Wafa, who was huddled in on himself to avoid attracting further notice. Homage was paid and courtesies extended, as Arian took note of the courtiers who kept up a lively stream of chatter.

Men with strongly defined physiques were dressed in long white tunics over matching trousers, rich bands of embroidery standing out in contrast to the stark simplicity of their clothing. Their skin was a range of shades from copper to gleaming ebony, their hair thick with soft, loose curls, their eyes liquid-dark with shining pinpoints of light. Mixing among them were women dressed in the manner of Kamali and Nuru, or in linen robes with patches of gold-stitched embroidery, their hair dressed in styles that indicated cultures at a crossroads. Apart from the spears carried by a handful of soldiers, there was scant evidence of militarization. Sinnia's people were at ease, at peace in the permanence of their traditions and the steadiness of their present.

"You have brought our daughter back to us." Queen Zoya offered the words as a compliment, a trust Arian had fulfilled.

"You were generous to send us a Companion whose presence not only graced the Citadel, but whose skill and endurance as a warrior saved my life too many times to count."

A pleased murmur met these words, the queen beaming at Sinnia with pride.

"A wise choice, husband."

The Negus patted Sinnia's hand. "A child of both the Tigra and Amhar could only bring glory to our court." He glared at Arian openly. "What did you think of our daughter's learning? Did we train her well?"

To combat his dislike, there was simple truth in Arian's reply. "The daughter of the Negus humbled me with all she had to teach me."

Speaking to the past, to the present. Learning even as she spoke, and seeing the response in Sinnia's eyes, their sisterhood not so easily damaged.

Sinnia was right about her stubbornness when it came to Daniyar. The difference was that Sinnia didn't know of the vows she and Daniyar had made to each other, nor of her hope that Daniyar would rejoin them before they set out for Timeback.

But how could she, if Arian hadn't told her?

Sinnia's rebuke may have hurt, but the hurt wasn't solely of Sinnia's making. It would take more than her few words of censure to sour the love between them.

The Negus folded Sinnia's palm within his own.

"You have made me proud, daughter. It must be an omen that you have returned in time for the festival." He raised his other hand. "Prepare refreshment for our guests." Then, to Sinnia: "I imagine you must have questions."

"I do, Eminence. And our arrival is indeed fortuitous, for the First Oralist and I couldn't have hoped to arrive in time for the Festival of Manuscripts. There is something of importance we are seeking—if we could visit the maqdas, the Glory of Kings might reveal it."

The Negus adjusted the white folds of his turban.

"You forget your roots, Sinnia. The Festival of Manuscripts does not take place at this time of year."

Sinnia glanced over at Nuru and Kamali. "No? I thought—" She fell silent as she considered the presence of so many soldiers at court. Surely the Negus didn't mean—

"You've arrived in time for the Festival of Courtship. Now that your duty to Hira has been discharged, your time of seclusion is over. Your marriage will be blessed before the festival ends. Most of the rites are complete; the final competition remains—your suitors will race for the privilege of being wed to you."

"Marriage!" Sinnia gasped the word.

Queen Zoya spoke. "We have a duty to your family, a debt that must be paid in return for all we have asked of you."

The whites of her eyes flashing, Sinnia jumped to her feet, suddenly aware that she was the focus of the courtiers' attention. She cast a helpless look at Arian, who tried to intervene.

"Your Eminence, Queen Zoya—Sinnia is bound by the oaths she took at Hira. Her Audacy is not complete."

The Negus sat up with the sprightly ease of a man decades younger, knotting his hands together in his lap with a dark frown upon his forehead.

"Did Sinnia not journey at your side throughout your Audacy, First Oralist?"

"Yes, Eminence."

"Did she not sacrifice time and youth and health in pursuit of your objectives?"

How could Arian claim otherwise? She nodded again, perturbed by the enmity the Negus made so plain.

"The wars of Khorasan are not the wars of the people of these lands. Axum is not at war. My queen and I are not at war."

Arian looked around the courtyard, to the courtiers held in thrall. She would have preferred to speak privately to the Negus and his queen, but that courtesy had not been offered.

"War comes to you across the Sea of Reeds. You must have learned of the Nineteen, gathering on the northern shore. Your people are well-versed in all that transpires across the Sea of Reeds."

"You forget the truce we signed during the Great Forgetting. The truce will hold. We will not be drawn into war."

Sinnia interrupted. "Father of our people, you do not understand. Once the Nineteen cross the Sea of Reeds, we will not have a choice."

The Negus unknotted his hands to study his palms. "Can one Companion of Hira stay the tide of this war?"

Sinnia's voice was sharp with relief. "I will certainly try."

The Negus came to his feet, extending his hand to his queen.

"But that is *not* your Audacy, Sinnia. You were sent to serve the High Companion, not to fight the First Oralist's battles."

Instantly, Sinnia made a choice. She moved from the Negus's side to stand next to Arian. "My Audacy is to defend the First Oralist. To follow wherever she leads."

The Negus frowned at Sinnia. "How quickly your loyalty has shifted. Has it taken less than a year for the First Oralist to win your allegiance? I wonder at her use of the Claim."

The insult froze Sinnia in place. "The First Oralist would never supplant my will."

The Negus's cold eyes met Arian's. "War is not the only rumor that has been brought to my court. The High Companion rescinded your rank. You are outcast from the Council, thus your Audacy is moot. You no longer possess the authority to compel our daughter to your side. She will withdraw from Hira, and her marriage *will* take place at the conclusion of the festival, where one competitor has won our favor."

Sinnia's hand gripped Arian's so tightly that she knew her bones would be bruised. They were caught in a trap, unable to speak of events at Ashfall without betraying the workings of their Council, or the High Companion's trespasses. Yet Sinnia had no intention of allowing her fate to hang on the whims of a man who, though old enough to be her father—her *grandfather*—was no actual relation to herself. Even if he had been her blood, she would still insist on deciding her own course.

Wryly, she conceded she was more like Arian than she'd realized.

"I'm sorry, Eminence. Despite the poison you may have heard, the First Oralist is the heart of the Council, and I am bound to defend her. I cannot marry now. I do not choose it."

Another voice spoke from somewhere behind Sinnia, deep, rich, drawling.

"I wasn't expecting a Companion of these lands to defy your wishes, Eminence." Quiet approval in the words. "Her disinterest in the festival intrigues me."

The two Companions turned to view the speaker.

He moved closer from his place under the shadow of the palms, his head brushing the fronds as he passed beneath them. Torchlight cast lambent flames upon a handsome, well-shaped head, burnishing dark brown skin until it seemed to gleam with fire. The man was tall and firmly built, head held high, eyes glinting with something that could have been malice, but which seemed closer to curiosity.

He was one of the few present wearing armor and weapons, and he moved with a warrior's sense of finely calibrated power. His approach was casual, indolent, but beneath it Sinnia sensed unbending purpose. When he was close enough for them to see his face, her eyes widened in appreciation. The man was a bronzed god, a warrior of the old world, eyes sheened with flame, cheekbones sharply angled. Despite the armor, his arms were bare, his forearms covered by gold cuffs marked with unfamiliar runes. He was holding a staff whose tip was carved of blue stone and inscribed with a word that he covered with his hand.

He stood before Arian and bowed, respectful, impersonal. "First Oralist. Your presence honors the people of the Negus."

There was a layer of flame over his clouded eyes that made it difficult to perceive their true color. When he turned to Sinnia, his expression shifted, all formality banished. Now a man's appreciation of a woman shaped the full curve of his lips.

"Do you fear you will be claimed by one who is unworthy, Sinnia?"

He didn't bow before Sinnia as he had before Arian. Instead, his eyes roamed over her face, then dropped to study her warrior's attire, the whip and daggers at her waist, before returning to hold her gaze, his appreciation deepening.

She tilted her head back to look at him, her face carefully blank.

"I am not a prize to be claimed, nomad." Pride in every word. "I am a Companion of Hira."

Movement now around the courtyard as soldiers filtered in to form a circle around them. Like the stranger, some were competitors in the Festival of Courtship. Others were the stranger's aides, dressed in a similar manner, carrying spears that were embellished like his staff.

"Nomad?" He sounded surprised.

Sinnia gestured at the runes on his cuffs. "I recognize the symbol."

"Do you?" A thoughtful glance as the man now observed her with a soldier's awareness. He rolled his forearm, raising it to her face. "Do you recognize this as well?"

The symbol he showed her illustrated a maze, circles contained within circles.

Ignoring the circle rune to focus on a series of slash marks across his cuff, she answered, "A warrior?" Her eyes flashed up to meet his. "What tribe are you from, nomad?"

He settled back on his heels, a gleam of amusement in his eyes.

"An intriguing question from one who would withdraw from

the festival. Do you seek to learn the lineage of a man whose suit you refuse to consider?"

Unthinkingly, she shot back, "Any man who would court me should be willing to answer my questions."

"Agreed," he said at once, his voice soft and deep.

Confused by his ready acceptance of her challenge, Sinnia turned to face her queen. "I refuse to be treated as an object of no value, my fate decided by others."

The stranger responded before the Negus could object. In a voice as rich as honey, he told her, "Then you mistake me, Sinnia. I cannot think of anything I would value more than the chance to win your favor. Why else would I travel to Axum to compete?"

Something beneath the surface of the question pricked at her awareness—fleetingly present, then just as swiftly gone.

Discomfited, she touched her circlets briefly, rubbing her palms against the words imprinted on each band. When he followed the gesture with his flame-shrouded eyes, she had the strangest impression that he was reading the inscription.

She straightened her wrists, speaking curtly. "I haven't given you leave to call me by my name, nor do I recognize your suit. My duties as a Companion do not permit me to do so."

The Negus clapped his hands sharply. He reproved her before the stranger could demur. "The duty you owe is to me, not to Hira, and in my name, you will treat Sidi Yusuf with respect. The Lord of Shining Gate honors you with his notice."

Sidi Yusuf bent closer to Sinnia, his voice low and compelling in her ear. "As you would honor me with yours. Take some time to consider the wisdom of the Negus." His attention shifted to Arian, measuring something Sinnia couldn't see. "The First Oralist would not compel you to complete an Audacy against your own desires. I've no doubt she wishes joy for you." His beautiful eyes held hers. "I would give you joy, Sinnia. So much so, you would ask for nothing else."

Astonishment brought a flush to Sinnia's skin. She had never been courted by a man who declared himself so plainly or with such self-assurance. Her heart beating hard against her ribs, she shook her head in reply.

She repeated her earlier vow. "I am a Companion of Hira."

The curve of Sidi Yusuf's lips deepened. "You are also a woman, Sinnia. One I intend to win, a victory I will ensure you have no reason to regret."

The courtiers surrounding them cheered his pronouncement. Even the Negus smiled.

Very much on her dignity, Sinnia stated, "That will not happen in this lifetime, Sidi Yusuf. Nor in the one to follow."

Yusuf laughed softly in reply.

With a courteous dip of his head, he said, "I accept your challenge."

34

THE COURTIERS DISPERSED AFTER THE EVENING MEAL, LEAVING SINNIA and Arian with Queen Zoya and a handful of her trusted aides. Wafa had been claimed for a game by a group of children with mischief in their eyes, and for the first time, he responded in kind, his sense of play awakened by Ajani's promise of a kite.

An attendant began preparations for the coffee ceremony that followed the meal, scattering freshly cut grass on the ground. Placing himself on a stool in front of a small charcoal stove, he began to roast coffee beans in a pan, while incense smoked nearby. Sinnia bent forward to draw the smoke into her lungs, praising the aromatic scent. The attendant smiled at her, bashful and modest, before returning to his task.

A cousin of Sinnia's named Ife passed around tiny porcelain cups on a tray engraved with depictions of Queen Makeda. Arian perused these at her leisure, allowing Sinnia the time to catch up on news of her family. She had a pressing request to make to Queen Zoya, but in the middle of the coffee ceremony was not the time to make it. Two of the queen's aides came to sit across from Arian and plied her for stories of her travels in other lands. With a smile, Arian began to regale them with tales of the Wandering Cloud Door, and the horselords' thunderous game of buzkashi, a game that involved chasing the carcass of a goat across a frozen tundra.

Sinnia interrupted with a teasing smile as more courtiers came to join them, drawn by the scent of fresh coffee. Ife poured out the cups, adding a healthy dose of sugar to each.

"You should have seen the Aybek of the Cloud Door. Now *there* was a man."

Her cousins begged her for more. Sinnia obliged with her description of a golden-haired giant with a laugh that boomed through the valley.

A porcelain cup was offered to her by a man's dark hand. She glanced up to find herself looking into Sidi Yusuf's face. Without asking her preference, he added sugar to her cup.

"Sweetness to balance the spice."

She knew he didn't mean the coffee, but to refuse the cup from his hands would have been an insult to a guest. The Negus had already warned her to treat Sidi Yusuf with respect—no matter that he took liberties she hadn't granted; she kept his warning in mind. Yusuf held the cup as she raised it to her lips. After she'd sipped from it, he asked, "Is that the kind of man who attracts you? A foreigner with little knowledge of your value?"

She was mortified to hear her cousins giggle. It was hard to sound severe with a mouthful of coffee, but she tried. "You've only just met me, Sidi Yusuf. What do *you* know of my value?" She made the words a dare, a challenge in her eyes.

"More than a king of yak-mules, I would hazard. Your praise has sounded in my ears since the day I arrived for the festival. That is why I set myself to winning every contest."

Her eyes caught his. There was an undercurrent beneath the

surface of his words. He was giving her his whole attention, but she sensed he was holding something back. To bring it to the surface, she questioned, "Why venture so far from home?"

He tipped up Sinnia's cup, making her swallow the rest of the coffee. The gesture was unexpectedly intimate, and though they were surrounded by others, his flame-lit, cloud-dark gaze wove a spell of seclusion around them.

"It was worth the journey, Sinnia."

He accepted a porcelain cup from Ife, pausing to thank her. Then he took Sinnia's empty cup from her fingers and offered her the full one, his eyes steady on hers. Her skin felt tight across her bones as the depths of his gaze drew her in, and though she tried to show him she wouldn't be easily won by a man she'd just met, her eyes dropped to her cup; she tasted cardamom on her tongue.

He was leaning in close enough to smell it on her breath, and it took all her self-possession not to draw away or to reveal her discomposure. She looked over at Arian, as she so often did, to gauge the appropriate response for a Companion of Hira, but Arian was occupied with the queen, speaking with quiet deference.

She would be attempting to win Queen Zoya's permission to peruse the manuscripts kept in the house of worship. Perhaps she hoped to win access to the ark that held the Glory of Kings. Most of their history was transmitted through their oral tradition, but the ark held manuscripts written in a script called manaqib—a script that recorded the sacred beliefs of the communities who had sworn themselves to the One. On important communal occasions, panegyrics that drew from these manuscripts were sung by a holy class similar to the Bloodless who had sheltered the Bloodprint in their safehold.

"I've lost you." The deep voice spoke into Sinnia's ear, inciting a flash of awareness. His features were remarkable, his eyes a flickering enchantment, but his deep, soft voice was *beautiful*.

"You never had me," she said, feigning indifference, but she didn't refuse the third cup of coffee he pressed into her hands, urging it to her lips. When she was finished, he took her cup and pressed his lips to the place where hers had touched it, a smile lighting his enigmatic eyes.

"Baraka," he said, and she stared at him, alarmed.

He'd given her three cups of coffee from his hands, but she'd forgotten that the third was the blessing cup in the ritual of courtship. While she'd been trying to suppress her unexpected response to him, he'd claimed her before the courtiers and the queen.

She watched in amazement as Ife refilled Yusuf's cup for the third time and gave it to Sinnia to hold, removing her empty cup.

"It's your turn now."

Sinnia blinked up at him, beguiled by the flames in his eyes. She raised the cup to the beautiful line of his lips, heavy now with sensuality as he waited to taste the coffee. She could sense the restrained power in his limbs, see the veins that stood out against his forearms, feel the warmth that pulsed beneath his armor, a warmth that engulfed her as she offered him the cup.

The rim of the cup touched his lips. His eyelids lowered as he pursed his lips to sip, and with the flames in his eyes doused, the spell between them was broken. Sinnia snatched back the cup before he could take a taste.

"No!" His eyes snapped to hers, an unexpected wariness in them. She flung the cup to the ground, rising to her feet. "I am a Companion of Hira. And even if I wasn't, I would not cede my right to choose. I shouldn't need to tell you this again."

He came to his feet beside her, the movement fluid and controlled, his gold cuffs blazing in the firelight. His body overshadowed hers as he nodded at the queen.

"I came from Shining Gate to fight for the right to win this woman, Companion of Hira or no. I came here on your word that I would have that right. Yet she refuses me baraka."

Though his tone was quiet, there was no mistaking the pulse of authority behind it.

Angry words rose to Sinnia's tongue, her dark eyes flashing fire. The queen silenced her with a look. She touched Arian's hand. It wasn't quite a gesture of deference—it was something else, a private communication . . . perhaps a request for trust, or for Arian not to interfere.

"You cannot expect Sinnia to accept you without a demonstration of your skill. You will have your chance to compete and to prove yourself the victor." A raised hand silenced Sinnia's swift objection. "I gave my word to Sidi Yusuf. Do not dishonor me, child."

Sinnia felt Yusuf's powerful body shift behind her. His shoulders loomed over her, his bare arms nearly brushing hers, as he asked, "Would you gainsay the wishes of your queen?"

Feeling trapped and resenting it, Sinnia swung around to face him. "Are you unable to persuade a woman of your merits unless duty compels her to accept you?"

She expected him push his advantage, to use it to force her compliance. Instead, his voice became serious as he asked, "Is that what you wish, Sinnia? To be persuaded rather than coerced? Then give me leave to do so."

The encouragement of the courtiers, the queen's vivid interest in the scene playing out before her, Arian's compassionate glance at Sinnia—everything faded away until only she and Sidi Yusuf were left. Yusuf's head was tipped to one side, patiently waiting for her answer. Sinnia's gaze dropped to the runes on his golden cuffs.

Nomad. Warrior. Desert-dweller. *Stranger.*

The thrumming murmur of the Claim tinged her blood, an awakening begun at the Wall that had come to fruition in Ashfall. It sang to her, advised her, *promised* her . . .

It was a silent source of power within her, yet Sidi Yusuf's gaze sharpened, becoming clear for the briefest instant before he turned his face away, reaching for his staff to grasp the blue stone at its tip.

When Sinnia still didn't speak, he murmured to the stone, "I am the Lord of Shining Gate. Does nothing about my suit appeal?"

Her confusion and anger melted away at the quiet regret in his voice, and she answered him with an openness she hadn't expected from herself.

"I mean no offense to the Lord of Shining Gate, nor to the man who would grant me an offering of baraka. My path was set long before we met. I promised to defend the First Oralist to my last breath of life." Keeping her gaze on his stone-tipped staff, she finished, "I hope the Lord of Shining Gate does not doubt the First Oralist's authority, or the duty I must honor above any other, may the Negus and Queen Zoya release me."

Her admission brought her back to the company of the others who were with them. They reminded her that the journey ahead remained obscure, with their allies still undetermined. Where she'd worried that Arian's unyielding insistence on her Audacy might somehow offend the Negus, now she realized that Arian had done nothing untoward, nothing to offend the customs of her people. But there had been no welcome from the Negus—there had been nothing that was due the First Oralist of Hira when the people of the Negus were a people of belief.

She had told Arian she would be fêted in these lands. Instead, she'd been met with suspicion. For the Negus to receive a guest in this manner—why should Arian have been the first? Had the truce struck with the Rising Nineteen demanded some other form of payment? Had the Negus been *expecting* their arrival? If he had, why had there been no official welcome?

Could Najran have played a role, insinuating suspicion into the Negus's court?

Her mind made another connection as her skin turned cold at the thought. In Ashfall, they had stopped to observe the Banquet of the Victorious, when the city should have been preparing to defend against the Talisman assault.

Now the Negus of her people insisted on the Festival of Courtship, though its outcome would strip Sinnia of her rank. She had been sequestered from men all her life, to ensure that she would be granted status as a Companion. But unless she could convince him otherwise, if the Lord of Shining Gate triumphed at the race, she would be given to him like a prize. Hira would lose a Companion, and Arian would be left to complete her Audacy alone. Without Sinnia's gift with the Claim, a power that was rooted deep within her.

To weaken an opponent in the midst of war was a stratagem that reeked of Ashfall's Nizam . . . and perhaps of the Iron Glaive, who might still be on their trail.

To compose her anxious thoughts, she made the Claim a subvocal sound pitched to Arian's ears. She was calmed by Arian's reply, peaceful yet resonant with power.

Sidi Yusuf stepped around her to Arian, his stone-capped staff in hand, his armor stretched over his shoulders. Cautiously, Sinnia moved her hand to the whip at her hip. If the Lord of Shining Gate intended any harm, his staff would be at her feet with one swift flick of her wrist. Ignoring her subtle movement, Yusuf spoke to Arian, the flames in his dark eyes banked.

"Do you know what it is you are seeking, First Oralist?"

"I do." Her answer, unruffled and certain.

His big hands relaxed, held loosely on his staff. "Then *I* do not doubt your authority. Your wishes are sovereign in these lands. You may command me as you choose."

"I thank you for your gallantry, Sidi Yusuf," came Arian's reply. "But it is the sanction of the Negus that Sinnia and I require."

Sinnia moved to Arian's side, placing herself between Arian and Yusuf, her body angled to block any sudden move of his staff. He moved his staff to one side, a promise in his eyes.

"I would not harm the First Oralist when she is a light unto these lands."

The words should have reassured Sinnia. When they were relayed to the Negus, they would mean more than her own protestations, given his eager reception of Sidi Yusuf's suit. Yet a kind of hollowness struck at Sinnia's insides. If Yusuf accepted Arian's mission, why not accept hers? Why not accept her role as a Companion when he willingly acknowledged Arian's?

And then she chided herself for having expectations of a man whose courtship she had just refused, despite his attempts to persuade her.

Queen Zoya intervened, to advise Arian. "To receive the sanction of the Negus, you will need to fulfill our customs. It is only the matter of a day. The festival begins at dawn. By sunset, you will have your answer."

The queen offered her hand to Yusuf. He raised it and kissed her wrist. She smiled at him as she told him, "And perhaps, Sidi Yusuf, you will also have yours."

35

Arian and Sinnia conferred in their private quarters, shared rooms in the palace where one side opened onto a courtyard of miniature fountains and palms. Wafa was asleep on a sturdy rope-cot covered in thick cotton cushions. A thin shawl covered his body, all that was needed in the ambient warmth of the night. Though Arian and Sinnia were just as much in need of rest, they were driven by a sense of urgency, determined to confront the perils that waited for them ahead.

"What is your counsel, Sinnia?"

Arian had bathed with care, mindful of the wound in her leg. She reapplied the salve Daniyar had given her, then wrapped it in a fresh bandage. Her body was dark with bruising, but the warm water had eased her. Now she was wearing a gown that was a gift from the queen. It was made of thick white cotton that should have abraded her skin, but its touch was soft against her limbs. A pattern of gold crosses embroidered the gown at her neck. Her circlets glimmered through the loose sleeves of the robe.

Sinnia had bathed as well, then dressed in armor because she'd decided on a plan.

Despite what she had told Yusuf, she could not ignore the wishes of the Negus if he insisted on the race. So she would observe the race and pretend to be in favor of its outcome. A night's rest would do them good. And it would give her a chance to carry out her mission.

"My cousins will meet you here. They're clannish, but they will take you to heart."

"Because you have taken me to heart."

Words of apology from Arian that Sinnia was quick to accept. "How could it be otherwise?" A shadow of her jaunty smile. "Ask them what they've learned from whispers they've heard at court. Prepare them for the Rising Nineteen. This may be a court at peace, but our soldiers should be ready. My cousins will alert others, but you will have to persuade them."

"What will you be doing?"

Arian settled herself on the rope-cot next to Wafa. Sinnia read the exhaustion in her eyes but knew better than to comment on it.

"I'll slip into the maqdas to search the ark. It may contain a reference to the Sana Codex. Timeback is not just a city; it's a region. We need to narrow down our search."

Arian reached for a shawl to wrap around her shoulders and nodded her approval.

"See if there's any reference to the Mage of the Blue Eye. Where will we find him? How should we approach him?"

"With fury?" Sinnia suggested. "He should have been in this fight from the beginning. What use is a sacred manuscript if there's no one left alive to read it?"

"He must have his reasons. Will *you* be able to read the manuscripts in the ark?"

Sinnia tested the fine edge of her blades, then sheathed them at her hips. "My manaqib is rusty, but I'll manage. Better still, the manuscripts are illuminated, so that will speed my search."

Arian shifted closer to Wafa, stroking his hair. "He exhausted himself with play. He hasn't done that before."

"He still managed to bolt down an entire beef stew." Sinnia stroked a hand over Wafa's curls. "He's filling out." And then with a frown, "Keep him safe, Arian. Najran is on our trail."

"I will. And you be careful too. If you encounter Najran, use the Claim before he gets anywhere near you. Whatever his gifts may be, I haven't learned to defeat them."

"You will, in time."

"There must be a way," Arian agreed.

Her eyelids began to droop. Sinnia tutted a warning.

"You should have had more coffee. My cousins will be here soon."

A playful light shone in Arian's eyes. "That isn't *my* fault, Sinnia. Sidi Yusuf didn't offer his third cup of coffee to *me*."

Sinnia refused to laugh. She could still hear the quiet regret in his voice. And even now, that sense of premonition colored her awareness. "I don't know what he was offering, but I'm not certain it was baraka."

"Why not?"

Sinnia hesitated. "I thought perhaps . . . there was a calculation behind his interest."

Arian's bright smile was such a rarity that it warmed Sinnia to her core, their earlier discord forgotten.

"Because you don't see yourself as I do. As Sidi Yusuf was bound to see you."

Sinnia sat down beside Arian, her gaze searching. "I am a Companion of Hira."

"As am I," Arian returned gently. "That doesn't deter Daniyar."

It wouldn't, Sinnia thought. The Silver Mage was a law unto himself. But Sidi Yusuf was a man she didn't know, a man she had no reason to trust.

Or to distrust either, an inner voice reminded her.

"What are you saying, Arian?"

"I'm wondering why you doubt his interest is sincere."

Sinnia adjusted her daggers impatiently. Apart from that slight awakening of the Claim, there wasn't anything she could point to. She contented herself with saying, "I don't think he's all he seems."

"Because he asked you for baraka?"

"Because he asked me for baraka when I'd already refused him."

When Arian stayed quiet, Sinnia nudged her shoulder. "Well? Is that not suspicious?"

She scowled at the smile Arian tried to hide.

"Why are you amused at my expense?"

Arian's voice shook with laughter. "I'm not, Sinnia. I'm amused by the fact that you seem to have no awareness of your remarkable allure. That a handsome lord should desire to court you is not suspicious at all."

Sinnia blinked at this. But she was quick to point out, "He refuses to accept my status as a Companion of Hira."

"Sinnia. He was welcomed to Axum by the Negus and his queen. He was promised a chance to win your respect—"

"*More* than my respect," Sinnia cut in.

Arian was smiling when she answered, "More than your respect, then. Sidi Yusuf is abiding by the rules of your festival; he did not *make* those rules. If he seeks your favor while the festival plays out . . . I would take that as your due." She stifled a yawn, curling up against Wafa. "The rites of Hira may bind us, but we are still who we were before we became Companions—there is no shame in that." She nodded at Sinnia once, returning to the subject of their earlier discord. "You know what I feel for Daniyar, so you know I would understand if you've wondered about a life beyond Hira. A life with that would allow for a man like Sidi Yusuf at your side."

"I don't," Sinnia said sharply.

Her eyes closing, Arian suggested, "Then shall we leave it at that?"

36

SINNIA'S THOUGHTS WERE FULL OF ARIAN'S COMMENTS WHEN SHE STOLE through the gardens to follow the trail of mosaics halfway to the gate. There was movement in the garden, the wings of birds fluttering against leaves, the songs of bullfrogs camped out in the rushes. And the night air, jewel-bright and warm, was a glorious caress against her skin.

The moon was still rising when she made her way to the maqdas in the center of the sleeping city, where families and livestock were at rest. The maqdas wasn't guarded—no one would presume to enter it without the permission of the Negus. The holy class who recited the scriptures did so only on feast days.

But the maqdas *would* be locked to guard its treasury of manuscripts, though Sinnia was fairly confident that she could slip in through a window. But as she circled the building, she found no easy point of entry. The maqdas had been part of an entire complex once, a stone obelisk marked with ancient runes standing sentinel. The wars of the Far Range had collapsed most of the structures of the city, save for the round-domed building with its thick wooden door. The windows above the door were set too high in the wall for Sinnia to scale. She backtracked to the rear, where she found a door that, while unlocked, was welded to its frame.

With the quakes that had followed the wars of the Far Range, those structures that survived had suffered permanent damage. No one since had attempted to enter the maqdas through this door.

Sinnia tried her weight against it, realized it was futile, and drew out one of her knives, which she wedged between the door and its frame. Birds called from the acacia trees that surrounded the maqdas, the moon revealed itself as a crescent against a luminous night, and still Sinnia worked at loosening the door from its frame. Her hand began to ache. When it slipped, her blade snapped in two. She muttered a curse to herself.

She shifted up her other knife, but she could tell that no matter how long she chipped at the door, the welded wood wouldn't budge. She retraced her steps to the front, considering the distance to the windows. A fallen obelisk could have helped her now, if she could have found one to balance on, except that its solid weight would make it too heavy to shift.

Her knuckles brushed against her whip. In the Nightshaper mines, she and Arian had tangled with a party of Ahdath. She'd used her whip to leap onto a moving platform buried in the depths of the mines. Perhaps she could do so again. If one of the windows had an exterior latch, could she use her whip to anchor her weight for a climb?

She searched the facade of the maqdas carefully, unable to find a latch. The entire facade was unbroken, which brought Sinnia back to the door with its heavy iron lock.

A rueful smile crossed her lips. A little more mastery of the Claim and perhaps her voice could sunder it. She couldn't read or recite at will, but she was lightning with a whip.

A terrible thought occurred, then: she could shatter a window with her whip. If parts of its frame fell outward, she would have the anchor she sought. But permanently damaging the maqdas would be a desecration.

She flexed her arm, stretching out her muscles. Then she uncoiled her whip. The throw would have to be a good one. She felt the onset of fatigue. Despite the coffee she had drunk, three small cups were not enough to vanquish her need for sleep.

It didn't matter. It had to be done, if they were to leave for Timeback armed with information. She stretched once more, then raised her whip.

Before she could strike, a shadow loomed up before her to grab hold of the knotted handle of her whip.

Najran!

Her heart leapt with such fear that her voice dried up in her throat. She choked out a word or two of the Claim, but then she recognized the man whose hand was on her whip, and the Claim fell silent in her mouth. His gold cuffs glinted in the moonlight, but his armor was covered by a cloak of midnight blue.

"What harm were you intending to inflict with your whip?" His voice was soft and intense. It shivered along her nerve endings. "More to the point, why would a daughter of the Negus need to steal into the maqdas under the cover of night?"

A lithe twist of her wrist, and the whip slipped free of Sidi Yusuf's grip. She took a step or two away from him, her eyes scanning the darkness for Najran.

"Why are you following me, my lord?"

The flames in his eyes sparked to life. "You have my leave to call me by my name, Sinnia. It seems appropriate in the circumstances."

She slipped past him to the door of the maqdas, all her senses alert.

"My definition of *appropriate* would appear to differ from yours."

His teeth flashed white against his skin. "That would be a pity if I could not convince you otherwise. Why have you come here, then, silent as a thief in the night?" The thunder in his eyes quenched the flames. She found herself looking into a face whose darkness was intriguingly opaque. The pulse at her neck throbbed.

"Don't call me a thief."

"Yusuf."

"What?"

"'Don't call me a thief, *Yusuf*.'"

He was wasting valuable time, so she gave in. "What do you want, Yusuf?"

A pleased glint in those unusual eyes. He thought he'd won a victory that earned him the right to move closer, so he did. She inhaled the clean male scent of him, surrounded by his warmth. Something intrinsically feminine within her pushed her to respond. She thought of Arian's insight into the uncertainty she'd refused to acknowledge. Then she drew upon the Claim to remind herself of who she was and why she'd come to the maqdas.

"Please." It was more a dismissal than a plea. "What I'm doing is important."

"*Not* a thief, then." His hand glided over one of her circlets, tracing the graceful inscription of the opening words of the Claim. She shivered at the touch, and he smiled.

Ridicule?

No, the curve of his lips was gentle, soft with understanding.

And with an intimacy that now reawakened the Claim. Its dormant power surged to life, throbbing through her veins.

Did he feel it, too? And if he did, what did it mean?

His glowing eyes found hers. His expression thoughtful, he removed his hand from her circlet. "Tell me what you're doing here, and I'll do my best to help you."

She resisted the urge to run her hand over the circlet he'd traced. "Why would you want to, Yusuf?"

His eyes sparked in response to her voluntary use of his name. "To prove myself worthy as your suitor."

Careful with the framing of her answer, Sinnia replied, "I would not offend your pride for the world, but I have told you that I am bound to Hira."

He didn't presume to take hold of her, but his voice became low and rough. "Did I imagine the way you looked at me when I offered you the cup of baraka? Am I mistaking it now? Is this only the delusion of a man who seeks what will never be his?"

There was nothing in Sinnia's experience that allowed for a response. Isolated from men until her assignment to Hira, she had never considered a calling other than that of Companion. It was all she knew and all she wanted.

He hadn't mistaken her response. He'd mistaken who she was.

But her quick-wittedness deserted her, and she stood before him silently, biting her lip to prevent herself from saying either too little or too much.

As if he sensed her turmoil, something in the atmosphere changed. His eyes became veiled, his voice detached, as politely he said, "You need not decide anything at this moment. Shall we let the festival play out?"

Without waiting for her answer, he shifted around her to test the lock at the door. Her sense of confusion cleared. His sudden remoteness wasn't because her silence had wounded his pride. In her bones she knew that Sidi Yusuf had made a calculation of his own.

To confirm her suspicions, she asked, "As the Lord of Shining Gate, you must know the city of Timeback."

He glanced at her over his shoulder, his eyes narrow and dark. He nodded without speaking.

"You may even have visited Timeback, perhaps on more than one occasion."

Now he turned around fully. He nodded at her again, without giving her anything else.

Sinnia waited, hoping for more. When he held his silence, she posed a direct question that came out sounding like a challenge. "Have you ever had dealings with the Lord of Timeback?"

His eyes cleared of shadows, the flames languid and deep. "Why fence with me, Companion, if what you wish to know is where to find the Blue Mage?"

Forgetting herself, her hands gripped his cuffs at his careless response. The night stilled into silence, the stars above their heads a river poured from a silver carafe. Yusuf watched her without blinking, his overcast eyes aflame. For a moment she felt as though she wasn't seeing him, the Claim muffled in her throat.

"Do you *know* where I might find the Blue Mage—the Mage of the Blue Eye?"

He freed himself from her grip, a dark shadow bending to the door where his strong hands tried the lock again.

"What do you seek inside the maqdas?"

Sinnia drew a careful breath, considering how far to trust him. Then she took a risk. "I need to look at a manuscript."

"Which one?"

"The Glory of Kings."

His mouth tightened, but he didn't object. He flung the door to the maqdas wide, though she'd missed how he'd managed to open it. "Help yourself, Companion."

She brushed past him, making her way to the sanctum of the maqdas, where the ark that held the Glory of Kings and the tablets of law was kept.

He watched her raise its lid, moonlight painting blue shadows on his cheeks. She stared at him for the briefest span of time, then made herself look away, pushing the lid aside.

He moved so that he was facing her across the ark, his eyes intent on its depths.

"What would the Negus say if he found you breaking into the ark? Why didn't you ask for his permission?"

Questions she couldn't answer. To deflect them, she said, "You should leave me if you fear his displeasure."

His quiet laughter sounded in the sanctum. "What a miserly impression that would give you of my courage."

Sighing, she reached inside the ark to search for the Glory of Kings. When her fingers touched its binding, she removed it from the ark with care to set it upon its stand. She viewed its illustrations with a smile upon her lips. Red, gold, blue, and green inks marked out separate spheres, the colors bold and distinct, the parchment mellow with age. Gingerly, she turned over a folio, searching for a reference to the Sana Codex or any sign of whether it had survived the destruction of the holy cities.

Her gaze fell upon an illustration of the Paradise Stone in its original setting, as a cornerstone of the House of the One. Tiny lines of manaqib script were crammed beneath the illustration. She squinted at them in the moonlight.

The rich intonations of Yusuf's voice reminded her of his presence. "What you hold in your hands isn't the Glory of Kings. The royal portraits and royal saga are absent."

Sinnia frowned, separating the pages with delicate persistence. Closer inspection revealed that Yusuf was right. The manuscript was a travelogue of some kind, with several pages of description missing and with the name of its scribe undeclared.

Yusuf hoisted the lid all the way off the ark. His hands reached in and came up empty.

"No rod, no jar of manna, no tabot. None of the treasures sacred to the ark."

Sinnia returned her attention to the page that featured the Paradise Stone. "I wonder why this travelogue was placed here."

Yusuf's head came up from his search. "That's not the only question. What you should be asking is what happened to the Glory of Kings. Who would have had the right to take it?"

She thought of the black-market trade in manuscripts that took place in parts of Khorasan. Fear colored her thoughts, as she remembered something worse.

The Authoritan selling the Verse of the Throne a single letter at a time.

Could the Glory of Kings have faced a similar fate? Would its secrets have meant as much? It was moored to a time, to a place and people. Could the One-Eyed Preacher have found something within it that spoke of universal power? Would the Negus have traded it to preserve the peace of his people?

She needed to discuss this with Arian, out of Sidi Yusuf's hearing. She scoffed at him to put him off. "What would *you* know of it, nomad? It would surprise me to learn you are literate."

She sensed his sudden stillness in her bones, but all he said was, "Perhaps I know a literature of memory."

His words stirred a long-forgotten story of rural schools known as mahadhras, where students wrote down the lectures of their teachers with their own commentaries in the margins—generations of learning passed down.

Shining Gate. The city where manuscripts were written on the skins of gazelles. But as with the city of Timeback, few of those histories survived. In an attempt at preservation, a citizenry of librarians had converted the very sands into graves for their treasures.

From these treasures, a proverb had sprung.

Lightning is buried here.

Sinnia studied the manuscript in her hands. Someone had stowed it in the ark to hide the disappearance of the Glory of Kings. But why *this* manuscript? And why in this place, now? Was the Lord of Shining Gate suggesting it had come from his city? She traced the parchment between her fingers, her head bent to inhale its subtle scent.

Not that of the skin of a gazelle.

"A literature of memory?" she echoed, considering his ability to distinguish between manuscripts. "Surely a nomad does not read."

His handsome face tightened, censure clouding his eyes. "Do you think that by belittling me you will not have to admit what you know exists between us, however little you may want it?"

Color swept up her skin. "No, I—"

He cut her off. "Every man understands eloquence in his own dialect. And though you consider me unworthy, the library *is* my country." He nodded at the page she held. "As I cannot serve you with my ignorance, consider whether the manuscript may be of greater use."

He strode out of the maqdas, his proud head held high, and

Sinnia felt ashamed of the arrogance she had displayed, arrogance unsuited to a Companion of Hira.

"Do better," she chided herself with a more poignant regret than she wanted to feel.

A half hour later, one of her questions was answered. The page with the Paradise Stone had given up its secrets when she'd carried it over to a spot where moonlight spilled into the maqdas. Now she had to consider the import of what she'd learned.

The Sana Codex had been stored in a chamber beneath the House of the One, a chamber whose entrance lay beneath the Paradise Stone. She cast her memory over her explorations of the holy city. She'd been distracted by the Well of Zamzam, but like Arian, she'd wanted to walk in the footsteps of those who'd come before their entire history had been expunged. She had made seven perambulations, circling the place where the Paradise Stone had been found. She had done so on her own, a quiet, secret pilgrimage that had warmed her, soothed her, clarified her purpose, a recommitment that reinforced her connection to the Claim. She had walked that ground not with her eyes turned to the sky but with a wild yearning to discover some further trace of a once-proud history brought low. But she knew that even before the wars of the Far Range, the Keepers of the House had destroyed that history themselves.

She had paid attention to the lessons, the Paradise Stone the final remnant of an ancient glory, now lost. She had searched through the center of the crater with care—the basement of the structure had been crushed into rubble, along with every other trace of it.

There was no conceivable chamber where the Codex could have been kept. So unless it had been destroyed during war, some wise scholar with foresight to spare had spirited it away some-where else.

The last line on the page in Sinnia's hand was written in a hurried script that suggested the scribe had been under some duress. He'd managed two hasty sentences.

The heart of wisdom and knowledge reside in Timeback.

A clue? To the hiding place of the Codex?

A strong sense of intuition told her not to disregard it.

But what of the final sentence? The warning etched in dull red ink, if indeed it was ink.

Beware Those Who Sign With Blood.

37

A HOT, BRIGHT MORNING DAWNED, BUT BEFORE ARIAN AND SINNIA could confer on the past night's discoveries, Sinnia was taken away by her cousins to be dressed for the conclusion of the festival. Wafa asked permission to follow the race with Ajani, who had come calling after breakfast, and because Arian wanted to spend time alone in prayer, she agreed.

Sinnia's cousins had told Arian very little the night before, but when she'd raised the issue of the ships amassing on the northern shore, they'd urged her not to worry.

"We are a seafaring people. Nothing that happens on our shores is unfamiliar to us."

With this cryptic reassurance from Kamali, Arian had to be content. A private audience with Queen Zoya had been refused, though not with the same hostility that she'd experienced from the Negus. One of the queen's attendants had come to Arian's quarters with a message that left Arian confused and more than a little worried.

"*This isn't your time, First Oralist. When the festival is over, we will talk.*"

She was just about to leave the rooms she shared with Sinnia and Wafa when Sinnia returned, attired like a queen of the Negus, in a long gold robe that clung to her body and whispered over her curves. Along her hairline, she wore a headpiece made of coins bound together by filigreed links. The headpiece was from a set that included a choker, a ring, a cuff, and strings of coins that served as earrings. Kohl had been applied to Sinnia's eyes and color to her cheeks and lips to highlight the rich tones of her skin. She looked like a golden goddess, but the expression in her eyes contained her usual humor.

"They were trying to match my circlets. Do you think it's too much?"

She didn't trouble to look at herself in any of the room's mirrors; she had her answer in Arian's rapt response.

"If anything, it's made me see you as you truly are: a warrior-queen of old. So beautiful and strong that even the sun dare not face you."

Sinnia looked pleased by the compliment, but then she grimaced. "Except they took my weapons—I'm meant to pretend submission as the prize to be won in this race."

She sat down on the rope-cot beside Arian, who had dressed in her customary armor, her pack ready beside Sinnia's for the journey ahead.

A gentle note of warning from Arian. "You look like a bride at her wedding. What follows after the race? If Sidi Yusuf proves to be the victor, will he have the right to bind you?"

Sinnia's glance at her was moody. "He can try. But I'm still going to Timeback."

"Sinnia—the Festival of Courtship, the idea of a woman being awarded to a man as a prize—it doesn't seem in keeping with the independence of the women of Axum."

Sinnia's hands smoothed down the folds of her robe, a frown pleating her brow under the golden headpiece. "It isn't. The festival celebrates couples who are courting. By winning one of the contests, a man is able to prove his devotion to his beloved. If he loses in one endeavor, he tries again in another, and if he wins, his beloved is pleased to accept him. I don't know why things have changed." She shook her head, and the coins on her earrings chimed. "I *do* know that I will not be abandoning my duties as Companion."

When her hands began to bunch the fabric of her robe, Arian covered them with her own. "Why are you so agitated?"

"Because we need to be on our way, and this foolishness delays us." The curve of Sinnia's lower lip was sullen. "Especially since I doubt that Yusuf will be entering the race. I managed to insult him last night. He left me at the maqdas in a huff." She described the result of her nocturnal activities.

Arian patted her shoulder, a knowing look in her eye. "You know what I said to Daniyar before I left him in Ashfall."

Sinnia nodded, her bright eyes curious.

"You were right, I was unjust to him. Yet he followed me across the desert."

Sinnia sighed. "The man has adored you for a decade; of course he followed you. He'd follow you into the fires of Jahannam." A hasty glance of apology. "Not that you would end up there. But Yusuf has no history with me. His interest is inexplicable."

"I thought I explained this to you," Arian said with a smile. "As Lord of Shining Gate, he's looking for a suitable partner. Who better than the Companion Sinnia, renowned throughout these lands? Also"—she urged Sinnia in front of a mirror—"just look at you."

Sinnia tossed her head, setting the headpiece jingling. "I'm not an object to be ogled. Nor should my rank affect his estimation."

"Ah, I see." Arian pretended to agree. "He shouldn't admire your beauty *or* appreciate your character—truly, the man is uncouth."

Sinnia shot her a wry glance. "Very funny." She leaned against Arian's shoulder for a moment, then sat up straight, defiance sparking her eyes. "Out of respect for the Negus, I will wait for the end of the race, but once it is over, we should hurry." She refused to dwell on the Negus's insistence that she remain behind. She knew her destiny now. It wasn't at Yusuf's side. "What I can't understand is why the Negus has taken so strongly against you. Or why my people seem oblivious to the danger of the Nineteen."

Nuru appeared at the entrance of their quarters to escort them to the race. Both women gathered their packs. As they followed Nuru from the tent, Arian murmured for Sinnia's ears alone, "We'll know more after the race. Queen Zoya has agreed to see us then."

An hour passed in formalities before the race began, as Sinnia was kissed on both cheeks by every cousin or courtier she encountered, followed by a dose of good-natured teasing. Arian scanned the race track for a sign of Queen Zoya, but though Nuru and Kamali were present in warrior dress, the Negus presided over the race on his own. He sat cross-legged on a wooden platform decorated with palm fronds and huge, jewel-like flowers that scattered petals on the dais. His closest aides included men and women, yet Arian noticed that none overlapped with the courtiers who waited on the queen.

She set the thought aside, as the competitors brought their horses to the track to the sound of great anticipation. These horses were similar to the Marra's horses, but they were built for speed rather than for endurance, with agile feet suited to sandy terrain. The oval track was short: from the dais on which the Negus reposed down to an arcade of palms, it was less than a mile in length, ending at a roof of acacias. The horses paced the ground behind a barrier, waiting for the signal to start.

A dozen or so competitors lined up, men whose skin ranged in color from ebony to gold; their features suggested the intermixed heritage that had come to define these lands. Many wore amulets or braids or other markers of tribal affiliation, but nearly all submitted to the rule of the Negus. Yusuf was the sole exception, clad in a form-fitting race uniform, his white shalmas left behind at the dais. His eyes as melting-dark as quicksand, he gave Sinnia a glance of frank male approval, before his gaze settled on her pack—a sign she didn't intend to be handed over like a prize. Staring at the pack, he frowned. Though she was surprised to see him, Sinnia chose to ignore him. She took her seat beside the Negus, while Nuru invited Arian to the far side of the track to watch the horses round the curve.

Arian considered the speed of the horses, measuring it against the distance she needed to travel to Timeback. She thought of the urgent need of her presence in Ashfall, and of the Citadel in ruins. She thought of Larisa and Elena mounting their firm resistance behind the Wall, and she wondered what that resistance would mean for Lania's plans to wage war upon the Talisman. Then there was Hudayfah, the brother who had wanted to save her but whose motives remained shrouded in mystery, and whose life was as opaque to her as Lania's. She'd been abandoned by both her siblings, left to Hira's care, as if the bonds of family hadn't mattered. The reasons Hudayfah had offered for his absence hadn't persuaded Arian. Somewhere inside, she still bled.

They didn't choose me, she thought. *Was it something about me that made my family forsake me? Was it the presence of the Claim, so deeply ingrained in my soul? Did it sever the early bonds of kinship?*

If Daniyar were here at her side, he would tell her that these were the outcomes of circumstance that had nothing to do with who she was or who she hoped to become. But he wasn't here to console her, so she brushed her despair aside. She had to keep her mind on her self-appointed Audacy. She would find the Sana Codex. She would return with it in time.

She was startled to attention by the blowing of a short, sharp horn. The race began without further fanfare. She'd thought that Sidi Yusuf might request a token of Sinnia's to wear, or at the very least assure her again of his determination to prove himself worthy. Instead, he'd ridden straight to the starting line, ignoring Sinnia, as he leaned over a magnificent thoroughbred with traces of khamsa blood.

With another blast of the horn the horses exploded into action, thundering down the track toward Arian. She caught a glimpse of Wafa's excited face in the crowd before her attention was wrenched back to the race. The riders shouted encouragement to their mounts, their knees pressed into their flanks. Manes and tails fanned out in the wind, like a falcon's plumage.

A moment later, the horses were at the curve, the ground shaking beneath Arian's feet as noise roared up in her ears. She caught a glimpse of Yusuf bent over his black horse, his hard face set in lines of concentration, the hooves of his horse churning up the sand.

Her heart in her mouth, Arian whispered to Nuru, "Are you sure this is safe?"

Nuru laughed as the horses roared past their position, a few feet away from the curve, behind another flimsy barrier. The breeze that blew up in their wake tumbled the barrier and caught at both women's clothes. The exuberant calls of the crowd sounded over the noise.

Two of the horses faltered off the track, nudged aside by riders who were more adept. The rest raced to the finish, almost flank to flank. Another two were routed by the whips of riders, stumbling across the center of the track to a chorus of screams. Three were left, as Yusuf and two of the competitors now raced to the finish line, their mounts lathered with sweat. Arian almost couldn't watch. The horses were so closely locked together that their riders were bound to fall under the tumult of their hooves. She gasped aloud as one of Yusuf's competitors struck at him with his whip. Yusuf shrugged off the blows. An angry Nuru cheered him on.

At the last possible moment, Yusuf broke away from the others. His steaming black tore through the banner a length ahead of the others to ecstatic cries of victory. He vaulted to the ground without a smile, summoning two of his aides—one to attend to his horse, the other to give him his staff. The noise of the festival swept over them like a wave, but even from this distance, Arian could see Yusuf's face. Instead of pride in his victory, his brow was dark as he made his bow before the Negus. Then the banked thunder of his eyes rolled over to Sinnia, his face unreadable.

A premonition of impending harm struck at Arian's heart.

38

THE NEGUS CLAPPED HIS HANDS. "LET THE PREPARATIONS BEGIN. YOU have earned the right to pledge yourself to our daughter, *former* Companion of Hira."

Sinnia opened her mouth to refuse the Negus's demand, but Yusuf spoke before she could, throwing down his spear. His tunic had been ripped open by another rider's whip. Now he ripped it from his back, his dark skin gleaming with sweat, his sinews rippling like silk.

Sinnia looked away from this demonstration of his power. All was not as it seemed. There were undercurrents that warned her, the same undercurrents she had sensed in their previous interactions. Yusuf's eyes were cloud-dark, thunder-cold, the flames extinguished from their depths.

He stopped at the edge of the dais, where he'd placed his spotless shalmas. He wound it around his torso and head, so that he assumed the appearance of a mystic.

But nothing could douse the heat that burned from his powerful limbs.

He used the edges of the shalmas to wipe traces of blood from his back. Then he reached for his staff, his fingers hard and fierce around it.

With an inscrutable look at Sinnia, he gave a curt nod to the Negus. "This was an honorable test of a man's endurance and skill; I thank you for deeming me worthy." His voice was quiet as he added, "But I regret I will not be claiming the prize you offer in marriage."

Sinnia went still, the Claim awakening in her blood. It whispered a word into her mind: *subterfuge*. And it told her to stand firm.

The Negus came to his feet. "You *dare* dishonor a daughter of the Negus? The one we favor above all others—the one we deemed worthy of Hira?"

Sinnia knew she should speak up, should intervene to put an end to this charade, but the Claim simmered quietly within, warning her to bide her time.

Yusuf turned his head, his dark eyes contemplating Sinnia. She noted the involuntary movement of his hand, as it covered the rune of the maze on his cuff. It reminded her of the way she centered herself by pressing her hands to her circlets.

"I thought to court the Companion at her quarters last night, but instead I found her at the maqdas. She breached its inner sanctum. She stole the page of a manuscript from the sacred ark while you slept." His hands tightened on his staff. "I have no wish to withdraw my suit, but I am the Lord of Shining Gate. I cannot pledge myself to a thief."

The Claim turned to ice in Sinnia's veins, so brittle that she feared it would break if she tried to contradict him. With forced calm, she said, "You know that isn't true."

For answer, he upended her pack with his staff. Before she

could react, he spread its contents on the ground. She carried spare clothing and items she needed on the road, but she frowned as the sun struck sparks over something covered by her linen.

Kamali raced over to stand with Sinnia, her eyes glinting in defiance, her spear planted in the ground.

The Negus pointed at Kamali. "Show me."

Kamali bent over Sinnia's linens. Her elegant brown hands stilled as they touched upon parchment. She withdrew the parchment from hiding; its brittle folds peeled open to disclose a painting of the Paradise Stone. It was the same painting Sinnia had viewed at the maqdas.

A collective gasp sounded from the gallery of courtiers.

Kamali passed the parchment to the Negus, her smooth face bewildered.

"I don't know how that came to be in my pack." Sinnia gathered up her belongings. "I would not steal from the father of my people, nor would I despoil a manuscript when my life has been dedicated to the keeping of the written word." She looked around the circle of faces that surrounded her. "Ask Sidi Yusuf how he knew the parchment was there."

Yusuf looked at her but spoke to the Negus.

"When I paid court to the Companion before the contest began, I saw the parchment in her pack."

Cold and implacable those eyes, hard and withdrawn as he faced her.

Whispers of disbelief at the accusation rustled through the crowd, but when she looked to the Negus, his jaw was set, he seemed to age before her eyes, his cheeks hollow with shame. A painful silence fell as courtiers waited for his judgment.

"Will anyone else have her?"

Riders shuffled away.

"Is there no man among you who will pledge himself to our daughter?"

Though the Negus's loss of face was painful to witness, Sinnia kept her composure. When no one spoke to claim her, she put a question to Sidi Yusuf, the words weighted with resolve. "If you believed me a thief, why did you compete in the race? Why carry out such a farce?"

And in the name of the One, why accuse her of such a crime but remain silent about their encounter? Had he done something in the maqdas that he sought to blame her for? Did the sense of premonition she'd felt earlier signify he was covering some dark crime of his own? Who, after all, had stolen the Glory of Kings from the ark?

Yusuf angled his staff so that it stood as a barrier between them. "It was a matter of honor. Having given my word, I would not have the Negus believe I lacked the courage to compete. But I couldn't have guessed that a Companion of Hira would choose to stoop to theft. Or that you would then refuse to concede the truth."

Losing her grip on her composure, Sinnia snapped, "I am telling the truth. I have always told the Negus the truth."

"Have you?" Yusuf's fingers tightened on his staff, and she read that as a denial of her claim. "According to your account, the First Oralist was not stripped of her rank. Which would mean that her Audacy has the sanction of the High Companion."

Sinnia drew a shaky breath at the weakness he'd exposed. "I can explain our . . . reticence."

The eyes of the Negus dulled. His chin trembling, he raised his arm to point into the distance.

"No one will wed you here." He kicked out at Sinnia's pack.

"Sever your bonds and leave my sight—you are henceforth banished from Axum."

She threw back her head with pride. "I am Najashi, Eminence. I did not agree to this contest, and I do not accept exile."

Yusuf's admonition stopped her from saying more. "Your lies dishonor the Negus." He said it as though concerned for her, then gestured at her pack. "Your actions give you away."

Sinnia set her jaw. She would puzzle through this nomad's deceptions once she'd given the Negus his due. She kissed the Negus's hands, trying not to feel stung when he jerked them roughly away. She glared over at Nuru, who was approaching with Arian. "Don't believe it," she said. "Don't believe any of this. Do not take the word of a stranger over one of your own."

Sidi Yusuf interfered again. *"Stand up for justice, even if it is against yourselves."*

A tremor raced up Sinnia's spine. The words he'd offered were daunting—a formidable verse of the Claim—a verse she'd learned only upon her training at Hira. The ice in her blood liquefied, seared by the beauty of the Claim.

She countered his words with a verse that proclaimed her innocence, breathed over the heads of her cousins, whose dark eyes were filled with tears. Yusuf's head turned to Arian. His lips moved without sound, his fingers configuring a pattern on his staff.

Sinnia gathered up her pack, thinking of the stolen page. She reflected upon Najran. She considered Sidi Yusuf's courtship, the soft words of persuasion he'd offered her in company, more persuasive still when they had been alone.

Her fiery nature demanded she take action, but she could feel the heft of the Claim weighing down the vessels of her blood. Her thoughts were multifaceted, suspicion rife in her veins. She modulated the Claim and leaned close to whisper in his ear. "The One will unravel your deceptions, Sidi Yusuf. I need only bide my time."

"Sinnia—" She caught the hesitation in his voice, the realization that he may have miscalculated. She glanced up to look at him, this time unaffected by the fire in his eyes.

Gripping Arian's hand, she withdrew from the dais, tossing her final words back over her shoulder.

"If any part of your pursuit was sincere, you should know that you will never receive baraka from me."

39

THE BATTLE FOR ASHFALL RAGED WITHOUT RESPITE FOR A FORTNIGHT. The Dark Mage had risen and with each new trial of his powers, another advantage was won. Despite Maysam's earlier miscalculation, the gates of Ashfall had held. On both sides of the wall, a full range of tactics had been tried: siege towers brought to bear, flaming catapults to burn both armies, boiling oil flung from the heights of the parapets, captured innocents murdered by gruesome means to dishearten the defenders. Grim losses on both sides, though the impact on the Zhayedan was greater: four brigades of Cataphracts and an entire company of Teerandaz taken by surprise by the strike of soldiers from a tower.

The Zhayedan thrust the Talisman back, but their numbers were too large to overcome, their troops fortified by a well-defended supply train, cushioned by a second flank.

The Black Khan used his powers ceaselessly, but it was only an approximation of what he'd been able to achieve when bolstered by the other Mages. And according to Toryal's report, the One-Eyed Preacher would soon have the means to vanquish Ashfall with a word. But he didn't entirely trust Toryal or the other

Talisman defectors, so he set them to work in the barracks, responsible for feeding his troops, but nowhere near the battle. It had been made clear to the former Talisman that if any of them were seen near the gates, they'd be executed on sight. He could promise the Silver Mage no more lenience than that.

There was still no word from Daniyar or Arian, and no time left to wait. The night sky was clear of clouds, the timeless beauty of the stars blazing in myriad combinations. The moment had come for Rukh to try the full extent of his powers. He summoned two of his commanders to the war room: Arsalan and Maysam, each of whom had pledged his loyalty anew, heartened by Rukh's efforts at the walls. But Khashayar followed, as well, his presence welcome to Rukh.

They went over the plan again, Rukh's fingers tracing the quadrants of the armillary sphere they had moved to the outer terrace, so that it was positioned beneath the light of the stars.

"You've lined up the catapults?" he asked Maysam now.

"We've only a few left, but the Cataphracts are ready," he said, a low growl at the suggestion that he would fail his Khan a second time. "We'll wait for the signal from the walls."

Arsalan nodded, his face pale with fatigue, his dark eyes clouded. He leaned forward to place his hands on the southern quadrants of the sphere. "Will it work?"

It was a question Arsalan should have known better than to ask in the presence of the others, because Rukh couldn't lie to him. So he sidestepped it. "If it worked for Darius, there's no reason I should fail."

A pulse of encouragement along the bond of the Mages. The whisper of jade-green rain.

Rukh inhaled sharply. He could do this. He *would* do this. He ordered the others back to their posts. Khashayar stayed behind, something unsettled in his posture.

"Excellency." His gaze traced the outline of the Sacred Cloak on Rukh's shoulders, the cloak Khashayar had briefly worn in an early battle against the Talisman.

"What is it?" Rukh made an adjustment to the armillary sphere, revolving it by a degree.

"I'm not certain that Maysam's tactics are sufficient to exploit the opening the sphere is sure to provide."

Rukh's hand stilled. "Why are you bringing this to me? Arsalan would have warned me if anything was amiss."

Khashayar took a deep breath. "Commander Arsalan has been at the walls. I've been on the ground with the Cataphracts."

Both men jumped as sparks traveled through Rukh's fingertips to light up points on the sphere. Khashayar took another breath.

"This meeting is the first time the Commander has left the walls in days. He hasn't rested; he barely takes time to eat."

"He's the general of my army; I would expect nothing less." At the worry in Khashayar's face, Rukh went on to ask, "Do you have a complaint against the Commander's performance?"

Khashayar swallowed. Only a fool would test the bond between Arsalan and the Khan. But Khashayar's duty was to Ashfall, so he quashed his disquiet and pressed on.

"The catapults are misaligned. They won't reach the designated target. Commander Arsalan would have caught this were he not so fatigued."

Khashayar paused. The Black Khan raised a silky brow. "Is there more?"

"Captain Cassandane is still imprisoned in Qaysarieh. We need her back on the walls."

"What does Arsalan say?"

"That's just it." Khashayar swallowed the fear in his throat. "He knows that Cassandane should not have been relieved of command, but he's failed to reinstate her."

The sparks beneath the Black Khan's fingertips brightened with his anger. "You underestimate the Commander. Our focus must be on the strike, not on Maysam and Cassandane's rivalry. Arsalan will address that once Ashfall has earned a reprieve."

Khashayar wasn't convinced. And there was still the matter of the catapults. It was time to tell his prince the truth. He looked the Black Khan in the eye.

"Excellency. Something is *wrong* with the Commander. He seems to have lost his focus . . . His mind has lost its clarity as if some outside force acts upon him." He shook his head, puzzled. "I say this with concern for nothing other than Ashfall's survival. As for Maysam—twice now his actions have endangered the city's defense—first with the Emissary Gate, now with the misalignment of the catapults. You know that Commander Arsalan would not miss this. He should have done something about it. He's the only one who can."

Left unspoken was, *Other than you, Excellency.*

Rukh frowned heavily. "Where should you be at this moment?"

"With my division of Cataphracts. We're currently engaged with repairs. The walls around the Zhayedan Gate suffered consecutive blows. The gate is vulnerable—the *Tower of the Mirage* is vulnerable." His eyes sketched the Sacred Cloak again, reassuring himself. With the gifts of the Dark Mage and the Sacred Cloak upon his shoulders, he had to have faith that the Black Khan could hold Ashfall until the First Oralist returned.

Rukh flung up his hand at Khashayar. "Go. Deal with the catapults—everything depends on the success of our strike."

"My prince, Maysam will not accept my authority. He will only heed the Commander."

Rukh's fist closed tight. His head turned to survey the Talisman's army, but he wasted no more than a breath. "No matter his current state, Commander Arsalan is the one man who cannot be spared from the walls." He removed his onyx ring from his finger and dropped it in Khashayar's palm. "Maysam will accept the symbol of *my* authority."

"And Captain Cassandane?"

Rukh's voice turned to stone. "*Get this done.* Signal me when Maysam has corrected the catapults; then go after the Captain, but return to your division as quickly as you can—we cannot afford to spare a single man."

It was enough. For the moment it was enough, so Khashayar gave a quick nod, sliding the ring onto his finger. "I will carry out your wishes at once, Excellency."

He turned on his heel, leaving Rukh to his preparations.

Rukh studied the stars. Perhaps neither Arsalan's weakness nor Khashayar's fears would come to matter in the end. As the power of the Dark Mage continued to rage through Rukh's senses, he considered whether Ashfall's deliverance might rest solely in *his* hands.

Arsalan would chide him for his arrogance, would caution him against it, but Arsalan wasn't privy to his thoughts. Nor had Arsalan ever commanded power of this kind.

Rukh murmured an incantation. The sphere began to glow. Light arrowed down from the sky, focused and vividly blue.

Awareness beat at Rukh's mind, as he waited for Khashayar's signal.

And somewhere in the depths of Qaysarieh, another consciousness awoke.

40

THEY THOUGHT THEY COULD CONTAIN HER. THEY THOUGHT THEY
could *destroy* her. Tied to this cold stone slab by the Assassin's
silver thread, tensile yet utterly unyielding.

The ghul's dead eyes snapped open.

She tested the strength of the bonds she had forged, tasting
Arsalan inside her. His firm resolve with its deep core of integrity.
Strong, proud, honorable, fiercely beautiful, and *hers*.

She linked her thoughts to his, wandering into his mind.

But there was Rukh to consider. What was her brother doing?

He was using his gifts as Dark Mage. She recognized the power
he had called upon to tame her, a power derived in part from the
Claim, felt the stirring of the magic that the Dark Mage had awoken. But in the ghul's consciousness, the magic was dark, altered
to thwart her brother's aims.

No! some part of her screamed in protest. *I am a daughter of
Ashfall. I will not bring harm to my city. I will not stand against
my brother! I will not hurt the man I love.*

And a deeper, more secret part of her spoke forlornly of the
vision she had seen when she had beheld the Bloodprint.

Come to me, child of Hira.

The magic wasn't dark. It was the gift of Hira.

A gift twisted by her reawakening. Just as Darya was twisted, ruthlessly suppressed by the ghul.

The corners of the ghul's mouth drifted up in a smile. Her fingertips ignited, tingling with pinpoints of light. A slight shimmy of her shoulders aimed her fingers at the webbing that bound her. The tensile netting caught fire, dissolving over her in seconds. She slid from the marble slab, adjusting her bones with a grimace.

She was wearing the same white robe that Rukh had shredded to pieces when he'd used his magic against her. Darya didn't mind. As she drifted through the Qaysarieh Portal, her state of undress distracted the few guards she encountered. A quick twist of her wrist was enough to disarm them. Or perhaps to destroy them. The ghul didn't know the difference. Nor did she care.

She moved with singular purpose, gliding just above the ground. Not to Arsalan at the walls. Nor to her brother in his war room. No, she'd been ill-used by each in his way. Arsalan had pretended to love her, but now the ghul knew she had always been a substitute for Rukh.

She'd seen Arsalan's face as her brother had embraced him. The intensity of his yearning had struck at the ghul's dark heart. Just as her brother's regret had torn away another veil. Their loyalty was solely to each other. The ghul didn't belong. The *Princess* didn't belong.

And Rukh hadn't given her the chance to seek out another home.

No matter at all.

She would revenge herself against the men who had abused her, with a single blow that would strike against each. First, at her brother's inheritance from their father. Secondly, at Arsalan, son of a Companion of Hira, instructed in the written word since childhood. And finally, at the Assassin, who had revived her from death only to imprison her. Like her brother and Arsalan, he venerated the scriptorium at Ashfall. Though it wasn't his duty to protect it, he acted as though he'd had a part in its expansion.

The Zhayedan sought to defend the people of this city, and by extension, the empire itself. But more than that, they fought to defend the glory of Ashfall's heritage—the symbol of an ancient line, the symbol of dynasties to come.

She whispered into Arsalan's mind.

My love, I give you a gift.

She was at the door to the scriptorium. The Khorasan Guard tried to stop her. She waved them away with a hand. Dead, dying, what did it matter? Soon they would all be one.

The Zareen-Qalam was next to confront her. He gasped aloud at her attire.

She twisted her wrists and hissed at him. His turban rolled from his head, his head from his elegant body.

Cries from the Warraqeen, the Zareen-Qalam's pupils. Swords pierced her ribs in quick thrusts of agony, but she drew on her brother's power with flagrant sorcery. As Rukh had called on his magic, the dawn rite had thundered in her bones. Now it slew the Warraqeen to a man.

The scriptorium fell silent. The Darya-ghul looked around.

What a beautiful space it was—the gorgeous concave arches, the sea-blue glass of the floor, the fractured light of the stars falling through stained-glass windows—and the ambient glow of lanterns like small ships drifting at sea.

The Bloodprint's pedestal was empty, but in every other nook, rolls of parchment abounded. Lore, history, fables, magic. Philosophy, arithmetic, science. Nature and cartography. Poetry and art. An astronomer's delight. And portraits of their family in the Shahnameh, the history of Khorasan's kings. Another wave of her hand summoned the Shahnameh from its nook.

Banished from the scriptorium, Darya had rarely studied it. She didn't even know if the manuscript recorded her birth. She placed it on the Bloodprint's pedestal. As her fingers brushed the spot where the Bloodprint had lain, her vision splintered in two. She was looking outward at the Shahnameh but also inward to another place . . . perhaps to another dimension.

She saw herself, innocent and kind, wearing a white silk dress, gold circlets bound about her arms. A woman with soft gray hair called to her, her voice resonant with warmth.

Come to me, child of Hira.

Blue waters enclosed her, dancing in dizzying patterns. Tears clouded her eyes.

She was wanted. She *belonged.*

The ghul wrenched the vision from her mind. She was staring down at the Shahnameh, the manuscript open to the register of births. Beneath their father's name, she picked out the names of Darius and Rukh. But the space for her own name was blank.

"Princess, may I assist you?"

She looked up to find a thin young man with loose dark curls standing beside the pedestal. His pain-filled eyes were kind. He made no mention of her dress or of the carnage in her wake. His generous offer was sincere. He read the notations on the page out loud, and this time the names of the men of her family—and *only* of the men—sounded softly in her ear.

In another room of the palace, Rukh touched the armillary sphere.

The ghul's fingers caught fire. They burned the Shahnameh to ash. Darya ran to one of the nooks. Astronomy, medicine, science.

When she'd found the nook for geography—the nook prized most by empire—she set the alcove alight. Flames roared to life from her fingertips, racing along from shelf to shelf.

The young man who'd read the Shahnameh to her leapt forward to stop her, his agonized cry in her ears. But that, too, was swallowed by the roar of fire as his body fell under clouds of smoke. And when the smoke had risen to the heights of the hall, and the stained-glass windows had imploded to scatter shards of color on the sea-glass floor, the ghul beat a hasty retreat.

Darya paused at the entrance to Ashfall's crowning glory.

A terrible smile on her lips, she watched the scriptorium burn.

41

"Rukh, fire!"

At first Rukh thought that this was the signal he'd been waiting for from Khashayar. But it was Arsalan who alerted him, shouting from the Maiden Tower, protocol forgotten as he roared Rukh's name along the wall.

The Black Khan's head swiveled to the palace, following the direction of Arsalan's out-flung arm. Nothing seemed amiss at the Divan-e Shah, the palace safe from attack. Then his wandering gaze caught it. The second gallery above the palace—the site of the scriptorium. Flames poured from the arcade, a blue-tinged crimson inferno unlike anything he'd seen.

Horror swept through his frame. Ashfall's history—its *legacy*—was imminently at risk, the Talisman's work done for them. If it came to pass—he couldn't grasp the immensity of his empire's loss.

"Rukh!" Arsalan called out again.

Arsalan had spent countless hours in the scriptorium, when he and Rukh had studied there as boys. His mother had been one of the scriptorium's custodians. This loss would hollow him out. But for the moment, Arsalan was thinking as the Commander of the Zhayedan.

He was calling men from the walls to take up the fight against the fire before it could spread to the Divan-e Shah and engulf the Messenger Gate, exposing the city to the west.

Which left Rukh to wonder who would have had the audacity to strike this blow from within? Why had he not paid attention to the plots laid by his Nizam? The Nizam's plans had been defeated by the Companions of Hira, but he must have left men behind who might even now be planning to assist the Talisman's army. His plans for the armillary sphere forgotten, a likelier thought flashed into Rukh's mind.

The Talisman defectors.

Those the Silver Mage had pledged his loyalty to.

He checked himself at once. The Silver Mage had risked himself at the loya jirga at *Rukh's* request.

But what had he done there, on his own with the Talisman commanders?

Why had he asked Rukh to harbor the enemy within Ashfall's unvanquished walls?

The power of the Dark Mage tore through a veil in his mind—power that touched his thoughts with the essence of something familiar.

Darya.

Brother. How is it possible that you refuse to see the truth?

His frame jolted as he heard the sinful pleasure in her whisper.

How was she able to reach him?

You know how.

That half-familiar pressure pushed against his mind. Touching him. Troubling him. Spiky fingers of crimson light scratched at the walls within. Ready to brutalize him.

His thoughts blanked out, a midnight shroud flung wide over the crimson.

You will not intrude here, Darya. You have no rights over me. Oh but I do, brother.

Crimson streaked through the midnight veil, throwing him back against the wall so hard he thought he felt his spine crack.

Arsalan shouted his name, pointing to a figure that had stumbled out from the smoke that shielded the scriptorium from view. A man who moved like a shadow, a steel mask covering his face. He was chasing another figure, this one dressed in the tatters of a white robe, her smoke-tinged face seized with rapture.

Rukh's eyes flashed to the flames that were consuming the scriptorium.

How could *Darya* have done this when she had wanted to be literate? When she had begged to spend every moment she could spare studying at the scriptorium?

You wouldn't let me, brother. And isn't your punishment fitting?

He threw the midnight veil up again, shielding his thoughts from Darya's intrusion, the battle around him now marked out with rapier-edged clarity. The Talisman's forces battering his walls like the waves of a tide breaking against the gates. Arsalan at the tower shouting orders that moved men from the walls to the scriptorium. Khashayar and a complement of soldiers in the square below ordering Maysam to adjust the catapults' counterweights to ensure they reached their target. Maysam neither helped nor hindered Khashayar, a detail Rukh set aside as the fire began to envelop the whole of the western wall.

Arsalan ran from the Maiden Tower.

And that was when Rukh knew only *he* could prevent the fall of Ashfall.

He surged up from the wall, the Sacred Cloak flying around his shoulders, his face dark with concentration as he faced the western wall, his arms raised high above his head.

The roar that rumbled up from his throat felt as though his chest had cracked in two. His lungs labored for air, his armor tight around his ribs. Words flamed through the terror in his mind, outlined with crimson rage.

He drew another breath to recite them.

Khashayar shouted up at him from the square, holding the hand that wore his signet ring aloft. "My prince, we are ready! Command the armillary sphere!"

But the sphere was at Rukh's back now, its sparking starlight quenched.

No matter. The moment would come again. An indigo light streaked from his fingers to the walls of the scriptorium. Where fire licked at the outer walls, the blue light swallowed the flames, leaving smoke in its wake.

Tiny scraps of parchment rode the currents of the wind, drifting over the giant square like flakes of newly fallen snow. The written word in all its incarnations now reduced to ash by a ghul the Assassin had chosen to recall from the dead.

History devoured.

Legacy destroyed.

The annihilation of all that was Ashfall, of all that Ashfall stood against.

Another ruined capital for the Talisman to collect.

A cold fire raging in his thoughts, he brought down his hands to strike.

"Go toward the threefold shadow that will offer no shade and be of no avail to you against the flame."

The words were directed at Darya, the threefold shadow death, resurrection, and the judgment of the One.

With the Sacred Cloak on his shoulders, the words rang with deepest faith.

It wouldn't last. But it was enough for now.

The Assassin watched as Darya stumbled to the end of the upper gallery, her feet taking her to the very edge. Her face and limbs had been blackened by the fire; she was choking on the smoke in her lungs. The ghul's campaign of destruction had been ended by the Black Khan's formidable strike. Now the delicate line of Darya's spine was braced against the outer wall, just to the right of a gap that opened onto the courtyard.

She didn't move as the Assassin glided closer, loosening the laces of his gloves with unmistakable intent. When he was no more than a breath away, she raised up an arm to feebly fend him off.

Her soft, sweet voice roughened by smoke, she cried out, "You don't have to do this. I *know* what I did. I know what I've become." Tears cut a silver trail through the grime on her cheeks. "I am not a child of Hira. I *couldn't* be. Not when I acted as an enemy of the word. Not when I destroyed our legacy for the sake of my pride."

"Do you make excuses, Princess?"

A sob surged up in Darya's throat, stealing what was left of her dignity. She shook her head rapidly, the words trembling on her lips.

"Nothing could excuse what I've done."

"Agreed."

The silver laces snapped tight in the Assassin's hands.

He heard a rumble behind him. Footsteps gathering speed. The force of a man's powerful body preparing to launch itself at him.

Darya's eyes moved beyond him. The Assassin took a half-step to the side.

"I'm sorry." Her voice was choked with tears. "You'll never know how sorry I am."

The words were offered to Arsalan, who grabbed the Assassin's arm. But with an agile twist of his torso, a movement the eye could scarcely follow, the Assassin wrenched himself free.

For a moment Arsalan's head turned to the ruined scriptorium, a gaping hole in the wall that continued to spew out clouds of smoke. The agony of loss was heavy on his brow, tears trembling at the fringes of his thickly studded lashes. But where there should have been a rage to rival Rukh's, Arsalan simply said, "It wasn't *you*, Darya. It wasn't you who did this."

But she refused to be absolved of the enormity of her crimes.

"I didn't listen," she whispered. "You tried to tell me, but I didn't listen. I used you. I *hurt* you. I did things to you that I wouldn't have survived if they'd been done to me." Her hand reached out for a moment, as if she would touch his cheek. But she checked the tremulous gesture before she could make contact. "You were always so kind to me, Arsalan. And look at how I've repaid you." She dropped her head again, flinching from his compassion. "But I didn't *know*. I didn't know that the darkness was inside me. I didn't know that I was more like Darius than Rukh. He was right not to send me to Hira. When I think of the damage I might have done—"

She took a shivering breath. Then with a last look at Arsalan, she pushed her fragile body through the gap, her footsteps gliding on air for a frozen instant in time.

Arsalan's shout of grief was unintelligible, as he stood there, too slow to react.

But the Assassin leapt into the gap, where his swift hands spun out his web.

42

THEY STOOD IN THE RUINS OF THE SCRIPTORIUM, THE WARRAQEEN DEAD around them, the treasury of manuscripts lost, the pedestal of the Bloodprint shattered by the heat of the flames.

The Sacred Cloak was drawn across Rukh's mouth, smoke hanging heavy in the hall. Arsalan stood beside him, his features bleak with weariness and grief, as he took stock of the damage, his limbs aching with fatigue.

Even Rukh's hand on his shoulder was poor consolation now.

Nothing had survived the ghul's ferocity.

Not a single sheaf of parchment, nor a vial of ink.

The stained-glass windows had imploded, scattering brilliant shards over the bodies of the dead. The scent of charred flesh was a contagion in the air. Arsalan drew Rukh closer to the burned-out windows to escape the stench, but the Assassin remained in the hall, fallen to his knees, his forehead pressed to the ground amid the rubble of the Bloodprint's pedestal.

He ripped his mask from his face. When he raised his head to search for the Black Khan, his scars stood out in sharp relief.

"I should have left the dead alone. The scriptorium would have survived. This—*all* of this—was my father's gift to yours. Now that link is gone, destroyed by my own hands. By my arrogance in thinking that I was worthy to command the unassailable power of the One."

His shoulders trembled with grief as he pushed himself to his feet.

Rukh answered the Assassin, unfazed by this admission, unfazed by the sight of a man whose face was unknown to him but whose eyes were impossibly familiar, soft as a clear jade rain. He pointed to the body that lay upon the floor of the gallery, bound in silver webbing.

"Yet you saved her. Why, Hasbah? With everything you know yourself guilty of, why did you spare Darya again?"

The Assassin's mask slipped from his fingers to the ground, the sound of steel striking stone. He pressed hard at a spot between his eyebrows that was undamaged by fire. His eyes moved from Arsalan to answer the Black Khan's demand.

"She was your father's daughter—she was your *sister*. I know what it is to have a sister you love, no matter that you are powerless to give her what she needs."

What the Black Khan might have offered in response was interrupted by Khashayar, who made his way through the smoke, his helmet tucked under his arm, his thick hair in disarray, as he brushed an arm across his forehead.

As he caught sight of the destruction inside the scriptorium, his head jerked from Arsalan to seek out the Black Khan. His gaze remained steady, his voice without expression. "Excellency. The catapults are ready, and Captain Cassandane has returned to her post. She is at the Emissary Gate, waiting for your command." And like a true soldier of the Zhayedan, he added, "The Talisman are pressing us. What delays the strike?"

He removed the Khan's ring and offered it back to his prince.

Rukh fixed it firmly on his finger. "I'm coming to the gate now."

He stepped around the bodies in his path, moving out onto the parapet, Khashayar at his side. He barked out an order as he left. "Do not repeat your mistake. Kill the ghul before she wakes."

The Assassin's body jolted in surprise.

But it was to Arsalan that Rukh had issued his command.

43

"WE REGRET TO LEAVE YOUR COURT ON THESE TERMS."

Arian's apology to Queen Zoya was sincere. She had viewed the outcome of the race with dismay and with more than a trace of confusion. She'd tried to find a way to comfort Sinnia, suggesting that there was more at play here than they guessed, but Sinnia hadn't been in need of reassurance.

Together they had come to pay their respects to the queen, who had called them to her receiving rooms inside the palace. Now Arian paid scant attention to Axum's melding of maghrebi and mashriqi architecture, palms and fountains indoors as well as outdoors, as Queen Zoya waited on her royal divan, surrounded by the women of her court.

Arian frowned. Unless she was mistaken, more than half the women assembled were related to Sinnia. She recognized many of the cousins who had greeted her. But none were dressed as casually as they had been the previous night. These women were wearing armor. To assist in the Companions' departure?

Or to prevent their return?

"Tell me what happened, Sinnia." An order from the queen.

But there was no way for Sinnia to speak without disputing the conclusions of the Negus. She had seen the darkness in his eyes; she couldn't bear to burden her queen with it.

The queen stood, dressed more formally this morning. She should have been stooped under the weight of coins she wore in layers over her neck, an equally weighty headdress delineating her brow. But like the Negus, her old age was vigorous, her brown face shining with health, the bronze coins of her eyes glittering with lively intelligence.

As Sinnia chose not to speak to the allegations leveled by the Negus, Arian offered, "The Festival of Courtship ended without Sinnia's hand being claimed."

"What of Sidi Yusuf? He was most insistent in his suit. Did he prove to be inadequate?"

In too many ways to name, Arian thought. But she kept the thought to herself. Najran would find them soon. It wouldn't augur well for their Audacy if the Lord of Shining Gate set himself against their course as well. Yusuf's actions perplexed her. How had he known that there was a manuscript page in Sinnia's pack unless he had placed it there himself? But what reason would he have for doing so?

Many of the women in the room had been at the festival grounds, and now a murmur of dissatisfaction made itself known to the queen. Kamali whispered in her ear. Then Arian saw something that neither she nor Sinnia had expected to witness. Queen Zoya's anger, her spine snapping straight, her necklace of coins shimmering as her breathing quickened with rage.

"He called our daughter a *thief*? And my husband of six decades *believed* him, that foolish and useless old man?"

"Queen Zoya—"

The queen's hand slashed down. "It is *my* turn to speak, First Oralist. The pair of you will listen."

Unaware that she was doing so, Arian straightened her shoulders so that she stood before the queen like a soldier at attention. A sideways glance showed her Sinnia had done the same.

"Eminence," they said in one voice.

The women of the court arranged themselves in rows that fanned out from the queen's divan, their posture military-straight, their fine spears gripped in their hands.

"Have you recited the Claim since you arrived at our palace?"

The queen's sharp question demanded an answer. Arian felt a stirring of the Claim. Was it the queen's voice . . . ? She jumped as Queen Zoya clapped her hands. "No, Your Eminence. It would have been my honor, but no blessing was asked of me."

"You need not speak so formally, First Oralist. It won't help us get to the truth."

"I don't understand." Ribbons of flame raced out from her mind to spiral down her arms. It was like nothing she'd ever felt, even when challenged by the One-Eyed Preacher. The power of the Claim was rising like a song, but it was also something more.

"Because we take a different path to the One than the Companions of Hira, my husband chooses to believe that our people cannot benefit from the blessings of the Claim."

The queen's distaste for this belief was obvious. And Arian noted also that instead of giving the Negus his title, Queen Zoya spoke of him in his family role.

"Yes." Queen Zoya nodded. "I knew you possessed wisdom beyond your years when you refused to be baited by my husband."

How had she read Arian's thoughts?

"Pay attention, First Oralist! That hardly matters now. My husband was unwilling to receive you, hence the rudeness of your reception. But you are here by *my* will. And when you depart, you will do so with my blessing."

Kamali tried to ease the queen back onto her divan. Queen Zoya pushed the warrior aside with a careless flick of her wrist. "I'm quite capable of carrying out my responsibilities while remaining on my feet. I have a duty to the First Oralist. And a greater duty to my daughter."

"What duty?" Arian whispered, though the tide of history was shifting in her mind, the pages of manuscripts turning one by one, pressing their weight against her thoughts.

The queen's eyes bored into hers. "Why did you come here, First Oralist? Why did you bring our daughter here?"

At last a question that Arian could answer without obscuring the truth. "We were fatigued from the battles we had fought, but our Audacy pressed upon us. We needed a place of safety."

"You were besieged on all sides."

Arian nodded slowly. The Claim rose in her mind, spilling out golden light. Without knowing it, she crossed her arms and raised her hands to her circlets.

"You needed respite, *sanctuary*."

Arian nodded again.

"So you came to the lands of the Negus, *as was your right*. Just as it was my duty to grant sanctuary to the Companions."

Sinnia broke in, bewildered by the queen's pronouncement. By the majesty with which she uttered it. "Why do you say this, Eminence? What do you mean by this? Axum is my home. I brought the First Oralist *home*."

"*She* knows." Queen Zoya's frail arm pointed straight at Arian.

"The First Oralist knows whose path you followed; she knew why the lands of the Negus would be a place of sanctuary for a Companion of Hira."

Sinnia looked to the faces of her cousins, to the pride that radiated out from each of the queen's courtiers. Kamali and Nuru disappeared for a moment and returned bearing a pair of lanterns inside gilded, ornamental frames. These they placed on either side of the queen's throne.

Something eased inside Arian's chest, a weight she hadn't known she'd carried from the holy city to Axum, grief bearing down each step.

And now that grief was gone. She turned to Sinnia, the Claim glowing from her eyes, stealing every color save light.

"We didn't have enough time for you to read the histories of Hira, but the lands of the Negus are the lands of the first hijra. I knew your city would be a place of refuge, because it was the first in our history to have offered sanctuary."

Sinnia had been taught similar stories as a child. "Those are myths, Arian. The hijra is a fable."

"Like the Paradise Stone?" Arian asked, only light in her eyes. She beckoned to Kamali and Nuru, who brought the lanterns forward, standing to either side of Arian and Sinnia.

"We followed the path of Dhu al-Nurayn, the One Who Possesses Two Lights. And in his honor—his *tradition*—we found our way to sanctuary here." She thought of that moment when she had stood before the All Ways at Hira, when she had sworn to fulfill the Audacy assigned by the High Companion, in the presence of the Black Khan. They had told her to seek out the Bloodprint. From that moment to this, she had been walking in its light.

"We follow the path of the one who preserved the Bloodprint.

He was a Companion of Hira, at a time of persecution. He, too, fulfilled an Audacy—he was told to seek safety in these lands. So he was received by the Negus, a man of great wisdom and mercy."

"And the Two Lights?" Sinnia breathed.

"The two women he loved more than any on this earth. His title is taken from *them,* not the other way around."

The spell Arian had been weaving was interrupted by a sniff from the queen.

"Women must lead in times when men are easily deluded."

The power of the Claim stilled; its halo of light dispersed. From futility and fear, Arian found herself firmly anchored. No wonder she'd felt such peace in the presence of the women of this court. The sanctuary they offered sprang from their mutual history, deeply revered by both.

"Yes. Though the early Companions were men and women alike, now only women serve." With sudden perception, she asked the queen, "Do you rule in place of the Negus?"

The queen swept out her arms to indicate her courtiers.

"My warriors have not been blind to the maneuvers of the Rising Nineteen. They sent emissaries to our shores. The women you see before you were quick to send them on their way."

"The Negus does not believe the Rising Nineteen are a threat. He trusts to the truce between your people and theirs."

"His mind has been overthrown." Queen Zoya spoke without apology. "The Nineteen sent a commander known as the Angel of Blood."

She paused when Arian recognized the name. "Najran."

"Najran is the name of a region where our people once flourished. His true name, no one knows. The Angel of Blood was able to beguile my husband, though the beguilement has been measured. Perhaps because Najran is busy reaping carnage in the east."

She was describing the siege of Ashfall, Arian realized, a new respect in her eyes. There was little that happened in her realm that this queen of the Negus did not know.

"What did he want?" Arian was eager to depart. They had been supplied with provisions. She had called for Wafa's return from the gardens where he played with Ajani. They needed to resume their quest; Ashfall's survival—and Hira's—depended on their return.

"He took our holy treasures from the maqdas. I do not know his reason."

Another shock of realization—of understanding. Of how Najran had worked the Claim against her. Because he'd had access to the treasures of the maqdas and used them in conjunction with the Claim. Manuscripts she hadn't read, whose power she'd failed to confront. And if Najran had taken Axum's treasures from the maqdas, why had a manuscript that described the treasures of the holy city been left behind in the ark? Why had Yusuf come to Axum? Whose ally *was* he? But when she asked the question of Queen Zoya, the queen stated simply, "I believed he came here for Sinnia because of her renown in these lands."

A contemptuous sound from Sinnia had Arian hurrying to ask, "So the Negus granted Najran the treasures of the maqdas, but what did you gain in exchange?"

"Improvidence," the queen replied. "Though we knew better than to leave our safety to a mind overthrown."

The queen should have been grief-stricken by the blow delivered to the Negus. Instead, she sounded impatient with the time-worn frailty of men. Testing this out, Arian said, "It could just as easily have been you, Eminence, that Najran twisted with his curse."

Queen Zoya snorted. "He tried. I dismissed him from my presence at once."

Luck then, had spared Queen Zoya the use of Najran's jeweled daggers. Or the tortures of the Iron Glaive.

"You think it was merely fortune, with my warriors around me? Kamali, Nuru. Show her."

The two women set down their lanterns to circle around the Companions.

"What on earth are you doing?" Sinnia challenged her cousins.

But before either Sinnia or Arian could react, the two women danced around them without sound, moving with scarcely a breath. An instant later they opened their palms to display the circlets of the Companions in their hands.

Thunderstruck, Sinnia stared at them. "How—what—"

Kamali slapped Sinnia's circlets back into her palm.

"We've learned a few tricks since you left, cousin."

At last, the queen sank back upon her divan, a gleam of satisfaction in her eyes.

"It wasn't merely fortune. When Najran tried to persuade me, I told him to go and sweep the desert. And when that entreaty fell on stubborn ears, I showed him what my warriors can do. What I failed to perceive is that he possessed the power to keep my husband in thrall."

Arian accepted Nuru's gentle touch as she shyly refastened her circlets, trying to hold back her amazement. This silent, bashful girl had just ambushed the First Oralist of the Claim without so much as disturbing a single one of her braids.

"We've had news of the Nineteen for more than a year," Queen Zoya continued. "My warriors have carried out attacks against their ships."

A huge smile broke out on Sinnia's face, her earlier turmoil forgotten. "They say not to doubt a queen of the Negus. Mother, you do us proud."

Kamali picked up her lantern, taking her place beside the queen. "We spoke to the First Oralist at length. She has shared her intelligence of the strength of the Nineteen. It may benefit Ashfall if we engage the Nineteen on *our* shores, instead of theirs."

At Sinnia's astonishment, a fine look of arrogance settled on Kamali's features. In that moment, she wasn't merely one of the queen's guards. She was a warrior with unshakeable confidence. "I trained *with* you, cousin. I am no less than you. Neither are any of our sisters."

Arian focused on what was important. "Have the people of the Negus formed an alliance with the Prince of Khorasan? Are you allies of the Black Khan?"

If they were, this was another secret the Black Khan had kept to himself. But perhaps he'd meant to keep the secret from Ilea. Arian shook her head at herself. No, if he'd wished to confide in her, he could have found a moment to do so, just as he had in the past. He told her what suited the aims he conspired at, never anything more.

Think of what happened in his chambers. Remember that he bled you, that he drank of your blood. He was never a true ally.

"Alliances are made and unmade every day." Kamali spoke, shifting Arian's perceptions again. The queen's guard wasn't only a warrior. She was also the strategist behind Queen Zoya's diplomacy. "We've been thinking like you, First Oralist."

The first to ever do so, if true.

Queen Zoya laughed, and Arian reminded herself of the vulnerability of her thoughts.

"Show her," the queen said to Nuru.

The courtiers rearranged themselves, several of the women bringing forth a table. On its surface they spread a large sheaf of deep blue parchment, covered with tiny lines. Sinnia studied it, covering her mouth with one hand. She clapped Nuru hard on her shoulder. "You did this?"

"I *am* the shipbuilder of this court." A modest reply.

Arian couldn't understand the markings. It looked like a map with the points of a compass, but its wiggling lines were unfamiliar.

"Tactics of marine warfare," Sinnia supplied. She pointed to various patterns. "Defense. Offense." Her hand shifted. "Our shore. Theirs." She considered the maneuvers Nuru had laid out with such skill. "Their resources are greater than ours—we cannot match their ships. In terms of sheer strength, they'll defeat us."

Nuru shrugged, her braids cascading over one shoulder with the music of cowry shells. "Let them try. We've been sailing these seas all our lives."

Arian's lips quirked up. "I once heard a similar refrain."

Nuru flashed her a shy smile. "Good. When you meet a woman of the Negus, the first thing you should notice is her self-reliance."

Arian cast a fond glance at Sinnia. "It's hard to miss."

Even the accusations cast by the Lord of Shining Gate hadn't dimmed Sinnia's fire. Arian turned back to Queen Zoya.

"You didn't answer me about the alliance with the Black Khan."

She nodded at Kamali, who adjusted the locket at her neck.

"We place no faith in the Khan as an ally, though his general is a man known to honor his word. But that is beside the point, First Oralist."

"Why?"

Kamali's candid eyes met Arian's. "You know it as well as we do; that is why you persist on your Audacy despite those who stand against you. Talisman, Nineteen—we cannot allow their doctrine to flourish. First they will take the empire of the Khan. Then they will come for us." Compassion lightened her expression. "But I sense that this is a lesson you have already learned."

The bond of sisterhood that sprang up between Arian and Kamali was as sudden and fierce as the one she had formed with Larisa. A sisterhood of suffering. And the unwavering commitment to end it.

A glance at the queen, who watched them both.

"How did you know the Nineteen for an enemy?" Arian asked. "They assert their own prerogatives over the Claim. Why not accept their truth? What if they were the ones who had been in need of sanctuary?"

Cold, cold wrath turned those bronze eyes to flint.

"The insult they delivered before they stole the Glory of Kings is of a kind that cannot be forgiven." She pretended to spit into her palms.

"What insult, Queen Zoya?"

The queen rose to her feet again, this time leaning on Nuru, who had leapt into place at her side, her tactical plans forgotten.

"They call themselves the Nineteen, the holiness of the Claim reduced to a blind arithmetic. But did they honor the Nineteen?"

Arian's heart jerked to a stop before it broke into a furious rhythm. "You asked them about the Adhraa. You asked them to give the blessing of the nineteenth chapter of the Claim."

The Queen inclined her regal head.

Arian fought hard not to show her excitement. Until this moment, she hadn't known how deep sisterhood could run. She hadn't known that the earliest hijra had woven a bond that the wars of the Far Range had not had the power to destroy: the children of the Claim and of the Esayin, one people for all time.

"To them the holy mother of the Esayin—*our* mother—is of no value. They did not know of her seclusion; they could not speak her name at all."

But Arian could. And *did*. In their language and hers, the language of the Claim.

She did as her predecessors had done, those who had made the first hijra. She gave them the story of the Adhraa; she sang of her highest honor in the Claim and then of the child the Adhraa had borne though chaste and untouched, the miracle of the Esayin.

The story gave grace to her voice and hope to her heart, and when her recitation had ended, each of the queen's fierce warriors had fallen to her knees to weep.

But Queen Zoya came to Arian and asked her to lower her head.

When Arian did, she kissed her forehead. "Verily," she breathed with great emotion. "Verily, your message and our message come from the same source of light, the light that we call mishkah."

And Arian echoed her forebears. "This is a land of sincerity in faith."

There was nothing she could have uttered that would have given the queen greater joy, the memory of the hijra a joyous bond between them, a heart whose blood was shared.

Queen Zoya kissed her again, then drew back to look her in the eyes.

"You are not just the First Oralist of Hira. Henceforth you are our daughter." She looked for Sinnia, and kissed her on both cheeks. With a stern warning, she said, "You will guard the First Oralist with your life, until she has returned dignity to these lands." A softer look at Arian. "But guard *our* daughter as well. She is the pride of our house, and also of my heart."

Crying openly, Sinnia hugged her queen. "The Negus has disowned me. He would have sold me in the Festival of Courtship."

The queen snorted again. "A foolish contest that *we* permit to satisfy the vanity of men. We would not give a daughter of our house to a man without her consent."

"Then why did you insist that I allow his suit?"

Queen Zoya raised a disdainful eyebrow. "We thought him worthy *because* he was enamored of you. The moment he spoke against you, he fell from our favor forever. Nor did *I* decree that your tenure at Hira was over. The Sidi knew this. No matter how he teased you, he told me he was prepared to wait."

It wasn't enough of an answer for Sinnia. "My allegiance must always be to Hira."

Queen Zoya scowled at Sinnia's refusal to understand. "Perhaps your time at Hira has clouded the truth. It would certainly serve the High Companion for you to believe yourself bound to your vow of chastity for all time."

"I'm not?" Sinnia's confusion was mirrored in Arian's eyes.

Drawing herself up proudly, the queen touched the coins at her hairline. "The vows you take—the allegiance of the Companions wasn't meant to be to Hira."

When Arian and Sinnia both remained silent, she clarified her point as if she was speaking to children. "The allegiance the Companions owe is not to the Council of Hira but to the All-Seeing One."

They stared at the queen, stunned.

44

Their leave-taking was brief. For the third time on their journey, sanctuary was offered to Wafa so he would have no need to share in the Companions' Audacy with the Iron Glaive on their trail. And for the third time, the offer was refused, this time by Arian, who held her brother's words in her mind.

You took him as your ward. Now his destiny is bound to yours.

To her surprise, Nuru followed them from the palace with a roll of parchment in her hands. "What route will you take to Timeback?"

Sinnia paused in the act of coiling her whip at her waist. "Let's see. We have no horses or camels. The Great Bend is inconsiderate and refuses to bend our way, so we'll be forced to travel by foot."

Nuru's eyes rested on Wafa. "The boy, too?"

Sinnia tugged Wafa's loose curls. "The boy, especially. He provides entertainment."

Wafa turned into her caress. "What's a Great Bend?" he asked.

"A river that covers much of the west. Different tribes call it by different names—the Joliba, the Isa Ber, the Kworra. But whatever its name, and though it flows through Timeback, it doesn't travel east. On both ends its empties into the great seas." She anticipated Wafa's next question. "No, not the Sea of Reeds."

A grin at Wafa's comical relief.

Nuru interrupted. "It would take weeks for you to reach Timeback on foot." She hesitated, looking around to make sure that no one was listening in on their conversation. "There are rumors that the Nineteen have reached Timeback. The road may have perils that you are not expecting." She unrolled the parchment in her hands, holding it flat against her torso. "There may be another way."

Arian peered at the map. It depicted a trail from Axum to Timeback, with few landmarks to serve as signposts. Not until the city of Timeback did the Great Bend hove into view.

"I'm not sure how this helps us, Nuru."

Nuru shook her head, the cowry shells on her braids clashing in her agitation.

"First Oralist, look at this spot." She pointed to an incline on the map. "See these hills? They're made of rock, and they encircle a closely guarded valley. I've been . . . experimenting . . . with a vessel in that valley."

"There's no water anywhere near that enclosure," Sinnia snapped.

"You won't need water," Nuru snapped back.

"Then what?"

Nuru's thumb slipped to reveal a sketch at the top of the map—a model of a sailing ship.

"It's not for the Sea of Reeds," she said quickly.

"Does it ride the sands?" Arian asked, thinking of their hair-raising journey on Rim-Sarah's sandsail.

"No, First Oralist." Another hint of that bashful smile. "This ship rides the air—you see the sails?" Both Companions nodded. "The thing is, no one has tested it. It hasn't been flown—though my calculations suggest that it should be possible for the ship to sail the air currents."

The drawing was too generic for details, but one question was paramount to Arian.

"How does the ship sail the skies? How does it overcome inertia?"

Nuru's pretty face fell. "That's where the difficulty lies. I rigged the sails just as I would for a ship on the Sea of Reeds—the airship even has an anchor—but I haven't solved the question of gravity. Water we know how to ride; our skills in the air are nascent."

Sinnia considered the drawing with pursed lips. After a moment's quiet study, she turned to Arian, a wicked light in her eyes. "A sailing ship is powered by wind, Arian. Who's to say you couldn't power it?"

Arian looked blank.

"Why am I doing all the thinking?" Sinnia said with a bad-tempered scowl. "The aesar, Arian. You called it up in the desert to hold off the Nineteen's pursuit. Perhaps you could do the same with this ship."

"That was a firewind," Arian protested. "I hardly think fire will assist in keeping us aloft. Most likely, it will tear through the sails."

"I'll help you. We'll turn the aesar to our purpose."

"It's taking a chance, Sinnia—we have so little time."

"A chance worth taking," Sinnia rejoined. "And the valley is on our route, so to make a stop there won't be taking us out of our way."

Sinnia snatched the parchment out of Nuru's hands without

formality. "If we are able to use the Claim to power the ship you've designed, the map and the Claim will guide us. How fast will we be able to reach Timeback?"

"It depends on how strong your source of power is," Nuru said.

Wafa had been following their discussion, and now he jumped in with an answer, fusing himself to Arian's side. "It's the strongest thing in the world."

Smiling, they strapped the parchment roll to Sinnia's pack, when another thought occurred to Arian. "Nuru, do you know of the Silver Mage?"

The shells on Nuru's braids danced. "By reputation only."

Arian described Daniyar. "If he should come here, please tell him of our route to Timeback. It's my hope he'll reach the airship in time, but if we fail to launch it, he'll be able to track our trail."

Nuru nodded but offered a warning. "He won't be the only one." She made a slashing gesture. "If the Angel of Blood is tracking you, you should know the airship will not fly if its sails are damaged."

Arian's lips firmed. "We'll be careful."

She took Wafa's hand in her own, giving the cousins a moment to say farewell.

It was late at night when they reached the valley of sand, pausing for a break to eat.

"We call this place Al Rimal because there is nothing in it but sand," Sinnia told her.

Arian panted her reply, her wound throbbing. "It's quite a climb through these rocks. My body needs more conditioning." Her eyes were on Wafa, who scampered through the rocks with a mountain goat's surefootedness.

A man's voice spoke into her ear, causing Arian to jump. It

contained laughter, warmth . . . intimacy. "May I offer my services with that?"

Arian whirled around. "Daniyar!"

"Arian."

He was swift to embrace her, pressing a line of kisses to her forehead, his hands smoothing down her back with the warmth that was uniquely his. Her need for him was a whip of flame through her body, but his nearness meant more to her than this all-consuming desire. It was hope, safety, tenderness . . . the chance to ground herself in his love.

He looked well to her eyes, as well as she could tell in the dark, though when the clouds shifted to allow a glimpse of moon, a bruise marred the beauty of his face. He captured the hand she raised to touch his bruise and kissed it, his lips lingering on her palm.

"It's nothing. And by some miracle of the One's, you seem uninjured also." A respectful nod at Sinnia, a fond wave to Wafa in the distance—both an almost unwilling interruption of his focus on Arian.

She sank into his embrace as Sinnia gave them a moment to speak privately, running after Wafa. When Arian had heard his tale of escape from the Sea of Reeds and told him of their reception at Axum, she asked, "Did Nuru put you on our trail?"

"She offered me the chance to rest. And the queen was generous in her reception. But I was so close, I didn't want to miss you." His arms tightened around her. "*Are* you well?"

"Now that you are with me, yes. Did Nuru tell you of this valley?"

He shook his head. His hair had grown long and wild again, well past the collar of his armor, and unable to resist the temptation, Arian found herself threading her fingers through its length.

It felt cool and silky to the touch, yet heavier than hers. He stood utterly still as she touched him, but his eyes told her of the storm within.

"Tell me now."

She made quick work of the telling, then they followed Sinnia and Wafa down from the roof of the red-black canyon whose walls were like cliffs of fire. Despite the narrowness of the passage, Daniyar held on to Arian's hand until they reached the floor of the valley. Here the airship loomed up against the night, a frightening, dark hulk.

Daniyar frowned. "Heavy to lift." His hand reached up to caress her throat. "I haven't known a qari like you, but will your recitation be equal to this test?"

She wasn't certain it would, but she tried to feign confidence. "I'll take a closer look."

She left him with Wafa, whom he drew close, while she and Sinnia circled the ship that rested in the valley of sand. Despite the drawing Nuru had shown her, the ship wasn't what she had expected.

Instead of sails rigged over a flat deck, the sails flared out like two giant wings at the stern, attached to wooden ribs angled like the bend of a bow. She thought at once of a falcon in flight, the sails rigged to open and close like the furling of the bird's wings.

The deck was bare, narrowing to a prow shaped like a steel-tipped arrow. A phalanx of similar arrows armored the hull on both sides, and below these mooring lines were cast out on the sand. A small pilothouse near the stern was protected by a series of arches that locked together. Arian and Sinnia boarded the airship from the companionway. There was seating inside the pilothouse, and a steering system comprised of pedals and a wheel. A trapdoor led to a hold below. The steering perplexed Arian, but Sinnia's question was a practical one.

"*Could* we lift this from the sands?"

Arian considered the canyon walls that surrounded them. "Even if I could call the wind to this valley, the wind would break against those cliffs."

Sinnia did a slow spin to take in the obstacles before them. Then she shrugged. "We'll need to ride the vortex. High enough to circumvent these walls."

Arian tried the wheel. It was too stiff to move, so Sinnia called down to Daniyar and Wafa. Wafa was given the task of securing their packs and weapons in the hold. Daniyar put his shoulder to the wheel.

It spun easily in either direction, but there was a groan as the rudder shifted.

"This would be safer on water," he teased.

Sinnia laughed. "Where would be the fun in that, my lord? You should be used to us by now: we've yet to learn to keep our heads down."

Daniyar reached out. He brushed Sinnia's beautiful curls, then Arian's long, dark hair.

"These two heads are precious. Take better care of them for me."

He found himself looking down at Wafa, who had finished his task and was now glaring up at Daniyar, his arms crossed over his chest. Daniyar obliged him by rubbing his head, affection plain in the gesture. "Three heads," he amended. "Take care of yours, as well."

Arian's eyes blazed with love for him. "Now that you're with us again, Wafa will worry less. The two of us can't stop ourselves from getting him into scrapes. Tell the lord Daniyar about the games at the festival, Wafa. Sinnia and I should consider how best to use the Claim."

The Companions drew away to explore the deck, so Daniyar hoisted up Wafa, giving him a chance to try the wheel, as the boy who had once been so suspicious of him—who had plainly resented his connection to Arian—chirped out story after story, the name "Ajani" quick and familiar on his lips.

"Did you win the kite-flying contest?"

"Ajani did." Only pleasure in his young voice. "I want to learn to fly like him."

"One day you will." With the air of a conspirator, Daniyar whispered, "I bet Ajani hasn't flown an airship through the skies." But he was conscious that such a task might be beyond their powers too.

He dismissed his worries from his thoughts, aware that someone new had made his way to the forefront of Wafa's stories.

The Lord of Shining Gate—could he be a possible ally?

At Wafa's description of the final race, Daniyar commented, "Quite a warrior, then. His reputation must be fearsome."

Wafa's curls shook with his earnestness. "Ajani says he's *not* a warrior. The only festival he comes to is the Festival of Manuscripts." He stumbled a little on the last word, fastening his hands onto the spokes of the wheel. He told Daniyar what had happened at the end of the race—how Sinnia had been accused by the Sidi who had refused to claim her.

Daniyar's interest sharpened. "Did you see the page yourself?"

"Everyone did."

Then the Lord of Shining Gate was a man to be wary of, his discovery of the page too convenient—he and Arian should discuss this. Shining Gate and Timeback were geographically close:

the Sidi's interest in manuscripts was something they needed to assess.

But why had the man claimed to have come for Sinnia only to refuse her hand?

He wouldn't know until he'd had a chance to speak to both Arian and Sinnia, though Sinnia might be sensitive on the subject. He asked Wafa more about it, expecting the boy's ire at the Sidi's insult to Sinnia. But Wafa seemed unmoved by the entire spectacle.

"Lady Sinnia didn't want to marry him anyway." A careless shrug. "Ajani said that the Sidi is always welcome at the court. An . . . honored guest." He pronounced the words with care. "Ajani trusts him—he says he is kind and tells lots of good stories. He always gives Ajani coins to spend at the market."

"What do Ajani and the others buy?" An idle question.

"All kinds of sweets. Stones from the market—blue, green, red, mostly white. We played marbles with them. Ajani said sometimes the Sidi plays, too, but he plays for blue."

The hairs on Daniyar's forearms were stirred by a chill.

Jeweled daggers, colored stones. Was there a connection to Najran?

"Describe him to me, Wafa."

The boy obliged, but his description did nothing to illuminate the matter, except at the end when he paused.

"Sometimes when I was looking at him, it felt like I couldn't see him. Not properly."

"What do you mean?" But the description was an echo of something Wafa had once told the Black Khan. Wafa had been interrogated by the Khan until Darya had come to his defense.

He'd said that the One-Eyed Preacher was more than just a man. That somehow he *made* himself. To be sure, he confirmed it with Wafa. "Did the Sidi look like the One-Eyed Preacher? When he called the lady Sinnia a thief, did he *feel* like the Preacher to you?"

Confused, Wafa let his hands slip from the wheel, fighting free of Daniyar's grip. His frank blue eyes were troubled.

"What is it?" Daniyar asked.

Wafa shook his head wordlessly.

"Tell me, Wafa." A softer coaxing, intended to reassure the boy.

"Ajani said the Sidi is good, but I don't know if he is or he isn't." His face pinched tight, he tried to find the right words. "I don't want to call him bad if Ajani says he isn't. The lady Arian told me to be someone who speaks the truth."

"But you felt something," Daniyar guessed.

But whether or not he had, Wafa couldn't be urged to say more than he had. The boy's enthrallment with Arian allowed for nothing else.

Daniyar couldn't blame him when he suffered from the same complaint.

45

In the end, Arian deemed it unwise to rely on the verse of the Claim she had used to summon the firewind. If the fire erupted beyond her control, it would destroy the sails. Without sails, as Nuru had warned her, the airship would not fly. Instead, she and Sinnia settled on a verse of the Claim that offered an allusion to the oceans.

Her voice rang out, radiant and clear.

"Behold! In the creation of the heavens and the earth; in the alternation of the night and the day; in the sailing of the ships through the ocean for the profit of humanity; in the rain that the One sends down from the skies . . . in the change of the winds, and the clouds that trail as servants of the wind between the sky and the earth . . ."

Sinnia completed the verse. *"Here indeed are signs for people who reflect."*

A slight stirring of the winglike sails, before the wind dispersed.

"Perhaps if we recited together?" She stretched out an arm to Daniyar. "Could you use your gifts to anchor us, my lord?"

She took a position beside the bow-like mast on the starboard side of the deck. Daniyar came to join her, linking his hands to Arian's and Sinnia's so that the three of them stood in a circle, Wafa sheltered in their midst.

She opened her mouth to try again, feeling no pain in her larynx for the first time since her escape from the Ark.

Light had transferred from Queen Zoya to herself when the queen had spoken of mishkah. A power Arian had guessed at, without the luxury of time to consider it.

Something cold brushed her cheek, a swift, transient touch— and she wondered if the wind was stirring. Just then, a blade flew past her head to the mast, where buried steel found wood.

Daniyar pushed Arian and Sinnia behind him, his body a wall of pure strength, his sword in his hand, his shield in the other, before she'd noticed him move.

Nothing stirred in the shadows, the moon illuminating the valley where scruffs of grass touched eddies of sand.

A quick glance at the mast revealed the hilt of a quivering sapphire dagger, the same one Najran had pressed to Arian's throat during their battle at Jabal Thawr.

"Take cover!" She pushed Sinnia and Wafa to the pilothouse, but Daniyar refused to give ground, and this time Arian knew better than to hesitate with the Claim.

Grabbing hold of the sapphire hilt, she intoned, *"Consider these messages sent forth in waves, and then storming on with a tempest's force! Consider these messages that spread the truth far and wide, thus separating right and wrong with all clarity."*

The knife shattered, blade and hilt, sapphires scattered on the deck.

With great satisfaction, Arian called out to Najran, "Your weapon of silence is no more."

The second blade embedded itself in Daniyar's shield, inches from his throat, flying in from another angle.

This was the emerald dagger, the one Najran favored for severing hands.

Arian's use of the Claim became thunderous. She shouted it into the valley.

"Go on toward that resurrection that you were wont to call a lie! Go on toward the threefold shadow that will offer no shade and be of no avail against the flame . . ."

The emerald blade shattered as perfectly as the first, scattering gems at Daniyar's feet.

Silence from the valley. Not a whisper of movement.

Arian edged up on her tiptoes to Daniyar. "He won't use his daggers until he's close enough to carve out my heart, but I worry that if he flings wide he might tear through the sails."

Daniyar turned his head slightly, his voice a low murmur. "Can you use the Claim to compel him to show himself?"

She shook her head, a movement he felt against his back. "I could try, but if it doesn't work, he'll have time enough to determine where our vulnerability lies."

Daniyar made a lightning-swift assessment. "Get to Sinnia, chant the wind verses, but do it so that he can't hear you. I'll distract him."

He shielded her until she slipped inside the pilothouse, then moved to the companionway, the only entrance. Unless Najran had devised a way to fly above these sands.

A shadow moved before him. He lowered his shield an inch to offer Najran a target.

This time the blade drew blood, skimming across his collarbone. He shrugged it off, kicking the blade behind him. Najran streaked up the ramp to the deck. For a moment he was out in

349

the open, trapped by a shaft of moonlight. Then he disappeared behind the pilothouse.

Daniyar planted himself by the door. What Najran wanted so urgently that Daniyar could taste it, was the chance to destroy Arian.

He'd seen something in that brief spell of moonlight—the reason that Najran had missed with every blade he'd aimed: Arian must have damaged his throwing arm when she'd fought him off in the Cave of Thawr. He'd reached for another dagger, the joint of his shoulder stiff.

Daniyar needed to consider whether Najran's left hand was as deadly as his right.

The glaive was strapped to Najran's back, a weapon of last resort perhaps, but one that hindered his balance.

His sword in his right hand, shield in his left, Daniyar reflected on what this weakness might mean. Possibly that Najran's training was not as lethal as the corps of the Assassins. He may have been used to having a host of men at his back. And remembering what Arian had told him of Najran, he knew his enemy was used to preying upon the vulnerable—women and children incapable of meeting him in fatal combat.

A hard smile touched Daniyar's lips. Najran had underestimated Arian at the Jabal Thawr. He did so again at his peril.

Daniyar shifted his weight with grace, predatory and prepared. A blade whisked past his head, striking at the cabin door. Daniyar ignored it. A creaking board betrayed Najran's sudden rush, and now Daniyar lunged forward to meet it, sword locked against sword, shield thrust hard at his foe. Najran stumbled but regained his footing, his sword slashing down from high above his head to the left. Daniyar swung his shield up to meet it, leaving his right side exposed.

Najran's left hand moved quicker than his eye could follow, the dagger in it driven through his armor to his ribs. He grunted but didn't fall back. His sword moved in a dangerous arc, striking hard at the other man's forearm.

A hiss spilled from Najran, his hood falling from his head, his eyes bright and feverish with rage. But he took the blow without losing his sword, and now Daniyar was forewarned about his agility with either hand.

He lunged forward again, yanking Najran's left leg forward by hooking his own behind it. He followed this with a swipe of his sword to the left. His timing was a moment too slow. Najran jerked back his hand and kept his dagger, this one ebony black.

A quick spin put Najran out of Daniyar's reach. For a split second, his attention shifted to something behind the Silver Mage. Daniyar felt it but didn't turn, pressing his advantage. But Najran's target changed, his cloak billowing behind him in the wind that had risen in the valley.

Not the vortex of fire this time, though. No, now the wind was freezingly cold. Buoyed by insistent pressure, falcon-winged sails flapped at Daniyar's back.

Smiling grimly, Najran drew back his arm to aim his dagger high.

Daniyar threw himself at Najran, his entire body left open. Forgetting the dagger, Najran slashed Daniyar's chest with his sword.

The blow took Daniyar to his knees, the ground shifting beneath him. The airship tipped to one side. Both men slid down the deck, Najran's ebony dagger spinning toward Daniyar. He grabbed it as it flew past, his left arm pressed against his chest, his right aiming with deadly accuracy. With momentum in his favor, the blow struck Najran hard.

The hilt of the dagger protruded from Najran's chest, just beneath his collarbone.

The airship tilted farther. Najran sailed over the side, hitting the ground with a thud.

Daniyar dragged himself over to the side, just as Arian and Sinnia raced out from the pilothouse, their arms raised to the sails, their voices joined in the Claim.

Daniyar found Najran in the shadows. He'd yanked the ebony blade from his chest and thrown it aside, his ruby dagger now in his hand.

The wing-sails opened wide, the airship began to rise.

"Hurry!" Daniyar shouted, feeling blood seep over his arm.

Najran's dagger flew forward, missing the left sail by inches. The airship dipped, swayed back, then righted itself again, rising from the sands at an agonizing pace.

Gripping the rails of the ship, Daniyar focused on Najran.

Smiling with sheer malice, the other man unbolted the steel-tipped glaive from his back. Daniyar shouted another warning, rolling his body into the path of the sails. His face sheened with sweat, he made a furious leap, trembling at the effort. The airship lurched up and out of reach, buoyed by the icy winds. Fifty feet below, Najran fell back onto the sands.

His chest soaked with blood, Daniyar hit the deck hard, pain shooting up his knees, as his torso burned with fire. But the agony was worth it.

He'd caught the iron glaive in his hand.

46

THE VERSES OF THE WINDS BUOYED THE AIRSHIP OVER THE PILLARS OF the canyon walls and shallow dunes of dry grass, with lanky lines of thorn trees and palms waving over tributaries that trickled through the desert landscape in patches of green and turquoise blue.

Their ability to sail the airship was dependent on their use of the Claim. No matter the effort they expended, mastering the air currents was difficult and taxing, a trial-and-error process through which Arian learned that neither she or Sinnia could steer the airship alone: she was stunned they could fly it at all. They required frequent rest and set down precariously in depressions of rock in the shelter of pockmarked mesas, or in the cradle of riverbeds shaded by thriving acacias. Time on the ground was used to hunt, eat, and see to their needs, but Arian spent most of it tending to Daniyar, who slept feverishly through their journey, as she treated his injuries with Alisher's precious gift.

While Sinnia and Wafa were busy searching for their next meal, Arian remained at Daniyar's side in a cabin in the hold, where the three of them had managed to carry his body. At the first opportunity to rest, she and Sinnia had stripped his armor from his torso, and Arian had cleaned the blood from his chest, spreading the loess like a salve as Daniyar had taught her in the cavern. Then she'd wrapped him in both their cloaks, their duties exchanged now.

His skin was flushed with heat, but he shivered with tremors of cold, the veins in his arms standing out in relief, his teeth chattering, and once he muttered in delirium that he couldn't find a way to get warm.

She didn't hesitate. She lay down next to him, resting her head on his undamaged arm while she held him in her embrace. He stirred uneasily, but as he inhaled the scent of her hair, he subsided into a deeper sleep. Arian stayed awake, watchful for signs of distress. Soon, his tremors eased as his body drew heat from hers. She stroked a hand over his heart, reassured by its steady beat, her cheek pressed to his chest.

Daniyar was so beautifully made, so strong and undiminished despite the blows he had suffered, that her heart thudded as she stroked him. His skin was a gold deepened by the sun, lightly covered with hair that caught against her fingers.

So many scars, she thought, tracing muscle and sinew and bone. So many battles he'd fought against the Talisman ascent. So much power in the strength of his limbs, such discipline in how he used that strength. Not against the weak, but rather to defend her, standing firm at her side.

She felt that power flex beneath her hands, his body tense and muscled, his lashes drifting up over clouded silver eyes. His voice rough with disuse, he asked, "What were you just thinking?"

A wave of relief crashed over her. But when his eyes heated, she became aware that her hands were caressing his chest, stroking over his body with more than a touch of possessiveness.

"How beautiful you are." The heat in his eyes flamed into an inferno. He shifted her over his body with an ease that belied his injuries.

"Careful! You'll reopen your wounds." She couldn't banish her fear. At the Ark, Daniyar had raged against the worst tortures of the Authoritan. To see his eyes closed, his body restless as his masculine power was tamed, had been as if she'd suffered his injuries herself.

He didn't listen, drawing her against his body.

She felt herself coming to life.

"I was protected by my armor—now all I feel is you. Touch me, Arian." Focused intensity and dark male warmth, a pull she couldn't resist. Lashes lowered, she did as he asked, pressing her lips to his collarbone, his scent in her every breath. Her hands smoothed from his shoulders to his chest to the sound of an indrawn gasp. Pain? Or pleasure? There was a rare hesitation in his eyes.

"Is this what you truly want? Or do you think to give me comfort?"

Had she ever wanted anything else? Daniyar in her arms, at her mercy. Hers to pet and indulge, hers to conquer and claim.

A little wrathful, she said, "I was comforting *myself,* if anything. I needed to know you were safe."

A possessive hand settled in the center of her back, firing her body with warmth.

"We're alone?" He didn't look around.

She nodded, color rising to her face. She had contrived this time alone. She had wanted this more than anything, her body locked to his like a lover's.

"And the vows you took at Hira? Are you choosing to renounce them?"

"Don't you want me to?" Uncertainty colored her voice. She hadn't expected his insistence that she face up to her choices to tell him boldly of her needs. Lying flush against him, she tried to find the right words. "I wasn't thinking that far ahead; I just needed to be near you."

"I don't want you to have regrets." Eyes dark and sincere, lips a breath away from hers, but he didn't kiss her, letting her decide. It took him only a moment to see that she hadn't yet come to a place where the promise of a future outweighed the needs of their present. Quietly, he said, "Nothing that passes between us should feel as if you didn't have a choice."

"Does it matter so much why? Do I matter so much?"

"Yes." Firm, unshakable conviction. "What I want from you, Arian, won't be satisfied with only this." Silver fire between heavy eyelids, lips firm and sensual, daring her self-restraint.

She gripped his face between her hands and stole a kiss for herself. Then she rubbed her cheek against his beard in pretend complaint. "Why couldn't you just accept this? Why must you ask for so much?"

Easing the tension between them, he teased, "I didn't know you would come to me when I lay broken in your arms." His eyes were clear, his body poised beneath her touch: she knew his healing had begun.

"You don't feel all that broken to me." Words of praise as she caressed him, the ghost of a smile his response.

"It's no trouble to change my mind." His hand found the curve of her hip and squeezed. But when he groaned at her involuntary movement, she shifted her weight off his body. He caught her before she could escape, strong fingers trapping her wrist, lightning sparking where he touched. He was too beautiful to resist, too beloved to oppose in anything that mattered.

"Arian." He waited for her to meet his eyes. "This isn't a rejection."

"I know—I'm not giving you up; I was trying not to hurt you." Tenderness filled his expression.

Her hand curled into his, her fingers stroking his palm. Suddenly, she wasn't in as much of a rush to put distance between them. She settled against him in her earlier pose, her head tucked against his chest, her fingers splayed across his jaw.

"You're right." She could see the confession surprised him. "When the moment comes, I'll have to think of Hira. But for now, it's enough that you're here with me—enough to know that you're safe." Her skin warm with color, emotion caught in her throat. "It's more than I've had in years, when even the thought of seeing you was an impossible hope."

"Arian."

Her voice thickened. "No, let me say it. I was consecrated to Hira, but I knew what was truly sacred."

He turned to his side to enclose her in his arms, ignoring her protest about his injuries. She felt the exquisite ache of being his without being able to claim him. They were lying face-to-face, and something stretched tight between them, a yearning shaped by years of isolation.

"We could make vows of our own," he told her. "Just as you chose your Audacy, you could take your own path in this."

Her face became somber, considering the possibility. She had held to Hira as long as she could, but what was Hira now with Ilea determined against her, the Citadel's captains dismissed, and whispers abounding as to the Black Khan's influence?

The High Companion had conspired with Rukh to send her to Black Aura. Not to find Lania but to face the Authoritan's wrath.

What loyalty could she hold to Hira in the aftermath of that?

Though it was no easier to walk away.

She thought of her earlier discussion with Sinnia about the restrictions placed on them by the Council. For a moment it had seemed as though Sinnia, too, had found someone who could stand at her side—who could see her as more than a Companion, though she and Sinnia had always believed there was no status as honorable.

Arian's thoughts whispered over a name. *Arsalan*. His mother had been a Companion of Hira. She must have given up her position on the Council when she'd chosen to marry. A woman who showed no disloyalty to the Council during her time as a Companion was accorded the honor of her former status.

So Arian and Sinnia were bound by their vows for as long as they chose to serve the Council. But she *could* walk away from Hira, if she chose.

What choice she would make when that moment came, she couldn't know until she'd made her stand against the One-Eyed Preacher. There was much that would have to be weighed.

Daniyar was watching her face, one hand raised to her forehead to play with strands of her hair. "Tell me."

She placed her hand on his forearm, gently tracing his veins. "The ranks of the Companions have thinned over time; there are so few of us left." Her thumb pressed against his pulse, which quickened at her touch. "Were I to leave, there is no one who could take my place."

Before Daniyar could protest, she pressed her fingers to his lips.

"I should have been training novices," she confessed. "When the Talisman began their purges, preserving our knowledge became urgent. Had I spent the past decade in the scriptorium, others may have been ready to take over my duties by now. Instead . . ."

Daniyar caught her fingers with his own, his eyes steady on

hers. "Instead, you broke slave-chains! What would have become of the women you returned to the safety of their families?"

Arian's eyes widened, the pale irises darkening to jade.

"Are you saying I made the right choice? You believe my Audacy was worthwhile?"

"If anything could account for the misery of separation, surely it would be this."

She looked away, wanting to shield her thoughts.

"You don't believe me?" He kissed her fingertips, turned her hand upward, and placed a kiss to the center of her palm. "Why not?"

"Because . . ." Her lashes drifted up. "You were so *angry* in the Black Khan's throne room. You cut me with your words."

Sorrow and regret in those eyes like silver flames. "I was blinded by pride. 'How could she leave me again?' I thought, 'After all I gave her? After I pledged myself to her.'" His beautiful lips compressed in bitterness. "My arrogance is a flaw I haven't overcome."

"No." Her own voice soft because she couldn't bear his self-flagellation. "I didn't know you'd gone to Hira to ask for leave on my behalf. Ilea used it against you. She used it against us both." She made up her mind to say the rest. "If we were bound to each other formally, she wouldn't be able to set us against each other. She couldn't interfere."

He gripped the nape of her neck and pulled her in for a kiss that altered the foundations on which she'd built her life. She met him kiss for kiss, touch for touch, until a small sound of protest recalled his wounds to her mind.

"Stop." She didn't want him to, but her hands pushed at his shoulders. He continued to nuzzle her with his jaw, his beard softly abrasive against her skin. "We were talking."

More open with each other than time and circumstance had ever before allowed.

Kisses along her jawline attempted to change her mind. "I like this kind of talking."

"Daniyar." She raised her head for a kiss. "This isn't helping."

"No?" He bit at her lower lip. "I'm feeling much better already."

A helpless laugh from Arian and he stilled, drawing back to look at her again. "What is it?" A plea not to say anything that would ruin the sweetness between them.

"Your laughter—" He shook his head. "It's been too long since I've heard it. I've missed it." A tug at her long dark hair. "I've missed everything about you."

Her whole body softened in his arms, as she breathed a prayer of gratitude for the boundless gift of his love. "Have you?"

He bit her lip again for having the temerity to ask. "And you?"

They looked at each other, serious now, Silver Mage to First Oralist of Hira, a binding unlike anything in Khorasan's history.

"I told you what it was like for me in the throne room."

Where she'd left him behind, pushed too far by his rejection.

What do you know of how it felt to cut out my heart from my body?

And he'd answered her by stealing her rage. *You cut out my heart too.*

"I need to hear it again." His mesmerizing smile flashed against his dark skin. "In kinder words."

All thought of restraint left Arian. "I would have given anything to have you. The time I spend on my own in prayer, I spend asking for you, asking to be shown a path, a way, *any* way, in which I might keep you by my side." A bittersweet smile touched her lips. "The One has yet to answer, but that doesn't stop me from asking. Perhaps I should consider a Night Journey to seek out the knowledge I need."

"I wish there was truth to the fable." His longing as deep as hers.

It was a moment of unalterable intimacy between them; they looked at each other, spellbound. Arian felt a tightness in her chest, the weight of all she was feeling.

She felt her breath leave her body in a sigh when his empathy shone through, answering her concerns about Hira, a response that moved beyond their quiet seclusion in the cabin.

"Ilea will not be able to succeed in removing you from the Council on the grounds of affection for me. As you said, there is no other who could take your place, and without your gifts the Citadel is weak. Even were that not the case, Ilea would not succeed in poisoning your sisters against you, when she herself has transgressed the Council's rules by her congress with the Black Khan. In accusing you, she accuses herself."

Arian shook her head at his use of the word *affection* to describe the emotion that blazed so fiercely between them.

"Our Jurist might well rule that both Ilea and I are in violation of the oaths we took."

"Ash is too wise to think of weakening Hira at its darkest hour. More, she must know of a circumstance where dispensation would apply. She was there when I made my appeal."

"If your appeal was denied, Ash must have ruled against you."

"Ilea didn't afford me an open deliberation. When I made my petition, Ash said she needed time to access rulings on the question."

"And Ilea overruled her?"

Daniyar's hold tightened. "Given what we've learned of Ilea, we shouldn't be surprised. What could it matter, Arian?" His silver eyes were grave. "Why is not possible for a Companion of Hira to be consecrated to a man she loves in an honorable bond?"

Arian's heart beat frantically in her chest. "Would you wed me?"

"This instant." His hands smoothed up her back to cup her head. "Isn't that what I've been saying? Didn't I attempt to bind you with my ring?"

She was taking them off the subject again, but Arian didn't mind. "What would I bind *you* with?"

Laughter in those magnetic eyes. "Your hair." He tugged at it, wrapped its silky strands around his fingers. "The beauty of your eyes. The sweetness of your kiss." His lips traced the rim of her ear. "The murmur of the Claim on your lips. Any of those. *All* of those."

"Then we are bound," she said with a smile.

"And Hira?"

She remembered Queen Zoya's caution about Sinnia and the Lord of Shining Gate and recounted it to Daniyar. "When we serve as Companions, our first duty is meant to be to Hira. We commit ourselves to chastity so there will be no question of conflicting allegiance."

"Such as yours to me." He kissed her, his lips moving over the wings of her brows. "Not that you have been particularly obedient to my wishes."

Arian shushed him. "But what if Queen Zoya was right when she said the allegiance we owe is *not* to Hira but to the All-Seeing One? What if the Council imposed itself between the Companions and the One as a means of control? *Then* where would our loyalties lie?"

From the light that entered Daniyar's eyes, she knew he shared her hope.

"Since I've held you in my arms like this and taken these untold liberties, have your circlets given you pain? Do they bind your arms more tightly or burn you with their light?"

"No." She flexed her arms slightly and realized it was true.

An irresistible tug brought her lips to his. "Then you see," he murmured into her mouth. "My love for you, yours for me . . . our pledging ourselves to each other . . . *cannot* be an act against the One, though I will think on it more." Tired now, he released her and rolled onto his back. She tugged her cloak around them again to keep his body warm. But also to keep them cocooned in this moment of utter peace.

"We will find a way."

She burrowed into his side, her hold a fierce avowal that she wouldn't give him up again.

"And when we do?"

"*I will be your garment just as you are mine.*"

47

IN THE HEART OF THE SAHEL, THE LAND WAS STILL, SAND-BRUSHED dunes and mud-baked earth lying undisturbed, a landscape of ochre and gold. At other places, there were startling signs of life in green oases that sprang up wherever the Green Bend touched. Ospreys rested above tall grasses that swayed at the edge of the river. Small rivercraft were moored in clumps at tributaries that leaked west from the great river as it made its arc, but those who steered them were absent. The isolated settlements that passed beneath their transport appeared abandoned. There was no one to point to the airship that sailed through the sky, no crowds of boisterous children to call out greetings as they passed.

The air was bone-dry, made hotter and wilder by the Claim-winds that Arian and Sinnia summoned, while Daniyar watched with Wafa for signs of attack or pursuit. There was none, though Daniyar took the time to destroy the iron glaive and scatter its pieces across the hushed landscape below. The Sahel may have been silent at times, but now the north felt dead. No matter where Daniyar swept his spyglass, there was no sign of the riverboats from the south or of the caravans that ferried loads of salt from the north. The slow-moving canoes that should have carried goods to city markets were missing along the water. The tapestry below was of a magnificent gold and blue and green field, a primordial land enclosed in silence.

Hours passed before they arrived at a barren plateau. At the northeast end of the plateau were two pillars of limestone surrounded by acacias, the pillars flanking a gate, the entrance to an unbarred city.

Sinnia pointed to a spot. Together, she and Arian brought the airship to rest, having learned the trick of balance, though the deck still tilted south.

"The gates of Timeback. From here, it is a half day's walk into the city itself."

Daniyar lowered the ramp, and their small party moved into the burning heat of the day.

"I thought there would be more life here. Like the welcome of Axum."

"Something's wrong," Sinnia said. "It was nothing like this when I came here as a child."

They made their way to the gates, each carrying a pack.

Arian glanced at Daniyar. She'd felt something upon their approach to Timeback—a call as powerful as the summons to Hira, yet somehow specific to who she was as First Oralist of Hira.

She considered the distance to the city beyond the gates, and felt the urgency of that pull. She brushed her hands over her circlets, seeking an explanation. "I don't know if the Codex is here, but I sense a presence here."

Daniyar's spyglass swept the plateau. "Is it hostile?"

Arian paused, running her fingers over the inscriptions on her tahweez. "I'm not certain, though I sense its anger."

"It could be Najran. He may have found a way to track us."

Sinnia objected. "The airship we commanded was Nuru's prototype. There haven't been any others. And who else is there who could offer such mastery of the Claim?"

Arian motioned them on, their shields raised, their swords ready. "We know better now than to underestimate Najran. As a disciple of the One-Eyed Preacher, his gifts are an echo of ours."

Sinnia kept walking, moving smoothly ahead, but Arian heard the words she tossed over her shoulder. "There *is* no other ship."

Daniyar's face was grim. "Najran wouldn't need a ship." He paused, raising his head, as a restless wind blew over the plateau, carrying a crisp new scent.

Arian took his hand in hers. "What is it?"

He gave it a reassuring squeeze, a slight frown on his brow. "It's nothing. I thought I recognized something . . . someone, but there's no one here."

Wafa circled back to them, and clutched at Daniyar's arm. "There's someone. There's many someones."

He pointed to the path that led into the city from the opposite side of the gate. Perched on small dunes that loomed over the path were figures whose spears were poised above their shoulders but whose faces couldn't be seen because they were covered with masks. Black fabric shielded their faces, the eyes and mouth picked out with shells in menacing patterns. Their chests were bare save for straps made of dozens of small white stones that ran down from their shoulders to feathered skirts dyed in shades of fuchsia, with outer fringes of amber.

Sinnia signaled to the others to wait. "Let me." Without hesitation, she spoke in a dialect of the region, calling out greetings to the men.

A man larger than the rest moved down from his hiding place, his spear still raised, his mask distinguished from the others by a pair of reddish fox ears.

Sinnia threw back her cloak to reveal her circlets, bowing her head at the man.

"Greetings from the Council of Hira to the Lord of Foxes. Peace be upon your people. May your family be well, your livestock healthy, and your bodies strong."

"Sahabiya." The man set his spear in the ground. A rapid conversation followed. He listened to Sinnia's explanation before he pointed his spear at Arian with what sounded like a demand. Daniyar pushed Arian behind him, his hand on the hilt of his sword.

The Foxlord stirred but made no move forward. He held up one arm, his mask swiveling to the dunes. His warriors stayed in place.

Sinnia gave him a friendly smile, then spoke to Arian in the language of the Citadel. "He asks for a blessing of the Claim over his people and their prophets. They venerate the fox. A blessing over the natural world would assure them we mean them no harm."

Arian eased out from under Daniyar's arm. She offered the verse at once. Sinnia knelt on the ground, searching for something in her pack. She produced a small leather pouch, cinched with a sturdy string. When Arian's recitation ended, she offered the pouch to the Foxlord.

"Gris-gris." She made the word sound like a promise. "You can walk the Sahel, one end to the other, and no one will be able to harm you. Blessings on you and your gods."

The Foxlord's hand closed around the pouch. Behind him, his warriors began to chant a song of welcome. Sinnia and the

Foxlord conferred a little longer before he gave them a blessing in turn, calling to one of his warriors.

A lean warrior skidded down the dune to give Sinnia a gift. It was the forepaw of a fox. She turned so the warriors could see her and pressed it to her forehead and bowed.

"The Lord of Foxes honors me."

The warrior gave her a slightly larger bundle wrapped inside a cloth. He indicated Sinnia's companions, and she amended her statement.

"The honor—and the gift of food—is for all of us. It will see us safely into the city."

Clouds had begun to amass over their heads, dark and heavy with rain that would not fall. A sudden crack of thunder followed by a bolt of lightning made them jump. To their surprise, the Foxlord began to laugh, a sound that boomed from his chest. Then he spoke to them in the Common Tongue, the tips of his fox ears quivering.

"*Usman,*" he said, his spear aimed at the sky.

Sinnia nodded, perplexed.

His shoulders continued to shake, as he placed a giant hand on Sinnia's slender shoulder.

"Your lover will come for you soon."

48

When they had left the Foxlord and his warriors behind, Arian slipped her arm through Sinnia's.

"You knew them," she said.

"They come to our markets to trade."

"What did the Foxlord mean about the lightning?"

Sinnia grimaced. "It's an old superstition of these lands. Lightning signifies that a woman has a distant lover." Her hands tightened on the straps of her pack. "But it can also mean an unrequited love." Her dark eyes flashed with anger at the inadvertent prodding of a wound.

Daniyar moved to Sinnia's other side, and Arian asked him, "Was it the Foxlord you thought you recognized?" She knew it wasn't their presence that she had sensed earlier.

Daniyar shook his head, his attention on Sinnia. "What did he tell you? Does he know why the city is deserted?"

"Not just the city, the Sahel." The light left Sinnia's face. "I haven't been to Timeback since I was a child. The people of the Negus have a tradition of exchanging visits with the Salaf. But there was no sign of the Mage of the Blue Eye—even then he must have been a recluse."

Daniyar said nothing to this, impatient for the rest of Sinnia's explanation.

With a sigh she continued. "We may have come too late. The Blue Mage hasn't been seen in these parts for a decade. The Fox-lord said Timeback was attacked by a plague."

Arian's brows drew together, but when Wafa caught at her hand, she softened her expression. "It's not possible. The plague was trapped behind the Authoritan's Wall. It couldn't have crossed the sea."

Sinnia dug for the bundle of food in her pack. She passed it to Daniyar.

"He didn't mean an actual plague; he was describing a calamity. A war was waged across the Sahel by a group he called Those Who Sign With Blood."

She accepted a piece of dried meat from Daniyar and passed another to Wafa, who took the time to chew it.

Arian came to a halt.

"The words you found on the manuscript hidden in the ark—they warned the readers of the manuscript to beware of Those Who Sign With Blood."

Sinnia faced her. "They came here ten months ago and swept across the Sahel. The Foxlord said they were enemies to the tribes who lived here. They broke their idols, insulted their beliefs—they burned the temples of the Foxlords and drove the people of Timeback into hiding." She hesitated, her glance settling on Daniyar. "What he described sounded much like what the Talisman did in Candour."

Daniyar considered this, still caught by that sense of recognition. "The Talisman haven't journeyed across the sea."

"They wouldn't need to." Arian shivered at the implications. "Not with the Rising Nineteen at the threshold of the Sea of Reeds."

Sinnia balked at this. "Are you saying that the Rising Nineteen and Those Who Sign With Blood represent the same entity? There hasn't been a battle in Axum."

"We've seen their ships, Sinnia. They could have crossed the sea far north of Axum and traveled west."

"But why wouldn't they have taken their war to Axum first?"

Arian resumed her pace, the others falling into step beside her. "Perhaps they wanted to conquer the maghreb before they broke their truce with the Negus." She touched Sinnia's shoulder in apology. "As Queen Zoya told us, they laid other plots in Axum by infiltrating the court."

Sinnia's face darkened at the reminder. "Axum will not fall," she said.

Arian stared into the distance, seeing the ruins ahead.

"Timeback already has."

A great red ring ran around the outskirts of the city, perhaps a road in earlier times, still framed by jacaranda trees, their scent a mark of freshness on a city where no one lived.

On the other side of the ring was a warren of houses, low and flat, made of mud and clay to withstand the brutal heat. There was no movement from any of these, no livestock grazing in courtyards, no residents to greet them from within the shelter of awnings, no coffee prepared in communal ceremonies, no offer of hospitality.

Just red markings painted across the doors of some of the houses, two vertical lines with a diagonal slash across.

Sinnia nudged Arian, reminding her that she had found the same symbol on the manuscript in the ark of the tabot. She'd been caught off guard by Yusuf's deception, she hadn't paid attention to the manuscript itself, a weakness she recognized now.

Perhaps he had tried to tell her something of use. But his accusation of theft belied his efforts to help.

"What do you think the symbol means?" Arian asked her.

"It must be the mark of Those Who Sign With Blood. They've marked many of these homes, but the animists we encountered don't live in cities, so the Foxlord couldn't tell me more. Could this symbol be a warning of some kind?"

Sinnia felt frustrated by her lack of answers, by the confusion that sat heavy on her heart. She had wanted to rediscover the city she remembered from her youth, a city of color and laughter, where different tribes lived together with ease, their religion gentle, their tradition a welcoming thing.

This utter emptiness—this desertion—made Sinnia fear annihilation.

Arian turned to Daniyar, nodding at the homes they passed. "Is one of these the home of the Blue Mage? Is there a chance he's here?"

Daniyar shook his head. "I met him at the center of the city, at a house of worship under his protection. It served as a scriptorium, but there weren't many treasures in his care. We should head in that direction, keep an eye out as we go. We could knock on a few of these doors."

Their party split up, Arian and Sinnia to one side, Wafa and Daniyar to the other. No one answered as they knocked, red dust stirring at their heels as they made their way into the interior, the heat bearing down upon them, hemmed in by the stifling cloud cover.

"What now?"

Daniyar pointed to a low rise on the horizon, blanketed by clouds. "Look there," he said. "The house of worship still stands."

49

"THIS IS IT." DANIYAR TRIED HUGE TIMBERED DOORS DECORATED IN the maghrebi style, with silver inlays on the frame. He wasn't surprised that the silver hadn't been stripped away; the inscription above the doors warned that opening them on any day other than a holy day would herald a cataclysm that would lead to the Day of Resurrection.

"You're taking our fate in your hands." Sinnia studied the ground beneath the doors where dirt and mud had piled up, undisturbed for centuries.

"This isn't the traditional entrance, so it seems safer to take it." Daniyar shoved hard at the unlocked doors. He rubbed his shoulder with a grimace to meet Arian's look of reproof.

"I could have helped you with that."

He caught her close, kissed her, heedless of the presence of Sinnia and Wafa. Arian had promised him a binding—in his mind they were already bound.

"Save the Claim for when we need it."

They entered the adobe structure, choking on clouds of dust that arose as they passed.

"No one's been here in ages," Sinnia said. "We won't find the Blue Mage here."

"He may have vaulted the walls of the outer courtyard, or he might know another entrance. When I was here last, he wasn't disposed to share his secrets."

They moved farther into the dusty interior, passing through the great hall to come out into the first of three courtyards. Daniyar kept Arian's hand in his, and she tugged at it to ask him, "Will you tell us about your conference with the Mage of the Blue Eye?"

Daniyar scrutinized the cool, spare structure of the complex as he answered.

"He wanted to consult the Candour, so he asked me to come to Timeback. When I did, he showed me the book that is the trust of the Blue Mage, the book that teaches him his powers."

Arian's breath caught. "Not the Sana Codex?"

A quick look of regret. "No, my love. The book of the Blue Mage is called the Pearl. Its full name is the Pearl of Timeback, named for the Baba who made the city a place of renown. The Pearl is written on a parchment so delicate that its pages seem to glow with light." His voice roughened with emotion. "The Blue Mage granted me the privilege of reading several pages."

He smiled down at Arian as her hand gripped his.

"It reflected the learning of its age. The title pages were decorated with floating ornaments and letters inlaid with gold." He shook his head in remembered wonder. "And notations were made by different hands in various scripts and tongues. It was exquisite, Arian. I wish you could have seen it."

He led them across the courtyard to a low building shaped from the same patchwork of mud and adobe brick. They passed the stairs of a minaret whose facade was pierced with dozens of spindles made from bundles of sticks. A gray-winged falcon rested at the top of these.

"A tower of the Claim," said Sinnia. "But the Call hasn't sounded here for over a thousand years."

Daniyar pushed open the door to the scriptorium. He asked Sinnia and Wafa to guard the door, while he guided Arian into the antechamber. "This is where the Blue Mage showed me the Pearl of Timeback." His eyes scanned the destruction within. The cabinets and trunks where manuscripts had been stored were smashed and looted. Not a single sheaf had escaped annihilation. An all-too-familiar sight after the destruction of the Library of Candour.

The same pain was felt by Arian. "They left the house of worship intact, but not the means to worship by."

"They must have been afraid of anything that could challenge their doctrine." Daniyar crouched down, pushing aside one of the uprooted shelves. His hand came away discolored. He held it up to show Arian a red mark.

A new voice spoke, warmed with cadences of the maghreb. "It was done by Those Who Sign With Blood. They chased out the White Fathers who were trusted with guarding the word."

Arian and Daniyar whirled, swords in hand, to see a man advancing into the antechamber from a door at the rear of the room. He wore a loose, indigo-dyed robe that covered him from neck to ankles. His turban was a lighter shade of blue, the ends left unwrapped to drift down either side of his head, his skin a rich dark brown in a face with harshly carved cheekbones and eyes that blazed a piercing blue.

Daniyar sheathed his sword and moved close to embrace the other man.

"Amghar. It's been too long."

"Daniyar. I've told you to call me by my name."

Arian took a step back. "Sidi Yusuf? The Lord of Shining Gate?"

But this couldn't be the man they had met in Axum. His eyes were brightly blue, his accent and dress altogether different. Confused, she glanced at Daniyar.

"Arian, this is *Amghar* Yusuf, the Mage of the Blue Eye. Yusuf, the First Oralist of Hira."

Arian stared into eyes so fiercely blue they caused an ache behind her eyelids. Gone were the flame-lit clouds that had struck her as unusual in Axum. She had thought more than once that she wasn't seeing Sidi Yusuf clearly. Now she knew why. The Blue Mage had somehow disguised the clarity and power of his gaze.

He gave her a warmer greeting than he had given her in Axum, bringing his forearm to his chest and holding it out, in the manner of the Companions.

"First Oralist. I regret the deception."

Arian explained it to Daniyar with some haste, conscious of Sinnia in the outer chamber. He related his surprise in turn—Wafa had mentioned the Lord of Shining Gate, but he had never used his name or Daniyar would have guessed sooner at the presence he'd thought he'd sensed.

Arian considered the title Daniyar had used, a title accorded by nomadic tribes. *Amghar*, chief of the clan. She considered also that the hands of the Blue Mage were perfumed with parchment and ink: his skin was scented with manuscripts.

"Amghar Yusuf. Why was the deception necessary at all? Sinnia and I have been searching for the Blue Mage—we could have used your assistance."

He made a quick bow. When he realized that Arian was having

trouble sustaining his gaze, his eyes shifted from searing blue to clouded shadows.

"We can't speak here, it's too exposed. I'll take you somewhere where we can." He arranged the tails of his tagelmust, so that his face was veiled, the glimmer of his eyes showing through. "Say nothing to Sinnia yet."

Daniyar checked him. "What happened to the treasures of Timeback's scriptorium? There have been rumors of trade from the Great Bend to Black Aura."

The Blue Mage shrugged. "What good are manuscripts when people are starving?"

Arian gasped. But at a signal from Daniyar, she turned to fetch Sinnia and Wafa.

Daniyar studied the other man. "Was that for the First Oralist's benefit? I remember the vows you took."

I have sworn to protect the manuscripts for as long as I live.

"Just a test of her commitment."

Daniyar stiffened at the implication, but for the moment he brushed it aside. "Then the treasury is safe?"

The Blue Mage lowered his scarf from his mouth to speak.

"We discussed the Harrowing the last time you were here."

Daniyar remembered it well. He and Yusuf had spoken into the night about the long-ago period when Timeback's historic treasury had almost come to ruin. The forerunners of the Talisman had come to burn its libraries. In response, the people of Timeback had banded together as custodians of their history. The manuscripts of Timeback had been sent downriver from the city to be buried in the desert.

"Those Who Sign With Blood brought a second Harrowing. These lands were bereft of the Claim, but they took what remained of the written word and burned it in the city center."

The bitter defeat in the Blue Mage's voice resonated with Daniyar, an echo of his failure at the Library of Candour when the Talisman had burned it to the ground.

"They chant the name of the One as they wreak destruction on the world."

Perfect understanding from the Blue Mage.

"They offer recitation without meaning." The Blue Mage cast a glance around the wanton destruction in the room. "Those Who Sign With Blood were an offshoot of the Nineteen, too many to withstand on my own. But the collection that mattered, I sent to safety." When Daniyar tensed, the Blue Mage held up a hand. "Not here. Not yet. The Companions must hear it too."

He wrapped his face up again as Arian and Sinnia returned . . . a blue-eyed boy in tow.

50

AN HOUR LATER, AN HOUR THAT HAD PASSED IN SILENCE, THEY FOUND themselves making their way through a labyrinth of tunnels beneath the complex. They emerged on the eastern side, far from the center of the city, at the grassy banks of a fast-running, olive-green river. Under the shade of acacias and palms, a round-eyed girl was tending a cooking fire. The girl wore a long tunic over loose trousers, her hair covered by a headcloth.

Arian lingered behind the group with Sinnia, hoping to prepare her before the Mage of the Blue Eye made his identity known. She knew Sinnia had guessed that something was amiss from the sharp looks she shot at Daniyar and herself, so she sent Wafa to assist the girl who was preparing a meal and drew Sinnia back into the palms.

But her efforts were defeated when the Blue Mage unwrapped his tagelmust and dropped it on a mat at his feet.

Sinnia gripped one of her knives. But she let her hand fall when the stranger raised his head to pin her with his eyes—eyes that pierced through their mantle of clouds until a burning blue remained. Sinnia froze in place. Then she turned her head to stare at Arian, deep distrust on her face.

"What is this?" And then steadying her voice, "*Who* is he?"

"The Blue Mage said he would explain once we reached this oasis," Arian said.

"*The Blue Mage?*"

The words were stark with horror, Sinnia aghast. Her gaze whipped to Daniyar. "Is this man a Mage of Khorasan, my lord?"

Daniyar knew enough of the story now to make sense of Sinnia's anger. He touched her hand lightly, trying to impart calm. "Amghar Yusuf is from the maghreb, which makes him one of our own."

"Amghar? The title of nomadic clan chief?" Sinnia drew herself up, fine and proud, as her dark eyes flayed the man who had dared to deceive her. "You called yourself the Lord of Shining Gate, Sidi Yusuf. Yet here you are the Mage who is said to govern Timeback."

He took her anger as his due, saying only, "Forgive me. If it had been possible to reveal the truth to you in Axum, know that I would have done so. Come." He invited them all to sit under the shelter of the trees, as river birds swam up to the banks. "We'll eat as we speak. It will be long before you have another chance for rest. Serve the zrig, Tafalkayt."

Daniyar and Arian sat side by side on the mat, but Sinnia stayed where she was, one hand on her hip, the other poised above her whip.

The Blue Mage glanced at her, his expression unreadable, before he placed wooden bowls for each member of their group in the center of the mat, as Wafa helped the girl called Tafalkayt carry a stone jug. Arian had the sense that the girl was letting him help—her arms were twice as sturdy as Wafa's.

When Tafalkayt bent to pour a thick liquid mixture into each bowl, Arian had a closer look at her. She was older than Wafa by several years, her thickset body flushed with health. When she passed Arian a bowl and smiled, the right side of her face didn't move, stretched tight by a pattern of scars. These weren't tribal motifs like the lines of black henna on her chin. They spoke of the fire, of disfigurement. She flashed a look of concern at Sidi Yusuf, but his attention was focused on Sinnia.

"Join us, Sinnia." Arian stretched out her hand, knowing that Sinnia was wary of the Blue Mage, given all that had passed in Axum. But after a moment, Sinnia eased down on the mat next to Arian. Ignoring the Blue Mage, who seated himself across from her, she thanked the young girl who poured the zrig into their bowls.

The zrig was a mixture of goat milk and millet, sweetened with a rare quantity of sugar. Feeling the kiss of Daniyar's eyes on her lips, Arian drank without restraint. She realized that she should have waited to give a blessing, but the Foxlord's gift had not sufficed to ease her hunger. She could smell the spicy scent of fish being cooked over the campfire—she would offer the blessing over their meal instead.

Everyone drank except Sinnia. The Blue Mage prodded her, sipping from his bowl. "Is the zrig not to your liking?"

Arian's fingers froze on her bowl, anticipating Sinnia's response.

But Sinnia's reply was unruffled, and all the more calculated for it.

"I wonder that it behooves you to take your meal with a thief."

The Blue Mage set down his bowl with a thud. "I regret that my actions in Axum caused you offense, Companion."

Coolly, Sinnia replied, "*Now* you seem to remember the appropriate form of address."

A tense silence fell over their company.

The Blue Mage broke it by asking, "Would you prefer me to call you Sinnia?"

Ignoring the gentle pressure of Arian's hand on her thigh, Sinnia shot back, "I would prefer you explain why you accused me of theft. Or why you carried out *any* part of your deception."

Yusuf's blindingly blue gaze swept from Arian to Daniyar before it came to rest on Sinnia. "A lieutenant of the Rising Nineteen called Najran has spent the past year whispering into the ear of the Negus. Forcing you into marriage was a scheme he devised to isolate the First Oralist—to leave her bereft of your protection." His gaze touched briefly on Wafa, then on Daniyar. "I didn't know then that the Silver Mage was sworn to the First Oralist's service." His attention returned to Sinnia, who had finally taken up her bowl. "I entered the festival to ensure you would be able to continue your journey at the First Oralist's side."

Sinnia sipped from her bowl. She closed her eyes to savor the sweetness of the zrig. When she opened them again, the Blue Mage was watching her with an intensity that reignited the spark of the Claim that she had tried to tamp down. A subtle flinch at the corners of his eyes told her he felt it too. But neither of them chose to speak of it.

"Understood." Her acknowledgment was flat. "But why continue your pretense when we were alone at the maqdas?"

She tried not to notice when Daniyar slid his bowl across to Arian. He'd left more than half his zrig for Arian, a gesture of the tenderest care. But with the same mark of tenderness, Arian passed the bowl back to Daniyar, urging him to finish it himself.

A surge of nameless emotion arose in Sinnia when the Blue Mage noticed the silent interaction, and refilled both Arian's bowl and Daniyar's from the jug in the center of the mat. To give herself a moment, she looked over at Wafa, chatting happily with Tafalkayt as he helped her tend the fish in the pan. The company of other children at Axum had been good for him; he was no longer as shy, nor as certain of enmity everywhere he turned.

"I couldn't tell you who I was or why I was in Axum, because Najran's spies are everywhere—I didn't know if we would be overheard, or whether, unbeknownst to you, you would confide in a courtier or cousin he had turned. I planted the page in your pack because I knew an accusation of theft would disrupt Najran's plan to keep you trapped in Axum."

His strategy *had* been effective. Instead of insisting on her marriage, the Negus had banished her at once.

When Sinnia silently conceded his point, the tension in his posture eased.

"A temporary victory only," he warned. "Once Najran learns of it, he will seek out your trail again."

Daniyar interrupted. "The Companions are well-acquainted with the Angel of Blood."

The Blue Mage muttered a choice phrase under his breath. "How so?"

Daniyar gave him a quick summary of their past encounters with Najran. Then he described the battle in the valley north of Axum, the Blue Mage observing him with heavy-lidded approval.

"There are very few men who could best the Angel of Blood. What did you do with his glaive?"

"Broke it into pieces and scattered it over the Sahel. It had a resonance. Opposite that of the Candour or the Pearl."

The recognition of a shared burden passed between the two men. Then the Blue Mage eased back on the mat, making room for Tafalkayt and Wafa to join them.

"Is Tafalkayt your daughter?" Arian asked.

Sinnia looked down at the communal plate heaped with catfish browned with herbs. She tried not to react to Arian's question.

Had the Blue Mage carried out his feigned courtship though pledged in marriage to another? And why would it matter to Sinnia if he had?

"My niece. She was with me at the scriptorium when the Harrowing began. She burned herself in a foolish attempt to rescue manuscripts from the blaze." Sinnia looked up in time to see Yusuf brush his knuckles across Tafalkayt's scarred cheek.

The girl bowed before Arian, urging her to take some fish from the communal plate. When Arian finished the blessing, the girl unwrapped her headcloth. Her curls bounced loose and free, her neckline open to reveal a silver necklace looped around her rich brown throat. The amulet that hung from it was deeply etched with runes.

"I swore to protect the library with my life," Tafalkayt said. "The scars were a small price to pay."

Her voice was so sweet, her accent in the Common Tongue so charming, that Arian could see why Wafa had begun to fall under her spell. Even now, he was picking up pieces of fish to set aside for her, an act of self-control from a boy who'd been hungry too long.

"I commend your bravery."

Daniyar's praise left the young girl tongue-tied. She flicked an astonished glance up at his stunning face, then dropped her eyes to the fish Wafa kept passing to her.

"Eat," she told him with the air of a girl who was used to having other children to boss. "*Then* I will do the same."

This youthful echo of Arian and Daniyar's interaction caused tears to sting the backs of Sinnia's eyes. *Kindness,* she thought. *Tenderness. Love. All of it was possible.*

Perhaps one day she *would* consider a life beyond her duties as a Companion of Hira.

They finished their meal and cleaned up. Tafalkayt showed the Companions a place to bathe and a small enclosure where bedrolls were laid out near a pair of speckle-winged terns.

"Rest for a while if you can." Yusuf offered the words to Arian, though his gaze stayed on Sinnia. "I'll take you to what you seek as soon as the skies are dark." He turned to Daniyar. "There are still things I need to tell you."

Gravely, Daniyar asked, "Was the Pearl of Timeback destroyed?"

"We have more than that to discuss."

51

A TRACT OF STARS, CLOSE AND UNUTTERABLY LOVELY, FORMED A CAN-
opy for the arms of thorn trees and shrubs, the palms dwindling at
the black bend of the river as the temperature plummeted, dunes
rising and falling in cosmic, oceanic waves. Stars shone across
the belt, ice-blue points of light, or bands of yellow and red, and
it was difficult to imagine a more beautiful landscape than this
abandoned desert, ravishingly silent and wild.

"This journey was a thousand miles across once," the Blue
Mage confided to Daniyar. "We would have needed camels to
cross this expanse, but the wars of the Far Range broke up most
of the continent. They upended the course of the river, these val-
leys collapsed in its wake. We should be at our destination before
the break of dawn."

The words reminded Daniyar of the possibilities of the dawn
rite. He hadn't spoken for hours, trekking beside the Blue Mage,
while Arian, Sinnia, and Wafa hiked on some distance ahead.
They had left Tafalkayt in Timeback for purposes the Blue Mage
didn't share. She'd asked Wafa to stay with her, and though for
the briefest moment the boy had seemed willing to consider be-

386

ing parted from Arian and Sinnia, the Blue Mage had cautioned against it.

"The boy needs to come with us. He was destined to be on this journey."

Daniyar hadn't pursued it, preoccupied by the questions that had kept him silent. But as the Blue Mage struck his staff into the sand, he thought it was time to speak.

"The One-Eyed Preacher's war has taken Candour. Hira and Ashfall are also at dire risk." He described the impact of the dawn rite on the forces of the Talisman's army. "We could have used your help at the Conference of the Mages. Why didn't you answer the summons?"

The Blue Mage used his staff to dislodge a scorpion that had skittered over his sandals. "I might as well ask why you or the Golden Mage stayed so long in *your* lands when Timeback was under threat. Like the other Mages, I had my own concerns. Without me, there is no one else to stand against the encroachment of the Nineteen. The Harrowing was the beginning of their war, a war that is separate from—though occasionally aligned—with the aims of the Talisman."

Daniyar had borrowed a length of cloth from Tafalkayt. Now he wrapped it tighter around his skull to ward off the chill of night, questions swirling. He settled on one he thought would be easiest for Yusuf to answer.

"Where are the people of Timeback? The city was deserted."

Yusuf's jaw hardened, his blue eyes turning to steel.

"The men were killed or conscripted. The women and children fled into the heart of the desert, to the safety they knew as nomads before they were welcomed to the city. The same thing happened to the people of Shining Gate."

"And the Lord of Shinqit?" Daniyar asked, using the name

that both men knew from the High Tongue. "Does a man with the title of Sidi Yusuf exist?"

The other man's shoulders slumped before he drew them up again. "He's dead. He was a fine and noble man killed by the Angel of Blood. I knew him from my earliest childhood—I was given his name to honor him."

Both men looked behind them at the beauty of a primeval land undisturbed by shadows.

"I took Sidi Yusuf's title as a means of disguise. The Negus knew no better, but I think his queen began to suspect my deception. Particularly when I arranged to be at the festival in time to vie for the Companion."

"You knew the Companions were headed to Axum?"

"I captured spies of the Nineteen who came from the Sea of Reeds. They were more than willing to speak of the women who fled from the Angel of Blood."

Was the Blue Mage alluding to torture? Disturbed by the thought of it, Daniyar asked, "Is that how you used your gift?"

A hard look from the other man. "Tell me you wouldn't have done the same."

But there had been a harrowing in Candour long before Timeback had fallen. And Daniyar had chosen not to strike against his kin or against any of the tribes. He hadn't used the Claim or the secrets of the Candour to torture. After what he'd seen at the Ark, the thought of it sickened his soul.

They had climbed another dune before Yusuf spoke again.

"Perhaps you found it hard to raise your hand against your own." His face tightened. "But despite our shared heritage, the Nineteen were not slow to exploit us. No black man or woman in these lands has forgotten their slave trade."

And Daniyar realized that the fire sparked by the memory of

oppression had not been quenched by the passing of millennia. He thought of the Hazara, brutally oppressed by men from Daniyar's own tribe. Given the untold scope of their suffering, how long might it take for them to recover from the Talisman's unabashed cruelty?

The Claim spoke of a reckoning, and it struck him deeply, painfully, that there would be no peace in his lands without an attendant accounting, which was what justice demanded.

The sands were not as quiet as he'd thought. Ahead of them on the rise, Sinnia's bow was in her hands, Wafa clapping his hands as her arrows brought down a pair of cape hares, defeating the prowling hopes of a pack of angry hyenas. When the hares' blood had settled, she strung them up on her back.

"Clever," Yusuf said, his admiration of Sinnia plain. "She's wise to think of food."

"There's been a famine in our lands. And Sinnia has been hunting the south with Arian for some time."

"Hunting?" A narrow-eyed look from Yusuf.

Daniyar's reply was succinct. "Slave-chains. The Companions have a particular hatred of the trade."

Something in his words settled Yusuf, gave him reason to fall silent. Until Daniyar asked the question pressing on his mind.

"When you and I held a Conference of the Mages, our combined gifts awoke a power that even the dawn rite at Ashfall wasn't able to yield. Do you know why that might be?"

The low howl of a wolf shattered the silence of the night, the eerie music of the dunes. Daniyar picked up his pace.

"You're asking why three are less powerful than two."

Daniyar nodded. If the Blue Mage had been with them, perhaps Ashfall's desperate fate wouldn't have been assured.

"From what I've read in the Pearl, the answer is not as complex as you suppose. The power we call upon is rooted in the Claim. In that sense, we are like the Companions because the Claim is tied to who we are."

Daniyar frowned. "Meaning?"

"Your gift resonated with mine because we sought the same end. But if the Golden Mage or Dark Mage were driven by different motives, the power of the Mages would be weakened. They may have wanted to destroy the Talisman to a man, but the Black Khan's desire was to reinstate his empire, while the High Companion sought to extend the influence of Hira. Did you share either of these aims?"

"I was at odds with the other Mages," he admitted. "I don't expect that to change."

The Blue Mage touched Daniyar's shoulder, letting his hand linger.

A surge of vitality flared in Daniyar's chest, sending streamers of energy out from his core to his limbs. His headache began to clear; he shot a grateful glance at Yusuf. "I remember our connection from the Conference in Timeback."

"Do you remember the purpose of that Conference?"

Daniyar thought back to their first encounter. His discovery of the scriptorium at Timeback had been like finding a wellspring in the desert, pure, fresh, unfiltered. The walnut wood of the cabinets had shone, manuscripts piled high behind casings of glass. Yusuf had shown him a parchment made of fish skin, the letters on it painted in blue gilded with teardrops of gold. There had been a volume on elixirs derived from the animal world, others on esoteric remedies. Histories of the lives of kings and saints, volumes upon volumes of poetry, including an erotic manual that depicted the arts of love. Side by side with these were treatises on astronomy and jurisprudence, and one amazing work of philosophy that contained a diagram that had occupied his mind for weeks: circles filled with tiny lines of the most beautiful maghrebi script. The innermost circle detailed the philosophy of the first generation of scholars of the Claim; each of the outer rings were dedicated to successive generations. This was the manuscript that had come to his mind during his first attempt to bind his magic to the other Mages—perhaps he had thought of it in that moment because it held significance for him as a Mage.

"I answered your call because you were seeking protection for the manuscripts of Timeback. You thought the Candour might contain the incantation that would preserve them."

"Parchment and fire," the Blue Mage responded. "I learned no spell to undo that."

"Did the Pearl of Timeback survive?"

This was the second time he had asked Yusuf the question, sensing the other Mage's deep reluctance to answer. They were still moving with Yusuf's hand on Daniyar's shoulder, and now Arian paused on the ridgeline ahead of them, her hood thrown back, her eyes concerned. When she began to head back to meet him, the Blue Mage removed his hand.

"She cares for you." Yusuf sounded surprised. "She worries that I do you harm."

Daniyar's voice was soft when he said, "She would set the world ablaze before she would permit anyone to harm me." He smiled to himself. "Though I am not in need of her protection."

The Blue Mage looked startled. "Are you bound to each other?"

Daniyar's certainty of the answer settled into his bones. "We will be. With a dispensation from Hira when we've reached the end of our quest." He refused to be distracted any longer.

"You said there was a manuscript—one manuscript—that you sent into safekeeping. Was it the Pearl?"

Before he could answer, Arian joined them. Daniyar reached for her hand to bring her to his side.

"Your wounds—"

"Are not troubling me. What of you? Did you rest enough?"

Her fingers stroked his wrist, seeking reassurance. Then she glanced at the Blue Mage. "There's a strange pull in these sands. My feet seem to know where to go."

The Blue Mage raised his staff and pointed, his blue robe falling away from the thick gold cuff on his forearm.

"We're following a trail, First Oralist."

An electrifying light shot out from his staff. It danced across hard-packed sand and mud-baked earth, across the tops of the rounded domes that led into the distance until it disappeared from view. Yusuf lowered his staff. The blue light disappeared.

"These domes bring you greetings perfumed with exile. An exile that yearns after the soil where its history resides."

They paced down the descent of a dune that was fifty feet high. Sinnia and Wafa made no effort to join them, still some distance away, and Arian knew it was because Sinnia was still puzzling through their encounters with the Blue Mage.

"I don't understand."

"When the Nineteen brought the Harrowing, Timeback's treasury of manuscripts was taken to the sands, to be buried in chests wrapped with iron bindings." He rolled his forearm to show her the markings on his cuffs. He pointed to Sinnia. "She was right to call me 'nomad.' These runes signify the tribes of the desert who took the manuscripts into their safekeeping."

"And the domes?"

But from the light in her eyes, the Blue Mage could tell that the First Oralist had guessed.

"It doesn't take much to lose your treasure in a desert as vast as this. These domes tell us where the manuscripts are buried." He swept out his staff with a flourish. "The path beneath your feet is built on the history of Timeback."

Arian drew a breath, her hand gripping Daniyar's so that he felt the imprint of her nails. "Do you know the name Half-Seen?"

The Blue Mage looked at her, almost pityingly. His words came as a shock.

"The Sana Codex isn't what you think it is. Even if it was, you wouldn't find it here beneath your feet."

52

Dawn appeared over their heads in shades of desert blue that touched on bracelets of sand under an absence of clouds, the sky a ceiling of blunt, hard stone, still heavy with traces of cold.

"We're here."

The Blue Mage had brought them to the edge of a mesa whose saw-toothed pillars were split by skiffs of sandstone, the western-most edge giving way to a canyon where jagged cliffs had been carved out by a twist of river. They could hear the roar of rushing water, but the crater below the mesa was like a sea frozen in amber, the waves cast of gold-green sand, with rust-tipped rushes at the edge. Still touched with darkness, the western side of the mesa was a darkly gleaming cliff of blue.

Below the mesa, the crater was teeming with life. From the throaty calls of frogs to the soft growls of caracals to the flutters of sparrows and martins that darted over rills of sand.

It wasn't until they had crawled to the verge of the mesa that Arian understood what waited for them below.

"*Qalb al-rishaat,*" she breathed. "I thought it was a place of legend."

She was looking down at a deeply eroded geologic dome, nearly perfect in the symmetry of its concentric circles, circles that stretched over the plateau for miles. She remembered the rune on the Blue Mage's cuff. It depicted an image of this crater.

Daniyar whispered in her ear of a drawing formed of concentric circles that arrowed to the heart of the Claim. He spoke of his own discoveries, of what he thought they portended for the Mages of Khorasan.

Sinnia scrambled into position, lying lengthwise beside Arian as they peered into the crater. The outer layers of the crater were ringed in stardust blue, the inner circles gold, with ridges of white flaring out like sedentary waves. The crater was composed of dikes and sills of sediment and rock. Shining through the sediment were flashes of diamond-hard light.

Sinnia jumped to her feet with a cry, pulling Arian up with her. Incredulous at their discovery, the Companions looked down at the crater that wasn't a crater at all.

Her sense of discovery momentous, Sinnia tugged at the sleeve of Yusuf's robe.

"You can see what it is from this mesa—it's an eye staring up at the sky . . . *a Blue Eye*," she breathed in wonder. "You're the Mage of the Blue Eye. *This* is the Blue Eye." She looked at the outer ring of stone, then back to the Blue Mage.

Wafa's eyes were a beautiful clear blue, but this man's eyes blazed a turquoise so bright that it hurt her to look into them, the black of his pupils stricken by crystal-edged shards of blue.

"It's also called the Eye of the Desert," the Blue Mage said quietly. "I was born here. My family were nomads who camped on the eastern butte. When my mother saw the birthright in my eyes, she took me to Shining Gate where Sidi Yusuf raised me—that is why I was given his name. It was he who entrusted the manuscripts to me."

"But why have you brought us here?" Arian asked. "So far from the war we fight? So far from where our powers can do our people any good?"

The Blue Mage raised his staff high in the air, where it gathered all the light from the diamond-sparks below and reflected them into the center, a penetrating arrow that pointed to a deep black hole.

The giant massif they stood on shook beneath their feet.

Arian's body trembled from head to toe. Daniyar pulled her into his embrace.

"Stop it," he said to Yusuf. "Stop what it is that you're doing."

"No!" Arian protested. "No, it's all right—it isn't him." Her eyes alight with joy, she reached for Sinnia's hands. "*You* know what this is."

The same tremors shook Sinnia at the point where their hands were joined. Yet they didn't lose their balance, anchored by Daniyar's strength.

"When the Harrowing came, I could think of no better place of safety. I traveled to the center of the Eye. This is where I kept it safe."

"The Sana Codex?" Arian demanded. "Will I find it at the center of the Eye?"

A bitter twist to his lips, Yusuf nodded. "It's kept safe," he repeated. "Though there is more to your journey than just the Sana Codex."

"I journeyed here for the Sana Codex," Arian insisted. The Blue Mage *would* believe her after she'd shown him the sheaf in her possession, the green-inked Verse of the Throne. "A manuscript like the Bloodprint, this one penned by Half-Seen. One I can learn to recite to vanquish the One-Eyed Preacher."

Tears fell unrestrained to her cheeks.

"It's calling me," she said to Sinnia. "The Codex is calling me home."

When Daniyar's arms tightened around her waist, she twisted in his arms to face him. She spoke to him fiercely, gripping him by the shoulders.

"This is what we came for. This will undo it all. Ashfall, Candour, *Hira*. All our enemies vanquished. All of Khorasan free."

Awareness pricked at her skin, and she whirled back to face the Blue Mage.

"What is it? What aren't you telling me?"

She was hemmed in by Daniyar and Sinnia, while Wafa watched her from the edge of the mesa, a curious diamond tint sheening his candid eyes.

His voice soft, the Blue Mage answered, "You will find the Sana Codex bound in the style of the manuscripts of Timeback, in an encasement to protect it, its separate pages untouched. But you should be aware that it is . . . distinct from the Bloodprint."

But Arian's circlets were blazing on her arms, as firm as the rock on which she stood. The opening words of the Claim had caught fire—they were burning a path through her thoughts.

"It's *calling* me!" she almost shouted.

Daniyar's touch calmed the pounding of her heart. His hand was in her hair, stroking through its dark waves. He stared at the Blue Mage, his beautiful face unreadable.

Tell her. Finish it now.

The Blue Mage widened his stance. Like a soldier at rest, he placed his hands behind him, his staff pointed up at the sky.

"The Sana Codex was a name given to a collection of fragments. It was transcribed by many *different* hands—by those who knew it by heart. A verse or two here, whole chapters elsewhere. There is a palimpsest that includes both upper and lower text; one rendering may cancel out the other. I also found a coda added to the collection."

Arian swallowed, glad now of Daniyar's strength, firm and unyielding at her back.

"What did the coda say?" It wasn't her most pressing question, but she hadn't yet faced the painful truth that lingered behind Yusuf's description.

The sharp blue eyes that watched her iced over with disappointment . . . with a regret she instinctively shared.

"The collection that constitutes the Sana Codex is made up of fragments from other records of the Claim. The Codex may also include fragments of works *beyond* the Claim. The only way to know for certain would be to compare them."

Angrily, Sinnia confronted the Blue Mage.

"*Compare* them? Compare them to what?"

Yusuf's face softened marginally as his blue eyes shifted to her. The connection between them flared to life again.

"To the only accurate record of the Claim." His breath whistled out from between his teeth. "You will need to compare the Sana Codex to the Bloodprint."

The tremors under their feet intensified, a fracture opening up in the mesa. Daniyar pushed them back from the edge, beckoning to Wafa, who scrambled to his feet.

Arian locked eyes with Sinnia. "This doesn't change anything for us. I can feel its power. We'll be able to tell what is real from what is counterfeit."

The Blue Mage shook his head at this characterization. "It isn't counterfeit, First Oralist. Simply older. The Codex reflects attempts to record the Claim *before* a single reading was standardized by the Bloodprint. The Codex represents variants. Recorded by those who were devoted to the words they transcribed."

A touch of wonder in eyes that had seen the Harrowing. "To compile the Claim from memory—what a task it must have been."

Arian pressed her circlets with her palms, her inner certainty deepening.

"You may be the Blue Mage, but I am the First Oralist. Trust me when I tell you that I will be able to distinguish the Claim from any other text preserved within the Codex. And should I have any doubt, Sinnia will guide me to the truth."

Sinnia leapt across a fissure at her feet. When she caught her breath, her voice was colored by an inflection of the Claim that throbbed with untapped power.

"May the One be pleased with those who came before us, with those who kept the Sana Codex safe, and with our sister Half-Seen who thought to preserve this collection."

But the Blue Mage was shaking his head again, as he turned to lead them down the mesa, finding a path he had marked before their coming.

"Why do you believe the Codex was under Half-Seen's protection?"

Sinnia bristled. "The Companions of Hira are well-acquainted with the desire of men to erase our efforts from history."

The Blue Mage held up a branch so that Sinnia could pass beneath it. "I only meant that Half-Seen's legacy is tied to the *Bloodprint*. The Sana Codex hails from a house of worship southeast of the Rub Al Khali. In the High Tongue, that place is called Sana'a."

Daniyar had given this some thought, and now as he followed with Arian and Wafa in the footsteps of Sinnia and Yusuf, he offered, "With so much of our history lost to book-burning purges, it's nearly impossible to know how the Codex was transmitted. Or where it may have been taken."

Yusuf glanced back at him, blue eyes narrowed to slits. "The

Pearl of Timeback records that it was stolen—spirited away to the House of the One, when war came to the countries that shared the Rub Al Khali."

A particularly ugly period of history when the holy city had seen fit to declare war upon the people of Sana, widening the gap between believers.

"Then how did the Codex come to Timeback?" Daniyar kept his eye on Wafa, something about the boy nudging at his sense of awareness.

Yusuf kept up his momentum as he answered, moving nimbly down a sandy ledge that carved around the mesa down to the canyon floor.

"There were rumors that the Far Range intended to destroy the holy cities—rumors that flourished for years before the wars began. So one who was faithful to the written word journeyed west to bring the Codex to Timeback."

When they reached the canyon floor, the Blue Mage finished his tale. "The woman who saved the Codex had heard of our libraries in exile. She thought Timeback a fitting home."

He gestured to a path that led to the center of the Eye. "We're nearly there."

Though anticipation at reaching the end of their quest was thrumming through Sinnia's veins, she couldn't understand why, when the Blue Mage had come to Axum to intercept the Companions, he'd failed to bring the Codex with him. Was the collection too vast, or was it too fragile to be moved? His decision to leave it at the center of the Eye had cost them valuable time. And if the Codex wasn't what they believed it to be, that loss of time would strike deeper.

Her palms went damp as she asked herself whether war had come to Hira. And whether it would strike at the lands of the

Negus as well. Despite the joy she'd felt upon her return to Axum, her tension hadn't eased, and now she knew that her longing for a place she'd left wasn't a longing to return to the lands of the Negus. It was the Citadel of Hira that she thought of as her home. She ached to return to the one place in Khorasan where the veneration of the Claim required no explanation and demanded no defense.

Salikh's gift, she thought. *He opened the Claim to me. Now I am truly a Companion. Just as Arian had promised, Sinnia would be able to discern the Claim from any imitation or falsehood.*

Wafa grabbed one of her hands, urging her to move faster. Her heart beat harder against her rib cage. In the ecstatic light of a rose-tinged sky, something strange had happened to Wafa's eyes. His beautiful blue irises were limned with a silver mist. And then as she watched, the rare blue of his eyes was split by thin silver lines.

He stumbled over a stone and looked down; when he glanced at Sinnia again, the strange illusion had vanished.

It took longer to reach the center of the Eye than any of their party expected. The layers of quartz-rich sandstone were tricky to navigate, giving way to false bottoms or murky pools of quicksand. More than once, Daniyar pulled Arian or Wafa out of danger.

Their path was set, dawn ripening in the sky against the blue darkness of the mesa. The pink light of early morning tumbled against the clouds. Small pools of water sprang up from time to time, and once they surprised a herd of gazelles picking their way to a pool. Occasionally, the Blue Mage would point to a pool of great clarity and tell them it was to safe to drink.

The ground continued to rumble everywhere they stepped.

"It's you," he told the Companions. "This hasn't happened before."

The chill of the desert night was giving way to a shimmering veil of heat. But before they could experience its full effect, they arrived at the center of the crater, where an opening gleamed from the ground, a tunnel formed of polished obsidian infused with diamond sparks of light. The path they followed disappeared into darkness.

They had reached the center of the Eye. A wind rose in the crater, white clouds tossed above gleaming cliffs, the wings of sparrows trapped against bold currents of air.

Arian felt the tug sharpen—at the center of the earth was the Codex her brother had promised she would find. Whatever its true nature was, it was bound to be of value in the battle that lay ahead. The Blue Mage had power in his own right, but *she* was the First Oralist of Hira. She could almost see the fragments in her mind. The Claim would reveal itself to her.

"I'm ready," she told the others, taking a step into the dark—

An arrow whistled through the last traces of night to split the ground at her feet. It brushed her cheek as it fell, striking pebbles from the sand.

An instant later, she and Sinnia and Wafa were pushed behind Daniyar and Yusuf. They raised their shields against a threat that had appeared without warning. A dozen arrows followed the first, striking harmlessly against the men's shields, but in the shock of the attack, Wafa tumbled through the opening into the darkness below.

Sinnia called after the boy while Arian wheeled to face the threat. She looked up and out over a quartzite ridge sharply distinguished in white.

Eighteen men stood atop the ridge, their bows raised in their hands. The man they waited to hear from was the nineteenth, and he stood at the center of their line. He might not have carried his glaive or worn his brace of daggers, but he held one knife poised in his hand, its blade obsidian black—aimed straight at Arian's heart.

Najran.

This time he wasn't alone. He'd learned that lesson, at least.

The Blue Mage let out a cry of rage, bounding forward from his place.

Najran's lips curved in a cruel smile, as the first rays of sunlight struck hard off something looped around his neck. A necklace with an amulet carved with significant runes.

Tafalkayt's necklace, its markings stained with blood.

"First Oralist." His voice was cutting. "You shouldn't be so careless with the children you leave behind. I believe you have another in your care—the blue-eyed boy intrigues me."

Her voice as sharply honed as his blade, Arian replied, "Just as I was shielded by the One at Jabal Thawr, Wafa is under my charge. I would never let you harm him."

Najran's laughter mocked her. "I nearly killed you at Jabal Thawr. The boy is unlikely to prosper if that is all you have to offer."

A roar of fury sounded from Daniyar. "Mine will be the sword that cleaves your head from your body."

Najran ignored Daniyar's warning, his focus on Arian. Taunting her, he said, "I, too, bear the protection of the One. I escaped Jabal Thawr unharmed."

Arian hesitated. The power that had saved her in the cave apparently also had spared Najran.

Daniyar jerked her close, whispering in her ear. "Do not allow his deceptions to cause you to doubt yourself."

Her shoulders straightened. Whatever tricks Najran had studied, whatever sorcery he commanded, *she* was the First Oralist of the Claim. Its power flooded her veins.

The smile died on Najran's lips, as he responded to the threat.

He raised his hand in a lethal gesture. A trail of arrows marked the dawn.

53

"Go!" Daniyar shouted at Arian. "Go and we will hold. Take Sinnia and find Wafa."

She flashed a desperate glance at him—no matter what her Audacy demanded, she wouldn't leave Daniyar again.

He pushed her into the opening with a quick kiss to her temple. "Go, jaan. I won't be far behind." He smiled. "You are not abandoning me, if I'm the one who asks you to go."

She gave him a last burning look and then moved swiftly inside.

Daniyar's attention turned back to the battle when the Blue Mage gripped one of his hands while holding fast to his staff with the other. He'd lost his shield, but the incantation that rumbled from his throat was picked up by Daniyar, a blue and silver light arcing between them to separate them from the Nineteen with a piercing, electric veil.

Only their backs were exposed. Yusuf spoke rapidly to Sinnia, who hesitated at the center of the Eye. "Help us augment our powers with your command of the Claim."

Sinnia swiftly turned her back on the opening, dropping her

pack at her feet. She grabbed Daniyar's free hand on one side and clutched Yusuf's over his staff on the other, so that the three of them formed a circle, now wholly enclosed by the veil.

Arrows rained against it, but none were able to penetrate. The three defenders raised their hands as the Nineteen advanced, aiming bolts of silver-blue lightning all along the ridge. A handful of their assailants fell back while the others pressed forward, Najran at their head.

The eyes of the Silver Mage met those of the Blue Mage.

"Remember the Pearl!" the Blue Mage shouted. "Remember what you read!"

For answer, Daniyar called out a verse of calamity he had found in the manuscript entrusted to the Blue Mage.

It was echoed by Yusuf's deep drum of a voice and welded together by Sinnia's powerful use of a melody of the Claim taught to her by Salikh.

Fired with a singular purpose, three were greater than two. Power blazed from their throats, racing along their arms to erupt into a fiery lightning. Six of the Nineteen fell dead. Then the rest were through the veil.

Calling to Wafa, Arian sprinted down the tunnel into the dark, gleaming bits of diamond striking sparks through the rock. The walls of the tunnel pressed around her, leaving no room for more than one person to pass. There was no sign of Wafa ahead of her, no sign of the others behind, and still she ran, dropping, down, down, into wretched darkness, afforded a minimal light by the whip-tailed flick of the Claim.

It issued not from her own dry throat but whispered along the walls that pressed hard and bright around her. The air should have been close and stale; she should have been terrified by her long, cold drop to the bottom, as if she was falling down to the very heart of the earth.

Instead, she felt buoyed, her heart lightened by joy. She caught the trickle of water murmuring over stone. She ran for another ten minutes, until the ground fell away beneath her feet into a sheer drop. She gathered herself and fell.

To land on the softness of sand.

She eased out of her crouch to find herself inside a cavern, cool and impossibly bright. Far above her head opposite where she'd landed, the light of dawn arrowed down, a slender column of purity that illuminated a rock-carved plinth at the center of a pool.

Crystal-blue waters lapped at the edges of the chamber, where Arian knelt on the sand. Slowly, she rose to her feet. There was no sign of Wafa, nor of any receptacle that might have held the Sana Codex. There were no traces of parchment at all; her heart stuttered in her chest.

The Blue Mage's description of the Codex hadn't reached her senses as a lie. And if Yusuf *had* lied to them, Daniyar would have known at once.

There was no trace of deception in the chamber—no taint of darkness or evil, just the slender column of light dancing upon hard stone.

She touched the waters of the pool with her hand, setting off a flurry of ripples. She studied the bottom of the pool that lay at the heart of the Eye. The ripples fanned out to ice-cold peaks of light.

She reached in with both arms to touch the pool's shallow bottom.

The instant her circlets struck water, the bottom of the pool began to shine. Dipping her head beneath the water, she opened her eyes to see. The entire basin of the pool was formed of a thick vein of carbon. Its cubic crystals winked at her: the floor was solid diamond. Gasping at the realization, she flung up her head from the pool.

Trails of long black hair lay wetly against her arms.

Now from the tunnel she had fled through, she heard the roar of conflict. Threats filtered down the opening, a shout warning her to flee. But the tunnel was the only entrance that led to the secret pool.

Had she taken a wrong turn?

The voices behind her sounded louder—something was coming through the tunnel. Something steeped in wickedness and dread.

Then she was distracted by a movement from the plinth. She looked into the column of light whose source she couldn't divine to find Wafa standing at the center of the plinth. His hair and clothing were dry.

He was holding a collection of fragments in his hands, bound not in soft, supple leather wrapped with twine, as Arian would have expected, but rather encased in fragile sheets of gold held together by a turquoise-studded spine. His head was turned to the sky: he was staring up into the light.

"Wafa!" she called, hope and disbelief commingled in her voice at the sight of the book.

He dropped his head, his small frame surrounded by light. When his eyes widened with joy to see her, Arian's heartbeat stopped.

Wafa's eyes had changed. She was staring into irises of metallic blue and silver, the colors carved out in arrow-thin wedges against his pinpoint pupils. His eyes held her transfixed, just at the edge of the water.

With one hand he indicated that she should join him. "Come," he said to Arian. "It's safe for you to come."

"Wafa," she gasped. *"Are you holding the Sana Codex?"*

At first he was confused, his loose curls flying around his skull as he shook his head. But then he looked into the light again and slowly nodded at Arian. And Arian didn't know how she knew to ask him, *"Who promises you safety?"*

He looked across the pool at her, then back up into the light.

"The one who says we have to take a journey, far away from here."

The voices from the tunnel grew more desperate. Arian whispered a prayer. She waded through the pool over to the plinth, keeping her gaze locked on the silver-blue spears of Wafa's.

The thrumming she had felt from the Codex now began to sound in the pool, ripples turning into waves as the walls of the cavern shook, shrinking the entrance to the grotto.

"Are we going to Hira?" She was held by the pinpoint splinters in his eyes.

His fingers stroked the Sana Codex, quickened the silent thrumming of the Claim.

The clash of a silver sword. The call of a beloved voice.

"Arian! *Arian!*"

She reached the base of the plinth, then hauled herself onto its surface, feeling a twinge of pain in her leg. She kissed Wafa, easing the book from his grip. She stroked one hand over the book's spine. The pull she had felt on the sands, the power that had called to her from the depths of the Blue Eye, was magnified on the plinth, the Sana Codex a living heart between her palms. A bolt of lightning shot through her body, the Codex gleaming in her hands—the Codex *fixed* to her hands. She recognized its power as the uncorrupted cadence of the Claim. Knowledge sang through her body, the hidden dimensions of Hira's rites suddenly as clear as truth.

As clear as the pool she had crossed to reach the plinth, as pure as the waters of the cistern beneath the Qaysarieh Portal. As pure as the waters of the All Ways.

For the first time, answers streamed through her mind in place of questions, brilliant filaments of light that arranged the verses of the Claim, opening up layers of mystery, of philosophy and glory, purpose and power that up until this moment had remained undisclosed.

It was like the crack in the mesa from which the river had bounded free.

She knew her purpose as First Oralist, though she had yet to read a single word.

She waited no longer to do so. Her heart in her throat, she released the catch that bound the fragments together. The collection fell open at the very heart of the book, and she knew this because she looked upon verses written in ink that had faded, in a language as old as the sands she had crossed to reach the Blue Eye, and she read those verses fluently. The years of her life that had passed until this moment, her tutelage under the guidance of her parents, her years in Hira's scriptorium, the months she had spent at the Library of Candour, the moment she had held the Bloodprint in her hands—each step on the journey that had brought her to the Sana Codex—had led her to the heart of this book.

A book written in the High Tongue. A language she read as easily as though the guiding hands of the One had poured it down her throat. Her breast cut open, her heart removed from her body to be bathed in a golden basin of faith before her spirit was restored. All of this done by a guardian of light who had taken the form of a boy.

This was taught to you, First Oralist.

She had found the center of the book.

She had found the heart of the Claim.

The majesty of the Claim sang out from the plinth, covering Arian in glory, inflaming her senses with joy. As her eyes moved down the page, through the loops and slashes that formed the words that were all of Khorasan's inheritance, she came to the crux of the answer she had searched for all these years—the answer to her despair in the face of the Talisman's supremacy.

Is the reward of good anything but good?

Then which of the One's favors will you deny?

Wafa tugged at her wrist.

"You must take the Night Journey," he whispered, his eyes spiked silver and blue.

He was telling her something she should know, something she should be able to grasp from the weight of the Sana Codex. He raised his hands to the Codex, turning its fragile pages as Arian balanced the delicate sheets of gold between her quivering palms.

He found what he was seeking, his fingers tracing a line of script in an emerald green whose shine had dulled. Then the boy who couldn't read raised his head and recited in the shining rhythms of the High Tongue.

"Limitless is the glory of the One who transported the servant of the One by night from the Sacred Place of Worship to the Distant House of Worship, whose surroundings the One has blessed, to show the servant of the One our signs."

"*I* am a servant of the One," Arian whispered.

"Then you must take the Night Journey," Wafa urged.

"Arian!" Daniyar's voice called to her from the depths of the tunnel.

"I'm here!" She aimed her voice at the entrance into the cave. "I'm safe, Daniyar. I'm here at the bottom with Wafa."

She'd turned away for the briefest instant, and when she looked back, she was standing alone on the plinth, holding fast to the Codex, holding fast to the rope of the faithful. Her heart jerked in her chest. She gazed at the pool, before searching the wider expanse of the cave.

Wafa had vanished. He wasn't in the cave.

A thud, a cry, alert at last to danger—a searing pain in her side, she fell to her knees on the plinth, sheltering the Codex with her body. She heard Daniyar's cry. Then the strident ring of steel. Followed by Sinnia's voice, ordering Arian to protect her wound, as she cut down the soldier of the Nineteen who had followed them into the cave and hurled his dagger at Arian.

Taking one hand from the Codex, Arian tested her ribs. Her palm came away dry.

Daniyar waded through the pool to vault onto the plinth, his hands urgently seeking the wound, without sparing a glance for the Codex or the salvation it promised.

"It's nothing." She inhaled roughly before she managed, "It glanced across my ribs."

He helped her to her feet with care. "Where is Wafa?"

Just as Arian had done, his silver eyes searched the cavern, his head twisted away.

She caught Daniyar's head in her hands, stilling his urgent movements.

"Daniyar . . ."

His gaze sharpened on hers. "My love. Tell me."

She drew another gasping breath, struggling to accept the blinding truth she had seen. She held out the fragile fragments carefully bound in gold.

"Wafa found the Sana Codex. He read it to me."

Daniyar's hands gripped her shoulders. "*Read* it? How . . . *what* did he read?"

"Israa," she said simply. "Israa e Miraj."

Sinnia gaped at her, as Daniyar jerked her hard against his chest, the Codex pressed between them.

"Israa e Miraj?"

Together, they turned to stare at the column of light that poured over the plinth. Arian translated for them, though she knew that he and Sinnia had understood. Just as they would understand the nature of Wafa's disappearance.

"The Night Journey and the Ascension. Wafa told me to *take that journey*."

She dropped her head to rest it against Daniyar's shoulder. The Night Journey was the purest of fables, the story of a journey from the sanctum of the holy city beyond the Rub Al Khali to a distant house of worship in the holy city of another time. It was a journey that signified enlightenment; it promised answers to the deepest questions.

Daniyar's voice rumbled in his chest as he echoed her initial reservations. "The Night Journey and the Ascension? The histories I've read call the Ascension an allegory, whereas the Night Journey was a journey of the *spirit*."

"I think there may be more to it than that."

Held in Daniyar's arms, the Codex safe between them, Arian had never felt more at peace. She had never dared dream of such hope.

"Arian!" Daniyar shook her lightly to bring her back to the moment, to the imminent threat they faced. "Najran is skilled in the sorcerous arts—the Blue Mage won't hold him for long. We need another way out."

Arian's head tilted up. Her eyes tried to pierce the light that spilled upon the plinth.

"Arian!" Daniyar touched his forehead to hers. His eyes blazed with concern. For her—always for her. For all that she had risked, for all she yet stood to lose. "Najran means to stop you. He means to *kill* you, if he can. Then he will take the Sana Codex."

Her smile trembled against his lips, her mind full of marvels. "There is nothing for us to fear here. And we're leaving, anyway."

"How? Najran blocks the exit."

"There *is* another way out."

"Where? Show me what you mean."

Before she could answer, they heard the thud of something heavy and dull. The sound was followed by a body that rolled into the sand at their feet. The Blue Mage straightened from his roll. He pounced at the staff he had thrown through the tunnel ahead of his agile landing. Then he looked at the other three.

His grim eyes swept the cavern, and without being told, he understood what was wrong.

"Najran and his men are coming; you have to hurry. What have you done with the boy?"

Arian pointed to the column of the light whose source couldn't be discerned—couldn't be *possible*—here at ends of the earth.

"You knew," she accused him. "All along you knew."

"What?" Sinnia demanded, her anger at him rekindled. "What did the Blue Mage know?"

Arian was staring at the light, the column ethereal and hallowed.

"The Blue Mage wasn't entrusted with guarding the Sana Codex. At least—that wasn't his *sole* charge."

Daniyar's deep voice growled at the lie. "No? What else, then?"

But Yusuf waited for Arian to speak with preternatural stillness.

"The Blue Mage brought us here because he was guarding a secret of greater significance than the Codex: he was *guarding* the Blue Eye."

Yusuf adjusted his staff under his arm. He unraveled the tails of his headscarf, his eyes glinting sharp and blue, dismissing the sounds of pursuit.

"You are as wise as our legends hold, First Oralist." He pointed to the Codex clasped with such care in her hands. "Did you feel the source of its power?"

Her nod at him was regal, and he smiled.

"Then you will be the one to master it."

"Enough of your mysteries, my lord." Sinnia snapped the words. "Tell us the secret of this place." Her limbs were bristling with a strange energy, too potent to be contained. She moved toward the roughhewn pedestal, the beauty of the Codex awakening something within. Daniyar reached down to help her climb the plinth.

Once Sinnia had gained her feet, Arian passed the Codex into Sinnia's hands. She took a step away from the others directly into the light. The Blue Mage watched her without blinking, the power of his gaze unsheathed.

"If you would learn the secrets of the Codex, retrace the path of the Night Journey. Once you ascend, First Oralist, you will truly know how to wield the power of the Claim. You will be ready when the time comes to face the One-Eyed Preacher."

Arian raised one arm above her head, the index finger on her right hand pointed at the sky, her hand curled up in a fist. Her free hand reached for Daniyar's.

"There is no one but the One. And so the One commands."

Sinnia copied the gesture. But her voice was shaking when she said, "I don't understand."

Arian answered her with the power of the verse she had read from the Sana Codex.

"Which of the One's favors will you deny?"

The words didn't explain all that had transpired in the cave. Until Arian added, "With due respect, my lord, the Blue Eye does not refer to the anointment of a Mage."

Yusuf bowed at her, his dark face grave.

Arian now spoke to Sinnia.

"The Blue Eye is a *portal*. Once we have harnessed the power of the Codex, the Blue Eye will take us home."

54

East of Candour, in a cave inside a mountain so steeply treacherous that none attempted to scale it, a patient entity stirred. The entity sensed the opening of the portal, sensed the power of the woman who transgressed it, and raised his head from contemplation. He ceased his study of the manuscript before him, setting its bloodstained pages on its stand.

He tramped to the cave's opening, looking out over a cruel range of peaks to the arid plains farther east. He pointed to a pair of winged creatures who hovered at the cave's entrance. Their flattened eyes met his, the pupils as deadly and slender as a pair of unsheathed blades. Their mouths gaped open to display their teeth, edged by a yawning fire within: each of the winged creatures held a glittering gem on its tongue.

The man on the ledge threw back his hood, bracing himself against the cold. When he raised his head to gaze into the distance, one eye was missing from its socket, replaced by a pale, hard stone that blazed with a translucent light.

The One-Eyed Preacher turned to the creatures and issued a harsh command.

"Bring the First Oralist to me."
Hira's supremacy was over.
The Talisman's time had come.

HERE ENDS BOOK THREE OF THE KHORASAN ARCHIVES

Acknowledgments

I'M DEEPLY GRATEFUL TO THOSE WHOSE WORK INSPIRES MY OWN, TO those who do so much to help uncover these archives, to those who enhance my storytelling with their magical arts, those who delight me by falling into these books, and to those whose love and encouragement keeps me on this path.

Thank you always to David, Vicky, Natasha, and Danielle.

And dearest Uzma, thank you for reading this manuscript too many times to count, for making me laugh and helping me *see*. You've made everything about writing these books deeper in meaning and more joyful.

Thank you to Nader, the heart of my heart.

And with unfailing love to all our forgotten queens.

Cast of Characters

THE COUNCIL OF HIRA

Ilea: the High Companion
  Other titles: the Golden Mage, the Exalted, the Qari, Ilea the
  Friend, Ilea the Seal of the Companions
Arian: First Oralist, a Companion of Hira
Sinnia: a Companion from the lands of the Negus
Ash: the Jurist
Psalm: the General of the Citadel
Other Companions of Hira, the Affluent: Half-Seen, Mask,
  Moon, Rain, Saw, Ware, Zeb; and in the old world, Hafsah

CANDOUR

Daniyar: the Guardian of Candour
  Other titles: the Silver Mage, the Authenticate, the Keeper of the
  Candour
Wafa: a Hazara boy of Candour

THE TALISMAN

The One-Eyed Preacher
The Immolans
Baseer: an Immolan
The Spinzhiray: an Elder
Toryal: a Talisman soldier
Masoumeh: a prisoner of the Talisman

ASHFALL

The Black Khan: Rukhzad, Rukh
  Other titles: Commander of the Faithful, Prince of West
  Khorasan, Khan of Khorasan, Sovereign of the House of
  Ashfall, the Black Rook, the Dark Mage
Begum Niyousha: the Black Khan's mother
Darya: the Princess of Ashfall, sister to the Black Khan
Darius: the half-brother of Rukh and Darya, formerly the Dark
  Mage
The Begum: the eldest aunt of the Black Khan
Nizam al-Mulk: the Grand Vizier of Ashfall
The Zareen-Qalam: the curator of the scriptorium of Ashfall
The Assassin/Hasbah: the founder and leader of the Assassins
Alisher: a poet of Black Aura
The Zhayedan: the Army of the Black Khan at Ashfall
Arsalan: Commander of the Zhayedan
The Cataphracts: shock troops of the Zhayedan
Maysam: Captain of the Cataphracts
Esfandyar: a Zhayedan captain
The Teerandaz: the Zhayedan's all-female company of archers
Cassandane: Captain of the Teerandaz
The Khorasan Guard: the Black Khan's personal guard, the home
  guard of Ashfall
Khashayar: Captain of the Khorasan Guard

THE RISING NINETEEN

Shaykh Al Marra: leader of the Rising Nineteen
Najran: Sayyid of the Rising Nineteen
  Other titles: the Iron Glaive, the Angel of Blood, the Bone Shadow

THE RUB AL KHALI

Rim-Sarah: a girl of the Bani Shira'a

THE LANDS OF THE NEGUS

The Negus: ruler of these lands
Queen Zoya: his queen
Nuru: a shipbuilder, a soldier of Axum, and Sinnia's cousin
Kamali: a soldier of Axum and Sinnia's cousin
Ife: Sinnia's cousin
Ajani: a boy of Axum
Sidi Yusuf: the Lord of Shining Gate and Sinnia's suitor

TIMEBACK

The Mage of the Blue Eye
Tafalkayt: a girl of Timeback
The Foxlord

THE WANDERING CLOUD DOOR

Zerafshan: Aybek of the Wandering Cloud Door
  Other titles: Lord of the Wandering Cloud Door, Lord of the
  Buzkashi, Aybek of the Army of the Left

THE WALL

The Authoritan
  Other titles: Khagan, Khan of Khans

The Khanum: Lania, sister to Arian, the First Oralist of Hira
  Other titles: Consort of the Authoritan, the Augur

THE USUL JADE

Salikh: the founder of the Usul Jade
The Basmachi Resistance
Larisa Salikh: the leader of the Basmachi Resistance
Elena Salikh/Anya: second-in-command

THOSE WHO SIGN WITH BLOOD

The group responsible for the second Harrowing of Timeback.

Glossary of the Khorasan Archives

ab-e-rawan. A type of silk known as running water.

Adhraa. The most highly venerated woman mentioned by name in the Claim.

aesar. A hot desert wind.

Afaarin. A word of praise and appreciation.

Affluent. Those who are fluent in the Claim.

Ahdath. Suicide warriors who guard the Wall.

Akhirah. The Last Day, the Day of Judgment, the Afterlife.

Akhundzada. A member of the family of the Ancient Dead, guardians of the Sacred Cloak.

Al Qasr. Literally "the Castle," but in this case referring to the women's fortified quarters inside the royal palace at Ashfall.

alam. A flag.

Alamdar. A title of utmost respect given to an elder of the Hazara.

All Ways. The fountains of the Citadel of Hira, imbued with special powers, and a foundation of the rites of the Council of Hira.

Al Qasr. The women's quarters in the royal palace at Ashfall.

Amdar. A river of North Khorasan that flows on both sides of the Wall.

Amghar. Chief of the clan.

andas. Blood brother.

Ark. The stronghold of the Authoritan in Black Aura Scaresafe.

Aryaward. A territory of South Khorasan.

Ashfall. The capital of West Khorasan, seat of the Black Khan.

asmaan. Sky.

asmani. Sky-blue lapis lazuli.

Asmat. The secret names of the One.

Assimilate. The proclaimed law of the Talisman.

Audacy. A mission assigned to any of the Companions of Hira, a sacred trust.

Augur. One who foretells the future, a rank in the Authoritan's court.

Authenticate. A title given to one who can verify the truth. *See also* Silver Mage.

Authoritan. The ruler of North Khorasan, the land beyond the Wall.

Avalaunche. A Talisman warning horn used to defend the Sorrowsong.

Awazim. A tribe of the Rub Al Khali that keeps noteworthy flocks of sheep.

Aybek. Commander of the Buzkashi, leader of the people of the Wandering Cloud Door.

aylaq. Summer camp of the Buzkashi.

Axum. The capital of the lands of the Negus.

badal. Revenge in the Talisman code.

baraka. Blessing.

Basmachi. A resistance force north of the Wall who follow the teachings of the Usul Jade.

Begum. The highest-ranking woman at the Black Khan's court, in this case the Khan's eldest aunt.

Black Aura Scaresafe. The Authoritan's capital beyond the Wall.

Black Khan. The Prince of West Khorasan, the Khan of Khorasan.

Bloodless. The guardians of the Bloodprint.

Bloodprint, The. The oldest known written compilation of the Claim.

burnoose. A long, loose hooded cloak.

Buzkashi. The name of the people of the Wandering Cloud Door.

buzkashi. A game of sport involving the carcass of a goat chased by horsemen.

Candour. A city in the south of Khorasan captured by the Talisman, home of the Silver Mage.

Candour, The. The book of the Silver Mage, instructing him in the history, traditions, and powers of the Claim, as well as his responsibilities as Silver Mage and Guardian of Candour.

Cataphracts. The shock troops of the Zhayedan, the Black Khan's army.

chador. Shawl.

Citadel. The stronghold of the Council of Hira.

Citadel Guard. Warriors who guard the Citadel of Hira, assigned to the protection of the Companions.

Claim, The. The sacred scripture of Khorasan; also a powerful magic.

Clay Minar. A tower in the city of Black Aura Scaresafe.

Common Tongue. A language common to all parts of Khorasan and beyond.

Companions of Hira. Also Council of Hira, Oralists, the Affluent, sahabiya in the feminine singular, sahabah in the plural: a group of women charged with the guardianship of Khorasan and the sacred heritage of the Claim.

Council of Hira. See Companions of Hira.

Crimson Watch. An elite company of the Ahdath who guard Jaslyk prison.

dakhu. Bandit, disreputable person.

Damson Valley. A valley north of the Wall and east of Marakand.

Death Run. A chain of mountains that forms one of the boundaries of the Wandering Cloud Door, east of the Valley of Five Lions.

Dhu al-Nurayn. The One Who Possesses Two Lights, a title of the one who preserved the Bloodprint.

Divan-e Shah. The throne room at Ashfall where emissaries are received.

dunya. The world.

Eagle's Nest. The fortress of the Assassin, north of the city of Ashfall.

East Wind. A people of a sister-scripture to the Claim, also known as the Esayin.

Empty Quarter. The lands of southwestern Khorasan, destroyed by the wars of the Far Range. Also known as the Rub Al Khali.

Everword. A people of a sister-scripture to the Claim.

Far Range. The uninhabitable country beyond Khorasan.

fayruz. Turquoise in the dialect of the Empty Quarter.

Fire Mirrors. A mountain chain that forms the northern boundary of the Wandering Cloud Door, just south of the Wall.

First Oralist. A rank of highest distinction among the Companions of Hira, reserved for the Companion with the greatest knowledge of and fluency in the Claim.

Firuzkoh. The Turquoise City, lost to time.

Five Lakes. A territory of Khorasan, north of Hazarajat.

ger. Home, tent, yurt.

geshlaq. Winter camp of the Buzkashi.

ghayrat. Self-honor in the Talisman code.

ghul. A powerful and dark spirit brought to life by sorcery.

Gold House. A palace in the Registan where women are trained in the arts. *See also* Tilla Kari.

Golden Finger. A minaret at the meeting place of two rivers.

Graveyard of the Ships. A desert near Jaslyk where the lake bed has dried up.

Great Bend, The. A river of the southern maghreb, also known as the Joliba, the Isa Ber, and the Kworra.

gris-gris. A leather pouch said to contain blessings; an amulet or talisman of protection.

Gur-e-Amir/the Green Mirror. A tomb complex in Marakand.

Hafsah. A Companion of Hira, the Collector of the Claim.

Half-Seen. A descendant of Hafsah.

Hallow. A hall in the valley of Firuz-koh.

haq. Truth, right, justice.

haramzadah. An epithet that means "bastard."

Hazara. A people of central and east Khorasan, persecuted by the Talisman.

Hazarajat. A territory of central and east Khorasan, home of the Hazara people.

Hazing. A district of Marakand that is home to the Basmachi resistance. *See also* Tomb of the Living King.

High Companion. Leader of the Council of Hira.

High Road. A river of central Khorasan; also called the Arius, the Tarius, the Horaya, and the Tejen.

High Tongue. The language of the Claim.

hijra. Migration, also the name given to a historically significant migration.

Hira. The sanctuary of the Companions.

Ice Kill. A valley at the entrance to the Wandering Cloud Door, home to the Buzkashi.

Illustrious Portal. The entrance to the Black Khan's palace at Ashfall.

Immolans. Deputies of the One-Eyed Preacher, tasked with book-burning.

Inklings. Scribes from the Lands of the Shin Jang.

iqra. Read.

Irb. The language spoken by the people of the Wandering Cloud Door.

Israa e Miraj. The Night Journey and the Ascension. The name of an allegorical or metaphysical spiritual journey taken by the Messenger of the One from the Near House of Worship to the Distant House of Worship.

jaan. Life, love, beloved.

Jabal Thawr. A mountain near the holy city.

Jahannam. In the afterlife, a place of punishment for evildoers.

Jahiliya. The Age of Ignorance.

Jaslyk. A prison of the Authoritan's, northwest of the Wall.

jorgo. Fast mountain horses.

kaghez. Paper manufactured from mulberry trees.

Kalaam. Word, one of the names of the Claim.

kamish. A type of calligraphy pen.

karakash. Black jade.

khaeen. A Talisman word for "traitor."

Khagan. Khan of Khans or King of Kings.

Khamsa. One of five mythical mares.

khamsin. A desert wind.

Khanum. A consort of the Khan, the Authoritan's consort.

Khost-e-Imom. A protective cover or place for the Bloodprint.

Khorasan. The lands of the people

of the Claim, north, south, east, and west.

khubi. Bounty, spoils of war, an endearment meaning "enough/everything."

khuriltai. Council.

kohl. Black eyeliner.

Kufa. A style of calligraphy taken from a city of the same name.

kuluk. Load-bearing horses with stamina.

lajward. Lapis lazuli.

lajwardina. A lapis lazuli glaze.

likka. Raw silk fibers used in the practice of calligraphy.

loya jirga. A consultation of Talisman chieftains; also a council of war.

Maghreb. The lands west of West Khorasan, across the Sea of Reeds.

maghrebi. A style of architecture in the lands west of West Khorasan.

mahadhras. Rural schools of the maghreb.

manaqib. A script of the lands of the Negus.

Mangudah. A death squad of the Buzkashi, a regiment of the Army of the One.

maqdas. A house of worship in Axum.

Marakand. A city of North Khorasan beyond the Wall.

Mashriqi. A style of eastern architecture, east of the maghreb.

Mausoleum of the Princess. A tomb complex in the Hazing, an area of Marakand.

Maze Aura. A city of central Khorasan.

melmastia. Hospitality in the Talisman code.

mihrab. A prayer nook in the wall of a house of worship, indicating the direction of prayer.

minzar. A searchlight or spotlight.

mishkah. A niche that contains the light of the heavens and the earth.

Mir. Any leader of the Hazara people.

mllaya moya. My sweet, my love.

morin khuur. Horsehead fiddle.

Mudassir. Respected teacher, a form of address.

Mudjadid. A teacher of great knowledge, a form of address.

musaawat. Equality in the Talisman code.

naamus. The honor of women in the Talisman code.

naanawatai. Forgiveness in the Talisman code.

Najashi. A word for the people of the Negus in the language of the Empty Quarter.

Nastaliq. A type of calligraphy.

neeli. Dark blue lapis lazuli.

Negus. Ruler of the lands south of the Empty Quarter, also the name given to these lands; the leader of Sinnia's people.

Nightshaper. Site of the Poet's Graveyard, an abandoned city of Khorasan.

Nun (pronounced Noon). Inkwell, the name of the scriptorium curated by Arian's parents.

nurm. Soft.

One-Eyed Preacher. A tyrant from the Empty Quarter whose teachings have engulfed all of Khorasan.

Oralist. A Companion of Hira who recites the Claim.

Otchigen. The Prince of the Hearth, a title given to the youngest male member of the family of the Lord of the Buzkashi.

pagri. A thick wool cap worn by the Talisman.

Pearl of Timeback. The book of the Mage of the Blue Eye, providing instruction in the history, traditions, and responsibilities of the Blue Mage. A book that endows the Blue Mage with certain powers of the Claim.

Pit, The. The dungeons of the Ark.

Plague Lands. A northern territory of Khorasan destroyed by the wars of the Far Range.

Plague Wing. A section of Jaslyk prison where prisoners are held for experimentation with the effects of the Plague.

Plaintive. A warning horn sounded by the Buzkashi.

qalb. Heart.

qarajai. A dangerous form of the sport buzkashi.

Qari. One who recites the Claim.

Qaysarieh Portal. The prisons underneath Ashfall.

qiyamah. Resurrection, rising.

Queen Makeda. A revered and honored queen in the history of the people of the Negus.

rasti, rusti. Originally, "safety is in right"; the Authoritan's motto, "Strength is justice."

Registan. A public square in the heart of the city of Marakand, literally translated as "sandy place."

Rising Nineteen. A cult that has come to power in the Empty Quarter.

Rub Al Khali. Also known as the Empty Quarter, the lands of southwest Khorasan, destroyed by the wars of the Far Range.

Russe. A name given to the people of the northern Transcasp.

sabz. Green lapis lazuli.

Sacred Cloak. A holy relic worn by the Messenger of the Claim.

Saee. A pilgrimage ritual consisting of walking or running between two hills near the holy city.

Safanad. One of the five mares of the Khamsa, Arian's horse.

sahabah. A title given to the Companions of Hira in the plural; sahabiyah, feminine singular.

Sahel. A southern desert of the maghreb.

Sailing Pass. A mountain pass en route to the Sorrowsong Mountain.

Salaf. A scholarly class from the city of Timeback.

Sanam. Camel hump.

Sar-e-sang/Sorrowsong. The Blue

Mountain, location of the oldest continuously worked lapis lazuli mines in Khorasan.

Sayyid. A courteous form of address for a man among the people of the Empty Quarter.

Sayyidina. A courteous form of address for a woman among the people of the Empty Quarter.

Sea of Reeds. A body of water that divides the Empty Quarter from the Lands of the Negus.

Sea of the Transcasp. A body of water that divides West Khorasan from the Transcasp.

Shadow Mausoleum. A crypt used for storing the bones of the Authoritan's enemies. *See also* Shir Dar.

shahadah. The bearing of witness.

shah-mat. Checkmate.

Shahnameh. Ashfall's Book of Kings, a history of its monarchy.

shahtaranj. A chessboard.

shalmas. A gauzy length of white fabric worn as a veil and/or wrapped around the torso.

Shaykh. The title of a man among the people of the Empty Quarter.

Shining Gate/Shinqit. A capital of the maghreb.

Shin Jang. A northeastern territory of Khorasan.

Shin War. One of the tribes of Khorasan, allegiant to the Talisman.

Shir Dar. A former House of Wisdom in the Registan. *See also* Shadow Mausoleum.

shisha. A water-pipe with fruit-scented tobacco.

Shrine of the Sacred Cloak. A holy shrine where the Cloak has been stored for centuries and guarded by the Ancient Dead.

shura. A council or consultation.

Sihraat. The scrying room where the Khanum conducts her Augury.

Silver Mage. The Guardian of Candour, Keeper of the Candour.

Sorrowsong. See Sar-e-Sang.

suhuf. A sheaf of paper or parchment.

Sulde. The spirit banner of the Buzkashi.

tabot. Tablets of law sacred to the people of the Negus.

tagelmust. A garment of indigo cloth worn either as a veil or as a turban by inhabitants of the maghreb to prevent the inhalation of sand on the wind.

tahweez. A gold circlet or circlets, worn on the upper arms by the Companions of Hira, inscribed with the names of the One and the opening words of the Claim.

taihe. A princess of Shin Jang.

Talisman. Followers of the One-Eyed Preacher, militias that rule most of the tribes of Khorasan.

Task End. A city of North Khorasan beyond the Wall, the original home of the Bloodprint.

Technologist. The chief torturer at Jaslyk prison.

Teerandaz. A division of archers in the Black Khan's army.

thobe. A long, loose gown worn by the people of the Empty Quarter.

Tilla Kari. A former site of worship in the Registan. *See also* Gold House.

Timeback. A capital of the maghreb.

Tirazis. A city of West Khorasan.

Tomb of the Living King. A lost tomb in a district of Marakand known as the Hazing.

Tradition. The accompanying rites and beliefs of the Claim.

Transcasp. Lands of northwest Khorasan.

turah. Courage in the Talisman code.

usman. A form of lightning in the maghreb.

Usul Jade. The teachings of the New Method of studying the Claim, by Mudjadid Salikh.

Valley of Five Lions. A territory in central Khorasan, fought over by the Shin War and the Zai Guild.

Valley of the Awakened Prince. A territory in central Khorasan.

Wall. A fortification built by the ancestors of the Authoritan to ward off the plague, dividing North Khorasan from South.

Wandering Cloud Door. The lands of the Buzkashi in northeast Khorasan.

Warden. The administrator of Jaslyk prison.

Warraqeen. Male students of the teachings of the Claim at the scriptorium in Ashfall.

Well of Zamzam. A sacred spring near the holy city.

White Fathers. A group that protected manuscripts in the city of Timeback, akin to the Bloodless.

wisa. Trust in the Talisman code.

Yassa. The law of the people of the Wandering Cloud Door.

Yeke Khatun. Great Empress of the people of the Wandering Cloud Door.

yurungkash. White jade.

Zai Guild. One of the tribes of Khorasan, allegiant to the Talisman.

Zareen-Qalam. Title of the curator of the Black's Khan scriptorium, literally "Golden Pen."

Zebunnisa. A revered poet in the history of Khorasan.

Zerafshan. A river of North Khorasan, beyond the Wall.

Zhayedan. The army of the Black Khan, headquartered at Ashfall.

ziyara. A religious pilgrimage.

zrig. A drink of sweetened milk, often thickened with millet and seasoned with spices.

zud. Animal famine.

About the Author

AUSMA ZEHANAT KHAN holds a PhD in international human rights law with a specialization in military intervention and war crimes in the Balkans. A former adjunct law professor, she served as editor in chief of *Muslim Girl,* the first magazine targeted to young Muslim women. She is the award-winning author of the Khorasan Archives series and the Khattak/Getty mystery series, beginning with *The Unquiet Dead*. A British-born Canadian, Khan now lives in Colorado with her husband. You can learn more about her at ausmazehanatkhan.com and can follow her on Twitter at @AusmaZehanat, on Facebook at facebook.com/ausmazehanat khan, and on Instagram at @azkhanbooks.

Other titles from
AUSMA ZEHANAT KHAN

THE BLOODPRINT

"*The Bloodprint* is extraordinary. The book is wonderfully written; its poetic prose and mix of history, faith, and adventure reminiscent of a post-apocalyptic *Odyssey*. . . this time with a pair of women warriors at the helm."

—S. A. Chakraborty, author of *The City of Brass*

The first fantasy novel by the award-winning mystery author of *The Unquiet Dead*—the first in a four-book series that explores the very present topics of religion, gender, and politics, wrapped in the wonder, darkness, and hope that only pure fantasy can produce.

HE BLACK KHAN

cking up where *The Bloodprint* left off, the company that set out search of the Bloodprint is scattered. Arian is at the mercy of the thoritan's consort. Daniyar, the Silver Mage, is being held and rtured. And leaders of the Basmachi resistance are mounting a id to rescue Sinnia.

e second novel in Ausma Zehanat Khan's powerful epic fantasy artet, a series that lies "somewhere between N. K. Jemisin and orge R. R. Martin" (Saladin Ahmed), in which a powerful band of men must use their magic to defeat an oppressive dark regime.

THE BLUE EYE

A band of powerful warrior women continues its resistance against an oppressive dark regime in this penultimate installment in the Khorasan Archives fantasy quartet.

This third volume ratchets up the danger, taking the conflict to a darker, deadlier place, and setting the stage for the thrilling conclusion to this acclaimed #ownvoices fantasy.